SLEE___ ___

CELL

First paperback edition November 2018

www.indiecrime.com
Facebook.com/ChrisCulverBooks

SLEEPER CELL

An Ash Rashid novel

BY

CHRIS CULVER

ST. LOUIS, MO

Other books by Chris Culver

To Ash, my son.

Chapter 1

The FBI agent moved with the stiff-legged, halting gait of a man playing a role he didn't quite understand. It was late May, but the temperature most days already reached into the eighties. The grass outside my mosque bloomed green and lush from spring rains, and the dogwood trees the youth group had planted three years earlier swayed in the warm morning breeze. I should have been at home relaxing. It was the Friday before Memorial Day weekend. Already, hundreds of thousands of people thronged the city for the 102nd running of the Indy 500.

None of that was my concern.

I unclasped the firearm at my hip. The rusted hinges of the FBI agent's truck squealed as he slammed the door shut. It was an old Dodge with sky blue paint that had started flaking along the wheel wells. Water from the air conditioner's condenser dripped onto the pavement in an intermittent stream beneath the vehicle. Steam wafted from the smoldering pile of manure and black mulch in the back.

The FBI agent stood still for a moment, surveying the area. He was probably in his mid-forties and had the broad shoulders of an athlete but also the paunch of a man who had stopped exercising in favor of other pursuits. As I watched, he leaned against the side of the truck to light a cigarette.

This wasn't his first trip to the mosque. The week

before, he had come wearing a uniform from the local water utility. The receptionist let him walk right in and even gave him a tour of the building so he could find the water meter. He wasn't the only agent assigned to the surveillance detail, either. A second agent came by twice a day, ostensibly to walk a dog. In actuality, he was there to photograph the cars in the parking lot. I had no doubt the owners of those vehicles had their names cross-referenced against and added to internal Bureau watch lists.

That second agent hadn't been by yet today, but he would have found the pickings in the parking lot disappointingly slim. In addition to the first agent's truck, there were two sedans, a minivan, and an SUV in the lot. Two men had parked a pickup truck on the shoulder of the road in front of the mosque. They weren't watching anybody in particular. It was more like they were waiting for something.

I had parked on the edge of the lot beneath a basketball hoop to wait for my brother-in-law. I hadn't seen Nassir since I helped him move out of my sister's house a month ago. Technically, he and my sister were still married but had separated. I didn't know how much longer that technicality would keep them together, though. I was in my Volkswagen Golf, and I wore one weapon on my hip and a second in a holster on my ankle.

I was ready.

It was six-thirty in the morning and still comfortable outside, so I got out of my car and sat on my hood to read the news on my phone while I waited. Nassir was late, but he was always late. I had expected this.

As I watched, the FBI agent scooped large shovelfuls of mulch from the back of his truck and carried them to a flower bed near the mosque's front door. Even if he was spying through the basement's casement windows, he did make the flower beds look good. I couldn't fault him for that. If he stuck to the same schedule he had when pretending to be from the water company, he'd go around the back of the building and pull a couple of trash bags from the dumpster next.

My brother-in-law's Cadillac CTS pulled into the lot about fifteen minutes after I arrived. Almost instantly, one of the guys in the pickup out front stepped out of the vehicle. He wore a pair of jeans, heavy boots, and a gray T-shirt, making him look like a construction worker. He wasn't a construction worker, of course. The nearest construction site was at least two blocks away. Not only that, his eyes swiveled around the lot, and he held his left arm out from his chest, presumably so he wouldn't bump the pistol hidden beneath his T-shirt. I slipped my phone into my pocket.

Six weeks ago, the body of an undercover FBI agent named Michael Najam had been found floating in the Ohio River near Madison, Indiana. The death wasn't an accident or a suicide. Najam had been murdered while infiltrating a suspected Islamic terror cell in Indianapolis. The Bureau needed someone to investigate, but it also needed to keep things quiet so it wouldn't disrupt other related operations.

That's why Kevin Havelock, the special agent in charge of the local FBI field office, had come to me.

As a former homicide detective, I knew how to conduct a murder investigation. As a Muslim who spoke two different Arabic dialects, I also fit into the world the FBI agent had tried to infiltrate. More than any of that, though, I was the brother-in-law of the suspected terror cell's leader. The Bureau thought I was perfect for the role. Havelock thought I could waltz right in, ask Nassir what had happened, and be home for lunch. I wasn't that optimistic, but I thought I could do it.

The moment Agent Kevin Havelock proposed the assignment to me, I accepted. My wife, though, persuaded me to think about it further. Havelock had leveled serious accusations against Nassir, but his evidence was circumstantial at best. Besides that, if I went undercover to investigate men and women in my mosque and got caught, I'd become a pariah to people I had known my entire life. I'd lose friends, and my kids would be ostracized by the only community they had ever known.

It took time and a lot of thought, but I eventually made a much more informed choice about what to do. I still wondered whether I had made a mistake.

Nassir stepped out of his car. He was fifty-three, but he looked closer to forty. He had thick black hair with the barest hints of gray near his temples and a perpetual worried scowl on his face. He shuffled toward me, wringing his hands in front of him. I watched him, but I also kept my eyes on the FBI agents beside the pickup and the FBI agent shoveling mulch. Nobody acknowledged Nassir and me, but they tracked our movements just the same.

"Ashraf," said Nassir, holding out a hand for me to shake. I took it and squeezed. He looked down at the ground. "I didn't expect to hear from you. How's Rana?"

"Since you left her?" I asked, tilting my head to the side. He nodded. "Angry, sad, confused, take your pick. You married a strong person, though, and she's surrounded by people who care for her. She'll be fine. You don't need to worry about her."

"She's a good woman," he said, drawing in a breath. "She deserves good things. I wish I didn't have to do what I did."

"We all wish that. But I'm not here to talk about her," I said, looking at the FBI agent with the mulch. "I called you because there are a couple of things going on around here that you should know about."

Nassir followed my gaze to the supposed landscaper. Then he nodded.

"Okay. Let's get some breakfast and talk."

"Give me a minute. I'm going to do something I should have done weeks ago," I said, already walking. "I'm tired of having people watch us all the time."

"You don't need to do this, Ash," said Nassir, hurrying to walk beside me. "They're not hurting anybody."

"They're strangers with guns and itchy trigger fingers

11

watching a building my children play in. I'm not comfortable with that."

Ahead of us, the FBI agent leaned his shovel against the side of the mosque and stood straighter. A sheepish smile broke out across his face, and he wiped his brow.

"Hey guys," he said. "Gonna be a hot one, isn't it?"

"It is," I said, stopping about ten feet from him. Nassir and the truck were to my right. The mosque was to my left. Out of the corner of my eye, I watched the two men near the pickup truck. They hadn't made a move toward us, but they would eventually. "The flowers look nice. Agent Havelock pick them out, or does he leave that up to you?"

The FBI agent shook his head. "You must have mistaken me for somebody else. Sorry, buddy."

Nassir put a hand on my shoulder and gently tugged. "Come on, Ashraf. He's not worth it."

I shrugged my brother-in-law's hand off and took a step forward.

"I'm not mistaken, and we both know it. Kevin Havelock, the special agent in charge of your field office, asked you to perform surveillance on this mosque. You're digging in the front flower bed so you can switch out the batteries on the surveillance devices you've hidden near the basement windows. That's why you're really here."

He chuckled and shook his head. "You've got an active imagination, I'll give you that."

"And you've got access to trucks from both Duke Energy and the local water company. My daughter takes art classes here. This used to be her favorite place in the world. Now she doesn't want to come back because there's a scary man outside who watches her classroom. She's nine years old. Even she knows who you are. What do you even hope to accomplish here?"

The FBI agent drew in a breath and stood straighter. "I think it's time for you to move on, buddy."

"It probably is," I said. "You first, though. Nassir, get the man's shovel and throw it in his truck."

Nassir hesitated and looked at me.

"I don't know if this is the best idea," he said.

"This man is trespassing at our place of worship," I said, not taking my eyes from the FBI agent. "We're asking him to leave. We're well within our legal rights."

Nassir hesitated again and then began walking around the truck to fetch the man's shovel. The agent took a step back, probably so he could see us better.

"You two need to really think about what you're doing," he said. "This doesn't need to escalate."

"We're politely asking you to leave," I said, pulling my sport coat back to show him the badge clipped to my belt. In the process, I exposed my firearm as well. "I'm a lieutenant with the Indianapolis Metropolitan Police Department. Neither of us is threatening you in any way. If you'd like, I can call in some patrol officers and have them remove you by force."

He looked up and down at Nassir before reaching behind his back. "I don't like you sneaking up behind me."

"I'm not doing anything of the sort," said Nassir, holding up his hands. The two men near the truck started walking toward us. Nassir took a step back. "We're not here to cause trouble, my friend. We're leaving."

"I'm going to call in some backup. Please keep your hands where I can see them," I said, reaching into the inside pocket of my jacket for my cell phone.

Almost the moment my hand disappeared, the FBI agent whipped out a black semiautomatic firearm. He pointed it at Nassir.

I didn't even think. Time slowed. I dropped my hip back and had my own firearm in hand before the FBI agent could get settled. Nassir's face went white as he dropped to his knees.

"I'm a police officer!" I shouted. "Drop your weapon."

The FBI agents who had pretended to be construction workers sprinted toward us, their own weapons drawn. I pivoted, being sure to keep my firearm pointed at the ground.

"Police officer. Back off."

The two FBI agents raised their weapons simultaneously.

"Oh, shit."

I dove toward the truck's front wheels as they fired. The first round pinged against the truck, but the second hit the brickwork of the mosque in an explosion of dried clay, shale, and mortar. My heart pounded against my breastbone. Nassir huddled down with his hands over his head. The FBI agent who had once pretended to be a landscaper stared down at the both of us, his weapon pointed directly at me.

Adrenaline coursed through me. My hands trembled, but I started lowering them to the ground. I wanted to run and scream, but I held my breath instead so I wouldn't provoke anyone.

"You don't need to do this," I said, forcing my voice to remain as calm as possible. "I'm putting my firearm down. Please tell your friends that we're surrendering."

The FBI agent's finger slipped from the trigger guard to the trigger. He couldn't have been more than five feet from us.

"Please lower your gun," I said, my heart beating even faster. "Nobody has to get hurt today."

He didn't say a word. He didn't even open his mouth. He didn't need to say anything. I read the intention in his eyes. I saw the color of his finger change as he began to depress the trigger, I saw the hammer of his weapon pull back, and I knew he was going to shoot.

I raised my weapon and squeezed the trigger four times before he could get a shot off.

His coveralls exploded with red, and his gun clattered to the ground as he fell back. Immediately, Nassir started reciting the *Shahada*, the Islamic profession of faith. He thought he was going to die and was praying before his death. I should have joined him, but I didn't have time to pray.

I crept around the front of the truck. One of the

construction workers saw me and crouched behind the minivan in the parking lot. He fired another round and hit the truck once more. Only a thousand pounds of steel and wrought iron in the engine kept me safe. I couldn't see the second agent.

"Nassir," I said. My brother-in-law rocked on his heels like a Quaker as he prayed. "Nassir!"

He looked up. He had the terrified eyes of a wild animal caught in a snare.

"We're not safe here," I said. "We've got to make a run for your car. We'll drive to the police station in Fishers and tell them what happened. We'll be safe there."

He couldn't even focus on me at first, but then comprehension dawned on his face.

"We tried to talk to him, but he didn't listen," he said. "They're going to kill us."

"We're not going to let that happen," I said. "Get to your car and drive it back over here. I'll give you covering fire."

He covered his face with his hands for a few seconds but then nodded.

I crept to the end of the truck so I could see the parking lot. My brother-in-law wore gray slacks, a tailored white button-down shirt, and matte black leather shoes. His outfit wasn't made for running, but he'd get over that if he wanted to live.

On the count of three, he sprinted toward his car. Immediately, the FBI agent near the minivan popped up. I fired two shots at him, driving him back.

Then I found where the second officer had gone.

He stood up from beside Nassir's car. I pivoted hard and raised my weapon. His pistol barked twice in Nassir's direction. I squeezed off three rounds. The FBI agent's gray work shirt became a mess of dark red. Nassir fell to the ground.

"Come on, buddy, get up," I whispered. "Get up, Nassir."

Slowly, my brother-in-law pushed up from the ground and ran once more toward his car. The FBI agent near the minivan started running just as Nassir jumped into the front seat of his Cadillac. I lined up the shot and waited.

"Drop your weapon and let him go!" I screamed. "Nobody else has to get hurt."

The agent stopped in his tracks and pivoted toward me. As Nassir's car roared to life, I went to my knee to minimize his target.

"Don't do this!" I shouted.

The FBI agent fired. Inches to my left, the truck's front headlight exploded. Nassir's tires screeched as he rocketed out of his parking spot. The FBI agent sprinted toward the minivan behind which his partner had hidden. I tracked him with the barrel of my firearm.

"Drop your weapon!" I shouted. "Nobody else has to get hurt. We're going to the police station in Fishers. We'll surrender there. You can meet us if you want."

The agent didn't respond as he ducked behind the van. I held my weapon in his direction while Nassir put his car in a forward gear. The big Cadillac's tires chirped as my brother-in-law accelerated toward me. The FBI agent shifted his attention and then popped up from near the minivan's hood, his weapon pointed at Nassir's car.

"Don't make me do this."

Whether or not he heard me, he fired. The round slammed into Nassir's front window on the passenger side, causing a spider's web of cracks to spread through the glass.

I squeezed my trigger three times. The FBI agent went down just as Nassir screeched to a halt a couple of feet from me. I threw open the back door, dove inside, and heard the engine roar before I even came to a rest on the gray leather. The heavy car jolted forward, and my door slammed shut with acceleration. Within seconds, we were out of the lot and on the street.

For a few moments, neither of us said anything. Then I heard Nassir gasp.

"We're alive," he said. "Thank God, we're alive."

"Yeah. We've got to keep moving, though. We'll go to the police station and get some help."

"You murdered three FBI agents," said Nassir. "You shot them. I saw it."

"It wasn't murder," I said, looking around me. The round that penetrated the front window had hit the center of the backseat. Had it been just a foot to the right, it would have killed Nassir. That was too close. "It was self-defense. There's a big difference."

"They're not going to see it like that," he said, shaking his head and cranking the wheel to perform a U-turn. I held onto the door handle tightly so I wouldn't roll around inside the car.

"What the hell are you doing?" I asked.

"Getting us somewhere safe," he said.

"This isn't a good idea," I said, looking out the window at the scenery passing us by. "Running makes us both look bad."

"You shot three FBI agents. Nothing we can do will change what they think now. Just shut up. We'll ditch the car, and I'll call somebody I trust for a ride. We need to get rid of our phones, too."

"You don't need to get rid of your car," I said, reaching into my pocket for my phone and opening the text messaging app. "Every witness who could identify it is dead. We should be okay for a little while."

Nassir swore under his breath. "This is a nightmare."

A few moments later, I pointed to the side of the road as I typed in a text message. "Pull over here. There's a storm drain."

Nassir slowed the vehicle and glanced at me. "Who are you texting?"

"Hannah," I said. "I'm letting her know we're safe. She'll tell Rana that you're okay, too. Now give me your phone. I'll toss them both."

The car pulled to a stop as I waited for the message to send. Nassir reached beside him and handed me his cell phone.

I didn't know how cell phone carriers routed text messages across their network, so I didn't know whether the recipient of that message would receive it right away, or whether it would take a while. Special Agent Kevin Havelock would get it eventually, though, and he'd know what it meant.

I'm in.

I walked to a storm drain and dumped in two perfectly good cell phones and a replica Glock 22 firearm that could shoot only blanks. Then I walked to the front seat of my brother-in-law's car, knowing that if Special Agent Havelock were right, I was likely sitting beside the most dangerous man I had ever met.

Chapter 2

Hashim Bashear stepped off the Emirates Airline flight and onto US soil at Kennedy International in New York. It was just after eight in the morning, and bright sunlight streamed through every window in the building. Though it was something of a cliché now to mock America's infrastructure, Kennedy wasn't as bad as many airports Hashim had flown through. In Lagos, Nigeria, he'd had to hire armed escorts to drive him to his hotel, and he couldn't walk freely at night for fear of being robbed and murdered. New York, as bad as it was, didn't quite compare.

The cramped international wing smelled of body odor and burned coffee. He wheeled his carry-on bag down the terminal, heading toward the exit.

Hashim's body and face still didn't feel like his own. Over the past month, he had gorged himself on rich food to gain almost ten pounds. He had lost the gaunt look of a fighter and gained the soft, pudgy look of an aristocrat. A month ago, a surgeon in Dubai had reconstructed his nose, and he had sat beneath the desert sun for hours at a time to darken his olive-colored skin.

The American government had some of the most sophisticated pattern-recognition software in the world on its surveillance cameras. From the rumors Hashim had heard, those cameras could almost do magic. If they could see even an inch of a man's skin, the US government would instantly know his name and background. It wasn't magic, of course; their sophisticated abilities came from mathematical algorithms and nearly unlimited budgets devoted to spying on American citizens. Hashim wouldn't fool that pattern-recognition software, but he could fool a police officer who happened to have seen his picture.

When traveling under his actual identity, Hashim carried a British passport. Here, he carried a Canadian passport once owned by a Egyptian-Canadian academic named Faizan Mubarak. Even before Hashim had altered his appearance, he and Faizan were the same height, they had the same build, and they had similar facial features. After Hashim's surgery, their own wives would have had difficulty telling them apart.

Hashim's men had offered to buy the passport, but Faizan had refused. He died for that refusal. It was a pity he hadn't seen the opportunity God had placed in front of him.

The line to pass through customs took almost three hours, but Hashim didn't feel nervous. With God on his side, no man could stand in his way. When he reached the front of the line, a bored-looking customs agent scrutinized Hashim's stolen passport.

"You here for business or pleasure, Mr. Mubarak?"

"A bit of both," said Hashim. "I'm presenting a paper at a conference and visiting some family in Queens."

"What's your paper on?"

Hashim forced a smile to his face. This same customs agent had allowed the Asian family in front of him to pass through with hardly a question. More than likely, the agent's superior officers had trained him to scrutinize Arab men more closely than other groups in the mistaken belief that Arab men had a high likelihood of being terrorists. In the past, that might have been an effective technique to thwart men and women like Hashim from completing God's will, but the future rarely looked like the past.

A majority of the world's Muslims came from Southeast Asia, but Eastern Europe had more than its fair share. Hashim's men could just as easily train a Caucasian man from Armenia as they could an Arab from Saudi Arabia.

As tightly as the United States government squeezed its fists around men like Hashim Bashear, some would always wriggle through its fingers. It was inevitable. It was partly God's will, but more than that, it came from the hubris of an American political class that preferred to look as if it was combating terrorism rather than getting its hands dirty in the actual practice.

"My lecture covers topics in the architecture of the Latin East from approximately 1100 A.D. to 1600 A.D.," said Hashim. "If you're interested in the subject, my lecture Thursday evening will be open to the public. It's at nine in the evening. I can give you the address if you'd like."

The customs agent blinked and looked Hashim in

the eyes. He either wanted to look interested, or he genuinely thought he could root out deception simply by looking at another human being. Some people had a gift for that, of course, but the eyes weren't truly windows into the soul of a deceiver. The signs of deception were more subtle than that. A carotid artery that pulsed just a little faster than average due to stress, arms held tight to the sides to minimize movements and diminish one's size, a smile that didn't reach past one's lips.

Before the Islamic State's most recent troubles, Hashim had known men in Raqqa and Mosul who could spot a liar from across the interrogation room. No doubt the US government employed thousands of similar men and women in its vast law enforcement apparatus. The agent across from him, though, hadn't received the same training. He wasn't a threat.

"How long are you staying in the States, sir?"

"Four days. I have return tickets already if you'd like to see them. I have to get back to my students in Dubai."

"No need to see your tickets. Good luck with your lecture, and welcome to the United States."

He handed Hashim the passport and then waved the family behind him forward. He had let Hashim into the United States without even searching his bag—not that he would have found anything. Hashim and his men already had everything they needed in the country. This would work out fine. As he neared the exit, a large African man walked toward him and smiled.

"*As-salamu alaykum,*" he said, holding out his hand.

Batul had a French accent and a deep, sonorous voice. Hashim didn't know him well, but he trusted him. Batul was a believer, and he knew Hashim was on a mission from God. If he thought it necessary for Hashim to complete His mission, Batul would storm the gates of hell with a smile on his face. Every army in the world needed cannon fodder. Batul played the role nicely.

"*Wa alaykumu as-salam*," said Hashim, smiling as well. "How are you, my friend?"

Batul looked around and drew in a breath. "Better knowing you're here. The decadence of this place cries out to God."

Hashim caught Batul's eyes following a young woman—probably in her early twenties—walking past. She had black hair, and she wore a black pencil skirt that showed off her legs as well as a tight-fitting sweater that showed off a scant amount of cleavage. By the standards of the day, she looked demure, but the standards of the day were produced by men and women who would one day suffer the fires of hell.

Even still, God did make women wondrous companions.

"Do you have a car?" asked Hashim.

"Yes. My brother will drive. He's outside."

"Then let's go."

Batul had to call his brother, but eventually, a black four-door sedan pulled up to the curb to pick them up. It wasn't posh, but it was comfortable. Malik, Batul's brother, pulled into traffic a moment later.

"Have you had this car cleaned lately?" asked

Hashim.

"We can speak freely in here, brother," said Malik. "Your son checked it last night."

Then they truly could speak freely. Hashim's son, Hamza, had a master's degree in mechanical engineering and an aptitude for electronics. He understood the modern world. If Hamza had swept the car for surveillance gear and found none, there was nothing to find.

"How are our plans?"

"Our friends from New Jersey are already in DC," said Batul. "*Insh'Allah*, they will attack the Metro Center station during rush hour. It will be beautiful."

"And President Crane's campaign rally?"

"On schedule," said Batul. "As are all of our plans. Hamza has created the devices as you specified utilizing the parts you sent ahead. This will truly be a glorious day."

Hashim nodded, his mind already vaulting ahead several steps.

"How are our friends in Indiana?"

Batul drew in a breath but didn't say anything. Hashim cocked his head to the side and narrowed his gaze.

"Tell me," he said.

Batul blinked and looked down. "They were infiltrated by a man they believed to be an FBI agent, but they took care of it internally. Their compound is still safe. We can still use it when the time comes."

Hashim sighed and rubbed his eyes. "Can we trust them?"

"I've never doubted their loyalty."

"All right, then," said Hashim. "Tell them only what they need to know. Our work is too important to fail. We need to start calling mosques in DC to warn them of the metro station attack. Their imams will warn their flocks to stay away from the metro."

Batul said nothing, but he sat straighter. Malik looked in the rearview mirror at Hashim, his eyes narrow.

"You can't trust the people in this country, even those who call themselves Muslims. If we warn them of an attack, they'll tell the authorities."

Hashim nodded again and looked out the window. He didn't know New York very well, but he recognized the kind of neighborhood they were in. Mixed income, very likely with a mix of black and white and Hispanic residents. The homes were small but well cared for. It was smart that his team had rented a home in a neighborhood like that one. They would blend in.

"I'm counting on that," said Hashim. "I want the police to know of the attack."

"If they know of it, they'll stop it."

Hashim sighed. "Probably."

"Then why?" asked Malik. "We've worked too hard to fail."

"Do you ever play chess?" asked Hashim, looking forward.

"I know the game."

"Good. Then you'll understand this. Our friends from DC and Indiana are pawns. Regrettably, we have to sacrifice them."

"Our cousin is in Washington right now," said Malik, looking to his right to Batul. "He has a family. Why would you sacrifice him?"

"Because sometimes you have to sacrifice your pawns to kill the king."

Chapter 3

Nassir and I settled into the Cadillac for a long drive. Even though he hadn't said anything specific, I knew where we were going. It was a training facility deep in the woods near the Hoosier National Forest. Nassir had been living there with a couple of other men since leaving his wife.

The FBI didn't know what went on at the camp, but agents kept it under tight surveillance. A couple of times a week, they even flew a drone overhead to take pictures and video. In the last video I had seen, Nassir and his friends were using heavy machinery to build an earthen mound. They may have just wanted a giant pile of dirt, but I doubted that very much.

I had been a police officer in central Indiana for almost twenty years, and I had seen dirt piled up on properties in the middle of nowhere dozens of times. About half the time, the property owner had built a redneck swimming pool. He'd dig a hole, line it with a tarp, fill it with water, and have fun for a week or two. The other half of the time, the property owner needed a backstop for a shooting range.

My brother-in-law didn't swim.

In years past, I had always thought of Nassir as a bit of a kook, but I never would have considered him dangerous. When Havelock first approached me and said he suspected Nassir and his friends were terrorists who had murdered an FBI agent, I thought I was the butt of some kind of twisted joke.

Then he started showing me evidence.

Six months ago, Nassir and two friends had flown to Doha, Qatar, where they had met with a group of businessmen, several of whom had known ties to radical Islamic groups in the Arabian peninsula. Neither the Bureau nor anyone in the American intelligence community knew what they talked about, but at the end of their trip, Nassir and his friends created a holdings company on the Isle of Man.

A month after that meeting, Nassir's holdings company purchased a large tract of land in Brown County, Indiana, for almost three million dollars cash. Brown County was one of the prettiest parts of the state, so Nassir's property was prime real estate. If he and his business group had started applying for permits to build a bed and breakfast, the Bureau probably would have dropped its suspicions entirely.

Instead, Nassir and his friends started putting up concrete buildings themselves late at night and on the weekends. It was bizarre.

Then Nassir had joined Facebook. Facebook had billions of users, so it wouldn't have been strange to see Nassir on the site except that he had mocked me for years for having an account.

The Bureau didn't have access to Nassir's Facebook account, but its agents monitored many of the private groups Nassir was in. The people in those groups traded videos of men and women being executed in the Islamic State, they joked about mass murder, they promised retribution for American air strikes in Syria, and they cheered when terrorists murdered innocent people.

Nassir didn't just visit the pages of these private groups, though. He posted notes to them, he liked pictures and videos, and he responded to comments other people posted. By the standards of the groups he frequented, he was moderate, but it was disturbing all the same. He had been married to my sister for almost twenty-five years. I had sat beside him at Thanksgiving; I had helped him sand the hardwood floors in the crappy house he and my sister moved into when they were first married; I had helped him put together his last three barbecue grills. I had even helped him bury his daughter.

Despite all the years together, I felt like I barely knew the man.

I glanced at him and then focused on the road ahead of us. Nassir said nothing. The adrenaline had waned inside the vehicle, leaving me feeling almost sleepy.

"Do you want to talk?" he asked.

I nodded and looked out the window. "We probably should. Even without witnesses, it's not going to take the Bureau long to find out I shot its agents. Their guys will probably talk to Hannah first and ask whether I've contacted her. Once they find the text I sent her, they'll try to track me via my cell phone. We got rid of those, so we're good there. They'll talk to my co-workers next, but I'm officially on vacation right now. Eventually, they'll start questioning Rana. Does she know where we're going?"

"No," said Nassir. After a few moments, he glanced at me before focusing on the road again. "You don't look like you're on vacation."

"I always take race week off."

He glanced at me again, his brow furrowed. "I didn't know you were a race fan."

"I'm not," I said. "I've taken race week off every year I could just so I don't have to be on drunk patrol."

"You should have stayed at work."

"I'm starting to think that, too," I said.

We drove for another few moments. Then Nassir started drumming his fingers on the steering wheel.

"I have friends in Qatar who could take you in," he said. "We'd have to get you out of the country first, but they might even be able to get you a job working security. Hannah and the kids could move later."

I sat straighter. "You have friends in Qatar State Security you've never told me about?"

"No," he said, shaking his head. "They're business people, but they're well connected. Qatar isn't a big place."

I didn't doubt that. Money was power. It was one of those very rare societal norms that transcended both culture and time. If it came up, I'd ask him about those friends later, but for now, I had to keep him focused.

"I'm not leaving the country," I said. "I didn't do anything wrong. That was my mosque. Those FBI agents drew their weapons first, they shot first, and then they refused to back down when given a chance. I wish I didn't have to do what I did, but I don't regret it."

Especially because the men I "shot" were probably taking showers to wash away the fake blood even as Nassir and I were driving.

"We can't hide you forever," said Nassir. "We probably can't even hide you for very long."

"I'm tired of hiding," I said. "It's time to stand up and fight."

For a moment, Nassir didn't say anything. Then he put on his turn signal and pulled onto the interstate's shoulder. We were on I-65 just south of Franklin, Indiana. A semi whipped past us going seventy or eighty miles an hour, rocking our vehicle. Nassir didn't even blink. He stared directly into my eyes.

"I understand your anger and your frustration, but I need you to listen to me, my friend," he said. "You can stay with me, you can eat my food, and you can sleep in my home. I will share everything I have with you, but if you intend to hurt more people than you already have, get out now."

He looked sincere, but I had seen his postings online. Nassir was old enough to know how the world worked. He never advocated violence, and he never encouraged those who did, but at the same time, he played a role in a violent community. He didn't advocate violence online because he didn't have to. Other people did it for him. It was enough that he perpetuated the conversation.

I crossed my arms. "I never pegged you as a pacifist."

"And I never pegged you as an idiot. You already killed three FBI agents. You may have been justified, but they're still dead. If you want to hurt more people, I have no place for you in my life. My work is too important."

I looked at him and tried not to look too interested. "What kind of work are you involved in? We're out in the middle of nowhere."

Nassir gritted his teeth before putting the car in gear again and looking over his shoulder to pull into traffic.

"If you think this is the middle of nowhere, you have an impoverished imagination."

I waited for him to say something else, but he went quiet. He didn't need to tell me everything right away, though. I had time to work on him.

We took the interstate south for another twenty minutes and then exited near Columbus, Indiana. After that, we headed west through deep woods and across rolling hills on a two-lane highway. Very quickly, dense woods surrounded the road, leaving us to drive in shadows so deep Nassir had to turn on his headlights. After about fifteen miles on that two-lane road, we slowed and pulled onto a narrow pockmarked asphalt road cut through the woods. The street didn't have a name as best I could tell, but it followed a shallow creek through the woods.

Indiana may not have had majestic mountains or dramatic coastal cliffs, but it had its fair share of beautiful areas. Even though I knew Nassir and his friends were likely using their property to hide illegal activities, it felt peaceful and serene. One day, if I had a lot of money, I wouldn't have minded owning a little piece of property like that.

Hopefully, my property wouldn't have a terrorist training camp next door.

"This is pretty," I said, sitting straighter to see the rock-strewn creek to my right. Overhead, trees kept most of it in the shade, but I could see gentle rapids in the shallow water. "You and Rana thinking of retiring here?"

He sighed. "It would have been nice, but no. This is something else."

I didn't ask what he meant by that, and Nassir didn't volunteer the information. We slowed a few minutes later as we came to a gate.

Directly ahead of us, the road turned to gravel and cut through a grass field. A man probably in his mid-fifties sat atop a big green tractor and trimmed the lawn. He wore a blue Indianapolis Colts baseball cap, and he had draped a white cloth across the back of his neck. I didn't remember the guy's name, but he and his family attended services at my mosque. He was pretty well off, if I remembered correctly. Why he was driving a tractor and mowing the grass in the middle of nowhere, I had no idea.

Nassir rolled his window down and waved as we passed.

"How many people are out here with you?" I asked.

Nassir shrugged and hit the button to close his window. "Four or five at any given time. It varies."

The Bureau didn't know how big Nassir's cell was, but Agent Havelock had a list of nine suspected members. My primary responsibility was to find out who killed Michael Najam, but if I could verify Havelock's list, I certainly would.

"Are they all from our mosque?"

He glanced at me. "Have you always been this nosy?"

"The more people who see me, the more trouble I can cause," I said, lying as clearly and forcefully as I could. "I don't want these guys to be arrested."

"God will protect us."

"I hope you're right."

The gravel road led to an outcropping of buildings beneath some trees. There were three cars there: a Mercedes, a Land Rover, and an Audi. Judging by the price of their cars, I doubted these guys worked with their hands for a living, and yet, here they were on Nassir's little farm.

My brother-in-law parked beside the Audi, and I stepped out into a bucolic landscape. To my left was a concrete building with a big porch and bug screens where the windows should have been. To my right was a raised concrete pad covered with artificial turf and a metal rod jutting about six inches from the center. There was an identical concrete pad maybe ten feet across from it and two large rectangular pits dug into the earth nearby.

Aside from the holes in the ground, it looked like a

rustic resort.

I pointed toward the concrete pads. "Horseshoes?"

Nassir nodded. "Ismail built the set, but don't play with him. He's too competitive."

I recognized the name. Ismail Shadid was a sixty-two-year-old materials science engineer with Raytheon's Analysis and Test Laboratory in Indianapolis. He had a top-secret security clearance at work and five children and a spouse at home. He specialized in structural finite elemental analysis of military systems, which meant he had spent his life learning how military hardware broke when put under stress.

Hearing his name confirmed one thing: I was in the right spot. Ismail was at the top of Havelock's list.

I looked at Nassir. "What now?"

He blinked and then looked down. "I need to talk to my colleagues to tell them what happened at the mosque."

"They going to be okay hiding a fugitive from the FBI?"

He hesitated before speaking. "They may not agree with your methods, but they understand the world we live in. All believers in God are brothers. If you can't stay here, we'll find somewhere else for you. We'll do everything we can to keep you safe. I'm sure of that."

Had the circumstances been different, it would have been the kindest thing he had ever said to me. Considering the circumstances, it was a felony. Still, it was touching. I paused and then lowered my voice.

"Thank you, Nassir."

"Of course. There are rocking chairs on the porch behind you. Stay here. I'll be back."

I nodded and then watched him walk away. As I looked over the fields surrounding us, I memorized the landscape, knowing there was a very real possibility that I'd have to tell the leader of an FBI tactical team how best to attack it without getting shot.

Chapter 4

The property was almost three hundred acres, and Nassir's friends could have been anywhere on it. Not only that, cell reception was spotty at best, and the rolling hills and dense forest made two-way radios next to useless. Nassir would have to track down each man individually. That gave me some time to search.

Once he disappeared down a hill, I knelt down and unholstered the subcompact Glock 26 strapped to my right ankle. Unlike the firearm I had shot earlier that day, this one would kill if I pulled the trigger. Holding it and knowing I might have to use it on someone I once considered a friend made my situation real somehow. I felt almost ill as I slipped the firearm into my pocket.

Intellectually, I understood the situation. I was in the middle of nowhere in the base camp of a potential terrorist organization. If Special Agent Havelock was right, they had already killed a highly trained FBI agent. They wouldn't hesitate to kill me, too. At the same time, Nassir had helped me teach my daughter to ride a bike. The other men here looked just like me. They came from the same parts of the world my mother and father did. They worshipped the same God I did, oftentimes in the same mosque.

I hated this assignment.

For once, I hoped I was wrong about everything. I didn't want Michael Najam's murder to make sense. I hoped for something random—a gangbanger making his bones before joining up, a sociopath who killed strangers because it gave him a thrill. Those random cases were the hardest to solve, but it would have meant my brother-in-law wasn't a murderer. I would have taken that tradeoff in a heartbeat.

I turned to the northwest and headed toward a building they had completed just a couple of weeks ago. It was the largest structure on the property, and though it was far from the main gate, Nassir and his buddies had extended the gravel driveway to its front door. Based on the aerial photography taken during its construction, Agent Havelock's analysts believed it was made of reinforced concrete on a slab foundation. It was about a quarter mile away from the buildings suspected to be living quarters, which would have made it a good spot to store or make explosives.

Agent Havelock theorized that Nassir had became radicalized after his daughter died a couple of years back. It made sense to me, knowing Nassir as well as I did. When Rachel died, Nassir lost a part of himself he'd never find again. He was angry more often than not, he stopped going to work, and he even stopped going to Friday prayer at our mosque.

Instead of coming to his family for help, he apparently turned to the internet, where he found a radical Islamic community that encouraged him to hate the world. Rana, my sister, had told me he used to stay up for hours at night, just reading posts on Facebook and watching sermons from imams in Syria or Iraq. Losing his daughter had broken him. There was no way to come back from that.

I followed the gravel road to the building. While its core may have been reinforced concrete, the building had a painted aluminum skin, making it look like any pole barn on any farm in Indiana. It had three open garage doors and a white metal roof that reflected the sunlight. Nobody came outside to greet me, so I walked inside.

The interior was silent, attesting to the concrete walls. The air held a chemical odor. There was an oil slick on the ground near one of the garage doors but no equipment or vehicles. There were, however, enough bags of ammonium nitrate fertilizer stacked in the northeastern corner to turn the world green.

I bent down and pulled a prepaid cell phone from a holster on my ankle. That far from civilization, I couldn't get a cell signal, but I took a dozen pictures from as many angles as I could so the FBI's analysts could properly estimate how much ammonium nitrate Nassir had. Then I went outside again.

Nassir and his friends had to have fuel for their tractor, so I walked around the building until I found an elevated diesel storage tank. I took pictures of that, too.

Then I sat down on the grass in the shade cast by the barn. Nassir and his friends needed a tractor to take care of their camp, and they needed diesel so their tractor could work. What's more, they needed some fertilizer if they wanted to keep their fields healthy and lush. I knew all that, but I also knew that fuel and ammonium nitrate happened to be the two primary components of the explosive device Timothy McVeigh used to blow up a federal building in Oklahoma City in the mid-nineties.

I closed my eyes and banged the back of my head against the building's aluminum siding.

"Fuck."

Even if they were innocent, this was a bad look. The diesel I could understand, but they didn't need thousands of pounds of fertilizer to keep their plants healthy. They had that for some other purpose entirely.

When I agreed to this investigation, I had hoped I'd waltz onto the property and find real, concrete facts that put all of Havelock's circumstantial evidence into context. Despite all the theatrics it took to get here, I had hoped I could prove Nassir and his friends were innocent—stupid, maybe, but innocent. The more I saw, though, the more confirmation I had that Havelock was right.

I banged my head against the wall again. Even if Nassir had an excuse for the fertilizer and diesel, the case against him was building. I left the barn and walked back to the cars.

When Havelock had shown me aerial photographs of the property, we had named most of the buildings after places on a golf course. The barn I had just searched was the maintenance shed, eight small buildings on the east side of the property had become the sand trap, an identical set of eight buildings to the west had become the ninth green, and the building Nassir and his friends had parked beside had become the clubhouse.

Now that I stood near it, it struck me that clubhouse was actually a good name. It was concrete, but it had wooden trim around the windows and doors, which gave it a softer feel. Someone had put rocking chairs and a low table on the covered front porch. As I walked closer, I noticed a pair of coffee mugs and a chess set on the table. Had its owners not been plotting the demise of the Western world, it might have been a pleasant place to relax.

I pulled open the door and stepped into an open room with a vaulted ceiling and a couple of tables and chairs. Winters would be a bear without insulation or glass in the windows, but it was comfortable on a spring afternoon. A hallway on the eastern wall led to private bedrooms, each of which had a sign outside designating its occupant. Only two rooms in the hallway had locks. One was the bathroom, while the other was a heavy steel exterior-grade door with a padlock.

Nassir could have kept a lot of stuff behind a heavy door like that one. If he had purchased the ammonium nitrate and diesel for a bomb, he'd need a high explosive to detonate it. I probably wouldn't have kept high explosives so close to my living quarters, but if they had blasting caps or dynamite, that's probably where they kept it. One way or another, I needed to get in there. That would have to wait, though. For now, I had other matters to investigate.

I went to the room with Michael Najam's name on

the sign outside and opened his door. The bedroom was small but neat and reminded me of a college dorm. There was a metal framed bed against the far wall. Thin berber carpet covered the ground, and open windows gave him a view of the grounds outside. Like the rest of the building, bug screens kept nature outside but afforded little privacy.

He had a navy blue duffel bag beneath the bed and a footlocker beside it. Evidently, Michael used the footlocker as an end table because there was a lamp, a copy of the Quran, and an empty contact case on top. Two navy blue towels hung on hooks on the wall, and a laundry hamper rested near the foot of the bed.

And that was it. At least I wouldn't have to spend a lot of time searching.

I started by unzipping the duffel bag and running my hand between and around T-shirts, jeans, thick canvas pants, socks, and boxers—the usual things I'd expect from a man who spent significant amounts of time at the camp. Najam liked blue and green shirts, evidently, and he didn't keep secret messages with his clothes. Beyond that, I didn't really learn anything new.

Next, I dumped out his laundry bag. Mud caked most of his clothes, but if he had left a message in dirt, it was too subtle for me to see. I stuffed everything back in the bag and then began moving the stuff from the trunk.

I popped the lid on the trunk and found shoes, toiletries, a couple of books, and a gallon-sized Ziploc bag full of amber prescription drug canisters. The drugs gave me pause.

Everybody got sick, but even cancer survivors—my wife included—had fewer pill containers than that lurking around. I opened the bag and dumped it on the navy blue comforter of his bed. He had an antibiotic, a drug for lowering cholesterol, a multivitamin, and a drug for heartburn. If those had been all he possessed, I wouldn't have been worried.

Unfortunately, he had four canisters of oxycodone as well, and each looked about half-full. That was a lot of painkillers to have lying around, especially for an FBI agent under cover. In addition, he had two drugs I didn't recognize, and each had been prescribed to Jacob Ganim. Both had been filled at the same pharmacy outside Indianapolis. Havelock hadn't given me information on Michael Najam's real identity, but I had the feeling I had just discovered it.

And that was a problem.

When the FBI put someone under cover, its agents created an entirely new identity. They would have given him legal Social Security cards, a driver's license, a passport, even a birth certificate. If Ganim had needed a prescription, the Bureau would have had a trusted doctor write one to his undercover identity. That told me Ganim had hidden these drugs from his bosses. Our special agent had more going on than Havelock knew. I pocketed the two Jacob Ganim pill containers and stuffed the rest back into the Ziploc bag.

That was when I heard the door open behind me.

Chapter 5

I lowered my right hand toward the firearm in my right jacket pocket before standing and turning. Asim Qureshi stood at the door. He was maybe five foot six or five foot seven, but he was well built and nearly as wide as the door frame in which he stood. A bushy gray beard covered most of his face. Anger radiated from his flint gray eyes. Though I hadn't seen him for a while, he went to services at my mosque. He was not on Havelock's list.

"Ashraf," he said. "Nassir told me you were here. What are you doing in Michael's room?"

I looked down at myself, trying to come up with something. It wasn't hard given what I had done that morning.

"I've got dirt and gunpowder residue on my shirt," I said. "I was looking to borrow something, and this was the cleanest room in the building."

For just a second, the anger in his eyes broke, and a wisp of a smile came to his lips. Then he blinked, and the smile disappeared. His face, though, wasn't quite as hard as it had been just a moment earlier.

"I'll give you a shirt. Michael's not with us anymore."

I nodded and walked toward him, hoping he'd have a harder time reading a lie on my lips if I were moving.

"His wife make him come home, or did he get tired of you?"

Asim took a step back as I pulled the door shut

behind me.

"We don't know where Michael is. He left a couple of weeks ago and said he had to take care of something. He hasn't been back since."

"I'm sorry to hear that. Did he say what he had to take care of?"

Asim turned and spoke over his shoulder as he walked up the hall.

"No. He just told us not to worry."

We walked to Asim's room. Like Najam's, it was small and reasonably neat. I stayed in the hallway while Asim got me a T-shirt. I changed in the bathroom, and by the time I got out again, five men waited for me in the building's main public room. Including Nassir, I knew three of the men there. The other two were strangers, but I shook hands with everybody. I also confirmed two more names on Agent Havelock's list.

Eventually, we sat down at a table, and Nassir cleared his throat.

"We talked, Ashraf," he said, looking to his friends. "We want to help you, but you can't stay here. It's too dangerous for us."

I looked at him and then to the other men. "Does everybody feel that way?"

"It's not that we don't want to help you," said Asim. "It's that we can't. This place is important. We can't risk losing it by hiding you here."

I looked around the room. "And what is this place?"

All the men looked to Nassir. For a split second, his

eyes lit up, and he leaned forward. Then, he seemed to remember himself. His countenance became stern once more.

"A summer camp," he said. "It's for children."

"For Muslim children," said one of the men I had just met, speaking quickly. "We're building a place where children who have never felt safe in their entire lives can have a childhood for the first time."

"It's for the children of refugees," said Nassir. "We're in the Rachel Hadad Community Center now. The boys and girls cabins are named after the children and grandchildren we've lost."

I looked at each of the men there. They looked sincere.

"You've all had children die?" I asked.

Most of them nodded.

"It's what drew us together," said Nassir. "I lost Rachel. Ismail lost two of his grandchildren to a suicide bomber in Lebanon. Asim lost his brother and his brother's family to the civil war in Syria. Jim's son died in the Army during a tour in Afghanistan. Qadi's nephew was a Marine who died in the Second Battle of Fallujah in Iraq. This place is our way of celebrating the lives of those we lost. I hope you understand why you can't stay here. We'll get you out of here. You can take my car and go to Mexico or Canada. From there, we can book you air passage to Qatar. Once you're there, you'll be safe for good."

This new information didn't explain why Nassir

frequented extremist private Facebook groups, but it did explain a few things.

"Where'd your funding for this come from?" I asked, looking to the men around me. "This property has got to be worth a couple million dollars."

"Does it matter?" asked Nassir, raising his eyebrows.

"Yeah," I said. "It matters a lot."

Nassir sighed and looked to his friends before focusing on me again.

"We all chipped in, but the bulk of our funding comes from Islamic charities in Qatar and Saudi Arabia."

And that explained his trip to Qatar, then. He was off fundraising. I looked at Nassir and then to the other guys.

"And none of you guys know where Michael Najam is?"

Nassir looked at his friends, perplexed, before looking at me. "No. Why? How do you know Michael?"

"I found him in Michael's room a few minutes ago," said Asim. "He said he was looking for a shirt."

"His old shirt was filthy," said Nassir. "I'd probably want a new shirt, too."

"Is the name Jacob Ganim familiar?" I asked, ignoring the two of them.

Nassir blinked for a moment. "Ganim is an Iraqi name."

"Good to know," I said. "You heard of Jacob?"

He paused and then looked to his friends. None of them nodded or shook their heads, so he turned back to me.

"No. Why?"

"I think Jacob Ganim was Michael Najam's real name," I said, pausing and considering what I wanted to say next. I looked down at the table and then to each of the men in the room. "The fertilizer in the barn to the northwest. Why do you have it?"

Nassir furrowed his brow. "How do you know about the fertilizer?"

"Please just answer the question," I said, allowing a measure of anger into my voice.

The group looked to Qadi with bemused expressions. He looked at them as if they were idiots.

"It's cheaper if you buy it in bulk," he said. "I explained that to you when I bought it. I saved us several hundred dollars. You put me in charge of the soccer field, and I'm going to give you a healthy soccer field."

"So you bought several tons of fertilizer for your soccer field?"

"They're big fields, and there are two of them," said Qadi. "I'd like to see you do better."

"I'm sure you're doing fine," I said, thinking that through and trying to put it into context. Havelock's case against Nassir might have been blowing up in front of me, but Jacob Ganim or Michael Najam—whatever he called himself—was still dead. These men were likely among the last to see him alive. "What did you guys know about Michael Najam?"

Nassir blustered for a moment. "He's a good

Muslim, and he came here to work. He was vouched for."

"By whom?" I asked.

"The imam," said Ismail. "They knew each other somehow."

Now that was interesting. The imam at my mosque was cooperating with the FBI in an investigation against some of his congregants. I didn't know what that meant in practical terms, but I filed it away as important information.

"Michael was murdered six weeks ago," I said. "He was an undercover FBI agent sent to infiltrate a terror cell. His real name, I think, was Jacob Ganim."

"What terror cell?" asked Nassir.

I tilted my head to the side, raised my eyebrows, and stared right at him. Gradually it dawned on him. He opened his eyes wide and then touched his chest.

"Us?"

"Yeah," I said, nodding. "The case against you was weak but still worth investigating. That's why they sent in Jacob—or Michael, as he called himself here."

For a moment, nobody said anything. Then Ismail leaned forward and looked directly in my eyes.

"Michael's really dead?"

I nodded. "Yeah."

Again, we lapsed into silence. Nassir cleared his throat.

"I'm sorry to hear about Michael. I'll contact an attorney I know. We should get moving. You still need to leave."

"I agree, but not for the reason you think," I said. "This morning was a setup. It was fake blood, fake guns, fake everything. The Bureau needed to get someone in here to investigate Jacob Ganim's death. Given the situation, Kevin Havelock at the FBI thought I was a good choice. We thought you would accept me easier if I proved myself to you by killing some FBI agents."

"You have a very low opinion of us, don't you?" asked Nassir, lowering his chin.

"You dumped my sister, so I'm not your biggest fan," I said. "That aside, I'm here to work a murder, which means I need to interview each one of you individually. The others can wait in your rooms. Once I'm done, you can go back to whatever you were doing before I arrived."

"Do we have a choice in this?" asked Qadi.

I looked at him and shook my head. "No. You either talk to me now, or FBI agents storm this entire camp and tear it apart looking for anything illegal. Even if they don't find anything, they're going to make your lives suck for a while."

Nobody was happy about it, but they agreed to the interviews. It took about two hours to get through everybody. Over the years, I had arrested maybe a hundred people for murder, so I had a pretty good background in the subject. Nassir's friends didn't act like killers.

Qadi, the man who had been on the tractor as Nassir and I drove in, teared up halfway through his interview.

The other guys didn't look too much better. A lot of people cried during interrogations, but usually they were blatant and transparent attempts to manipulate me. I didn't get that feeling with these guys. They looked like simple men who'd just learned their friend had died.

More telling than their mannerisms, though, was the fact that Nassir was the youngest man there by at least a decade. It took quite a bit of physical strength to move a corpse around. Even I would have struggled, and I'm a pretty big guy in his early forties. Nassir's friends were all in their sixties. Working together, they probably could have killed a healthy, young FBI agent and then dumped his body in the Ohio River, but even that was a stretch.

None of these guys knew Ganim worked for the FBI, and even if they had known, they had no reason to fear him. They were men building a summer camp. Unfortunately, that left me without much to go on.

After interviewing each man individually in the dining hall, I let them get back to their chores. Nassir hung around and sat down heavily across from me when Ismail left. Even with just a bug screen to shield us from the outside, little air moved, making it feel warmer than it truly was.

"I need a list of everyone who's come to the camp and worked with Michael."

"You don't think one of us killed him, do you?" asked Nassir.

I shook my head and closed my eyes. "Not really. I'll need to clear everybody just the same, though."

"I'll get you the list, then."

Neither Nassir nor I had anything else to say, so we sat in silence for another moment. Then he stood. Before he could leave, I cleared my throat to get his attention.

"Hey," I said. He looked at me with his eyebrows raised. "This is a good thing you're doing. I wish I had come out here under better circumstances. I'm sorry I doubted you."

A wistful smile formed on his face as he shook his head. "An FBI agent told you I was a terrorist. Instead of talking to me, you decided to investigate me. Then you pretended to shoot three people because you thought I'd approve. I've known you for twenty-five years. Even after all this time, you have no idea who I am. We're strangers. Please don't try to pretend we're anything more."

I deserved some of that, but he carried his fair share of blame, too. I laced my fingers together on the table in front of me.

"I investigated you because the FBI had very serious evidence against you. I wanted to disprove it. I wanted them to leave you alone. Instead, I found that you follow radical clerics on Facebook, you comment on the pages of people who advocate violence, and you engage in theological debates with people who joke about mass murder. You're exactly right, Nassir. I've known you for twenty-five years, and I have no idea who you are. After what I've seen, my concern is whether you're a threat."

Nassir screwed up his face. "The FBI is monitoring my Facebook account?"

"No," I said, shaking my head. "They monitor the radical groups in which you post. You happened to show up in places you shouldn't have."

For a moment, Nassir covered his face with his hands. Then he leaned forward and rested his palms on the table so our faces were only a foot or so apart.

"And what if I am a threat? Are you going to arrest me?"

I locked my eyes on him. "Without hesitation. Now get me a list of everyone who had contact with Michael Najam."

Nassir stood straighter and nodded. "Is this how it's going to be from now on? We'll be adversaries?"

"Until you can prove to me that you're the man who married my sister twenty-five years ago, yes."

He looked at the ground and drew in a heavy breath. "I'll write down the names for you. I assume your friends at the FBI will have most of them under surveillance anyway."

"Thank you. While I'm here, do you have a computer with internet access I can use?"

"In the office," he said, sighing heavily. "Follow me."

I followed him down the main hallway and into the first room on the left. The office was a little bigger than the bedrooms, and it had actual glass windows, but otherwise it looked like every other room in the building. There were two desks pushed against the east wall. Both had computers. Nassir pointed to the one nearest the door.

"You can use that one, but please don't install malware to track the things I view online."

"I'm pretty sure the FBI doesn't need me to install anything on your computer to monitor your internet usage," I said. "If you'd like me to pretend that's what I'm doing, though, I certainly can."

Nassir shook his head. "I'm going for a walk. I'll get you the names when I return."

"Sure," I said. "Thank you."

He grunted and left. I pulled the pill canisters from my pocket and opened a web browser to look up the first drug: alprazolam. It was the generic name for Xanax. Physicians prescribed it as a treatment for anxiety disorders and depression. I looked up the second drug, escitalopram, next. It was the generic name for Lexapro, an antidepressant.

I left the screen open and pushed back from the desk to think. Going undercover was one of the most stressful things an FBI agent could do. Because of that, the Bureau had strict protocols for its undercover agents. If Ganim had a history of depression—which the pills clearly indicated—he never would have passed those protocols. Not only that, he had enough opioids in his room to keep an NFL team pain free for a week. That should have been a red flag, too.

He lied to his superiors to get here. He knowingly risked his job, his pension, and his life to get to this summer camp. I spun around in the chair to think.

Ganim didn't come here to spy on old men as they

played horseshoes and mowed pastures that would one day become soccer fields. He didn't come here to work, either. Ganim disguised his identity and came here for a reason. Then, presumably, he was murdered for that reason. This wasn't a homicide investigation, or at least it wasn't just a homicide investigation. This was something else.

I wasn't certain about anything except one fact: Nassir and his friends were in trouble. If a man was willing to kill an undercover FBI agent, he would certainly be willing to kill the hapless old men who gave him cover. No matter what else was going on, that left me with a very cold feeling.

Chapter 6

Though he had only been in the United States a few hours, Hashim Bashear was already behind schedule. He and his son, Hamza, stood in the basement of their rental home. Around them were heavy tables strewn with all manners of equipment and firearms. Foremost among them, though, were a pair of vests laden with explosives.

When bomb makers in the Islamic State made a vest, they typically used whichever high explosive was available to them. Most commonly, that was TNT. It worked well for most purposes. With its relatively low detonation velocity, TNT created a low-pressure wave that pushed outward, shattering everything—including human tissue —within its blast radius. Because the low-pressure wave propagated slowly, it lasted a relatively long time and traveled farther out than a pressure wave created by explosives with higher blast velocities. When one was relying upon the blast wave itself to kill, TNT was a fine choice.

Hashim needed something special, though, and he had the resources to procure it. The two vests on the table in front of him had six compartments, each of which contained a kilogram of dime-sized steel ball bearings. In addition, they had ten kilograms of Chinese-sourced RDX. RDX detonated with a velocity nearly two thousand meters per second faster than TNT. Though it made a poor mining tool, it was an excellent weapon.

Once the RDX ignited, its fast-moving pressure wave would impart a significant percentage of its blast velocity to the ball bearings. The ball bearings would then shred everything around them like a blast from a shotgun. Where a vest made with TNT alone might have a lethal blast radius of ten meters—not bad for use in a crowd— a vest with RDX and ball bearings would be lethal to almost two hundred meters. One was an easily manufactured weapon of terror, while the other was a weapon of war. This fight had stopped being a terror campaign long ago.

Hashim looked up from the vests to his son.

"You used only the components I provided?"

"Yes," said Hamza, nodding.

"It's very important," said Hashim. "You didn't buy anything from RadioShack, you didn't purchase anything that could be traced to you? We can't afford to be caught at this juncture."

"No," said Hamza, humoring his father with a smile. "I understand our mission. I used only what you gave me."

"I didn't doubt you," said Hashim, patting his son on the shoulder. He drew in a breath. "Can you bring our two soldiers down here?"

Their two soldiers were a pair of young Somali men from Minnesota. Hashim had spoken to them almost a dozen times over the phone. Neither boy had much of an education, neither had a good job, and neither had much of a future. They were isolated and scorned by the community to which they had moved, but they were intelligent. They realized they were just as smart and industrious as the men and women around them, but unlike them, they had no real prospects. Alone and isolated, they became resentful. They were perfect recruits.

Hamza disappeared upstairs and returned with the boys. They had very dark skin and hair cropped close to their scalps. More than anything else, their eyes stood out to him. Upon seeing the explosive devices laid out on that table, their eyes sparkled with hope. It filled Hashim with contentment to see young men such as these.

When western journalists had visited the Islamic State, they had oftentimes remarked on how polite and happy the soldiers seemed. They were surprised—shocked even—to see men so willing to die. If those journalists had even a tiny fraction of understanding, though, it would have been obvious to them. The men and women inside the Islamic State had given their lives to God, just as these young men would give theirs. There was no higher calling or privilege. Of course they would be overjoyed to be the implements of God's will.

"*As-salamu alaykum,*" said Hashim, finding the smile came to his lips easily. "It's good to meet you in person."

"*Wa alaykumu as-salam,*" said both boys in unison.

"I'm proud to be here," said one, stepping forward to shake Hashim's hand. He had a weak grip. "I'm Abdullah. My brother is Yasin."

Hashim shook both of their hands and then stepped

back. "You entered this world as boys. In a few hours, you will join the martyrs in paradise. I'm sorry I wasn't here for your training, but know that I'm proud of you both. Your families will be proud, too, especially yours, Yasin. There's no better example you can give to your son."

Yasin looked to his brother. "My family thinks Abdullah and I are fishing in Wisconsin."

"Then we will tell them the truth of your heroism," said Hashim. He gestured toward the vests on the table. "Please, these vests are tailored for you. They're perfectly safe. They will not go off until you decide. Let's make sure you can wear them."

The young men walked forward and lovingly ran their hands across the equipment.

"The components are mostly ceramic," said Hamza, glancing to his father. It was a lie, but hopefully their Somali friends were too enamored to notice. "They will not set off the metal detector. Abdullah, you will enter the arena during the president's rally speech. As soon as you are close to the stage, ignite the device. God will welcome you home as one of His beloved martyrs."

Hamza turned to Yasin. "And Yasin, my friend, you will join the crowd of protestors outside. President Crane has been known to interact with those who jeer him. If you see him and get close to him, do not hesitate."

"What if he doesn't go outside?" asked Yasin.

"Then you become a martyr the moment you hear your brother become one," said Hashim. "You are God's tool to strike down the wicked."

Abdullah picked up his vest and looked at the containers of ball bearings. "It's heavy. These marbles look like metal."

"They're glass," said Hashim, hoping his voice sounded reassuring. "Don't worry. We have every eventuality covered. Now take your vests and go upstairs. Call your loved ones, but don't tell them what you are about to do. I will join you shortly. We have a long drive ahead of us before your holy work begins."

The two Somali boys walked upstairs with their vests, leaving four additional explosive devices still on the tables in the basement. Hashim let out a long breath. Hamza met his father's eyes.

"They're not as ignorant as we expected," said Hamza.

"It doesn't matter," said Hashim. "They'll play their role. How are things progressing in DC?"

"The team from New Jersey is in place. They can pull off the attack. It could work."

Hashim shook his head. "This isn't about destroying the metro station. All warfare is deception. We are playing a longer game than the Americans will understand until it's far too late. Have you heard anything new from our soldiers in Indiana?"

"No," said Hamza.

"Then we assume they're fine," said Hashim. "This will be a great day."

"I hope you're right," said Hamza. "I'd hate for all this work to be for nothing."

"Of course I'm right," said Hashim, smiling. "Don't

be so negative. This is the best day of our lives, for today, God will use us to bring down an empire."

Chapter 7

Nassir and his friends were holding back on me, but they weren't terrorists, and I doubted they had killed Jacob Ganim. I'd give the farm a more thorough search later, but for now, I had things to see. I took out my cell phone and held it up, hoping I could get some kind of a signal. For a brief moment, I had a single bar. Then it disappeared.

I went outside and climbed the tallest hill I could find and still remain on the property. My reception up there was weak but steady. A breeze blew from the woods behind me and rolled across the grass at my feet.

My position gave me a view of the entire camp. Hills rolled down to the creek we had passed earlier. Two men were clearing trees with chain saws near the water's edge, probably so they could build a dock or boat house for the camp. Forest surrounded us as far as I could see, like an undulating green blanket across the earth. Nassir's holdings company had spent three million on the land, and they had certainly received their money's worth.

My address book didn't have many numbers in it, so it only took a moment to find Special Agent Havelock's listing. He answered quickly.

"Ash, I got your text. You okay?"

"Yeah," I said, squinting in the sunlight. "They're building a summer camp for Muslim kids and refugees. That's why they were getting money from wealthy

Muslims in Qatar and Saudi Arabia."

"Yeah, we thought that might have been the case," said Havelock. "We're monitoring Nassir's credit cards. He ordered four trampolines two weeks ago. Terrorists don't usually do that sort of thing."

I gritted my teeth before speaking.

"You knew this was a summer camp, and you still sent me in here?"

"We had no idea what it was, Lieutenant," said Havelock, his voice sharper than it had been a moment earlier. "You may have forgotten this, but occasionally bad guys lie when they do business. For all we knew, the order could have been for automatic weapons labeled as trampolines on an invoice. Don't forget what your brother-in-law does online. Even if he is building a summer camp, he has ties to very violent people."

I closed my eyes and drew in a heavy breath. "He's active on radical Islamic Facebook pages. That doesn't make him a terrorist. It makes him an asshole. And even then, he's not advocating violence. He's talking to them. He probably thinks he's injecting a moderate voice into the conversation."

"I'm not going to listen to you defend your brother-in-law. If you can't do this assignment, tell me now. Michael Najam is dead. We need to know why."

I started pacing beneath an oak tree. "And by Michael Najam, you really mean Jacob Ganim, right?"

Havelock hesitated. "How'd you learn that name?"

"He had pills in his room under his real name. Who

is this guy, really? He had enough drugs in there to keep a house full of addicts high for weeks."

"Lieutenant Rashid, I need you to listen to me very carefully," said Havelock, his voice slow and measured. "You are not there to investigate Jacob Ganim. You're there for Michael Najam. Someone killed him. Find who and why."

"And if I need to look into Jacob Ganim for that?"

"You won't," said Havelock. "Good luck."

He hung up. On my end, it sounded like a gentle disconnect, but he had probably slammed his phone down. I understood and even respected where Havelock was coming from; he wanted to protect an undercover agent's privacy. Under other circumstances, I would have been completely on board. But this was a murder. If the evidence led me to Jacob Ganim, that was where I had to go. Havelock may not have appreciated it, but that was his problem, not mine.

I called up a web browser on my phone; opened the page for INSPECT, Indiana's prescription drug monitoring program; and logged in with my IMPD credentials. Jacob Ganim had received his first prescription for oxycodone three years ago from a physician with the Indiana University Hospital in Indianapolis. Before that, INSPECT had no records of him. Either he wasn't on any drugs, or he had moved from out of state. More importantly, though, INSPECT gave me his home address near Broadripple Park in Indianapolis.

I entered the information in my phone's address book and walked back to the administrative building, where I found Nassir on a rocking chair on the front porch.

"Hey," I said. "I need a favor."

He put his feet down on the ground. No smile touched his lips. "Anything for my favorite brother-in-law."

"I need a ride back to the mosque in Indianapolis so I can pick up my car. You should consider getting your front window replaced, too, before you get a ticket."

He crossed his arms and leaned back. "I assume the FBI will pay for my window."

"You assume wrong," I said. "At least for the moment. When this is over, I'll put in a formal request to reimburse you."

Nassir nodded. "If I do this favor for you, will I see you here again?"

"I don't know," I said. "Probably. If you don't want to do it for me, do it for Michael Najam. I'm going to find his murderer."

Nassir closed his eyes and sighed before standing and reaching into a pocket for a cell phone. "Fine. Let me get my keys. And give me your new cell phone number in case I need to reach you."

"I thought we threw out your phone."

He held his phone toward me and smiled a humorless smile. "You did. That was a very expensive phone, by the way, and I expect to be reimbursed for that, too. This is my work phone. What's your number?"

I gave him the number of my burner phone, and he started to walk toward the door. I caught his arm before he could pass me.

"Believe it or not, I am sorry it's turned out like this."

He looked me up and down before pulling his arm away. "Me, too. Let's just go before either of us does anything else to regret."

Though the Secret Service had well over three thousand special agents and another thirteen hundred uniformed officers, only a very small portion guarded US officials. It was an honor reserved for the most distinguished officers in the service, one the agents themselves took extremely seriously. As one of those agents, Special Agent Sean Navarro considered himself one of the luckiest men in the world.

He was also probably one of the most nervous.

As one of the senior-most agents within the White House's protective detail, he took the safety of the president and his family personally. He had known President Crane for almost nine years and had started protecting him before Crane even won the presidential election. He had met Crane's grandchildren and had watched them throw snowballs at one another on the White House's north lawn. He had seen their birthday parties. He had seen the first family grow up.

Over the years, he had grown to care for them, all of

them. They treated him with respect and even kindness. In return, he'd protect them with everything he had, even laying down his life if necessary. Agent Navarro may not have agreed with President Crane's politics, but he believed in the office of the president and the ideals of fairness and justice it represented. His job was the greatest privilege of his life.

It was a little after one in the afternoon when he walked into Horsepower, the Secret Service's command post directly beneath the Oval Office. It was a large room with a dozen monitors displaying camera feeds from within the White House and the surrounding grounds. Two agents watched those at all times.

Aside from the surveillance equipment, there were duty stations for communications officers, there was a desk for an intelligence officer, there was an armory to the south, and there was a conference room to the east. Navarro scanned his ID at the door to the conference room and passed inside to find a group of six agents around a table. The room smelled like stale coffee and even staler cigarette smoke. It was not a pleasant combination.

"Cohiba is in the Oval Office with Sunshine," said Navarro. "We anticipate him staying for at least an hour. Marine One is on the lawn. We'll depart when Cohiba is ready."

Cohiba was an odd code name, but the president had chosen it himself. Apparently, it was his favorite cigar brand. The first lady was Camus because she had a Ph.D.

in philosophy and an interest in French literature, while Crane's children and grandchildren were all given names from Winnie the Pooh. Sunshine was Megan Hill, Senator Dylan Hill's wife.

In other office buildings, people might have snickered at news of the midmorning rendezvous, but not here. President Crane's affair with Megan Hill was an open secret, one probably even known to Senator Hill. As a Secret Service agent, Navarro knew it wasn't his job to concern himself with rumors and innuendo. What the president did with his time was his business and no one else's.

"Thank you, Sean," said Special Agent in Charge Walt Baker. "Have a seat."

Navarro pulled out the nearest chair and sat while the rest of the command staff went over that day's threat analysis.

"If you haven't heard," said Agent Baker, "Homeland Security is on a heightened state of alert right now due to an anticipated terror attack on the DC metro sometime this afternoon. They've deployed agents throughout the metro system and city. So far, we have not heard any specific threats toward the president, but we need to bear in mind that we have a situation in town."

Baker reached to the table for the remote that controlled the room's presentation equipment. A map appeared on the video screen at the head of the conference room table.

"As we've discussed multiple times, Cohiba is holding

a campaign event late this afternoon at Westbrook Elementary in Portsmouth, New Hampshire. We'll fly Marine One to Andrews Air Force Base and then Air Force One to Pease Air National Guard Base. At the base, we will meet Cohiba's family. From there, we will depart via presidential motorcade to Westbrook Elementary. By the time we arrive, the locals will have closed off the streets that we plan to drive on. Upon finishing his speech, Cohiba will depart and return to Andrews Air Force Base via Air Force One. From there, he and his family will travel to Camp David for the duration of the Memorial Day weekend.

"In New Hampshire, should we need them, we have four emergency routes designated A, B, C, and D to return to Air Force One. In the eventuality that we have to evacuate, Agent Navarro will make the call as to which route we take. We've already gone all over this, and I don't anticipate problems. We have agents on the ground in all locations. Protestors have already arrived at the school. The locals have separated them and given them their own location.

"As far as specifics go, a chapter of the Ku Klux Klan has driven up from Georgia to march while President Crane is speaking. The local police are ready to arrest them for disturbing the peace as soon as they become a problem. We're actively monitoring both situations, but the New Hampshire State Police have both situations in hand. They are keeping us updated. Again, though, I don't anticipate problems. Questions before we go?"

Navarro looked up. "We have any more information about the metro situation in DC?"

"Nothing indicates a threat to the president. For several weeks now, the FBI has been monitoring a group from New Jersey that it believed was planning some kind of attack. The Bureau is tracking suspects and anticipates having them in custody shortly. At this point, they're a concern but not a worry. That said, we have diverted resources to that investigation as a precaution, leaving us a little thinner than I would like in New Hampshire. We don't anticipate problems, but we have ample staff in place should any occur. Anything else?"

"Any chance we can persuade Cohiba to avoid trying to make nice with the protestors?" asked one of the other agents.

Baker drew in a breath. "I have spoken to the president and voiced our security concerns, but he was unmoved We'll have CAT members on the roof with sniper rifles in case of an incident."

CAT was the Secret Service's counterassault team. While agents on protective duty carried pistols, their primary job was to protect the president by removing him from danger as quickly as they could. That meant they usually surrounded him and carried him to an awaiting escape vehicle.

The counterassault team, however, was a special forces unit that laid down suppressive fire in the eventuality of an attack by multiple gunmen. They rode in the rear of the motorcade and bought time for everyone else to get out of there. They were some of the baddest men on the planet. Navarro couldn't think of anyone else he'd rather have watching the president's back.

Still, the metro attack had him on edge. If it were up to him, he would have scrapped the afternoon entirely. It wasn't up to him, though. This was the president's call, ultimately, and the president would see no reason to postpone.

"Any other questions?" asked Baker. No one else had anything, so he nodded and looked to the six supervisory agents in the room. "Okay, then. You guys know what to do. Do your jobs and get everyone home safely. Let's roll."

Chapter 8

Nassir dropped me off in front of our mosque, and I immediately got in my car. Jacob Ganim lived near Broadripple Park on the city's northeast side of town. It was a middle-class neighborhood full of bungalows built in the thirties and forties on tree-lined streets. I had always liked that part of the city.

I parked about a block from his house and grabbed a pair of polypropylene gloves from the evidence collection kit in my trunk. Ganim owned a single-story bungalow with a big front porch and elaborate flower beds full of hostas and other shade plants. The yard was trimmed and neat, so someone was caring for the house while he was away. A faded red baby swing hung from a low-hanging limb on a tree out front. He had a family, evidently. Hopefully someone would talk to me.

I walked up the asphalt driveway to the front door and knocked hard. The air smelled like freshly cut grass. In the distance, a lawnmower droned. I waited for twenty or thirty seconds before knocking again and listening for voices from inside.

Nobody came to the door, so I peered through the front window at a cozy living room with a couch, a loveseat, and a coffee table. Despite his having a family, none of the pillows on the couch were out of place, the books on the coffee table were precisely stacked atop one another, and there were no toys on the floor. It looked like a home that had been staged for sale.

I knocked hard again and then watched through the window to see whether anyone was coming. Nothing inside moved, though, so I followed the driveway down the side of the home to the back. None of the doors or windows had visible sensors on them for an alarm system. Even more important than that, the neighbors all had single-story homes, none of which provided a vantage over Ganim's privacy fence. I was good to go.

I snapped on my gloves and took out my lock pick set from the plastic holder in my wallet. If this had been a normal homicide investigation, I would have secured a warrant for the victim's house and searched it without a problem. According to all official records, though, Jacob Ganim was still alive. That wouldn't change until Havelock got his head out of his ass and let me do my job. Based on all I had seen of the man, that could take a while. This job was off the books.

I picked the deadbolt on his rear door and stepped inside. The air smelled stale, and the room was warm. The back door led directly into a modern, clean kitchen with stainless steel appliances, stark white cabinets, and gray granite counters. A thin layer of dust covered everything.

I slipped out of the kitchen and into the hallway that connected the front and rear of the house. The decor was clean and modern. The oak hardwood floors creaked under my weight. I popped my head into rooms off the hallway, first into a bathroom and then into a bedroom with a toddler bed. Dust covered the flat surfaces in both rooms.

I followed the front hallway past another small branching hallway that led to two additional bedrooms and then to the front living room. It looked just as it had from the front porch, only now I could see pictures that hung on the walls. I had seen pictures of Ganim's body, but I hadn't seen pictures of him alive before. He was a light-skinned Arab man with straight black hair, dark eyes, and slightly inset cheeks. In nearly every picture, he held a little girl who looked just like him. They looked happy. I snapped a picture of one of those pictures with my cell phone.

A woman accompanied the two of them in many pictures. She had blonde hair, green eyes, and pale skin. She and the little girl had the same nose, although that little girl had clearly gotten her olive skin tone from her father. Whether the blonde woman was his wife or girlfriend, I didn't know. Based on the dust covering everything in the house, clearly neither she nor the girl lived here.

Though I had gotten a better picture of who Ganim was while walking through the house, nothing told me why he was dead. Maybe Havelock was right. Maybe I did need to focus on Michael Najam, Ganim's undercover alter ego.

Before leaving, I went back to the main hallway and started opening doors I hadn't yet tried. One opened to a linen closet, but the second opened to a stairwell into an unfinished basement. I couldn't find a light switch, so I took out my cell phone and held it in front of me like a torch as I descended.

The basement walls were bare concrete. Casement windows along the ceiling let in pools of light that did little to alleviate the gloom. It smelled just slightly damp. I flicked a light switch at the foot of the steps, and six bare-bulb light fixtures immediately bathed the room in harsh white light. Where the rooms upstairs looked like something in a magazine, the basement looked like a teenager's hangout. On the far end of the room, there was a threadbare rug over the concrete floor, a desk pushed against the wall, a bright orange sofa, and a coffee table. There was a beer bottle on the coffee table and an ashtray on the desk.

More interesting than any of that, there was a corkboard on an easel near one wall. I walked toward it and caught a whiff of marijuana as I did. Ganim had the remnants of a joint in the ashtray and a small Ziploc bag full of weed in the desk's bottom right drawer. In addition, there was an empty pill container in the trash can. The label said it was Vicodin 10/300. This guy was a walking pharmacy.

I put the pill container back in the garbage and took out my cell phone to snap pictures of everything down there. Then I looked at the corkboard. There were dozens of pictures, each of which was numbered. A few were taken at spots around Indianapolis, but most had been shot outside a familiar two-story motel. There was a man and at least one woman in hijab in every picture. I didn't remember the man's name, but he was the imam of a small mosque on the east side of town and had a seat on Indianapolis's Interfaith Council. I didn't remember seeing any of the women before.

I took pictures of the board and then looked around for a legend that would explain what I was looking at. I found it on the rug beneath the coffee table.

1. Fatima Jaffari
2. Milana al-Amin
3. Aisha Shalhoub

The list went on, but they were all names of women, presumably those in the pictures. He had six names on the list, although some of the women were in multiple pictures. I went back to the corkboard and took pictures of each individual picture in case I had to reference them later. Then I took a step back.

Before becoming a detective, I had spent a couple of years as a patrol officer. In that time, I had broken up fights at just about every dive bar in town. I had also been to more than my share of seedy hotels. I recognized this one from the tattered orange awning over the office. It was on the southeast side of town near the Marion County Fairgrounds. At one time, hookers used to hang out in its lobby and ply their services to truckers who stopped by for the night.

I didn't know who these ladies were, but Ganim watched and photographed them for a reason. He was studying them—stalking them, practically. This was an investigation, but I doubted it made it to any report that went to the FBI. More than that, it had nothing to do with Nassir and the men at his camp.

More and more, I wondered what game Ganim was actually playing.

I stared at the pictures for another moment before my cell phone rang. I almost picked it up without thinking, but then I stopped myself.

I had dumped my actual cell phone into a storm drain that morning. By now, it had probably floated to the White River or the Geist Reservoir. Nobody knew the number on this phone except Special Agent Havelock—and now Nassir. I didn't expect a call from either of those men, though.

I hesitated and then reached into my suit coat for the phone. According to the caller ID, it was my sister. I furrowed my brow before answering.

"Hey, Rana," I said. "How'd you get this number?"

My sister's voice, normally strong and confident, trembled as she responded.

"Please get out of that house, Ashraf."

I blinked. "What are you talking about?"

"I don't know," she said, her voice on the edge of tears. "There's a man here. He's got a gun. He told me to call you on this number."

A cold shot of adrenaline passed through me. The basement around me disappeared.

"Is he still there?"

79

"Yes," she said, her voice barely above a whisper.

"Hand him the phone."

Nothing happened for a moment, but then someone bobbled the phone, and my sister's voice came back on.

"He won't talk to you. Get out of the house, or he'll kill me."

"Did he say that?"

It took Rana a five count before she responded. When she did, her voice was barely above a whisper.

"Yes."

"Give him the phone. I want to talk to him directly."

"He won't talk to you," she said, her voice nearing hysterics. "He's got a gun to my head, Ashraf. Please."

"All right," I said, standing. "I'm leaving now. Ask him what he wants."

Rana paused. I heard her say something, and I thought I heard a voice respond, but I couldn't be sure. Then she came back on the phone. Her voice was shaky.

"He said that you're already giving him what he wants. In exchange, he'll leave here shortly."

Her voice trailed off just as I ran out the back door.

"Tell me you're all right, Rana," I said.

I could practically hear the tears in her voice when she spoke.

"He says that if you go to the police, he'll kill Hannah and the kids."

My heart thudded against my breastbone, and I could feel waves of cold sweat begin to form on my brow.

"Tell him I understand."

Rana hung up, and I sprinted to my car, my stomach churning. When I took this case, I had a voice in my mind telling me Kevin Havelock had held back on me, that he hadn't told me the whole truth. Like an idiot, I ignored it because I thought I could trust him. I didn't plan to make that mistake again. When I reached my car, I jumped inside, looked over my shoulder, and floored it out of there.

Along the way, I took my phone out and dialed Havelock. He answered after three rings, but I spoke before he could say anything.

"Havelock, we need to talk."

"You sound angry," he said. "Why do you sound angry?"

"Ask me again in a few hours. In the meantime, I need you to put a strike team together."

"You found out who killed Michael Najam?"

I gritted my teeth before speaking. "No. The guy who killed Michael Najam found my sister. Get a team together. We're taking him down. And send a car to my house. He threatened my wife and kids."

Chapter 9

I got to Rana's neighborhood a few minutes later and parked about a block away from her cul-de-sac. I wanted to rush onto her street and kick her door down, but I didn't know who I'd be going up against in that house or what he was capable of. He wasn't just some average guy off the street, though. He must have had Jacob Ganim's house under surveillance. Maybe he had even installed a silent alarm.

So I sat and waited outside, gripping my steering wheel hard enough that my knuckles turned white. The more I sat, the angrier I got. Aside from Nassir, my wife, and Kevin Havelock, no one should have known that number. Somehow, this guy did. And not only did he know the number, he knew my family. This never should have happened. There should have been safeguards in place.

About ten minutes after I arrived, a full-sized black SUV pulled up behind me. Havelock was in the driver's seat, and he rolled his window down as I approached his car.

"I asked for a team," I said.

"Your sister's alone," said Havelock, stepping out. "A helicopter from Homeland Security buzzed over the house with an infrared camera."

"Fine," I said, already turning and walking. My sister lived in an old Arts and Crafts home built when the twentieth century was still new. Over the years, she and Nassir had spent a small fortune restoring the home to its original state. In the process, they turned a drafty, dilapidated mansion into a comfortable modern home with accurate historical features. I wished their daughter had gotten to see it finished.

As I stepped onto the porch, I noticed the oak front door was open a crack. I reached to my ankle holster for my firearm and found Havelock behind me unholstering his own weapon.

"You sure she's the only one in there?" I asked.

"Aerial scan indicated only one person was inside."

Of course that didn't mean much. That person could have been my sister, but it just as easily could have been a bad guy with an assault weapon. I kept my pistol pointed at the ground and pushed the door open with my foot.

"Rana?" I called. "It's your brother."

Immediately I heard light footsteps upstairs. Havelock and I stepped into the foyer. The home's woodwork had a rich patina, and comfortable reproduction pieces of period furniture decorated the front room. My sister must have been in her bedroom because it took her a moment to come down the stairs. Her eyes were red and her cheeks were puffy, but she didn't look hurt.

Rana was nine years older than me. My father died before he even knew my mother was pregnant with me, leaving my mother to raise two children alone. My mom worked two jobs to keep my sister and I clothed and fed, which meant she wasn't around a lot when we were young. That left Rana to take care of me after school. She cooked, she cleaned, and she wiped my nose when I fell. She even learned to forge my mom's signature on school forms so I could go on field trips and other school events. She was as good a sister as anyone could ask for, and it hurt to see her upset.

"Are you alone?" I asked. She nodded. Havelock started to put his weapon away, but I kept mine out.

"I'm going to check the house," I whispered. My sister shut her eyes and shook her head. She wore a white, long-sleeved blouse and black pencil skirt, but she hadn't yet put on her makeup.

Rana rarely wore hijab. She was still a devout woman, but she argued that if men could dress modestly without covering their heads, so could she. A lot of Muslims—men and women—criticized her for going out without her head covered, but I admired her for it. Rana was strong enough to look graceful and elegant while weathering the misdirected criticism of her peers. I hoped my own daughter would grow up to have that kind of strength.

"There's no one here, Ashraf," she said. "He left. I'm fine. You don't need to play hero."

"Are you sure?" I asked.

She rolled her eyes. "He's gone. If he weren't, I'd tell you."

I nodded and slipped my firearm into the holster on my ankle.

"What happened?" I asked.

Rana started to say something, but then she stopped and closed her eyes as she drew in deep breaths. She tried to keep it from showing, but she was terrified. I softened my voice.

"He's gone," I said. "He's not going to hurt you."

"No, he won't," she said, opening her eyes. She swallowed and then looked to Havelock. "I was in my room getting ready for an appointment with my attorney when somebody knocked on the door. He wore a brown uniform, and he was carrying a package, so I thought he worked for UPS—"

"Was he driving a UPS truck?" I asked, interrupting her.

"You always interrupt me, Ashraf. Even when we were kids. You asked me to tell you what happened, and I am."

"I don't always interrupt you. It's an important question."

She took a breath and then crossed her arms while shaking her head. "Fine. No. I didn't see a truck, but I thought he had parked up the street and dropped off packages for multiple houses. They do that."

"Have you seen any unfamiliar cars on the street lately?" I asked.

"There are always unfamiliar cars on the street. Across the street, Beth can't keep a housekeeper to save her life, so we have a new car there at least every other week. Down the street, Melanie sleeps with a new personal trainer every time she goes to the gym, so there's always someone new there. The man next door is a psychiatrist in private practice, and he's started meeting clients in his home office. I don't even know if that's legal, but there are always cars there. And then Kathy—"

"I got the picture," I said, interrupting her. "You didn't see a new car."

"I was talking, Ashraf," she said. "That's twice you've interrupted me. How do you expect me to answer your questions if you keep interrupting me?"

I started to tell her I was just doing my job, but Havelock cleared his throat, getting my attention. He looked from her to me.

"Why don't I question Mrs. Hadad from here on out, Lieutenant? It might save us some time."

"Sure, fine," I said, taking a step back.

Havelock took over the questioning. According to Rana, a man pretending to be a delivery person had knocked on the door. When she opened it, he handed her a box, which she took. He then pointed a gun at her and told her to take a step back. It was a smart move, really. By giving her a box, he both distracted her while he took out his gun and tied up her hands momentarily to prevent her from fighting back. I had the feeling this guy had done that before.

She didn't recognize the intruder, but she said he had black hair, olive colored skin, and dark eyes. He was approximately thirty-five to forty years old, a little under six feet tall, and of a medium build. When she finished answering our questions, she asked to be alone for a few minutes, so Havelock and I walked to the front porch.

Once Rana closed her door, I crossed my arms and looked to the FBI agent.

"Who's Jacob Ganim?"

"You know who he is," said Havelock.

"No, I don't," I said, shaking my head. "I've only been working this case for a couple of hours, and already I've found enough pills and weed connected to Ganim to make me suspect he might have been dealing. He's freelancing a case, too. He had surveillance pictures of a lot of women."

Havelock narrowed his eyes. "Where'd you find these pictures and drugs?"

"I found drugs in his room at my brother-in-law's camp and in his house near Broad Ripple Park. I found pictures in his basement."

Havelock looked down. "You were told to investigate Michael Najam, not Jacob Ganim."

"I'm working a homicide and following the evidence," I said. "And the evidence tells me you're either a liar or you're incompetent."

Havelock closed his eyes and took a step back. "I'll ignore the insult for now. What else have you found?"

"My brother-in-law, the guy Ganim was sent to investigate for potential ties to terrorist organizations, is very likely clean. Every piece of evidence you have against him is circumstantial. You had no right to go after him the way you did. The only crimes I've found so far are those committed by your agent. If he were alive today, I could get arrest him for possession of a schedule I substance. I might even be able to get him for possession with intent to sell. And did you know he had a history of depression? He had no business whatsoever being undercover."

"I didn't know about his depression or the drugs," said Havelock, his voice low.

"What did you know about this guy?" I asked. "From what I'm seeing, it can't be much."

Havelock looked to his right and pointed to a set of white wicker furniture. I nodded, and he sat down on a loveseat. I continued standing but leaned against the thick, wooden railing that separated the porch from the yard. Then I crossed my arms.

"Ganim wasn't my agent," he said.

"Who was he?"

Havelock looked up and caught my eye. "I have no idea. I got a call from DC a couple of months ago telling me the Bureau's counterterrorism division planned to run an operation in my area. I found out later that operation involved Jacob Ganim. I didn't know him, I had never seen his personnel file, I had never seen his mission reports, and I had never spoken to his co-workers or his handler. Before he died, I didn't even know what he looked like. I supported the operation because that was my job. I called you in after Ganim died because I needed someone independent to tell me what went wrong."

I put my hands on the rail behind me. "Everything

went wrong. That's what happened. You're getting played. I don't know who's doing it or why, but Ganim wasn't working a case against Nassir or his friends. Not only that, the moment I got to Ganim's house and started getting somewhere with my investigation, a guy came after my sister and told her to call me on the phone you supplied, the one no one should know about."

Havelock stood up and started pacing the front porch.

"He must have had Ganim's house under surveillance."

"Since he knew my phone number, he has access to at least some of your files. I highly doubt he's working alone, either. We've got to assume somebody in your office is playing for the other side. Ganim was either involved with him or found out about him. Either way, Ganim's dead now, and somebody came after people I care about."

Havelock nodded and then stopped pacing.

"I should probably turn this over to the Office of Professional Responsibility for them to investigate."

He didn't continue. He was waiting for me to say something.

"But if you do that, you're afraid your higher-ups will bury it."

He grunted, nodded, and started pacing again. "If you want out now, I won't hold it against you."

"I don't think so," I said, shaking my head. "Whoever this guy is, he came after my sister. He and his friends are using my community for cover for whatever they're doing. This is personal."

Havelock returned to the wicker loveseat he had sat on earlier and took out his cell phone.

"I'm going to put a team together to search Ganim's house. We'll figure out what's going on there."

"You still have his body?" I asked.

Havelock thought for a moment and then slowly nodded. "We should. Why?"

"I'd like Dr. Rodriguez in the Marion County Coroner's Office to look at it. With everything else going on, we need to make sure we can trust the autopsy results."

Havelock blinked as he thought that through. "We can bring him in as a consulting pathologist. He won't get paid, but I'll make sure he has access to the body."

"It'd be better if we could ship the body to him so he can examine it without someone looking over his shoulder. I'm sure your pathologists are good, but you know the old saying. Too many cooks in the kitchen."

He sighed and cocked his head to the side. "I'll see what I can do."

"I need one more thing from you. Someone put a gun to my sister's head today. I need you to keep her safe until I find the guy and put him in custody."

"Of course," he said, raising his eyebrows. "I've got a safe house in town. She'll be okay there."

"If you know about it, so do the bad guys," I said. "It's not safe."

"What do you suggest, then?"

"Nassir's camp. It's remote and defensible. The main building is concrete and built on a hill. You'll have sightlines for at least a kilometer in most directions. Plus, if the bad guys know the situation as well as I think they do, they won't expect Rana to go there. She'll be safer there than anywhere you can put her."

"Somehow, I don't think your brother-in-law will appreciate more FBI agents showing up on his doorstep."

"He'll get over it for his wife's sake."

Havelock ran his fingers through his hair and then turned his back to me. "We're really doing this. I'm violating my direct orders and spearheading an investigation into the most decorated division within my agency."

"No," I said, shaking my head. "You're doing your job and following the evidence where it leads you. If the evidence leads us to someone within your own agency, tough shit for them. Now let's go. You have work to do, and so do I."

Chapter 10

Once Havelock and I had the outline of a plan together, I knocked on Rana's door and waited for her to open it. Her eyes were harder than they had been a moment earlier. When I first came to the house, she had been scared. Now, she was angry—and rightfully so.

"Agent Havelock and I have been talking. We're not sure that it's safe for you to be here right now."

She crossed her arms and nodded. "Okay. What does the brain trust suggest, then?"

Rana's angry expression made her look even more like our mother than usual. I blinked and took a stutter step back.

"The man who came to your house this morning seems to have access to information that he shouldn't. We can't put you in a safe house because we don't know whether they've been compromised. In our opinion, the best place for you is probably Nassir's camp. It's remote, it's defensible, and nobody would expect you to go there."

For a moment, she became as still as a statue. Then she narrowed her eyes and nodded.

"I appreciate your concern, Ashraf," she said, her voice almost artificially sweet. "But in the future, I humbly ask that you include me in any discussions involving my welfare."

"I'll make arrangements for one of my agents to—" began Havelock. Before he could finish his thought, Rana glared at him, and the FBI agent stopped speaking.

"I'm not done speaking," she said, looking from Havelock to me. "I will most certainly not be joining my soon-to-be ex-husband at his little playground. If I'm not safe in my own home, I will make arrangements on my own to go somewhere safe."

"I understand that you may not want to see Nassir, but Agent Havelock and I truly think his compound will be the safest place for you."

When Rana looked at me, her eyes practically flashed red.

"I would rather be tied to a stake and set on fire than spend time with Nassir. If you drag me to that camp of his, you'll have a new murder to solve very shortly after my arrival."

Neither Havelock nor I said anything for a moment as we thought. Rana's tone didn't seem to leave a lot of wiggle room.

"What do you propose, then?" I asked.

"I will go to Chicago, where I will rent a suite at the Drake Hotel. I will shop, go to museums, and have massages at a spa. My husband will gratefully pay for the entire trip."

I tilted my head to the side. "If the bad guys can track you to your house, there's a good chance they can track your credit cards."

"Then I will withdraw cash from my bank account and use that cash to purchase prepaid credit cards they can't track. I will not stay with Nassir, and that is final."

I knew Rana well enough to know she wasn't going to budge on this, so I looked at Agent Havelock. He thought for a moment and then drew in a breath.

"If that's what you want to do, you should be fine," he said. "I'll call the field office in Chicago to let them know you're in the area. I'd prefer if you rented a car instead of taking your own."

She closed her eyes and nodded. "I will."

Havelock looked at me and then to her before nodding and walking back to his car, giving us some privacy. I looked at Rana and softened my voice.

"Are you okay?"

She nodded. "I'm fine."

I knew she wasn't, but I didn't plan on pushing. I looked down so I wouldn't have to meet her gaze.

"I'm sorry about Nassir. I don't know whether I've told you that yet."

She drew in a breath and blinked away a tear. "I want to hate him, but I can't. He's the father of my only child. We had a life together. Things were starting to turn around. He seemed happy. And then he just discarded me like I was garbage. He didn't even give me an explanation. He just left."

"He's a fool," I said.

"Yeah," she said, nodding. "And I still love him."

I stayed with her on the porch for another few minutes, but we didn't say much. I wished I could comfort her in some way, but I was just her little brother. She needed time. Before leaving, I gave her a hug and told her to call me if she needed anything. She promised she would.

As I walked back to my car, I found Kevin Havelock walking back to the house, probably to help Rana make arrangements to disappear temporarily. Havelock and I might have disagreed about how to run an investigation, but he was a good man who would do everything he could to keep her safe. That made him all right in my book.

When I got back to my car, I focused once again on the case in front of me. Even after searching his house, I didn't know a lot about Jacob Ganim. It took time and planning to do the kind of surveillance work he did, though. The women he photographed and identified were important to him. That meant they were important to me, too.

I put my car in gear and headed to the city's southeast side, where I eventually pulled into the parking lot of a seedy, two-story hotel. Unlike on previous trips, no prostitutes loitered near the office, but neither did women in hijab. I parked beside a pickup on the edge of the lot. There was a fallow field across the street and the white barns of the county fairgrounds just beyond that. Modest family homes on large, rural lots stretched into the distance east and west.

As I got out of the car, I heard a cow mooing from the fairgrounds. They must have been having a cattle show.

I didn't know what to expect at the hotel, so I kept

my eyes open for threats as I walked to the lobby. Nobody came out of any nearby rooms or peered through the windows at me, though. It was just a crummy place to stay.

The lobby's interior smelled like stale cigarettes. There was a sofa pushed against the right wall with a chipped wooden coffee table in front of it. A television blared from a stand near the front desk. The woman behind the counter looked up at me and then down to the phone in her hand without saying a word. Her name tag said her name was Kylie.

"Hi, Kylie, I'm here looking for one of your guests," I said. "My sister's staying here."

The receptionist thumbed a final message in and then put her phone down. She had straight white teeth and freckles on the tip of her nose. Though she was probably in her mid-twenties, her skin still had the tanned glow of youth, and she smiled easily and well with just a bit of reserve. Her smile faded just a little as I drew nearer.

"We don't give out guest information, sir. Sorry. There are a lot of crazy people out there."

I nodded. "That's understandable. You don't have to tell me her room number, but could you call her for me?"

Her smile turned uncomfortable. "Okay, sir. What's your sister's name?"

"Fatima Jaffari."

It was one of the names from the pictures in Ganim's house. Kylie's uncomfortable smile didn't waver, but she shook her head.

"I'm sorry, but we don't have anybody by that name here."

"Are you sure?" I asked, leaning against the counter. "You didn't even check the computer."

She forced herself to laugh. Then she looked down. A lock of brown hair fell over her forehead.

"I'm not supposed to say this, but we've only got a couple of guests right now. Most of our customers arrive late in the evening and leave early in the morning. This isn't the kind of place you stay at for long."

"How about Aisha Shalhoub?" I asked, leaning forward to rest my arms on the counter. "That's my other sister. They might be staying together."

She looked thoughtful for a moment and then frowned before exhaling. "I'm sorry, sir, but we don't have anyone by that name, either."

"Well, who do you have staying here?"

She tittered uncomfortably. "Like I said, I can't give out information about our customers."

"How about Milana al-Amin?"

Her smile faltered for just a second, but then it came back as she regained her composure. She laughed softly.

"You have a lot of sisters," she said. "Bathrooms must have been challenging growing up."

"Milana's not a sister," I said. "I met her on Tinder."

She leaned forward and started running a finger down my forearm to my wrist and then to the knuckles of my hand. When she spoke, her voice was a little low and sultry.

"You don't look like the kind of guy who needs to meet girls on the internet."

I pulled my arm back. "I'm usually not. How about Michael Najam?"

She shook her head and shrugged. "Nope."

"Jacob Ganim? Is he familiar?"

For just a second, she tensed. Then she stood straighter and shrugged. Where previously her hand gestures and body language had been fluid and natural, this was a little wooden. She knew Jacob.

"Never heard of him. Sorry."

"You sure?" I asked. "He's a reasonably good looking guy. His skin is a little lighter than mine, and he has a slight build. He's maybe a year or two younger than me. You never saw him?"

She raised her eyebrows and shook her head. "Nope, and sorry. If you'll excuse me, though, I've got some work to do."

"Of course," I said, taking a step back. I pointed to the couch and television with my thumb. "I'm pretty sure my sisters are planning to stay here, though. I'm willing to wait for them, so I'll just take a seat and watch TV for a while. You won't even know I'm here."

She smiled as she considered. Then she leaned forward and looked around the lobby conspiratorially.

"You know, there's not really a whole lot going on around here right now. There's an open room right next door if you want to hang out with me. I can help you pass the time a lot better than the TV."

I took a step toward the counter and leaned forward so that our faces were only a few inches apart. She bit her lower lip and smiled just a little. It almost looked real. Her breath smelled like breath mints and something sweet. Strawberries, maybe. Then I unbuckled my badge from my belt and put it down on the counter in front of her.

"I appreciate that you're willing to go this far to protect these women, but it's time to cut the shit. Are they here, or are they not?"

She looked at my badge, and then to me, a blank expression on her face. Only when I looked down, did I see her thumbing a message into her phone. I grimaced, and she tilted her head to the side and shrugged.

"Sorry. They're not here. I've never even heard of them."

"Even if they're not here now, I know they were here at one time. They're not in trouble, and neither are you. Okay? I just want to talk to them. They may have information about a homicide."

She shook her head again. "I don't know what you're talking about. They've never—"

"Please don't lie to me again," I said, interrupting her and staring directly into her eyes. "Jacob Ganim, the man you pretended you didn't know, is dead. I'm working his murder. I know he was here. I know he took pictures of the women I mentioned. I want to know who they are and why he was interested in them. You're not in any trouble, and neither are the women. If they're in the country illegally, I don't care. I'm not going to tell anybody about them. If you make me get a warrant, though, I'm going to have to bring in a lot more people, and things will get complicated very quickly. It's your choice."

She blinked a few times and then licked her lips. "Get a warrant."

I had hoped she wouldn't say that, but I nodded anyway.

"If that's how you want to do this, that's how we'll do this," I said, reaching for my wallet and the business cards I kept in there. I put one on the counter in front of her. "Talk to your friends. I've seen pictures of them, so I know they wear hijab. If they have any contacts in the Islamic community in Indianapolis, have them ask around about me. I'm well known, and I'm fair. I can't protect them or you if you make me bring in my entire department."

She nodded, so I took my badge from the counter and hooked it on my belt.

"My cell number's on the back of the card. Be smart and use it."

She forced a smile to her lips as I walked out. In a perfect world, she'd carefully consider what I had to say and then talk to her friends. But that wasn't going to happen. She had something planned. She was either protecting those women, or she was exploiting them and keeping them hidden. Given that hotel's history as a flop house for prostitutes, I leaned toward the latter.

I walked back to my car and then drove about two blocks away, where I parked in the driveway of a single-story brick home.

I sat, waited, and watched the parking lot of the hotel for about fifteen minutes before anything happened. The first guest to leave a room was a guy, but I couldn't make out his features at that distance. He pressed his back against the exterior of the building and peered down the side like some kind of amateur spy. Someone probably should have told him he would have looked a lot less suspicious if he acted like a normal person.

After checking the building, he walked back to the room from which he had come and held open the door. Two women wearing hijab immediately came out and hurried toward a minivan on the edge of the property.

As those women ran, the man went to the room next door. This time, three women in hijab emerged and ran toward the minivan. None of them looked as if they were being held against their will, but there could have been some kind of coercion there I didn't see.

As the man got in the minivan's driver's seat, I backed my car out of the driveway and floored it back to the hotel, where I braked hard enough that my tires chirped. Then I backed up and positioned myself so that my car blocked most of the entrance.

The minivan's driver saw me and froze. He had backed his van out of its parking spot and was now in the center of the lot facing my car. His vehicle stopped moving as our eyes locked.

I started to open my door, but then the van's tires spun on the asphalt. The heavy vehicle rocketed straight toward me.

"Oh, shit."

I didn't have time to move, so I braced myself for the impact. At the last moment, the minivan screeched to a stop not more than a foot from my car. All of its doors flung open as the women inside ran.

I pounded on the latch of my seatbelt and tried to open my door but found it pinned against the minivan's front bumper. Before I could move, the van's rear door slid open and women ran out. I dove across the passenger seat of my car and threw open the door just in time to see the van's driver sprinting away.

"I just want to talk."

The driver looked over his shoulder but didn't stop. He was heading across a field straight toward the Marion County fairgrounds. I could lose him there, so I took off after him.

When I had gotten up that morning, I had put on comfortable black leather shoes. They were great for walking around an office, but they were heavy, and they didn't have the traction of a tennis shoe—which the guy I was chasing wore. By the time I got about halfway across the field, the guy had gained at least forty or fifty feet on me. Even if I had worn tennis shoes, though, I doubted I would have been able to catch him. He was fast enough that I never even had a chance.

So I stopped and put my hands on my knees while I

caught my breath. As the man I was chasing reached the edge of the field, he looked over his shoulder. The fairground's barns were just ahead of him. There were a few people walking around. He could have disappeared if he wanted. Instead, though, he turned and watched me, daring me to chase him.

He wanted me distracted.

I looked behind me toward the hotel. A woman in hijab closed the sliding rear door of the minivan as Kylie climbed into the driver's seat. The rear tires spun as she backed up and then floored it over the hotel's lawn toward the road out front. The man I had been chasing stood straighter and gave me a halfhearted wave before turning and running deeper into the fairgrounds.

I wanted to chase him down, but I didn't need to. He and I knew people in common. More than that, he was in nearly every picture Jacob Ganim took. He may have escaped for now, but very soon, this man of God was going to get a visitor, and I didn't plan to be nice.

Chapter 11

Abdullah had never felt his heart beat so quickly. His entire life, eighteen years, had led to this moment. The vest weighed heavily against his skin. For the past three months, he and his brother had lifted weights, run, and even boxed at a gym near their house to get in shape. He wore blue jeans and a wool sweater loose enough to conceal the heavy vest Hashim Bashear had constructed. To someone looking at him from afar, he would have looked fat, but beneath his outfit, he was strong and lean, more powerful than he had ever been in his life.

He stood beside his brother in front of Westbrook Elementary School. Hamza Bashear had driven them directly from the townhouse in New York. To his right, perhaps two hundred yards away, a raucous crowd had gathered behind police barricades. They held signs and shouted political slogans. Until this moment, nothing about the day had seemed real. Now, he knew his destiny was before him.

When Abdullah's parents had first brought him to the United States, they told him he would have a better life than he ever would have had otherwise. And they were probably right. In Somalia, he would have had to join a gang just to survive. He didn't have to do that in the United States, but he could hardly call what they did living. It was unfair.

People spray painted things on their doors. When his

mother left the apartment wearing hijab, people leered at her and called her a rag head. Though no one had ever physically attacked Abdullah yet, some drunk men beat up his father the night after a mass shooting on the East Coast. They broke two of his ribs and his nose. They could have killed him, all because they had seen him walk out of a mosque.

For a long time, Abdullah's life in the United States had left him confused. He had often wondered why God would allow bad things to happen to His people. Only later when he met Hashim Bashear online did he understand. Hashim showed Abdullah that he had a place in the world, that God cared about him, that God had created him for a purpose. Hashim taught him more than that, though; he showed him the truth of the world.

Abdullah, for the first time, saw politicians who lied so fluently they no longer understood truth. He saw governments that undermined God's authority. He saw a decadent, broken place beyond saving. God didn't want the world to be as it was, and for the good of humanity, Hashim told him, God had made men like Abdullah. God had created him to become a soldier, a martyr. Standing there with a bomb strapped to his chest was his entire reason for being.

At that moment, the president of the United States stood somewhere inside the elementary school, preparing to give a speech to elect another wicked man to a position of power. It would only lead to more suffering the world over. The cycle had to stop. Hashim Bashear had made him see that. It was his moral duty to set the world right.

"I'm nervous," said Yasin, his breath heavy. Abdullah nodded and looked to his brother.

"Me, too," he said. "But there's no wrong in what we are about to do. We have to be strong. This is why God created us. This is why He sent us to this country."

Yasin drew in a long, slow breath. "*Insh'Allah,* my son will know me for who I am and not the man I was."

"He will know you as a man of God," said Abdullah. "And he will know that you do this for him so that he and his children don't have to fight as we do."

Yasin nodded, his face distant. "Today, we go home. I'm sorry if I haven't been the best brother."

"*Inna lillahi wa inna ilayhi raji'un,*" said Abdullah, reciting a familiar verse from the Quran. "To God we belong, and to Him we shall return. You are the best brother I could ask for because you are the man who stands beside me now."

Yasin nodded. "I'm ready."

Abdullah looked at him and knew it would be for the last time. "May God give us the strength to do what we must."

The moment the words left his lips, the two young men began walking to their deaths.

Almost three thousand people had crammed themselves into the gym to hear the president speak. Each one made

Sean Navarro nervous, for each one could become a threat at any moment.

Ideally, they would have hand searched every person who came into the arena, but Senator Hill's campaign would have gone ballistic at the mere suggestion. Instead, the Secret Service had brought a portable metal detector and dozens of metal-detecting wands. Every single person who walked through the entrance went through that metal detector, and then every single person had a wand waved over his or her body for a closer scan.

More than that, every person who entered that arena had his or her picture taken by a camera hidden inside the top rail of the metal detector. Those pictures were then sent via an encrypted satellite link to the Intelligence Community Comprehensive National Cybersecurity Initiative Data Center near Bluffdale, Utah. Code-named Bumblehive, the data center officially cost the US taxpayers something around one and a half billion dollars. In actuality, it cost several times that and had computing power an order of magnitude greater than most members of Congress knew.

The data center processed all forms of digital communications from emails to parking receipts. Each of its Cray XC30 supercomputers could scan and compare thousands of images to dozens of federal databases each second. Matching the men and women who walked into the elementary school against images from a national terror watch list didn't even scratch the surface of what the facility could do, and yet it could save the life of the most powerful man in the world.

Agent Navarro didn't trust technology to replace human instinct, but he couldn't deny its utility. It was an amazing system, and already it had pointed out several potential troublemakers—two men with violent felony convictions, three suspected militia members from Idaho, and one woman with an outstanding federal arrest warrant for tax evasion.

Agent Navarro stayed near the stage, approximately fifteen feet from the president. He was close enough to protect him should the need arise but also far enough to give the president a moment of privacy with Senator Hill before both men began their presentations. In addition to his firearm, Navarro carried a tablet computer that allowed him to see video feeds from the body cameras worn by the uniformed Secret Service agents outside and the security cameras the advance team had installed a week ago.

He went through the various feeds but didn't see anything that stood out to him, so he keyed his microphone.

"We are ten minutes to magic hour. Exits one through four, sound off."

Early in his career, before the Secret Service had moved to digitally encrypted communications gear, Navarro and those with whom he worked had to speak in code in case anyone unfriendly tried to listen in. Agents could speak much more freely now, but they still tried to keep communication as succinct as possible.

"Exit one, clear."

"Exit two, clear."

"Exit three, I've got a lost family. They're moving to the main entrance. Otherwise clear."

"Exit four, clear."

No real threats, then. He flicked his finger across his tablet to view a feed from the body camera of one of the snipers perched on the building's roof. Due to the agent's position, Navarro couldn't see much except a line of trees.

"Overwatch, check in."

"I've got a family in the park approximately three blocks from the school. You want uniforms to clear them out?"

Agent Navarro tried to picture the area in his head. The only park nearby was southwest of the elementary school. Evacuation routes A and B ran on either side.

"What are they doing?" asked Navarro.

"Flying a kite. Mom, dad, grandpa, toddler, and bouncing baby in a car seat."

The locals were supposed to have cleared that park already, but Navarro shook his head. "Leave them be for now, but keep an eye on them. Main entrance, how are you?"

"We've got a few stragglers coming in late. Other than that, we are clear."

"And finally, Bamboo, what's your status?"

Bamboo was the code name for the president's multicar motorcade. In addition to the Beast—the president's armored limousine—it had decoy vehicles, radio vehicles, an ambulance, and various other vehicles for the president's security detail.

"Bamboo is ready to roll. Cowpuncher has engines running on the tarmac at Pease. Evac route on your order, sir."

Navarro flicked through his available camera feeds and scanned his eyes over the crowd. He had brought a detail of over fifty officers. Combined with the local and state police, they had almost four hundred armed law enforcement officers within a two-block radius. Given the state of the world, he would have preferred if the president never left the Oval Office, but he felt as comfortable as he could given the crowd size.

He looked over his shoulder at President Crane and gave him the thumbs up signal.

The president scanned the crowd and then walked toward Agent Navarro, his brow furrowed.

"Do you know where my wife is?"

Navarro looked to the roped-off set of seats for the first family. The first lady, her daughter, and at least one of the president's grandchildren were gone. Navarro keyed his mike.

"Janet, Cohiba would like to know the location of Camus."

"Piglet had a dirty diaper," said Special Agent Janet Westman. "So Camus and Eeyore took him to the ladies' room. They'll be out momentarily."

"Thanks, Janet," said Navarro before looking to the

president. He turned his mike off. "Ethan had a dirty diaper, sir, so the first lady and your daughter took him to the restroom. They'll be back any moment."

"Thank you, Sean," said the president. He joined Senator Hill on the side of the stage again. The first lady and her family returned to their seats within moments. Once the president saw them, he mouthed *I love you* to his wife and then clapped Senator Hill on the back. The two men walked out on the stage. Navarro keyed his mike once more.

"Showtime. Stay vigilant."

Yasin's breath caught in his throat. Faith had never come as easily for him as it had for his brother. Even as a young boy, Abdullah seemed to find himself within religion in a way Yasin never had. As a child, Abdullah had begged his mother and father to enroll him in their mosque's Arabic classes so that he could read the Quran. By the time he was twelve years old, Abdullah had half the book memorized. When asked questions, he not only knew the Quranic verse, he could quote applicable *Hadith*—the sayings of the Prophet—for many given situations.

Yasin had always imagined his brother would become an imam one day. He'd lead a congregation down the straight path and change people's lives for the better. Above all, he had pictured his brother as a peace-loving man who exemplified the merciful, generous spirit of their faith.

But neither Abdullah nor Yasin had been born into a peace-loving world. They lived in the world of *jahiliyyah,* a world ignorant of God and God's commands. Though Yasin didn't realize it until Hashim Bashear showed him the truth, the Islamic community had truly ceased to exist centuries ago. As believers, it was their job to bring it back —even if that meant dying in the process.

Yasin forced one foot in front of another as he walked toward the protestors. Like his brother, Yasin wore jeans and a bulky cable-knit sweater that hid the vest around his chest. He looked pudgy and soft, like most of the Americans around him, and like them, he held a handmade sign on a yardstick.

Put some balls in the White House.

When the other protestors saw Yasin's sign, they laughed and welcomed him into their group. Yasin looked like one of them, but he wasn't. He felt hot, and the vest seemed to weigh far more than it ought. Even as his index finger touched the switch in his pocket, he wondered whether he could go through with this. The people around him were lost and ignorant, but they didn't seem malicious. They had brought children and their wives. Did God need them to die as well?

Yasin wished he had his brother's strength, his brother's certainty. His legs began to feel weak, and his heart thudded in his chest. The crowd seemed to crush in around him. He wondered what would happen if he walked away. He wouldn't dump his vest, and he wouldn't go to the police. He wouldn't get anyone in trouble. Hashim Bashear had treated them fairly and well, after all. He respected them and even cared for them, but he didn't have a direct pipeline to God. He didn't know what God truly wanted.

Besides, the president was inside. If he had come out beforehand to greet the protestors, Yasin would have gladly given his life and become a martyr. If he couldn't decapitate the snake, though, he had no reason to die. He was barely twenty, and he had an infant son and a wife who depended on him. He had too much to live for and too much to lose. This wasn't his burden. This was a job for a childless man. He started to slip through the crowd, to leave.

He made it about three steps.

Abdullah stood in front of the elementary school. An arched metal awning with an old school bell at its apex covered the front entrance, while four squad cars from the New Hampshire State Police blocked the road out front. Soft, gray clouds stretched from horizon to horizon. Abdullah sucked in a deep breath, knowing it would be his last chance to smell the clean, sweet scent of a spring afternoon.

In a few minutes, he knew would die. Despite his faith, despite his knowledge that paradise awaited him, a growing trepidation began filling him.

"God, give me the strength to do what I must," he whispered as he stepped forward.

A wooden doorstop held Westbrook Elementary's front doors open. Inside, barricades had been set up to funnel crowds through a metal detector. Three men and two women in black suits stood behind those barricades. Each of them wore an earpiece, and each of them walked with a confident swagger. Though they pretended not to notice him, they still stared. Two campaign workers in red, white, and blue T-shirts smiled at him.

"Do you have a ticket, sir?" asked one, a woman a few years younger than Abdullah's mother. Suddenly, he wondered whether he could actually do this. The physical act of triggering the switch wouldn't be a problem, but the vest bothered him. Hashim and Hamza had said the vests were made from ceramic parts, but Abdullah wasn't so sure. He had seen the ball bearings they planned to use. They looked like metal. Surely Hashim hadn't made such an elementary mistake.

"Yes, I have a ticket," he said, feeling his pockets. His hand brushed against the switch in his pocket, and then he touched the glossy card stock ticket Hashim had given him that morning. He hesitated before pulling it out, though.

He was willing to die for his cause, but he wasn't willing to waste his life. Already, the Secret Service agents had begun watching him intently. If he had gone in earlier with a large crowd, maybe he could have slipped through the security gate unnoticed, but not now. Even if he didn't set off the metal detector, the Secret Service agents would pat him down. He'd never make it inside.

Abdullah took his hand out of his pocket and turned around as if he were searching for something on the ground.

"My mother gave me the ticket," he said. "I must have dropped it."

"That's all right," said one of the campaign workers. "We have some open seats, so you can come in with or without your ticket."

Abdullah stood straighter and shook his head. "No, my mom wants the stub back as a souvenir. I'll be right back. I need to find it."

The campaign workers started to say something, but Abdullah started backing toward the entrance as a Secret Service agent passed through the metal detector and into the lobby. Abdullah's heart pounded, and sweat began beading on his forehead.

"Put your hands on top of your head, sir," said the agent, his hand hovering over the firearm on his hip. Abdullah started backing toward the entrance.

"It's all right. I'll be right back."

The moment the words left his lips, his vest started beeping, and he realized how badly he had misunderstood his role in this mission.

Chapter 12

Agent Navarro's body went stiff. He keyed his microphone.

"Repeat, main entrance."

"Control, we have a young man here. He seems confused and disoriented. How do you advise?"

Navarro flicked his fingers across his tablet until he came across the video feed from the lobby. The video showed a man in his early twenties. He had very dark skin and hair cropped close to his brow. The young man's movements looked stiff, but that didn't worry Navarro. Most people got nervous when the Secret Service took an interest in them.

The clothes, however, stuck out to him. The man's sweater was bulky and thick. From the neck down, he looked like a man who would have had to turn sideways to fit through many doorways. His face, though, was thin. He had something under his clothes. For all Navarro knew, the man carried a shotgun.

"Take him into custody. Administer first aid if he's having a medical emergency, but first of all, secure his person and find out what he's got under that sweater."

"Understood, command."

Navarro kept his eyes on the tablet as one of his agents passed through the metal detector to step into the lobby. The young man hesitated and then held up his hands as he backed toward the front door. Then, both he and the Secret Service agent stopped and looked down. Navarro held his breath.

"Main entrance, what's going on?"

Before anyone could respond, three agents appeared from offscreen and tackled the young man. Navarro's heart started pouring.

"Main entrance, I repeat, what's going on?"

"Subject is beeping, Control."

For a split second, Navarro's breath caught in his throat as his mind processed that information. Then the reality of the situation slammed into him full force.

"Main entrance, secure his person and—"

Navarro never got the chance to finish the order.

Hashim smiled at his granddaughter. She had straight black hair, skin a few shades darker than olive, and brown eyes like her father. He hated to use her as cover, but sometimes he had to take risks to succeed.

Though the Americans claimed to take the moral high road, they profiled everyone within their borders and categorized them by race and threat level at both the local and federal levels. Where an Arab man sitting on a park bench alone might have garnered significant attention from the Secret Service, an Arab grandfather sitting with his beloved family would look as American as Thanksgiving dinner.

"*Habibi*, please watch your *ummi* for the next few

minutes," he said. "Can you do that for me?"

She smiled and nodded and turned toward her mother. Hashim looked to his son.

"Let's put up the drone."

Hamza handed the kite strings to his wife and daughter before walking to the double stroller he had brought and taking their drone from the rear seat.

Hashim knew very little about drones, so he had let his son do the research before they purchased anything. Hamza had settled on a professional quadcopter with an integrated high-definition camera on a gyroscope. With the extended battery, it could stay aloft for almost forty-five minutes and fly nearly four miles in any direction before losing a signal. At that point, it would use an integrated GPS tracker to return to the spot at which it had taken off.

In Hamza's tests, it had been able to fly to an altitude well over two thousand feet—outside visual range—and still take crystal-clear video of the ground with its digital zoom camera. It was a remarkable piece of surveillance technology, one that would come in very handy here.

Hamza put the drone on the ground and then used the remote control to take off. Sabah, Hashim's grandaughter, covered her ears at first, but the buzzing motors quickly disappeared. Hashim watched the video feed from his tablet. Every image that camera took was streamed live to a distributed network of servers on three different continents. The events today would be seen live by thousands of men and women around the world and recorded in high-definition video for all of humanity to witness.

"Yasin is in the middle of the crowd, but he's moving," said Hamza, looking up from the screen attached to his drone's flight controller. "He's going to run."

"I see that," said Hashim, reaching into his pocket for a disposable cell phone. "He'll still serve his purpose."

Hashim opened the contact list and selected the second of two phone numbers. He looked up at Sabah and smiled. She looked directly into Hashim's eyes, away from the school. The instant his finger hit the call button, a signal passed from his phone to the nearest cell tower and then to the disassembled phone on Yasin's vest.

The current that would have created the ringtone, though, bypassed the speaker and instead flowed through a circuit that collected and amplified it before sending it into a blasting cap attached to a brick of RDX explosives. It all happened within a thousandth of a second.

The explosion ripped across the park like a cannon shot, reverberating against the trees. For one single moment, the world passed into stunned silence.

Then the screaming started.

Sabah's mother grabbed her daughter and held her to her breast, crying. Hashim looked at the screen of his tablet. A nearly perfect ring of bodies surrounded the spot where Yasin had once stood. The windows of the school that were nearest them had shattered. Limbs and body parts lay across the ground like shells scattered on the beach after a hurricane.

For a few moments, nothing moved, but then people began pulling themselves from the ground. Most of them ran in random directions, away from the bomb blast, but a few brave souls ran toward the damage to check for survivors. They weren't Hashim's concern.

"Show me Abdullah," said Hashim, glancing at Hamza. Hamza nodded and moved the drone so it had a better view of the elementary school. He couldn't see through the glass, but Abdullah hadn't run out yet. He still had a job to perform. Hashim turned his attention to his phone and then looked at Sabah and her mother. "Don't look at the school."

Dalia, Hamza's wife, nodded and held her daughter close. Her eyes were almost glassy. Hashim wouldn't have involved his family if he could have helped it, but they provided him the cover he needed for the job he had to do. He opened the contact list on his phone again and thumbed in the first number. Almost the instant he hit the send button, the front windows of the school shattered, and a second ear-splitting blast reverberated around the trees and surrounding structures.

Already, in the distance, he could hear sirens. Hashim looked to Hamza.

"Take it up now, but we need to run. We can't get caught yet."

Hamza nodded once more, and Hashim turned his attention to the tablet before standing. He ran to the stroller and began pushing it. Hamza released their kite to fall where it would and urged his wife and daughter to follow Hashim.

They ran toward the street, all the while Hashim watched on the monitor as the drone climbed higher and higher, giving them an aerial view of the school and surrounding streets. Once the drone hit approximately two thousand feet, Hashim said they had gone high enough.

Now, the real work began.

The moment he heard the first explosion, every neuron in Special Agent Sean Navarro's brain fired at once, and they all screamed the same thing: move.

He sprinted across the stage and wrapped an arm around both Senator Hill and President Crane. The explosion had sounded distant but strong. Likely, it was outside the building. Once he had the two VIPs off the stage, he handed them off to a pair of agents who hurried them both out the back.

Then another explosion ripped through the building, this time much closer. It was from the north, very likely the main entrance. As loud as it was, he had very likely just lost people. He keyed his mike and looked down at the crowd. Half a dozen of his agents had sprinted toward the first family, sometimes carrying two children each.

A security team had scouted the area beforehand and

had secured a fallback location within the building. If he knew what kind of threat they faced, he might have suggested they hunker down and wait for additional security personnel to arrive. Already, though, they had two coordinated, powerful blasts. If they had too many more of those, the building could come down around them. Ultimately, that made the choice for him.

"Evac, evac, evac," he said, his voice straining to be heard over the screaming crowd. "Roadrunner, contact Magic. I want gunships in the air. Stagecoach, roll as soon as Cohiba is inside. Cowpuncher, we are wheels up as soon as Cohiba is secure. Overwatch, anything moves toward Cohiba, put it down."

As he shouted orders, smoke began filling the auditorium, bringing with it a scent that Navarro had smelled all too often when employed by the US Army in Iraq. Someone was burning.

He put it out of his mind and sprinted after the president and the rest of his security detail. The locals would have to secure the crime scene here and protect the civilians. His first priority was the president.

The hallways around him blurred as Navarro sprinted. He exited the building through a Secret Service checkpoint between the cafeteria and kitchen. His protective team had just secured the president and Senator Hill inside the Beast, the president's eight-thousand-pound limousine. Navarro dove through the open door and pulled it shut behind him. Instantly, the vehicle's climate control systems purged it of outside air

—a precaution in case of a biological or chemical weapons attack. Behind those eight-inch-thick hardened steel walls and five-inch-thick ballistics glass, they were safer, but not yet safe.

Navarro looked toward the front of the car. "Go, go, go, go."

The vehicle took off with a speed that belied its massive girth. Both the president and Senator Hill lay on the floor with agents on top of them to act as shields. Navarro looked out the window at the armored SUV behind them. Already, the protective detail had rounded up the president's family and secured them in the second car. They, too, were off.

"Where's my family?" asked Crane.

"They're right behind us," said Navarro. He keyed his mike. "Evac route Delta. Magic, where are my birds?"

"Five miles out. One minute," said a soft, female voice at the Helicopter Command Center at Pease Air Base.

"Roadrunner, I want everything but friendly signals jammed. I don't want anything getting through."

"Understood, Control," said a Secret Service agent in Roadrunner, the mobile communications center rolling behind them in the motorcade. Navarro exhaled heavily, trying to get his breath back.

"Are we safe?" asked Senator Hill.

Navarro looked at him, as if noticing him for the first time. "Not yet, sir. Hold on."

Chapter 13

Sabah cried big, terrified tears that neither her mother nor father could calm. Sirens blared in every direction as they walked. Hashim tried to comfort her, but she didn't want to hear from him. He hated to think it, but it probably helped that she cried. Any child would have cried in that situation. By crying, she helped them blend into the crowds around them.

And already, there were crowds.

People who lived near the park and elementary school had come out of their houses to see what had happened, while panicked audience members from the political rally sprinted toward the perceived safety of their cars. Hashim and his family fit in very well. As he pushed the stroller, Hashim glanced at his tablet on the stroller's rear seat.

Though he had already tossed the controller, Hamza had set the drone to hover fifteen hundred feet above the school, giving them an bird's-eye view of the unfolding scene. Once the drone's batteries ran low enough, it would gently descend and land in the same spot from which it had taken off. The police would find it, but that was part of the plan.

On his screen, Hashim watched as a pair of Secret Service agents escorted the president and Senator Hill into the back of the presidential limousine. The first family went into a full-sized SUV behind them. Within moments of their doors closing, the vehicles sped off. The farther they traveled from the elementary school, the more options their drivers would have to reach their destination, but for the first half mile, there were only four possible routes, and Hashim had a team member on each.

"He's taking Maple Avenue," said Hamza, glancing down at the tablet while also carrying his daughter.

"I see that," said Hashim, reaching for his cell phone. Every member of his team was on high alert, but he needed to give his men some advanced warning to make sure they were ready.

Before they left New York that afternoon, everyone had set their phones up to act as walkie-talkies, allowing instantaneous communication among group members. Hashim hit the button to talk.

"Batul, God has blessed you today. You will become a martyr. Everyone else, go to fallback positions."

"*Allahu akbar.* I'm ready."

Hashim recognized Batul's voice. There was no hesitation or catch. He was a true soldier. This would be a very good day for his cause.

Batul heard the sirens already. He knew he didn't have much time left. He sat on the side of the road near a tree approximately a quarter mile from Westbrook Elementary. Beside him rested a heavy canvas backpack.

He had a bachelor's degree in economics from Ohio State University, and he could have done any number of things with his life. This, though, was his duty. This was his moment.

The backpack held a surprise no one would see coming. Most of the bomb makers in the Islamic State had been ignorant of modern physics. They understood how to modify depleted uranium shells left over from the Soviet invasion of Afghanistan into IEDs, they understood how to follow a wiring schematic to turn a cell phone into a remote detonator, and they understood how to hide explosives alongside the road, but very few lived to old age, and even fewer survived with their limbs intact. Almost none could truly innovate.

Hamza Bashear, though, Hashim's son, had an analytical mind and the academic background to be a real force for good. He had made devices that would take down an empire. Inside his backpack, Batul had a large-diameter PVC pipe packed with twelve kilograms of RDX high explosive. Into that, Hamza had inserted an eight-kilogram conical copper liner he had shaped and welded himself. The tip of the cone, the apex, pointed toward the tree, while the large opening pointed toward the street.

The moment Batul ignited the blasting cap inside his backpack, the high explosive would burn with a velocity of nearly nine kilometers per second. According to Hamza, the explosive force would hit the apex of the cone first, sending it toward the street like a copper nail moving six thousand meters per second. As the force pressed against the base of the cone, it would invert the entire structure so that it took on the shape of a carrot.

The tip would hit the target first and physically push aside steel like a nail driving through wood. The remainder of the projectile would follow and splinter inside the target, shredding everything within its path.

Batul couldn't follow the physics of shaped charges, but he understood the concepts. As long as he detonated his device on time, he would strike a great blow for God.

He reached into the side compartment of his backpack for the switch. The infidels screamed in the distance, but their prayers and exhortations fell on deaf ears. They had turned their backs on God, and God had turned His back on them. For the good of humanity, they had to be purged.

"Ashhadu Alla Ilaha Illa Allah, Wa Ashhadu Anna Muhammad Rasulu Allah."

Batul repeated the *Shahada*, his profession of faith and promise of his obedience to God, as his finger hovered over the switch. He saw the motorcade speeding down the street. In the distance, a helicopter neared. It would arrive just in time to witness God's vengeance.

"Ashhadu Alla Ilaha Illa Allah, Wa Ashhadu Anna Muhammad Rasulu Allah."

Sirens blared in all directions. Batul's heart thudded against his breastbone. His hands shook, but he felt as alive as he ever had.

Two SUVs passed first, hidden police lights flashing.

They practically flew down the street. Batul readied himself. When they had practiced these maneuvers, they hadn't known how fast the presidential motorcade would move, so they had had to make educated guesses.

Even though they were trying to flee, the motorcade was still in a heavily populated residential area. The Secret Service wouldn't risk going eighty or ninety miles an hour for fear of hitting a civilian trying to cross the street. Not only that, the curve in the street and the generally poor condition of the asphalt wouldn't allow them to speed more than fifty or sixty. Batul knew when to strike.

"Ashhadu Alla Ilaha Illa Allah, Wa Ashhadu Anna Muhammad Rasulu Allah."

The president's limousine came next. Batul's finger hovered over the switch. He held his breath.

"Allahu akbar."

As the driver's door passed his position, Batul depressed the plunger on his switch and breathed his last, an exalted smile on his face.

Despite its massive weight, the explosion rocked the car. The rear end fishtailed violently, throwing the occupants against the doors and then back to the floor. The driver regained control of the vehicle and floored the accelerator. President Crane gasped and then coughed.

"I think I just broke a rib," he said.

"Can you breathe?" asked Navarro, already reaching

forward for an oxygen bag embedded in the divider between the front and rear seat compartments.

"Yeah," he said. "Get off me. Everybody get off me."

The Secret Service agents atop him repositioned themselves to give the president more room, but no one got up.

"I'm sorry, sir, but we're staying here until we're clear," said Navarro.

"Are we hit?" asked Senator Hill.

Navarro popped his head up to look around. A black, billowing cloud rose up behind them. Three black SUVs swerved around it, following them. His team frantically checked in, trying to ascertain the status of the president as well as the rest of the protective detail. Navarro keyed his microphone. As the team leader, he silenced the line with a push of a button.

"Stagecoach is rolling. Cohiba has minor injuries. Roadrunner, coordinate with locals. We need ambulances. Halfback, what is your status?"

Navarro paused for a moment. Halfback was the chase vehicle, one of the decoys. They had stashed the first family in it.

"Halfback, respond."

No voice came on the line. Navarro felt a catch in his throat.

"Halfback is down, then. Nichols, are you alive?"

He waited a second, praying his old friend could still breathe.

"Yes, sir."

"You have tactical authority on scene. Birds are inbound. Coordinate with Magic. We are proceeding to Cowpuncher. Stagecoach out."

The interior of the presidential limousine plunged into silence, but it lasted only a moment before three more explosions blasted behind them in rapid succession. These felt farther away than the earlier devices. Immediately, the tactical team on the ground began sounding off, but no one seemed to have been hit. His team would figure out what happened, but for the moment, Navarro needed to focus on the situation in front of him.

"Where's my family?" asked President Crane.

"We're working on that, sir," said Navarro. "I need you to stay down and calm."

"Where's my goddamn family?"

"Sir, you've got broken ribs and potential internal injuries," said Navarro, trying to sound soothing. "I need you to stay calm until we arrive at Air Force One."

The president struggled beneath the Secret Service agents and gasped and then shouted at them to get up. In addition to transporting the president to safety, the Beast could turn into a mobile operating theater with a few presses of a button. It had several pints of blood on reserve in a refrigerator built into the door in case the president was shot. It also had a full complement of surgical instruments and drugs. Normally, a physician would have traveled with them, but he evidently hadn't made it into the car in time for their evacuation. Navarro looked to one of the other agents in the protective detail and gave an order he never thought he'd give.

"We need to sedate him. There are syringes of midazolam and haloperidol in the cabinet. Get me a small one."

The agent hesitated, but then reached into the drug cabinet. Everything in there was already carefully measured for the president's physiology. He pulled a syringe out and handed it to Navarro. Navarro popped the cap and then hovered over the president's thigh.

"I'm sorry, sir, but this is for your own good," he said, jamming it into the muscle. The president kicked and fought at first, but then his movements slowed as the drugs passed through his body. The drug combination was often used in psychiatric emergency rooms to sedate patients who presented a danger to themselves or others. President Crane would have a hell of a headache, but he wouldn't hurt himself further by fighting them.

The drive to the airfield seemed like the longest ten minutes of Navarro's life. The base personnel had already cleared the surrounding area to half a mile, but a competent sniper could still make even that shot. The Beast skidded to a halt approximately five meters from Air Force One. Navarro stepped out and looked around. Nothing moved.

"Let's get him in the plane."

The president was conscious and aware, but he didn't fight what was going on around him. Two Secret Service agents carried him to the plane while Navarro escorted Senator Hill. The moment they were onboard, the truck with the staircase pulled back, and the massive jet started rolling toward the runway. Once they were airborne, the plane's physician would take a thorough look at the president, but in the meantime, Navarro handed him the syringe.

"President Crane needed to be sedated," he said. "This is what we used."

The physician shook his head. "That was dangerous. The president is not a young man. You should have waited until I was there."

"I kept him alive. That's my job. Do yours."

Crane's doctor didn't say anything, but he helped the Secret Service agents strap the older man into a beige leather seat. Agent Navarro ran to the communications center above the cockpit and strapped himself into a seat so he could monitor the situation on the ground. An Air Force communications officer synced the duty station at which Navarro sat with the Secret Service's encrypted digital system. As he did that, the pilot started taxiing down the runway.

At first, Navarro felt very little, but as the plane built speed, the momentum pressed him back into his seat hard. As the plane's wheels left the ground, the front of the plane lifted in a steep climb.

Through it all, Navarro listened to the teams on the grounds. Things were moving fast, but the attack seemed over. No one said anything, but listening to the chatter,

Navarro knew he had lost a lot of agents that day. Eventually, as the plane leveled off, a Secret Service agent entered the communications center and walked to Navarro.

"Sir, the president wants to know the status of his family."

Navarro had dreaded this moment because he already knew the answer. President Crane was never their adversary's target.

He cleared his throat and leaned forward and keyed the microphone.

"Roadrunner, this is Agent Navarro on Cowpuncher. The president is asking for a status report on his family."

The voice that answered his own sounded strained. It trembled.

"The situation is still fluid, sir."

"Tell me what you can," said Navarro.

Roadrunner coughed. "Uhh, Camus is down. Eeyore is down. Pooh Bear is down. Tigger is down. Owl is down. Piglet is down. Roo is critically injured but breathing."

"What about Christopher Robin?"

Navarro could hear the tremble in his communication officer's voice even as he tried to hide it.

"We can't find him. His mom was carrying him. We're looking."

"Do what you can do," said Navarro.

"We're going to get them for this," said Roadrunner.

Who or what they were going to get, Navarro didn't

know, but he nodded.

"Yes, we are," he said. "Good luck, Roadrunner."

Navarro hung his headset back up and looked to the Secret Service agent who had walked in.

"Did the first family make it out?" she asked.

Navarro swallowed hard and shook his head. "Is the chaplain on board?"

"I think so."

"Good," said Navarro, nodding. "We're going to need him."

Chapter 14

I walked back to my car and felt the sweat drip from my brow. My shirt stuck to me, and I had mud all over my shoes, but I didn't care. I had a lead to follow.

Once I sat down, I took out my cell phone, planning to call Agent Havelock for assistance in tracking down the imam. Before I could get him on the phone, I found I had three voice mails and two text messages from my wife. All of them said the same thing: *Please come home.*

New plan, then. I pulled my legs into the car, slammed the door, and drove out of the parking lot, a worried knot growing in my stomach. When I reached the house, I pulled to a stop and ran through the mudroom and into the kitchen.

"Hello?" I called.

"In the living room," said Hannah, my wife. I followed her voice and found her sitting on the couch. She had tear streaks on her cheeks. "The kids are in the basement playing. I didn't want them to see this. Maybe I shouldn't have called you. I don't know. I didn't want to be here alone if things got ugly."

"That's okay," I said, putting a hand on her back. "What's going on?"

She nodded toward the television. She was watching the news.

"What happened?" I asked.

"Nobody knows, but it's bad," she said, shaking her

head. "It's really bad."

I sat down beside my wife on the couch. I didn't know what channel we had the TV on, but it was broadcasting a live feed from a helicopter hovering over what looked like a school. Smoke billowed from multiple spots on the ground, while first responders sprinted across the grass. There was so much going on that it was hard to see any single thing until the camera focused on a particular spot on the ground. At first, it kind of looked like we were looking at a stick. Then the view zoomed in. It was a leg unattached from its body. Once the details became clear, the view pulled out quickly.

An anchor immediately came on and apologized. It was the aftermath of a bombing. Dozens of groups had claimed responsibility, but already the network analysts were jumping to conclusions. One said it was obviously the work of sophisticated terrorist groups, possibly working on behalf of North Korea or maybe even Russia. Another said it looked like attacks he had seen in Afghanistan. A third suggested it bore the hallmarks of a certain domestic terror group. I reached for the remote and muted it.

"Depending on what happened, this could get really ugly," I said. "We'll need to stay inside for a few days. If we need to, we can have groceries delivered."

My wife didn't say anything, but fresh tears fell down her face. She drew in a breath and nodded.

"I hate the people who did this," she said. She looked at the TV. "You know it's going to come back to us. It's going to be *al-Qaeda*, or *ISIS*, or *al-Shabaab*, or some group we've never even heard of. How do I tell people we're not like them? How do I do that? How do I protect my kids?"

"I don't know," I said.

We were quiet for another few moments. The analysts talked on TV for a while, but then they switched to footage of the actual attack. I didn't want to see it, but I couldn't look away. Hannah gasped every time something exploded. I held her hand without saying a word until my little boy came up from the basement. He looked at the two of us and then started to look at the TV. I grabbed the remote and shut it off before he could see anything. Kaden was five. He didn't need to know we lived in a world where people committed mass murder in God's name.

I looked at him and forced a smile to my face.

"You look sad, *Baba*," he said.

Hannah scooted close to him and took his hand so that she had mine and his. "We're glad to see you."

"Want to wrestle?" he asked, looking at me. I forced a smile to my lips.

"More than anything in the world," I said.

Some things were more important than work, so I stayed home the rest of the day. Hannah and I put the kids to bed that night at about nine. The White House press secretary had held a press conference that evening to say the president had survived the attack with minor injuries, but he gave few details about what had happened. We didn't tell the kids anything, mostly because we had no idea what to tell them. They weren't in school, so for the moment, we could control what they were exposed to. I appreciated that.

After we put the kids to bed, I held Hannah on the couch. I knew a lot of strong, intelligent women, and I was lucky to have them in my life. Hannah stood shoulders above everybody. No matter what happened, as long as I had her and the kids, things would be okay. We'd get through this.

At a quarter to ten, I kissed her for the last time that evening, and she went to bed. I wanted to join her, but I couldn't quiet my mind. I kept thinking about what I had seen on TV. The media focused on the president—and rightly so—but the attack had killed hundreds of people outside, too. That meant there were hundreds of families who had lost children or parents or siblings. I didn't want to think about that, so I forced myself to think about my assignment with the FBI.

At the time of his death, Jacob Ganim was working a case. His superiors thought he was hunting terrorists, but I hadn't found anything to substantiate that. Instead, I found pictures of women in hijab. If those women were being trafficked, I could certainly see him investigating. At the same time, though, he could have worked that kind of case under his own name. Instead, he lied to his superiors and hid within Nassir's group.

And even that wasn't enough to keep him alive.

I needed to go back to the beginning and rethink this. Motive, means, opportunity. That's what this case came down to. What was Jacob Ganim working on, who wanted him dead, and why?

Unfortunately, I had no idea how to answer any of that.

As I paced my living room, trying to put things together, a pair of headlights lit up the front of my house. Hannah and I lived in a sprawling neighborhood with streets that seemed to meander lazily across the landscape. Visitors got lost all the time, but since we lived on a cul-de-sac, they didn't have to pull into anyone's driveway to turn around. This was someone who was coming to see us. It wasn't a colleague or family member because they would have called first. It probably wasn't someone who wished us harm, either, or they would have pulled up with their headlights off. This was something else.

I walked to the front door so my visitor wouldn't get the chance to ring the doorbell.

The car in the driveway was a dark gray four-door Jaguar, and a tall but thin man in a suit stood near the hood. As I pulled the front door shut behind me, an enormous man stepped out of the passenger door. He was about six foot four and likely weighed well over three hundred pounds. Though he was in his early sixties, he could probably break me in half if he wanted.

In my internal monologue, I had dubbed him the

Hulk, but his actual name was Lev. I didn't remember his last name. It had been a while since I had seen him, but he was the brother-in-law of Konstantin Bukoholov, the largest supplier of cocaine in the region.

Though the Hulk was a dangerous figure in his own right, Bukoholov was the real threat. He was intelligent and politically connected at all levels of government both locally and statewide. It wouldn't have surprised me to learn he had people in the Department of Justice as well. I crossed my arms and leaned against one of the support posts on my porch as I looked at the Hulk.

"What do you want?"

"My uncle needs to see you," said the thin, tall man.

"And you are?"

"Michael," he said.

I raised my eyebrows, waiting for him to continue. He didn't.

"You got a last name, Michael?"

"Yeah," he said, nodding. "Now please get in the car."

I looked from Michael to Lev and then back. "It's late. If your uncle wants to talk to me, he can have his lawyer call me. We'll set up an appointment. That's how normal people conduct business. They don't show up at people's houses in the middle of the night with requests to get in cars. Consider that a tip in case you guys ever pretend to go legit."

"Get in the car, Lieutenant," said the Hulk. He had a high voice that made even the most ominous threat sound a little ridiculous. It was a bit like being ordered around by Mickey Mouse.

"I'm pretty good here, but thank you," I said. "If you guys would leave now, I'd appreciate it. I've had a long day."

"My uncle needs to see you, Lieutenant," said Michael. "It's important. Get in the car. Please."

I looked at him up and down, sizing him up. His voice was confident and strong. That surprised me. This was a man accustomed to giving orders and having them obeyed. If I had been holding my cell phone, I probably would have taken his picture and taken it to our organized crime section.

"Given your uncle's age, I'm guessing you'll be taking over soon," I said. "Good for you. I have the feeling we'll be seeing more of each other in the not-too-distant future."

Michael looked to his father and then back to me. "My uncle has terminal cancer. His doctors don't give him much time. He wants to see you before he passes away."

I closed my eyes and sighed. "His dying wish is to see me?"

"It's not a wish. It's a hope. He has something to tell you before he dies."

"I'm sorry for your loss, but wouldn't he rather be spending that time with his family?"

"Yes," said the Hulk. "Which should tell you how important he views a meeting with you. It concerns your brother-in-law."

The words felt like an ice pick in my side. I stood straighter and tightened my arms across my chest.

"How does he know Nassir?"

Instead of answering, the Hulk took a step back and opened the Jaguar's rear passenger door.

"Get in and find out."

As much as I wanted to tell them to leave, I couldn't. If he knew something about Nassir, I needed to hear it.

"Give me a minute. I'll be out shortly."

Before either of them could say anything, I walked into the house and went upstairs. The lights were out, but Hannah was still awake. She rolled over as I opened the door.

"I heard you go outside," she said. "What's wrong?"

"I don't know," I said, walking to the closet and kneeling in front of the safe in which I stored my firearm and badge. "I've got to go out tonight. A guy I know is sick. He wants to see me before he dies. I don't know which hospital he's at, but hopefully I won't be out too long."

"And you need to take your gun to see him?"

Though she couldn't see me, I shook my head even as I punched in my passcode and opened the door. My weapon was in its holster, right where I had left it. So was my badge. I attached both to my belt before standing and turning to face my wife.

"If this guy wanted me dead, I'd be dead already. I'm bringing it to remind everyone what side I'm on."

She sighed and then sank deeper onto the bed before

rolling over. "On the plus side, if he does decide he wants you dead, at least you'll be in the hospital."

I smiled and crossed the room to stand beside the bed. She didn't roll over, so I kissed her shoulder.

"I love you, honey."

"I love you, too, sweetheart. Try not to get shot."

"I wish you didn't have to say that so often," I said.

She rolled over then and flashed me a crooked smile I had fallen in love with many years earlier.

"Me, too. Stay safe."

I squeezed her shoulder before standing straighter and leaving. The Hulk and his son were still outside waiting for me.

"Get in, Lieutenant," said the Hulk, putting his hand on top of the Jaguar. I shook my head.

"I don't think so," I said, reaching into my pocket and then walking toward my garage, which I opened with a keypad outside. I unlocked my Volkswagen with a press of a button and looked at them. "If this meeting is as important as you implied, I'll meet you at the hospital."

The Hulk looked to his son. The younger man nodded.

"Fine. Let's go. I don't know how much longer Uncle Kostya has. But we're not going to the hospital. He's at his house. Follow us."

The two of them climbed into their car and backed out of the driveway. I followed maybe a hundred feet back. Intellectually, I knew I should have been focusing on the meeting ahead of me, but I couldn't help but think about Nassir.

Bukoholov may have dressed himself up as a businessman, but IMPD suspected his involvement in at least half a dozen open homicides. He was one of the most ruthless men I had ever met. Nassir had no reason to know a man like that, and yet he plainly did. Nassir had held back on me. With everything else going on, I really wished he hadn't done that.

Chapter 15

Despite their successful attack at Westbrook Elementary, no one in Hashim Bashear's car smiled. They still had too much to do. While Hamza drove, Hashim sat on the rearmost seat behind his grandchildren. His daughter-in-law sat beside her husband up front. Lights from Boston lit the horizon ahead of their vehicle. It was an evil thing they had done, and every adult in that car knew it. They also recognized its necessity.

In 2001, Hamza had been a graduate student at Georgia Tech. He had never hurt anyone in his life, and he had wanted nothing more than to finish his Ph.D., start a family, and become a college professor. He had wanted the American dream, and he had wanted his children to grow up in a tolerant and safe world where they were judged on their actions and the merits of their ideas rather than the part of the world their ancestors came from. For a time, he thought he and his wife had it. And then nineteen hijackers boarded four airliners on a September morning and changed the world.

On the morning of September 11th, Hamza was lecturing to a classroom of freshmen at the time the first plane hit. An administrator came by and told everyone what had happened. Hamza cancelled the rest of the class and sent his students home.

Since he lived near campus, he walked home to find his wife, Dalia, on the front steps of their townhouse, sobbing. Just an hour after the attack, someone had thrown a brick through the front window.

Detectives came and took a report so Hamza and his wife could file a claim with their insurance. The police acted professionally, but they looked at Hamza and Dalia differently than they had just a few hours earlier. In one tragic morning, they had become Arab-Americans instead of Americans. Hamza couldn't even blame his neighbors for being pissed; he was angry, too. He wished his neighbors would direct it at the right people, though.

Life changed after that. Hamza could hardly get on a plane anymore without having armed guards search his bags and person. For some people, even that wasn't enough. Even after he went through a rigorous security process, they would complain to the flight attendants or captain about him. They'd say they were scared of him and wondered whether the airline could do anything about him—as if he were a cockroach to squash rather than a human being.

At first, hearing those comments hurt, but he got used to them after a while. To forestall arguments, he even voluntarily left his flight a few times and caught a later one.

He and Dalia adapted to their new place in the world, but all the while, they couldn't help but think of what they had lost. Dalia had been born in New Jersey, and Hamza had come to the country legally and become a permanent resident, but the United States had ceased to be their home. The American dream was no longer their dream.

Once Hamza finished his master's degree, he and his wife moved to London, where they hoped to live in peace. Life was easier there, but it wasn't home. Hamza and his family had no home. His native Iraq was a shattered, broken country; Saudi Arabia was run by men who claimed to know God but who enmired themselves in regional politics. Turkey and Egypt teetered toward madness.

For the sake of their future children, Hamza and Dalia and all the world's men and women like them needed a home, an Islamic community not beholden to the capricious whims of dictators or men more interested in amassing wealth than living a godly life. Men and women in the West had carved out their own nations hundreds of years ago. Hamza and visionary men like his father planned to do the same. They would create a new world from the ashes of the old. Hamza wouldn't live to see it, but his children might. They deserved somewhere they felt safe.

"I don't want you to go, *Baba*," said a soft voice from the middle seat.

Hamza looked in the rearview mirror at his daughter. "I know, Sabah. *Giddo* has a very important job ahead of him, though, and I have to go with him. He needs my help."

"Your father is right, sweetheart," said Hashim. "I get lost so easily. I'm an old man. I need his help."

Hamza looked in the rearview mirror in time to see

his father leaning forward limply, as if he had no strength left. Hamza smiled. Though Hashim had more yesterdays than tomorrows, he was far from weak. He still had a sharp, tactical mind, which was more than most men could ever say.

"You're not so old, *Giddo*," said Sabah, giggling.

Truthfully, at sixty-seven, he wasn't very old. In a perfect world, Sabah would smile and wave to her grandfather at school and sporting events for the next ten or twenty years. In this world, though, once Hashim and Hamza climbed onto the airplane to Indianapolis, she may never see either of them again even if they did their jobs perfectly. That was too much to burden a little girl with, though. She still deserved to dream big dreams.

"You will always be my sweetheart," said Hashim. "Everything your *baba* and I do, we do so that you can grow old in a better world than we have now. Your *baba* and I are doing something that will make a difference. And you and your *ummi* have a special job as well in Washington. I'm counting on you to make a special delivery. I hope you understand that one day."

"I already understand," she said. "I love you, too."

"If you understand that, then you understand a lot," said Hashim. "Now hush, child. It's growing late, and I'm old and tired. Your *baba* and I have a long flight ahead of us once we reach the city, and then we have much work once we reach Indianapolis. I need my rest."

Chapter 16

We drove for twenty minutes to a gated compound on the northwest side of Indianapolis. A limestone fence about six feet tall surrounded the property, creating a private parklike yard that was likely big enough to house horses. It was impressive for a city neighborhood. The driveway meandered across the landscape, allowing me to see a pair of tennis courts, a massive pool complete with a waterfall, and a poolhouse that was bigger than any home I could imagine owning.

Then we turned the corner, and I saw the main house for the first time. It was enormous and had a limestone and steel exterior that made it look like an upscale ski lodge. I parked in the circular drive out front, right behind Michael's Jaguar. A pair of men immediately came from the house. I reached to my gun, but then one opened the car door for me and smiled.

"Would you like me to park in the garage for you, sir?"

I looked to Michael and the Hulk, both of whom were exiting their vehicle. Then I looked at the valet and shook my head.

"I won't be long," I said, pulling back my jacket enough to show him my badge. "If my car isn't in this spot when I return, I'm going to be annoyed. Clear?"

"Of course, sir," he said, taking a step back. "Have a nice evening."

I got out of my car and looked around for a moment, taking in the grounds while also looking for possible threats. I didn't see guards, but there were cameras on the corners of the building. I had the feeling that if I made a sudden move toward Michael or the Hulk, I'd have a lot of company very shortly.

"Uncle Kostya went all out on the property, didn't he?" asked Michael, walking toward me. "We just finished it up about a year ago. It's a shame he won't get to enjoy it longer."

I nodded and looked around again, this time marveling at the sheer size of the house and its gardens.

"I suppose any jokes I might make about compensating for physical inadequacies go without saying, right?"

Michael forced a smile to his face.

"My uncle's inside. I'm sure you'd like to get safely home to your wife, so we'll skip the tour."

"Fine. Let's go."

We started walking, and almost immediately the front door opened. Only as I walked inside did I see a member of the household staff there, smiling at us from the entryway. As much as I appreciated having doors opened for me, I felt exposed having all those people hanging out in dark corners, just waiting for me to pass.

We walked through the house for a few minutes before stopping outside a wooden door at the end of a long hallway. Modern glass sconces on the wall bathed the hallway in a subdued, calming light, while a skylight overhead gave me a view of the stars. I may not have approved of Bukoholov's profession, but there was something to be said about the man's home. He knew how to live.

Michael knocked on the door, and we stepped into a bedroom with panoramic windows overlooking the property. Bukoholov lay in a king-sized bed positioned along the north wall. His skin had a gray pallor, and his breath seemed weak. A monitor reported every beat of his heart on a screen beside his bed, while an IV snaked into his arm. For the first time in the all the years I had known him, he looked frail and tired.

Then he looked at me with the unfeeling black eyes of a predator, and I saw the strength still inside him. It made me shudder.

"Please come in, Ashraf."

Though his voice was weak, it still had a commanding presence to it that compelled me to move forward. Bukoholov looked to the men near me.

"Privacy please, gentlemen. Mr. Rashid is no threat to me."

"Are you sure, Uncle?"

I looked at Michael. "I'm here to talk. I'm not going to kill a defenseless old man in his bed."

"Go," said Bukoholov.

I watched the two men leave the room and pull the door shut behind them before turning to Bukoholov.

"Michael seems sure of himself," I said.

"That he is," said Bukoholov. "He's also brash,

reckless, and entirely too young for the life he's trying to lead."

"We can't have it all, I suppose," I said, looking around for a chair. I grabbed one from a nearby desk and rolled it over. "He taking over after you shuffle off this mortal coil, or are you still looking?"

Bukoholov chuckled and then shook his head. "No one's taking over. At one time, I had hoped you might pick up my mantle when I'm gone, but now I know that hope will never come to fruition."

"Yeah," I said, nodding and then scratching the back of my head. "I might get in trouble at work if I start leading a drug empire. The boss tends to frown on that sort of thing."

Bukoholov chuckled again and then started coughing. I waited for about a minute for him to stop.

"Do you need some water?"

He shook his head and paused to catch his breath before speaking again.

"No, but thank you. You and I are more alike than you realize. You're a genuinely good man, Ashraf, but you've got meanness inside you. You pretend it doesn't exist, but we both know it's there. You're one tragedy away from turning on everything you believe. I know. I've been in your shoes. I'm glad your life has turned out such that you've never been in mine."

I crossed my arms and raised my eyebrows without bothering to consider what he said. "Are we done with the armchair psychology lesson?"

"Of course," he said. "I called you here for a reason. Your brother-in-law manages a holdings company called Safe Haven, LLC. They lease a secure building from me."

"Secure in what sense?" I asked.

"Secure from police intrusions provided the leaseholder maintains a low profile. My people have an arrangement with some of your people. I'm sure you know how that goes."

I nodded, considering the admission. Bukoholov wouldn't have told me about the building unless he was confident I wouldn't be able to connect it to him officially. Very likely, there were layers of ownership and protection that would take a team of forensic accountants years to unravel. He'd be long dead by the time that happened.

"Why are you telling me this?"

"My nephew decided to lease the building to your brother-in-law's company. I didn't agree with it, but Michael will be taking over our real estate holdings. It was his choice. After the events earlier this evening, I'm reasserting my right to refuse to do business with certain types of people."

I allowed a mirthless smile to spring to my lips. "You'll sell drugs to children, but you won't lease a building to a Muslim-owned company? You had better be careful saying things like that. If the wrong people hear you, you'll have a serious PR problem."

He smiled, but it faded quickly. "At my age, I'm not overly concerned about my image. Nor am I concerned about your brother-in-law's religious convictions. I'm concerned about men who store explosive devices in populated areas."

I crossed my arms. "Do you have any evidence to back up that claim?"

Bukoholov blinked. "Yes."

I waited, expecting him to keep speaking. He didn't say anything.

"Can I see it?" I asked, raising my eyebrows.

"No," he said. I started to ask him why he wouldn't share his evidence with me, but he coughed again before I could. Then he cleared his throat. "Lev will give you the address and passcode to enter the building. I've pulled my own security team. If there's anyone in the building, he or she works for your brother-in-law. You should proceed with caution."

I nodded, already thinking about how best to approach this. If there were explosives or armed guards in the building, I'd need backup. Havelock would have wanted me to call him, but he had dicked me around enough. I'd handle this one with my own team.

"Anything else you want to tell me?" I asked.

Bukoholov blinked. "I've always liked you, Lieutenant. I wish you knew the man I was before I became the man I am. You would have liked him."

"I'll take your word for that," I said, standing. "Anything else?"

"Good luck."

I looked at the machines beside his bed and then to

him and nodded. When I spoke, I softened my voice.

"*Inna lillahi wa inna ilayhi raji'un,*" I said, reciting a familiar verse from the Quran.

Bukoholov smiled and allowed himself to sink into his pillow. "To God we belong, and to Him, we return. Thank you, Ashraf. It's a lovely sentiment."

I probably should have been surprised that Bukoholov recognized the verse in Arabic, but then he had probably learned Arabic while fighting in Afghanistan in the seventies while a member of the Soviet Army.

"Good luck, Mr. Bukoholov."

I left without saying another word. The Hulk met me outside Bukoholov's room and escorted me out of the house. My car hadn't moved. The big man handed me an envelope.

"Thank you," I said. The two of us stared at each other for a moment. As I reached to open my door, I hesitated, thinking.

"Your son Michael is a young man," I said, looking down at the concrete before looking up to catch the Hulk's gaze. "He doesn't have to keep going down the path he is."

The Hulk's expression didn't shift. "My son isn't the man you think he is. Do not presume to know us or what is best for us."

"You're right," I said, opening my door. I sat down but kept my legs outside and looked at the Hulk. "I don't know you or your family, but I know the world you live in. Your son isn't going to live to old age like you or his uncle. One day, if he keeps doing what he's doing, somebody like me is going to put him in a box."

"Are you threatening him, Lieutenant?" asked the Hulk, shifting his weight onto the balls of his feet.

I lowered my right hand to the pistol on my hip and shook my head. "I'm not threatening anyone. I'm stating a fact. Think about that when you go to bed tonight."

Before the Hulk could respond, I got in my car and shut the door. As I left the compound, I pulled out my burner cell phone. As the commander of the city's major case squad, I worked the most challenging cases our department came across. Unfortunately, due to some budgetary constraints, I didn't have detectives permanently assigned to my squad, which meant I had to borrow from other units. That meant I got to choose who I wanted to work with. I didn't mind that one bit.

I dialed a familiar number and waited for the other end to pick up.

"Paul, it's Ash Rashid. I know it's the middle of the night, so sorry I woke you up."

He coughed, clearing his throat. Paul Murphy was a middle-aged sergeant with over thirty years on the job. He smoked constantly, he swore quite often, and he had a love of deli meat that had expanded his waistline to epic proportions. He was also one of the few people on the planet I considered a friend. He was a good man, even if he tried to hide that fact.

"Don't apologize to me," he said. "Apologize to my wife. I'll put you on speaker."

I laughed. "You serious?"

A woman's voice answered. "Yes. It's the middle of the night, and you woke me up, Lieutenant. I think I deserve an apology."

"Sorry, Becky."

She grunted but didn't say anything else. Then I heard Paul sigh.

"What do you want, buddy?"

"Am I on speaker?"

He sighed again. "Nope. I'm walking to the toilet."

"You want to work an antiterrorism case?"

He paused. "Not especially."

"Would you meet me somewhere if I ordered it?"

"If you ordered me to meet you somewhere, I wouldn't have a whole lot of choice, would I?"

"Nope," I said. I opened the envelope the Hulk had given me and found a single paper with an address and a six-digit passcode scrawled across the top. I read both aloud. "I'm heading out right now. I need Emilia Rios there as well, so give her a call. And one other thing: This is an important case, but you need to keep it quiet for now. Don't call the dispatcher and tell her what we're doing."

"You're the boss," said Paul, his voice betraying his annoyance. "I'll see you in a bit."

I thanked him and then hung up. Even though he was annoyed for being woken up in the middle of the night, Paul was an excellent detective. He and Emilia would be there. I put my car into gear and drove.

Bukoholov's warehouse was in a mixed-use neighborhood near I-65 on the city's southeast side. There was a mobile-home park up the street and a body shop next door. The building itself had gray brick and a lot of rectangular windows. It looked like it could have been a cabinet maker's shop, or maybe the home base of a heating and air conditioning company. That was probably what made it attractive to men and women who needed a quiet place to store illicit goods.

I drove through the surrounding streets to get a feel for the area and to see whether anyone was around. At this time of night, the streets were empty.

About half an hour after leaving Bukoholov's house, I parked on the edge of the warehouse's parking lot to wait for my backup. Paul must have met Emilia somewhere because they arrived in her unmarked cruiser. Instead of parking beside me, though, they pulled to a stop directly behind my vehicle, boxing me in.

My shoulders tightened.

Emilia opened her door slowly and crept out, keeping her car's engine block between the two of us. Paul opened his door but didn't step out from behind it. Both detectives kept their hands near their weapons as I got out of my car.

"Hey, guys," I said. "You want to tell me why you're approaching me as if you're going to arrest me?"

"Sorry, Ash," said Paul, unholstering his weapon. He didn't raise it toward me, but the threat was still there. "Turn around and put your hands on your car. You're under arrest for the murders of three John Does in the parking lot of your mosque this morning."

I slowly turned and put my hands on the roof of my VW but looked over my shoulder.

"That isn't what you think it was."

"A guy walking his dog shot a cell phone video," said Emilia. She had her weapon out. I started to turn around. "We saw everything. We saw you shoot them, and we saw you drive off."

"We should probably talk about that."

She pointed her weapon at my chest. "Keep your hands on the vehicle. I don't want to hurt you if I don't have to."

I turned around and put my hands back on the roof of my car. Paul took the weapon from my hip and the cell phone from my pocket before securing my hands in front of me with cuffs. I swore under my breath.

"Something you want to say, Ash?" asked Paul, leading me to the backseat of his cruiser.

"Yeah," I said, looking at him. "I should have just called Special Agent Havelock for help."

Chapter 17

Emilia drove. Paul stayed beside her in the front seat, while I stared at the backs of their heads from the cruiser's rear. I wanted to tell them they were making a mistake, but suspects had yelled that same thing at me from the backseat of my own car so many times that I hardly heard it anymore. Emilia and Paul were two of my closest friends, but they were cops first and foremost. They were just doing their jobs. I didn't want to waste their time or my breath by screaming at them.

So I stared out the window at the changing countryside.

Eventually, Emilia tapped Paul on the shoulder and pointed toward the parking lot of a Baptist church. None of the overhead lights were on, leaving it dark and more than a little foreboding. There was a shuttle bus on the edge of the lot. The congregation probably used it to pick up senior citizens who couldn't drive to church events on their own. Paul nodded almost imperceptibly.

"What are you guys doing?" I asked.

"Driving you to the station for an interrogation," said Paul, glancing into his rearview mirror. "But first, I'm tired. I'm going to get some coffee. You're buying. I was having a wonderful dream when you called, by the way."

"Sorry to interrupt your dreaming."

"Me, too, my friend," said Paul. "Me, too."

We drove for another few minutes, and then, true to

Paul's word, we pulled into the parking lot of a fast-food restaurant, where Emilia ordered three large coffees in the drive-through. When it came time to pay, she rolled the car forward and pushed the automatic window down so the restaurant worker was just beside me. She was subtle like that. Once I paid and had my change—which was not an easy feat with my hands cuffed together—Emilia rolled up the window and put the heavy police cruiser in gear.

As Emilia pulled to the restaurant's exit, Paul pointed to the left. "He's half a block to the west in a red Ford sedan."

"Good catch," said Emilia, pulling into traffic. Instead of heading back downtown, she drove about half a block, turned into the parking lot of a grocery store that was open twenty-four hours a day, and parked in the fire lane. Immediately, she got out of the car and pulled open my door.

"Come on. We've got to move."

"What are you doing?"

"Buying groceries," said Paul. "Emilia needs someone to carry her bags."

I looked at Paul and then to Emilia. Paul mouthed for me to go. Both of them were very good officers, and they rarely acted without reason. More than that, they were my partners. I trusted them implicitly. There was more going on than I recognized, so I swung my legs out of my car.

"This is an inappropriate use of your time at work,"

I said. "When I get to the office, I plan to write you both up."

"I look forward to seeing the report," said Emilia. "Come on."

The moment I got out of the car, Paul got into the driver's seat and drove off. Emilia put her hand on my elbow and led me into the store. Even though there were few shoppers at that time of morning, the overhead lights illuminated every square inch of the building's interior as brightly as if it were the middle of the day. Emilia shot her eyes around and then pulled me toward the produce section.

"You do a lot of shopping here?" I asked.

"I worked here when I was in high school," she said. "I know the manager."

We walked through the produce section and then to the bakery, where she led me to the end of a display, effectively hiding us from view from the front of the store. Nobody in the bakery noticed us, but a woman near the butcher counter stared at us as if we were nuts.

"Police matter," I whispered. "Don't worry. We do this all the time."

Emilia snickered. The shopper nodded and then put down the package of chicken she had been inspecting before moving on quickly.

"We should probably get out of here," I said.

"They didn't follow us in, so they must have stayed with Paul."

I didn't know who "they" were, but I nodded anyway.

She started moving again, escorting me out of the bakery. A guy in a paint-spattered T-shirt caught sight of us as he walked up an aisle. Despite the fact that I had my hands in cuffs, he didn't even bat an eye. He just kept his head down and walked past. That was probably the sane thing to do.

"Who would be following us?" I asked.

"We'll talk once we're out of here," she said, squeezing my elbow and directing me toward a hallway between the dairy and meat departments. We walked past the bathrooms and then toward an employee-only section, where an older man in a red vest held the door for us.

"Hey, Emilia," he said, smiling at her. "*¿Cómo estás?*"

"*Bien, bien*," she said, hurrying past him. "Thanks for doing this, Mateo."

"Anything for my best bagger."

Emilia smiled as we passed. The room we entered looked like a warehouse complete with a loading dock in the back. We stepped around a pallet jack and hurried to an exterior door on the other side of the room. It was almost pitch black outside the store. The air smelled like stale smoke, and I could see cigarette butts on the ground in the moonlight.

There was a police cruiser beside the loading dock.

"Get in," said Emilia, hurrying toward the passenger door. "We don't have a lot of time."

"You want me in the front or the back?"

"I don't care. Just get in."

I got in the front, and the moment I sat down, Emilia took off but didn't turn on her headlights.

"You want to tell me what's going on now?" I asked.

"You pissed off a couple of people you shouldn't have pissed off," she said. "Paul's losing them now. I am going to try to avoid letting them see us. We'll talk in a second. I've got to concentrate."

We pulled out of the parking lot, still without her headlights on. The roads were empty, but I could barely see ahead of us in the dark. About five minutes after we left the grocery store, we pulled into the gravel lot of the church we had passed earlier. Paul wasn't there, but we parked on the far edge of the lot in the shadow cast by the building.

Emilia opened my door for me and then led me across the lot to the shuttle bus. There, she finally took off my cuffs. A cricket chirped nearby, and a warm breeze blew across the church's lawn. We were utterly alone. I rubbed my wrists and leaned against the bus.

"While I appreciate the tour through your grocery store, can you tell me what's going on now?"

"How about you tell me?" asked Emilia, crossing her arms. "We've got you on video shooting three people and then driving away in a Cadillac."

I softened my voice. "To be fair, I wasn't driving. That was my brother-in-law."

"Whatever," said Emilia, closing her eyes. "Tell me you didn't murder three people and run."

"I didn't murder three people and run," I said.

"There's a lot more going on there than you realize. I thought Special Agent Havelock would have cleared that up with IMPD, but apparently not. I'll tell you what I can, but where's Paul?"

"Like I said, he's shaking our tail," she said. "Since news of your shooting came out, we've had people watching us. Somebody in the prosecutor's office thinks Paul and I are too close to you to be trusted."

"I didn't kill anyone," I said.

"It's on video, Ash," she said, her voice growing harder. "Don't try to bullshit me. I saw you."

"If it's on video, where are the bodies?"

"We don't know," said Emilia. "Somebody swooped in and picked them up. They hosed off the parking lot, too."

While it was nice that the FBI cleaned up after themselves, it would have been even nicer if they'd told my department they had an operation planned.

"You didn't see a shooting," I said. "It's a long story. I'll tell it to you when Paul gets here."

"Fine," she said, turning and pacing alongside the shuttle bus. I stayed leaning against the bus, waiting. Paul finally pulled into the lot about five minutes later. Like Emilia, he had kept his headlights off. He nodded to me as he stepped out of the car.

"Lost 'em," he said, looking to Emilia. "He tell you why he shot three people this morning?"

"I didn't shoot three people," I said, raising my eyebrows. "But I can't tell you what's really going on

165

because it might be classified."

Emilia smiled, but there was little amusement in her eyes. "In the movies, people usually say they could tell us, but then they'd have to kill us afterward. Is that the line you were going for?"

I looked at her and shook my head. "I could tell you, but then I'd be sent to Fort Leavenworth's prison for the rest of my life. It's in the document I signed granting me a security clearance. You would then be taken into federal custody and debriefed by somebody from the US Attorney's Office. If you refused to sign their nondisclosure agreement, you'd probably end up in prison beside me."

Neither Emilia nor Paul said anything.

"You're serious?" asked Emilia, a few breaths later.

"Yes," I said. "For the past couple of weeks, I've been working an antiterrorism case with the FBI. Those men I supposedly shot this morning are FBI agents. The whole thing was a setup to make some bad guys trust me. Those FBI agents are alive and well. That's why you didn't find any bodies."

"There are people who can verify that?" asked Paul.

I nodded. "That cell phone you took from me is a burner. It's only got a few numbers in it, but one belongs to Kevin Havelock. He's the special agent in charge of Indianapolis's FBI field office. He's running the operation."

"If you're working with the FBI," said Emilia, "why did you call us tonight?"

"Because I trust you. I don't know if I can trust the Bureau right now."

Paul snorted and shook his head. "Let me guess: You can't tell us why you don't trust people there, either?"

"I'm already telling you more than I probably should. I'm investigating a suspected Islamic terror cell in Indianapolis. This terror cell rented that warehouse I met you at earlier. I had hoped you'd help me search it. Beyond that, I can't tell you much. If you don't want to help me, that's fine. I understand. You can go on your way. I need some help, though, and I called you two because I thought I could trust you."

Paul looked at Emilia. Neither said anything, but Paul nodded. Finally, Emilia looked at me.

"If it's important, we're with you," she said. "I wish we could help you with the department, but we've been boxed out of the investigation into your shooting."

"Who's stirring this up?" I asked.

"Tim Smith," said Paul.

Should have known. Sergeant Smith and I had a long history. He was the supervising officer of the investigative unit assigned to the prosecutor's office. He wasn't corrupt, but he worked under the supervision of a corrupt politician. We didn't always get to choose the men and women we worked for, so I could forgive him that. I had a lot harder time forgiving his strange preoccupation with having me fired or arrested.

"I've been home all evening," I said. "I'm not hiding. If he wanted to talk to me, he could have just knocked on my front door or called."

"If he did that, he wouldn't get the chance to shoot you," said Paul. "He sent an email this afternoon to department heads describing you as one of the most dangerous felons the department has ever investigated."

"That douchebag," I said. "I'll have Agent Havelock call Chief Reddington to see if we can figure this out. In the meantime, I need your help checking out that warehouse."

"Do you have a warrant?" asked Emilia.

"No, but a confidential informant told me to check it out. This guy wouldn't have contacted me without very good reason."

"So this is an illegal search to go along with your classified investigation. If we go in there, we'd be committing a felony, and we wouldn't even know why we're doing it," said Paul. "You're not selling this well, Ash."

"It's an antiterrorism case. You help me, you could save a lot of lives. If something goes wrong, I'll take as much responsibility as I can. Better?"

"Considerably," said Paul. "You should have led with that whole 'save a lot of lives' thing."

I ignored him and looked to Emilia. "You with Paul on this?"

"Yeah," she said. "You buried the lead. You should have told us that we could save lives earlier. It would have made for an easier decision."

I closed my eyes. "Your attempts at being funny

aside, are you with me or not?"

"Of course, boss," she said. "I don't lead just anybody handcuffed through the grocery store. You've got to be really special to receive that kind of treatment."

"Thank you," I said. "Let's just go."

Thankfully, neither of them attempted any other jokes before we headed out. I rode with Emilia in her cruiser in the lead while Paul followed. My heart sank the closer we drew to the property.

It started as a light glow, but the more we drove, the more that glow intensified. Then I saw the flashing lights of the firetrucks through the trees around the building. The warehouse was burning.

Whatever was in there, we were too late to find.

Chapter 18

Emilia pulled over to the side of the road about half a block from the fire. Neither of us said anything until Paul parked behind us, walked to our vehicle, and knocked on the window. Emilia and I got out. For a few minutes, we simply stood there and watched the building burn. Then Paul put a meaty hand on my shoulder.

"On the plus side, they didn't torch your car."

I exhaled a long breath through my nose. "Too soon, Paul."

"What'd you expect to find?" asked Emilia.

I shrugged. "Explosives, timing devices, bomb components…something, I don't know. Someone must have seen me near the building."

"You want us to start knocking on doors?" asked Emilia, nodding and looking around. "There are enough houses around here that somebody could have seen something."

"No," I said, shaking my head. "I'm going to bring the Bureau in on this. They'll be pissed if I don't. You guys have probably spent enough time with me. I don't want to get you two into trouble."

"We're not going to get in trouble," said Paul. "If you're working with the FBI, you didn't do anything wrong."

"Be that as it may, you guys were given orders to stay away from me," I said. "You don't want to be seen with me at the scene of a crime. Go home. I'll handle this."

They didn't seem to want to go, but eventually they agreed with me and left. I walked to the warehouse, where I flashed my badge to the fireman and got into my car so I could call Agent Havelock. He answered on the second ring, but I spoke before he could say a word.

"I'm in the parking lot of a warehouse leased by Nassir Hadad's holdings company. The building's burning right now."

Havelock paused. "We didn't know anything about a warehouse. How'd you find it?"

"Konstantin Bukoholov gave it to me. He's the landlord. Fire department's here now, hosing the place off. Once they're done, you should probably send some of your technicians through it."

"I'll put the call in. Thank you. Keep the scene secure for me. We'll be there as soon as we can. We'll need to talk about Bukoholov as well."

I turned toward the fire. Half the building was in flames. The other half had smoke billowing from its now broken windows. The firefighters were focusing their efforts on preventing the fire from spreading to nearby trees and buildings. I couldn't blame them. The whole place was toast.

"The scene doesn't need to be secured. There's nothing left," I said. "We'll talk about Bukoholov later. I've done enough for you today. I'm going to hang up, and then I'm going to go home. Once I'm off the line, please call my department and tell them I didn't murder three people this morning. Somebody took a video of our setup at the mosque. A detective in the prosecutor's office is telling anyone who will listen that I'm a dangerous, armed fugitive. I'm lucky I haven't run into a patrol officer with an itchy trigger finger."

"I'll call Sylvia Lombardo in the Office of Public Safety. Your video didn't hit the news yet. Hopefully it won't."

"We need to do better than hope. Get off your ass and make some calls. No one should have been around to film anything this morning. At the very least, you should have called my department before anything went down to tell them we had an operation going. It doesn't matter, though. I'm going home now. Send some techs out to my location. I'll pick up the investigation tomorrow."

I wanted to slam the phone down, but I gave him the warehouse's address. Afterwards, Havelock cleared his throat.

"I probably shouldn't tell you this, but in the past couple of hours, our signals intelligence unit has been picking up a lot of chatter about Indianapolis."

I looked toward the warehouse while shaking my head.

"I have no idea what that means."

"It means a lot of bad guys both within the United States and abroad are talking about Indianapolis. Our analysts haven't had a chance to dig through the raw intelligence yet, so they might just be talking about the Indy 500. After the attack on Westbrook Elementary today, though, the counterterrorism division isn't taking chances. They're coming to town in force, and they're going to scrutinize everything out of the norm."

I closed my eyes, understanding the implication without him having to mention it.

"Meaning, this warehouse and the man who leased it are going to get a lot of attention."

"Yeah. It's out of my hands. I just thought you should know."

For Nassir's sake, then, I hoped they didn't find anything. I thanked Havelock for keeping me up to date, and then I hung up. After that, I drove home. As I turned onto my street, though, I slowed to a stop and killed my headlights without even realizing it. None of the homes around me had lights on, and no one was on the road.

It had been a rough night. It wasn't too long ago that I had carried a bottle of bourbon in my glove box for nights like this. I didn't do that anymore, but there were days I wished I still did. I was an alcoholic. I used to go to meetings, but not anymore. Some days, I drank. Most days, I didn't. I wanted to get drunk every day, though.

As I sat in that warm car, I thought of Hannah, and then I thought of Megan and Kaden. For them, I could get through another day without a drink. They were my world and all I ever wanted. Every ounce of strength I had came from them. I wished I could show them what they meant to me.

I kept the headlights off but drove to my garage and parked inside. Hannah just barely woke up as I put on my pajamas and climbed into bed beside her.

"Everything okay, honey?" she asked.

I put my arm over her shoulder and felt her settle her against me. "It is now."

"Sleep tight."

Within just a few minutes, we were both out.

I slept until about nine the next morning when Megan, my daughter, poked me in the shoulder. She had brown hair and big brown eyes that sparkled with mischievous light. Every time I saw her, I couldn't help but think how much she had grown in the past few years. She was nine years old now. When she was younger, she had loved to draw and sing songs with my wife. She still liked those things, but now she had become my little engineer. Once she had found where I kept my tool set, she had taken apart everything she could reach.

The toaster had never recovered.

"Hey, Dad," she said, smiling at me. "*Ummi*, Kaden, and I are going to go to the grocery store. *Ummi* said I should tell you."

I smiled at her. It wasn't too long ago that she had called me *baba* instead of dad. In the grand scheme of things, it wasn't a big deal that she had started calling me dad, but I couldn't help but feel I had lost something important. My wife told me Megan did it to fit in with her friends. I understood that, but I still missed hearing her say it.

"What are you going to get at the grocery store?" I asked.

"Everything."

"Wow," I said, smiling. "You're going to have to get a big cart if you're going to pick up everything. Mount Everest alone is going to take up a lot of space."

She closed her eyes and shook her head. "Come on, Dad. That's not what I meant, and you know it. We're going to get everything on *ummi's* list."

"Oh," I said, nodding and trying not to smile. "That makes a lot more sense."

"*Ummi* wanted me to ask if you wanted to go."

"I would," I said, smiling, "but I've got to work. I could always use a hug, though."

She stepped toward the bed and held out her arms. I hugged her tight and whispered that I loved her. No matter how old she got, Megan would always be my little girl. I hoped she knew that. She bounced out of the room a moment later, and I got up to shower. I got out just in time to kiss my wife and hug my little boy before they left.

Of all the things I had to do that morning, one took precedence over everything else. I grabbed my cell phone from my bedroom and called Kevin Havelock at the Bureau.

"Havelock, it's Ash Rashid. Did you call my department last night?"

"I did. Your professional standards division might

have some questions for you, but your chief knows you're working for us. He sent out an email to his department heads telling them to back off on you."

I raised my eyebrows and started walking to the kitchen.

"Did you tell them I wasn't involved in a triple homicide?"

"We're keeping the details quiet. Suffice it to say, your chief and department heads know you were undercover working a case and that you didn't commit a crime."

I rubbed my eyes. "Until you tell them the truth, there are going to be a lot of police officers in this city who think I killed three people and got away with it."

Havelock drew in a long, slow breath before speaking.

"If we tell people the FBI staged a shooting to get inside an Islamic terror group in Indianapolis, how do you think the Islamic community will react? And bear in mind that if we tell your colleagues, it's going to get out."

I grimaced and poured a cup of coffee in the kitchen.

"We thought it was necessary to get inside Nassir's group."

"Nobody's going to care if it was necessary," said Havelock. "My agent is dead. You are tasked with finding his murderer. Are you going to do it or not?"

"Of course," I said. "What about the warehouse? You find anything?"

Havelock grunted. Then his voice softened.

"Rubble's still too hot to sift through. There are indications the fire was intentional, though. We'll work that end, and you work yours. Find out who killed my agent."

"I will."

Havelock hung up, and I took my first sip of coffee. It was so hot and bitter that I almost spit it out. I didn't know who had taught my wife to make coffee, but I sincerely hoped her teacher didn't make a habit out of the practice. My wife's coffee was the exact opposite of her character. Hannah was kind and sweet; it made my day just to see her. Her coffee was as black as death and seemed to suck the joy out of every room in which it found itself. I took a couple of deep breaths and forced another sip down my throat, but that was it. Any more than that, and I'd probably gag.

I poured most of the cup down the drain in the kitchen and considered what to do. Depending on what Havelock found at that warehouse, I might have to change my approach to the case. For now, though, I needed to focus on Jacob Ganim and those who knew him. He had a family. I didn't know their names, but if I could find them, they should be able to shed some light on the man I was investigating.

I went to Hannah's office and turned on her computer. I knew where Jacob lived, but I didn't know the first thing about his family. They could have different names, they could live out of state, or they might not even be alive anymore. Everyone leaves a trail when they pass through our lives, though, and everyone's information passes through the court systems eventually. That's where I'd find them.

I opened a web browser and navigated to INcite, the Indiana Court Information Technology Extranet. There, I looked for court cases in which Jacob Ganim was a party. I struck out at first, but then I looked at a database of protective orders. Again, I struck out. Finally, I searched the marriage license database and got lucky. Ganim had married Lauren Collier in 2013 in Johnson County. He divorced her two years later.

Once I had Lauren's name, I called my dispatcher. According to Indiana's Bureau of Motor Vehicles, there were fourteen Lauren Colliers in the state. We eliminated those who were over fifty and under twenty-five, which left us five women, one of whom lived in Franklin, Indiana—right in the middle of Johnson County. I had the feeling I had found Jacob Ganim's ex-wife.

I thanked my dispatcher and went upstairs.

Though the body of Michael Najam had been found weeks ago, Jacob Ganim was still officially alive. Had they been married still, Agent Havelock would have done the next-of-kin notification and called Lauren first thing. Estranged spouses, though, didn't get the same kind of courtesy—especially when their former spouse was undercover.

As I put on my suit and tie, I knew I was probably about to tell a woman that her ex-husband was dead. Worse than that, I was very likely going to tell a little girl that she would never see her daddy again.

The thought made me feel ill.

Chapter 19

The courier wore a bright orange jacket. It was the kind of thing a hunter might have worn so his fellow sportsmen wouldn't mistake him for a deer. He hated the jacket, and he hated the job.

Mostly, he delivered packages to law firms. It wouldn't have been so bad except those assholes almost never tipped him. Dentists were good customers. When he dropped off X-rays or a patient's medical file, dentists broke out their wallets.

Lawyers, though? Nothing.

They could afford a tip, too. That's what pissed him off the most. Some of them were billing out for eight hundred or a thousand dollars an hour. The courier didn't make that much money in a week, and he busted his ass every day. Rain, snow, blistering summer heat, it didn't matter. He got on his bike, and he did his job.

A couple bucks on top of his twelve-dollar-an-hour salary didn't seem like much, but a week of good tips meant he could buy his daughter new shoes or a new school jumper without having to worry about how they'd also buy groceries. Of course, nobody cared about that. He was just a guy on a bike.

Row houses surrounded him as he pedaled up North Carolina Avenue toward Lincoln Park in Washington, DC. A woman on the sidewalk pushed a black baby jogger and talked on her phone. Cars lined the streets. The assignment had come from a dark-skinned woman with two small kids, one of whom was still in a stroller. She was probably the personal assistant of an attorney or maybe a congressman. People like that came into the courier's office all the time.

There weren't too many businesses on this street, so he didn't make it up there often. He stopped in front of an old brick house a little more run down than the million-dollar homes around it. There was a printed sign on the second floor for *The DC Exponent*, a tabloid distributed for free around town.

The courier had picked up the paper more than once for its restaurant reviews, but he didn't read it on a regular basis. *The Exponent*'s primary reason to exist was to spread political gossip. The courier didn't care who was sleeping with whom on Capital Hill, because in the end, they screwed everybody with their legislation. He didn't need to know about their personal lives.

The courier locked his bike to a tree and carried his envelope to the door. Almost as soon as he rang the bell, a white guy in jeans and a red cable-knit sweater opened it.

"Yeah?"

The courier held out the envelope and a clipboard with the delivery label. "I've got a delivery for the *DC Exponent*. I need a signature."

"This for anybody in particular?"

The courier shook his head. "Just to the paper."

"All right," said the guy in the sweater. He signed his

name and then smiled. The courier waited for a moment and smiled back. "You need something else?"

"It's customary to tip for a delivery like this," he said. "I know we don't make it out here to often, so you may not know."

"You want a tip," said the man in the sweater, nodding. "You should have gone to college. There's your tip. Now go back to work."

The courier took a step back as the reporter closed the door.

"Asshole."

He was gone without a look over his shoulder.

Jeremy carried the envelope inside and ran his hand along the seal to open it. *The Exponent* got these kinds of envelopes a couple of times a week, usually from divorce attorneys. When women found out that their famous husbands had been sleeping with an intern and wanted some leverage in settlement talks, the *Exponent* got a new story complete with pictures. Reporters at places like *The Washington Post* looked down their noses at *The Exponent*, but while their paper bled money, *The Exponent* printed it. Jeremy never had to fear that his paycheck would bounce or that he'd be downsized. That was more than he could say of his colleagues at more "reputable" institutions.

As he pulled the documents from the envelope, he stopped walking. They were pictures, all right, but they didn't involve congressmen with their penises in places they didn't belong. They were surveillance photos of Westbrook Elementary, the school at which the first family died. Curious, he looked in the envelope and found a neat, handwritten note on lined paper.

Found in a mosque in Indianapolis. Our government knows more than they're letting on. - a concerned FBI agent.

Jeremy carried the envelope to his desk and brushed aside the empty soda cans to make space. He flipped through dozens of pictures of the school from before and after the bombing before coming to pictures of the devices themselves. Someone had placed them on the ground by the school. The photographer had then taken pictures of their design schematics.

Jeremy wasn't a bomb expert, but this looked like the real deal. His breath caught in his throat, and he looked toward his editor's cubicle.

Marcia sat at her desk with a smile on her face. She had been working on a slide show involving funny cats when he last saw her.

"Hey, Marcia, we've got something," he said, his voice trembling. "It's big."

She glanced up at him and humored him with a smile. "I'm on a roll, Germs. Give me an hour, and you'll have my full attention."

He shook his head and gathered the pictures as well as the note and took them to her desk.

"What are you doing?" she asked. "I'm working."

He reached forward and turned off her monitor.

"Now we're working on something else," he said, looking down at the pictures. "Look at this."

She gave him an exasperated look and then glanced down. "They're pictures of a school. Why do I care about pictures of a school?"

"Because an FBI agent just sent them to us. This is Westbrook Elementary, the school the president's family was murdered at. We've got proof Islamic terrorists assassinated the first family."

She flipped through the pictures slowly, just as Jeremy had. Her hands began trembling sometime after the tenth picture. Once she finished, she folded her hands together for a moment, her eyes glued to her desk.

"This is real news," she said. "This is fucking real."

"Yeah, it's real," said Jeremy. "What do you want to do?"

She didn't respond for a moment. They both knew what they should have done. Reporters at the *Post* or *The New York Times* would have called their sources within the government for verification, but neither she nor Jeremy had those kind of sources. And even if they had, they wouldn't have picked up the phone. They didn't know how many other news outlets had received similar information packets. They had to get this out before anyone else. She looked at Jeremy, her eyes distant for a moment before focusing.

"Did Roger finish our server upgrades?"

Jeremy nodded. "Last week."

"Good," she said, her breath still short. "We're about to get slammed."

Chapter 20

Lauren Collier lived in a single-story home with a big bay window out front and a hip roof. There were rose bushes along the base of the house to hide the foundation and a shade tree between the front walkway and sidewalk. Though she had used a different color palette and different plants, something about the symmetry of the home and yard reminded me of Jacob Ganim's place. Evidently, Lauren was the designer in the family.

I parked in front, but before I could even open my door, a blonde woman stepped out of the house. I recognized her from pictures in Jacob Ganim's living room, so I knew I was at the right place. I got out of the car and began walking up the paver walkway to her front door.

"Ms. Collier?" I asked. She looked at me up and down warily. I pulled back my jacket to expose the badge at my hip. "I'm Lieutenant Ash Rashid with the Indianapolis Metropolitan Police Department. Do you have time to talk?"

Her eyes snapped to mine. I stopped a few feet in front of her.

"What's this about, Lieutenant?"

"Is it possible we could go somewhere and sit down?" I asked.

"No," she said. I nodded and took a step back to show her I respected her wishes and personal space. I probably should have brought Emilia Rios for this. She was better with people—especially women—than I was.

"I understand," I said. "Like I said, I'm a lieutenant with the Indianapolis Metropolitan Police Department. I'm currently working on a task force with the FBI in Indianapolis. Has anyone from the Bureau contacted you about your husband lately?"

"I'm not married."

"Your ex-husband, then. Jacob Ganim," I said. She drew in a breath at the mention of Ganim's name. I took that as a sign of recognition. "Has anyone talked to you about him lately?"

She sighed and crossed her arms. "No."

I considered stopping the interview right there. She clearly didn't want to talk to me, and even more clearly, she didn't want to talk about her ex-husband. Still, the man was dead, and I didn't have a lot of leads.

As a former homicide detective, I had done a lot of next-of-kin notifications in my career. I had found a lot of wrong ways to do it, but never the right one. No matter what I did, Ms. Collier's world was going to fall apart as soon as I spoke. Early on in my career, I'd thought the best way to do this was to beat around the bush for a while, let the victim's family come to the realization on their own. I had thought that would be easier for them, but it wasn't. It was cruel. Ms. Collier needed honesty.

"Ma'am, I'm very sorry to inform you that your ex-husband has died. I'm here because I'm the lead detective in his murder investigation."

She blinked once, but that was the only indication that she had heard what I said. I waited for a ten count, and then she blinked again and again as tears welled in her eyes. She brought her hand to her face as her lower lip began to tremble.

"I'm truly sorry," I said.

She held up a hand to stop me from saying anything else. Then she leaned against her doorframe and drew in some deep breaths. We stayed there for a few minutes. Even if they were divorced, she obviously still cared about her ex-husband on some level.

"How did he die?"

"He was murdered while working a case," I said. "And that's why I'm here. I'm trying to find out what kind of a person he was. I'd appreciate anything you can tell me."

She closed her eyes and drew in a breath. "Are you really a police officer?"

It was an odd question, and I considered my answer before speaking.

"Yes. If you'd like, I can have someone from my department or from the FBI call to confirm my identity. I'm Lieutenant Ashraf Rashid with IMPD. My office is in downtown Indianapolis, and my supervisor is Captain Mike Bowers. Right now, I'm reporting to Special Agent Kevin Havelock of the FBI. I'm not a con man. I'm simply a detective trying to find out who murdered your ex-husband."

"Okay," she said, nodding and rubbing a tear from the corner of her eye. "I believe you. What do you want to know, Lieutenant Rashid?"

"Anything you can tell me," I said. "I have access to information about your ex-husband's work life, but I don't know much about his personal life. I need to know about the kind of things he did after work. Did he have problems with anyone? Did any of the men or women he arrested make threats? Did he ever have problems with drugs or alcohol? Anything you can tell me would be extremely helpful."

She blinked a few times and then drew in a breath. When she spoke, her voice was strong and clear.

"I appreciate that you came all the way out here to tell me about Jacob, but I'm not comfortable answering these questions. If you come here again, I'll call the local police and have you prosecuted for trespassing."

I paused, unsure what I had just done wrong. Then I nodded and took a couple of steps back, giving myself a moment to think. People got upset when I did next-of-kin notifications, but usually they yelled and screamed. Ms. Collier's request was cold and calculated.

"Thank you for your time. I'm sorry to have disturbed you. Would you like my card in case you change your mind?"

"No," she said. "Please just leave, Lieutenant."

I didn't think staying and arguing with her would have gotten me anywhere, so I got back in my car and drove off without saying a word.

Rarely did the spouse of a murder victim refuse to help an investigation. When it did happen, it usually meant he or she had other means of seeking justice in mind, or that he or she was involved in the crime. Ms. Collier's tears had looked genuine and spontaneous. I doubted she had known her husband was dead. Whether she had the means to seek justice on her own, I didn't know yet, but I planned to find out.

When I got back in my car, I called up the GPS app on my cell phone. Nassir's camp was only forty-five minutes away, and we needed to talk. I dialed his number, but his phone immediately went to voicemail. Given the remoteness of his summer camp, that didn't surprise me. He was probably out of range of any cell towers. At the beep, I left a message.

"Nassir, it's Ash. You and the guys at your camp are the only people I know who knew Jacob Ganim. We need to talk about his ex-wife. I need to know everything he's told you. Every throwaway comment, every gripe, every compliment, everything he said.

"We also need to talk about a warehouse leased by Safe Haven, LLC. The building burned to the ground last night, and the FBI has sent over technicians to sift through the rubble. I know Safe Haven is your company, and I know you were storing something there you shouldn't have been. We need to talk so we can sort this out. If you let the FBI investigation run its course, they're going to kick your door down and come in with guns drawn. Someone could get hurt. You don't want that, and neither do I. If you're not at your camp when you receive this message, get there. I'm coming to see you."

Once I hung up, I waited a moment to see whether he'd call back. He didn't, which was probably for the best anyway. Some conversations were best had in person.

The drive to Nassir's camp through the hills of south-central Indiana was uneventful but pleasant. There were a lot of spring wildflowers on the roadside, and the air smelled like freshly cut grass. When I arrived at Nassir's camp, the front gate was shut. Evidently, they didn't want visitors. I opened it and drove through anyway.

As before, there were a number of cars parked outside the clubhouse, including Nassir's Cadillac. No one came outside to greet me, so I went in. Nassir and three other men were in the mess hall, deep in conversation. They didn't notice me, so I cleared my throat. One by one, they nodded to me. Nassir waved me over. I stayed put near the door.

"Did you get my message?" I asked.

Nassir furrowed his brow. "What message?"

I looked at the other men in the room. I recognized Ismail Shadid and Asim Qureshi from my trip to the camp earlier, but I didn't know the third man. Evidently, my brother-in-law had more people involved in his project than anyone knew about. I looked at Nassir again.

"Tell me about the warehouse you leased from Konstantin Bukoholov."

The furrow on his brow deepened, and he tilted his

head to the side. "What are you talking about?"

"Your company, Safe Haven, LLC, leased a secure warehouse from a known gangster," I said, speaking as slowly and clearly as I could. "That warehouse burned to the ground last night in very suspicious circumstances."

Nassir looked to the other men around him. They looked as confused as he did. Bukoholov could have lied to me on his deathbed, but I doubted it. They knew more than they were letting on.

"We have no idea what you're talking about," said Nassir. "We don't have any rental property. This is it."

"If that's the story you want to stick with, that's your choice. Bear in mind that the FBI has some of the best forensic scientists in the world. They will find everything stored in that building. If they tie it to you and find something incriminating there, you're going to have a bad day."

"I told you already, Ashraf," said Nassir, gesturing around him and practically yelling, "this is a summer camp. What else do I have to say to you?"

"It is a summer camp, but I'm guessing it's more than that. I've searched this building. You have a room secured with a solid exterior door and a padlock up the hallway. Aside from the bathroom, it's the only room with a lock anywhere on the property as far as I can tell. What are you hiding?"

A couple of the guys sat straighter. One drew in a breath. That got their attention.

"Nothing," said Nassir, turning away so that his

shoulder pointed at me. A lot of people did things like that when they lied. A psychologist could probably explain the move, but I didn't need an explanation to know he was holding back.

"You don't put a door like that inside a residential building without reason. What are you storing in that room?"

Nassir sighed and shook his head, but he didn't look at me. Before he spoke a word, I knew he was going to lie to me.

"Donations and payroll," he said, turning his body so that I could see only his side. "It's where we keep our petty cash. Would you rather we keep that in the open?"

I looked to the other men there. "You think these guys are going to steal from you?"

"This isn't a secured building. People like you can just drive right onto the property."

I sighed and took a step back. If they weren't going to tell me the truth, I'd find out on my own.

"What do you know about Jacob Ganim's ex-wife?"

"Nothing," said Ismail. "We didn't know Jacob Ganim. Michael Najam never mentioned his wife."

I waited for Nassir or anyone else to say anything. No one did.

"This is your last chance," I said. "If you force me to find answers on my own, you might not like my methods."

Again, no one said anything, so I turned to leave. Before I could get more than a few steps, Nassir sighed.

"Please stop," he said. "We need your help."

I turned around and put my hands on my hips to push back my jacket. Everyone there could see my badge and the weapon on my belt.

"Are you going to cooperate with my investigation?"

The man I didn't recognize stepped forward. He was probably about fifty and had graying curly hair, dark brown skin, and a neatly trimmed beard. His irises were brown, while the whites of his eye were tinged slightly yellow. He moved with a barely perceptible limp. I hadn't seen him at my mosque, but if he was one of Nassir's friends, he was probably quite devout.

I nodded hello to him. He nodded back and then lowered his gaze.

"My name is Saleem al-Asiri. I'm the guidance counselor at a high school near Dayton, Ohio."

"Very nice to meet you," I said, glancing from Saleem to Nassir and then back. "I'm Ashraf Rashid. Nassir is married to my sister. As you can probably guess by now, I'm a police officer."

He looked back at his friends and then to me. He shuffled just a little and sighed. "I need you to talk to one of my students."

I raised my eyebrows. "I'm a detective in Indiana, and I'm already working a case. If you suspect your student committed a crime in Ohio, you need to talk to someone at your local police station."

Saleem shook his head. "He's not committed any crime, but he will. He's here. His parents contacted me after they found him ordering ammunition online. The family doesn't own any firearms. We think he's buying the ammunition for someone else."

I sighed. That was a problem.

"If he's acting as a straw buyer for guns or ammunition, that's a federal crime. I don't have jurisdiction. I don't even know that area of law well."

Nassir stepped forward. "He's not selling guns. We've been monitoring him online. He thinks God wants him to become a *mujahid*. We think he's stockpiling ammunition for some kind of attack. We need you to talk to him and find out who he's working with. Please."

Nassir was almost pleading. I didn't say anything. Instead, I let my mind work freely for a few minutes. Then I sighed as everything clicked all at once.

"That's why you post on radical Facebook groups," I said, rubbing my eyes. "You're not trying to moderate them. You're monitoring kids that you think are radicalized."

"Yes," he said, a smile breaking across his face. "Now you see. That's why I left Rana. I couldn't involve her in this. I didn't want her hurt. This is important work. Someone needs to do it."

"Yeah," I said, nodding. "Someone. The FBI, for instance. Not a bunch of middle-aged high guidance counselors and accountants."

Nassir seemed to shrink a little. "You're not going to help us?"

"I'll help," I said, shaking my head. "But first, we're

going to talk in private. Outside, right now."

Nassir nodded and followed me outside. Though I had marveled at what a nice day it was earlier, now the late morning felt somehow oppressive. The clouds seemed lower in the sky, the heat and humidity had begun to settle in, and the gray horizon looked almost foreboding. There was a storm building in the distance. Whether it would pass here was anyone's guess, but it would smack somebody and soon.

Nassir and I walked without saying a word. I didn't have a destination in mind, just a vague goal of getting out of earshot of Nassir's friends. We walked for about ten minutes behind the clubhouse to the hill at which I had placed a call to Agent Havelock the day prior. I had looked out over that hill just a little over twenty-four hours ago and wondered how I'd tell an FBI assault team to take the camp. After the fire at the warehouse last night, I wondered whether a tactical officer was making that decision without me.

I looked at Nassir and drew in a breath.

"It's time to come clean about everything. Did you know about the warehouse?"

He closed his eyes and then shook his head. "The curse of *Allah* be on him if he is one of the liars."

I nodded. "I know what the Quran says about lying. Did you know about the warehouse?"

He shook his head again. "No. I don't know anything about it. I haven't spoken an untruth to you since you got here. You're the liar. Everything you've done has been a lie."

I held up a hand. "This isn't about me. I'm doing my job. You don't like my methods, tough shit. We don't live in a pleasant world. Could any of your friends down there use your camp's funds to rent a warehouse?"

He hesitated, but then nodded. "We all have responsibilities, so we all have access to the checkbook. If anyone wrote a check, though, they would have told me. I'm the accountant."

"And nobody told you anything?" I asked.

He shook his head. "Of course not."

"Then go over your accounts and compare your funds available with the books. You're going to have a discrepancy somewhere."

Nassir considered me and then crossed his arms. "Why do you think the problem is on our end? Where did you get your information?"

"A confidential informant. He has no reason to lie to me about this, and he would have no reason to know your name unless you or someone close to you did business with him. Can we talk about the kid you guys are holding captive now?"

"We're not holding anyone captive."

I took a step back and raised my eyebrows. "Is the kid who bought ammunition free to go?"

Nassir uncrossed his arms and rubbed his forehead. "You and Rana are exactly alike. I couldn't talk to her, either."

That was probably part of why his marriage

imploded; saying that probably wouldn't have helped the situation, though.

"What do you hope to accomplish with him?" I asked.

Nassir sighed and then began pacing, all the while looking at the ground. If I had to guess, he had a speech prepared for moments like this, but he couldn't bring himself to say it.

"We want to help him," he said, finally. "We want to show him that holding on to his hate won't get him anywhere. We want to show him that there are ways back from the places he's been."

"If this kid is ordering ammunition and giving it to potential terrorists, there may not be a way back," I said. "Did you consider that?"

"There's always a way back," said Nassir, his voice soft. "Where there is God, there is hope."

"Is that the plan? You keep him here and hope?"

"No," said Nassir, shaking his head. "We keep him here, and we show him a better way to live. We show him what it means to submit to God."

"For all of our sakes, I hope that works out," I said, sighing. "His parents have given you permission for whatever you're doing?"

"Yes," said Nassir. "They play a key role. His father will come down on the weekends to work beside him. His mother will come down, too, when she's able. Together, we'll show him a better way to live. We've already started giving him projects, and he's responding well. He's at a lumberyard right now. He's buying wood so he and Asim can make bunk beds."

So they hadn't kidnapped him, at least.

"He's alone?"

Nassir nodded. "He's got the camp truck."

"What's his name? I'll call my contact at the Bureau and see if anyone else is monitoring his activities. The last thing you need right now is to give the FBI more reason to raid this place."

"Butler al-Ghamdi."

I took out my phone to see whether I had any bars. Not only did I have reception, my supervisor at IMPD had tried to call me four times. I looked at Nassir.

"Why don't you head back?" I said. "Tell Butler I'll be in to talk to him in a few minutes. I've got to make some calls."

Nassir left without saying another word, not that we had much to say to one another. I let him get about twenty feet away before I called my boss. He answered before his phone finished ringing once.

"Mike, it's Ash Rashid. I've been out of cell reception. What's up?"

"First things first—since I couldn't get in touch with you, I called the police in Fishers. They'll send extra patrols through your neighborhood to make sure there aren't people loitering around your house."

I paused for a moment, thinking. "Okay. Thanks, I guess. Why did you do that?"

"You haven't seen the news?"

I looked at the hillside around me and shook my head. "I'm in the middle of nowhere. I have to climb a hill just to get cell reception."

Bowers grunted. "Lucky you. About half an hour ago, a tabloid in DC published a package of photographs that purportedly outline the planning and staging of the attack on President Crane's family in New Hampshire. According to them, these pictures were found by an FBI agent inside a mosque in Indianapolis."

Immediately, my heart sank. I tried to say something, but my voice caught in my throat. Indianapolis had a lot of Muslims, so the chances were that I didn't know the people involved. Still, it made me feel sick. This was my community.

"You still there, Ash?" asked Bowers.

"Yeah, I'm here," I said, my voice soft. "What's the Bureau saying about this, and how did a tabloid newspaper in DC get the scoop?"

"Bureau's not saying anything officially. Unofficially, IMPD has been trying to get in touch with them, but it's something of a clusterfuck over there right now. Best we can tell, the story took them by surprise. They hadn't connected the attack on the president to anyone yet, let alone a group in Indianapolis."

Meaning they hadn't leaked the photos. I thought for a few seconds.

"That is a problem. Is that why you called?"

"No," said Bowers. "I called to ask what the hell you're doing in Franklin."

"I'm working a case for the FBI," I said, somewhat taken aback. "I'm not sure how much I can say. Officially, I'm supposed to tell you to call Special Agent Havelock if you have questions."

"As you can imagine, given the other news of the morning, Havelock isn't returning my calls."

Bowers was fifty miles away, but I nodded anyway.

"How did you know I was in Franklin?"

"Because I got a call from Colonel Nathan Carter this morning telling me so. He's a staffer on the National Security Council. He works at the White House." Bowers paused for a moment. "What the hell kind of case are you working?"

That took me aback again. As the ex-spouse of an undercover FBI agent, Lauren Collier would have had the number of a security officer at the Bureau to call for emergencies. That security officer wouldn't have worked at the White House, though, and he certainly wouldn't have worked for the National Security Council. This was just…weird. I had hoped visiting her would shed more light on my case and victims. Instead, it just revealed more shadows.

"That's a very good question," I said.

Bowers waited a few beats before responding. "I'm delighted you appreciate it. Are you going to answer?"

I shook my head. "I honestly don't know how to answer you. I have no idea what kind of case this is now."

"Then, as your colleague, I'd advise you to find out. You're not working for me right now, so I can't order you to do anything. That said, I'd advise you to avoid visiting Lauren Collier again. She's got the kind of friends who can bury you with a phone call."

I heard everything Bowers said, but I didn't respond. My heart started pounding.

My vantage on the hill gave me a view of the entire property, including the front gate. Three black SUVs and an armored personnel carrier had just barreled into the camp, hidden lights flashing in their grills. None had the markings of any law enforcement agency. Faintly, I heard the blades of a helicopter drawing closer in the distance.

"Hey, Mike, I'm going to have to call you back. I think I'm going to be arrested."

Chapter 21

Hashim Bashear's chest felt heavy. He took a handkerchief from the table beside his bed and held it to his mouth as a wet cough racked his body. Though he had told his son he had a bad cold, it was more than a cold. The wheezing, the pain in his bones, the exhaustion, the headaches…a physician in Syria suspected it was lung cancer, but he didn't have the equipment to confirm the diagnosis. Hashim didn't care. His time had come.

He closed his eyes and returned the handkerchief, now tinged with blood, to the end table.

"God, watch over your humble servant and give me the strength to complete your glorious work."

For a few moments after the prayer, he allowed himself to sink deeply into the pillow again. At his age and in his health, he should have been in the hospital. Barring that, he should have been at home, surrounded by loved ones. He was ready to die. Life had never been easy for him, but it was growing harder still now that he neared the end. God would never ask of him more than he could accomplish, though. Of that, he was certain.

After drawing in a breath, Hashim forced himself to sit up. It was the second time he had been out of bed that day, having already led his men through *fajr* earlier that morning. Some of the men had grumbled when Hashim woke them at dawn, but all of them understood their obligations to God. They were good boys. Some needed a firmer hand than others, but that was to be expected. All men were different, and yet God had room for everyone under His tent.

Hashim cleared his throat and dressed before leaving the room. He and his son, Hamza, had arrived late the previous evening to find that the men had reserved the master bedroom for Hashim and a guest bedroom for Hamza. The rest of the men slept on sleeping bags and sofas throughout the house. At his age, Hashim appreciated the courtesy.

He stepped into the hallway and heard voices whispering from the kitchen. Hashim didn't know who had rented the home, but it fit their needs. About twenty minutes west of Indianapolis, it sprawled across a wooded, ten-acre plot of land, giving them both the privacy and space needed to complete their mission. That it was comfortable after years spent in the Syrian desert was a very welcome bonus.

"*As-salamu alaykum,*" said Hamza, as Hashim entered the small kitchen. The young man Hamza had been speaking to stood straighter and repeated the greeting. Hashim smiled and put a hand on the young man's arm gently.

"*Wa alaykumu as-salam,*" he said. "I'm glad to see you, but I'd like a moment of privacy with my son."

"Of course, sir," said the boy, picking up a coffee mug from the nearby counter and leaving. With its open architecture, the house afforded little privacy, but Hashim would take whatever he could get. The young man he had just met joined two others in the living room. Hashim watched them for a moment, before turning to his son.

"He's young," said Hashim.

"Sixteen," said Hamza. "He's a good boy, though. He understands the importance of our mission here. Are you feeling okay? I heard you coughing."

"I'm fine," said Hashim, waving away his son's concern and glancing to the clock on the microwave. It was already after ten in the morning. "You shouldn't have let me sleep in this late. We have work to do."

"This work, I can supervise," said Hamza. "I can't replicate your leadership. God has given you a unique mission. You needed to sleep so you can better lead these men."

Without thinking, Hashim felt something in him swell. He brought his hand to his son's face and wistfully touched his cheek. It was an intimate gesture, a father to his beloved son. Then he dropped his hands to his side and took a step back.

"You are wiser than you have any right to be at your age," he said. "You remind me of your *ummi.*"

Hamza smiled. "I do get most of my good traits from her. A few come from you, too, though."

He meant it as a joke, but Hashim knew it was true. His deceased wife was the best woman he had ever met. He missed her every day and looked forward to seeing her again soon.

"How are things here?"

Hamza grunted and then reached for a coffee mug in

a nearby cabinet. He poured Hashim a cup of black, steaming coffee and drew in a breath.

"They've had setbacks."

Hashim nodded and sipped his drink. It was hot and bitter and thick, just as he liked it.

"Enough to endanger our mission?"

Hamza thought for a moment but then nodded.

"Yes, but there are contingency plans in place. They kept their supplies in a warehouse, but somehow a detective found it and tried to search it last night. They barely had enough time to burn the building before he got in."

Hashim sighed and put his coffee on the counter. "Any losses?"

"Guns, timing devices, and explosives. Our losses were material but significant. Thankfully, we didn't lose any of our soldiers."

Hashim closed his eyes, feeling his frustration build. Then he exhaled slowly.

"God will provide for him from where he does not expect. And whoever relies upon God, then He is sufficient for him. Indeed, God will accomplish His purpose."

Hamza nodded. "I know what the Quran says, but I'm still worried."

"Tell me about this detective," said Hashim. "How did he find us?"

"We don't know much about him, but he's a Muslim. Or at least he claims to be. His name is Ashraf Rashid."

"If he were a Muslim, he would be with us here," said Hashim, reaching for his coffee again. "He's an apostate. If this country had laws, he'd be executed, and his corpse would be burned. We'll deal with him ourselves. Are all of our soldiers here today?"

"The young men are here. The older men are at work."

"Then get the young ones. I'd like to talk to them."

Hamzah said he would. Hashim took his coffee to the dining room. His team had leased the home furnished, so he took a seat at the head of the dining table. Young men started shuffling in moments later. He knew their names from their Facebook accounts, and he recognized their faces from prayers that morning, but he hadn't gotten to speak to any of them. He was proud of every one of them, though. Even at sixteen or seventeen years old, they were ready to give up their lives to make the world a better place. He wished he had possessed the same strength at their ages.

Hashim greeted each man with a handshake and a smile. There were nine men in total, and they came from all over the Midwest. Hashim had recruited each of them —along with a number of local men who were currently at work—online. He had recruited the soldiers who attacked Westbrook Elementary the same way. These young men had a job ahead of them that was even more daunting than the one in New Hampshire, but it came with rewards beyond their imaginations.

He put his coffee on the table and stood.

"My friends, thank you for coming," he said. "I know it's been a hardship for many of you to come here today. I've not known many of you very long—six months, a year at most—but each of you has impressed me in your own way. I am as proud of you men as I am of my own son, and that is truly high praise, for my son is a man of God."

Most of the boys smiled and nodded, but their eyes darted around as well. They were nervous. Hashim understood it, but they had no reason to be nervous. Their place at God's side was assured by their righteous actions. He smiled at them reassuringly.

"Many of you asked me whether I could bring you to Raqqa or the Euphrates River Valley after Raqqa fell. You wanted to join your brothers in the fight," said Hashim, sweeping his eyes across the group. "I told you, though, that God had a plan for you, that you needed patience. This is the day you've been waiting for. This is the day God created you for."

He paused and smiled at each man in the room. Now, none of them looked away nervously. In fact, they looked eager and excited. Good.

"The world is changing. I don't need to tell you that. Our enemies are gathering strength. They've driven us from our homes in Iraq and Syria. They've murdered our friends. They've refused to allow us to worship God as He deserves. They've hurt us, but they haven't broken us."

Some of the boys nodded, while a few clapped. Hashim smiled good-naturedly.

"It's your time to stand up. You will continue the fight your brothers started in New Hampshire. Your brothers struck a mighty blow against the infidels. We exposed their weakness. Now, we will show them our strength. We choose to fight them in their heartland. We will attack where they are weak. And make no mistake, we will win."

Now, everyone in the room nodded and clapped.

"They'll call us terrorists, but we're not. Our goal isn't to inflict terror," said Hashim. "Our goal is to make them bleed. In New Hampshire, we committed a surgical strike designed to weaken their president. He's locked himself in his rooms in the White House and hasn't been seen since the attack. We've rendered the great man impotent.

"In Indianapolis, we will declare war. We will destroy their homes, we will shoot them in their streets, we will bury them in their places of business, and we will destroy their hospitals and schools. These aren't empty boasts or false bravado. With your bravery and your talents, we will make it happen.

"I understand you've lost supplies and weapons recently. Know that God will always provide, though. Even now, my son is enabling our contingency plans. We will have trucks and guns and devices so fiendishly clever our enemy will never see them coming. The infidels may have hurt us, but they have not taken us down. Soon, they will know what it means to be hunted, and then their tears and blood will flood the earth."

"*SubhanAllah*," said Hamza.

Glory to God.

Hashim looked at his son and smiled as the other boys in the room shouted and stomped their feet like a football team at halftime.

"Allahu akbar."

Hashim didn't see who said it, but it turned into a chant that sped up with every passing moment. The boys needed a pep talk, and he was happy to give it. At the same time, he had work to do. He nodded to his son, who encouraged all but two preselected boys to disperse. Hashim smiled at them. They were older than some of the other boys, probably in their early twenties. From their conversations online, he knew they had skills he sorely needed. There should have been three, though. He looked at Hamza.

"Where's our third team member?"

"It's a long story," said Hamza. "Suffice it to say, he'll be here when we need him."

Hashim didn't like how that sounded, but he kept his disapproval hidden behind a smile. At this moment, his team needed to see a confident and strong leader. He looked to the first young man.

"Kamil," said Hashim, holding out his hand to him. "I'm Hashim Bashear. I've enjoyed our chats online, and it's an honor to finally meet you in person. I hear you're quite the hunter."

"I am," said the boy, beaming. He had dark skin and hair and bright eyes. He was a handsome boy. If Hashim had a daughter, he might have introduced them. "I'm proud to be here."

"And I'm proud to stand in front of you," said Hashim, smiling. He turned his attention to the second boy. "And Daniel, it's an honor to meet you as well. I understand you're quite good with a bow and arrow."

Daniel stood straighter as Hashim shook his hand.

"My parents thought I could go to the Olympics, but I was never good enough."

Hashim reached forward and patted his cheek gently. "You're more than good enough, my son. God has a special job for you and Kamil. Your brothers are destined to become martyrs on the streets. You, though, will hunt apostates. Where the other men in the house are hammers, you are scalpels. Truly, I envy the day you have ahead of you. Now come, we have much to discuss."

Chapter 22

With a helicopter in the air and my car beside Nassir's Cadillac at the clubhouse, escape wasn't an option. I pulled out my cell phone and called Kevin Havelock at the Bureau. His phone rang four times before going to voicemail.

"Havelock, it's Ash Rashid. I'm at Nassir's camp right now, and I think I'm going to be arrested. If these are your guys, let them know I'm here. If they're not, I'd appreciate it if you called Homeland Security to let them know I work for you."

I hung up immediately and began dialing my wife's number. Trails of dust followed the convoy of vehicles as they sped across the gravel road. The helicopter I had heard earlier streaked overhead and hovered in the center of the property a couple hundred feet from the ground. Hopefully Nassir and his friends would know to give up without a fight. They didn't need to get hurt. Hannah's cell rang twice before someone picked up.

"Hello?"

It was my daughter's soft voice.

"Hi, sweetheart," I said, trying to make my voice sound calm. "Can you put *Ummi* on the phone, please?"

"She's in the shower."

I forced myself to smile and hoped it came through my voice. "Okay. Open the bathroom door and give her the phone."

Megan hesitated. "I'm not allowed. She'll put me in timeout."

"She won't put you in timeout, honey," I said. "This is an emergency. Open the bathroom door and give her the phone."

Almost the moment I finished speaking, the nose of the helicopter dipped as it began creeping toward me. In movies, my connection probably would have begun crackling or breaking in and out. That didn't happen. Instead, the connection simply dropped before my daughter could even say anything. The helicopter must have had some kind of cell-jamming device. We used them, too, when we attempted to arrest suspects who we thought might use their phones to call additional support.

I slipped my cell into my pocket and stepped out from beneath the canopy of trees. Already, one black SUV peeled away from the group near the clubhouse to close in on my position. The helicopter stayed overhead long enough for the SUV to skid to a stop near me. Four men jumped out. All four carried tactical rifles, and all four trained them on my chest. None of the men wore insignia for any law enforcement agency.

I got on my knees without them having to ask.

"I'm an armed police officer, and I'm on the job," I said.

Two of the men hurried behind me, while the other two stayed in front.

"Lie on the ground, and lace your fingers behind your head," said one of the men in front of me.

"I have a firearm and a badge on my belt," I said, complying with the order and slowly lying down. "I'm cooperating. Please don't shoot me."

"Face in the dirt. Lie on the ground."

The voice was close behind me. Before I could brace myself, pain exploded in my shoulder as a heavy boot kicked me. My teeth sliced into my tongue, drawing blood. I turned my head so that my ear was on the grass. I spit into the dirt beside me.

"I'm cooperating, assholes!" I said, shouting now. "Kick me again, and I'll file excessive-force complaints against all of you."

This time, they didn't kick me. Instead, a knee hit me in the lower back, nearly knocking my breath out.

"Keep your hands on top of your head."

I gritted my teeth before speaking.

"I'm not moving."

The guy with his knee on my back pulled my weapon out of its holster and then began running his hands up my torso. He pulled out my cell phone and keys and then tossed them to somebody behind him before reaching to my wrist and wrenching my hand behind my back.

Early on in my career, I had been shot in the shoulder while serving an arrest warrant on a murder suspect. Now, pain lanced through that same joint and into my neck and back. I tried to hold it in, but I gasped.

"That hurt?" asked the man, twisting my wrist to wrench my shoulder again. The ball of my shoulder nearly popped out of its socket. I had gone through a lot of rehab after being shot, and it always hurt. Never like this, though. I gasped again, and he chuckled under his breath as he tightened one side of a zip cuff on my wrist. Then he reached my for my other wrist and secured both behind my back. Finally, he let go and stood. I blinked away tears of pain.

"On your feet," said one of the men, reaching to my elbow and gently tugging. Thankfully, this guy seemed to recognize that I was subdued and didn't need more encouragement to follow directions. As I got to my feet, I rolled my shoulders and felt a deep, throbbing ache pass through me. I'd be sore for a long while, but I was alive. Hopefully Nassir and the others at the clubhouse were cooperating.

"Walk toward the vehicle and stop outside," said the guy to my right. "Bear in mind that you still have three men with rifles pointed at your back. If you cooperate, you won't be hurt."

I started walking to the car, but then a hand pulled my shoulder back. I started to turn around, but before I could, somebody behind me pulled a black sack over my head. The fabric was thin enough to allow light to pass through, but I couldn't see anything except blurred shapes in front of me. It smelled musty, like it had been used before.

"Is this really necessary?" I asked.

"Watch your head as you get inside the vehicle. Please sit in the center seat."

I guessed that was a yes. I got in the car. Immediately,

somebody pulled a seatbelt over my shoulder and then climbed onto the seat to my left. Then somebody climbed onto my right.

"Am I under arrest?" I asked. They ignored me, so I drew in a breath. "What are you charging me with?"

Finally, the guy in the front passenger seat spoke.

"You're being held as a material witness in the murder of a hundred and eighty-seven people in New Hampshire. Now shut up or we will pull over and gag you."

I swore under my breath and felt my shoulders slump. Essentially, the federal material witness statute allowed them to hold me without trial for as long as they wanted. It was the same legal justification the government used to hold men at Guantanamo Bay. Since I wasn't officially under arrest, they weren't even legally required to give me access to an attorney. This could be bad.

We drove for quite a while. We spent a big part of that drive on the interstate, but eventually we pulled onto smaller surface roads. Given our starting destination and the time in the car, we were probably in Indianapolis. We could have reached Louisville or Cincinnati, but something about the turns we were making felt familiar. I couldn't see much through the cloth over my eyes, but I knew this place.

"Can we stop by Hardee's before we get to your office?" I asked. "It's just off Allisonville Road. I'm kind of hungry, and I haven't had lunch yet."

The agent to my left laughed. "Sorry, buddy, but we

just passed it. Should have asked earlier."

I nodded to myself. "So we are in Indianapolis, and you guys are FBI agents. Good to know."

The agent in the front passenger seat sighed. "Both of you shut up."

Evidently, he was in charge. We drove for another few minutes before slowing, I presumed, at the security gate outside the FBI's compound. Our driver spoke to the guard in hushed tones before going inside. A few moments after that, we drove into an underground parking garage, where we finally stopped. It was cold, and the air smelled like exhaust.

One of the agents ripped the bag from my head, and I looked around. No cars occupied this level of the garage. Even if I wanted to make a run for it, I wouldn't have anywhere to go. They led me inside, and then we took some stairs down to a very bright corridor before they pulled open the door of a cell similar to those in a supermax prison. The bed, toilet, and sink were bolted to the wall. There were no windows save an opaque piece of plexiglass in the door that, presumably, was used for observation of prisoners.

"I'm a police officer. You can't hold me here indefinitely," I said. "This isn't right, and you know it."

My captors left the room without responding, locking the door behind them. The room was silent save the constant hiss of a vent near the ceiling. I halfheartedly pushed on the door, but it didn't even budge. I wasn't getting out of here until they let me.

For the first few minutes, I paced back and forth, hoping someone would come in and explain what was going on. When that didn't happen, I unfurled the thin mattress on the bed and lay down. It was cold, so I crossed my arms. My wife was a well-known author, and I was a well-known police officer. I had the money and position to fight an arrest. It was just a matter of time before I got out, but they never should have arrested me in the first place.

I didn't know how long I waited in that cell, but eventually my door opened again. Special Agent Kevin Havelock stood outside, motioning me out of the room. I slowly sat up and swung my legs off the bed but didn't stand.

"You want to tell me what the hell's going on?"

"I'm getting you out of here," he said, looking to his left before looking at me once more. "Let's move."

I put my hands beside me but didn't otherwise move.

"Where's my brother-in-law?"

"Right next door," said Havelock. "He's safe. Nassir and his friends surrendered peacefully, so no one was hurt. I'm going to do what I can to make sure their attorneys have access to them, but we need to move."

I leaned forward and slowly stood up. "For future reference, I'd prefer if you told your agents I was working for you before you sent them to raid a compound I was visiting. It might help us avoid these awkward encounters in a prison cell."

Havelock nodded and then put a hand on my elbow

to hustle me through the door. He shot his eyes up and down the hallway before leading me to the stairwell.

"My men didn't arrest you," he said. "You were picked up by the counterterrorism division. The attack on Westbrook Elementary was filmed by a drone. Agents found that drone yesterday and traced the serial number this morning. It was purchased on the website of a camera store in New Jersey and delivered to the warehouse you took us to last night."

I closed my eyes.

"Shit."

"Yeah. If we could connect the warehouse directly to your brother-in-law or any other person at his camp, you'd all be on a plane to Guantanamo Bay right now. Officially, the warehouse is owned by a holdings company in Hong Kong. We're still trying to unravel the ownership structure and see who might have actually been in control of the building."

"So you're saying my tip is the only thing connecting Nassir to the warehouse," I said, nodding to myself. "If I hadn't called you last night, I wouldn't be here now."

"Life is full of irony, isn't it?"

I shook my head and kept walking. "Thank you for coming to your senses and letting me go."

Havelock tilted his head to the side. "The FBI isn't letting you go."

"Hold up," I said, stopping on the concrete landing between floors. "Do the agents who arrested me know what you're doing right now?"

"There's a car upstairs waiting for you," said Havelock. "We need to move."

"You didn't answer my question," I said, lowering my chin. "Is this a prison break, Agent Havelock?"

He shook his head and spoke with a sharp tone. "No. It's a prison transfer. I may not get to have a say in the activities of the counterterrorism division, but I have operational authority over my own facility. In my professional judgment, I've decided it would be best if you were transported to a federal correctional institute in Sheridan, Oregon."

"So you're taking me to Oregon?"

Havelock sighed and closed his eyes. Then he looked down and clucked his tongue a few times before looking at me again.

"When you were in Jacob Ganim's house, did you find anything that linked him to the attack on Westbrook Elementary?"

"No," I said, shaking my head. "All I found were surveillance pictures in the basement."

Havelock's eyes went distant for a moment as he thought.

"Did *you* find something that linked him to the attack?" I asked.

Havelock nodded. "Yeah. We found pictures of Westbrook Elementary, the surrounding area, and explosive devices in the home. They're similar to the ones published by the *Washington Exponent*, but we think they were taken by a different camera."

I drew in a breath, unsure how to react.

"What about the pictures of the women at the mosque?"

He shook his head. "There were no pictures of women, but we did find surveillance equipment. It's high-end gear, but the serial numbers didn't match anything in the FBI's inventory."

"You sure it's not from your counterterrorism division?"

Havelock hesitated and then looked down.

"It's not the same gear we use. My guess is that we've got more federal agencies working on this case than we know about."

I covered my mouth with my hand, thinking for a moment. "I visited Jacob Ganim's wife, and right afterwards, my boss got a call from an Army colonel who told me to stay away from her. Would someone from the Army have access to the kind of surveillance equipment you found?"

Havelock blinked and then crossed his arms. "Maybe, but why would they be watching a dead FBI agent's house?"

"That's a very good question," I said. "We should probably try to answer it."

Havelock looked over my shoulder, his eyes distant as he thought. A moment later, he focused on me again as if he had made a decision.

"Officially, two of my agents are going to drive you to FCI Sheridan, a medium-security federal prison southwest of Portland. Unofficially, I'm breaking you out. Nobody in my office leaked the story about the attack on President Crane's family, but clearly somebody wants the world to think we did. I don't know what the hell's going on, but I think Jacob Ganim did. Somebody killed him to stop him from telling us. You've got about forty-eight hours before you're expected in Oregon. I'd advise you to use that time well."

Chapter 23

Havelock opened the door to the parking garage, where a black SUV awaited me. Before stepping out, I hesitated in the doorway and looked toward the older FBI agent. He had dark spots beneath his eyes, and his hair had gone to gray. I didn't notice that before. I had known Agent Havelock for a few years, and he had never struck me as the sort of guy who ever got tired. Now, he looked as if he could sleep for days.

"You remember the first time I met you?" I asked. "I was working a human-trafficking case. You were hoping to be reassigned to DC."

Havelock nodded and closed his eyes before speaking. "That was a long time ago."

"You let me go, you're never going to get that assignment. They might even fire you."

"I considered that," he said.

I looked around for a moment. "I could make some calls and get an attorney. It may take me a while, but I'm pretty sure I can get out of here if my lawyer makes a big enough stink."

Havelock blinked and seemed to think for a moment. Then he nodded, almost to himself.

"Some things are more important than my ambition. I'd rather be fired for doing the right thing than retire as a deputy director who let innocent people go to prison."

I held out my hand. He shook it.

"Good luck, Lieutenant. Now get out of here before the wrong person sees you."

"Thank you," I said, before turning and climbing into the backseat of the SUV. There was a woman in the driver's seat. She wore a navy blazer. A tie held her hair in a ponytail behind her head. Her partner sat in the passenger seat. Like her, he wore a dark suit, and he didn't look at me. Even though the windows were tinted, I slouched low in the chair as we began driving. The guy in the passenger seat turned his head for a moment, but he didn't look at me.

"There's an envelope on the seat beside you with your things in it," he said. "A forensic team is going through your car right now for evidence, so we don't have access to that. Agent Havelock authorized the use of a vehicle we impounded, so unless you want to go elsewhere, we're going to pick that up."

I nodded and then reached to the legal-sized manila envelope beside me. It was heavier than it looked.

"That sounds good. Thank you," I said, opening the envelope and reaching in. They had my firearm, keys, wallet, badge, and burner cell phone. I felt a little better having everything back.

We left the parking garage within moments. The sky was overcast and foreboding. Occasional droplets of water hit the windshield, and the leaves of nearby trees swayed. I had expected there to be news trucks around the property, but the streets were empty. As we approached the guardhouse on the outskirts of the compound, the car slowed, and I started to slouch even lower in my seat.

"You can sit upright, Lieutenant," said the driver, finally looking at me. She had a long, angular face and high cheekbones. "We have clearance from the boss to take you out."

I didn't know whether that made me feel better, but I nodded anyway and straightened my shoulders. In the end, the guard waved us through without saying anything, and I finally took a deep, relaxed breath.

"I kind of thought there'd be reporters here," I said.

The driver glanced in the rearview mirror before looking at the road in front of her again.

"News of your arrest has been kept quiet," she said. "The real action is at Islamic centers around town."

I grunted. That figured. Hopefully there wouldn't be rioting.

"You guys mind if I make a few calls?" I asked.

The guy in the passenger seat turned his head. "Go right ahead."

I started with my sister. Even though she and Nassir were going through a divorce, she needed to know he was in jail. I waited a couple of rings for her to pick up.

"Rana, hey," I said. "It's your brother."

"Ahh, Ashraf," she said, her voice subdued. "I can't talk long because I have an appointment to have my nails done. I just got a massage. It was wonderful."

"I'm glad to hear it," I said. "Listen, I'm calling because your husband is an idiot."

She sighed and laughed under her breath. "I'm glad we agree on that."

"He's been arrested for the attack on the president yesterday," I said.

For a few seconds, Rana said nothing. Then I heard her draw in a breath.

"Tell me he didn't do it."

"He didn't do it," I said. "I don't know who did, but it wasn't him. He's being set up. We don't know why yet. He never mentioned Michael Najam to you, did he?"

"No," she said. "But I don't know any of them in his little club. All of them kept their families away. That camp broke up my marriage, and I don't think I'll be the only one. As far as I know, Qadi and Fatima Hamady stopped talking weeks ago."

"I understand you're mad at him, but if you don't do something now, your husband is likely to end up in prison for a crime he didn't commit."

Rana sighed. "What do I need to do?"

"Look up John Meyers and Associates. They're a criminal defense firm. They're going to cost you some money, but they're the best defense firm in the Midwest. If they can't handle the case, they'll refer you to a firm that can."

"Nassir doesn't deserve a brother-in-law like you," she said, sighing again. "I can't even remember what I used to see in him."

I blinked, thinking through my response.

"You saw a good man. I think he still is that good

man, but I wish he had better judgment. When you talk to him next, ask him why he left you. If he refuses to tell you, I will. It might change your feelings toward him."

"I don't think anything could change how I feel toward him."

"Then it will put things into perspective," I said. "Good luck."

"You, too."

She hung up a moment later, and I rode for another couple of blocks in silence before we turned into the parking lot of a Denny's on 82nd Street. The driver stopped our SUV, while the passenger reached into his pocket for a set of keys, which he handed to me.

"It's the black Ford Mustang in the handicapped spot," he said. "Please be careful with it. Also bear in mind that the vehicle was confiscated from a drug dealer. It's been searched and cleaned thoroughly, but its previous occupant was gunned down in the front seat. You happen to find drug paraphernalia, weapons, or cash in the car, we'd appreciate hearing about it."

"Havelock will be my first call," I said, opening my door and stepping out. The occasional sprinkle had turned to a drizzle, making it uncomfortable to stand outside for long. The FBI agents drove off, and I walked to the car they had given me. I'd get a little more attention in a jet black Mustang than I would have in my Volkswagen, but it beat walking everywhere. I opened the front door, sat down, and took the handicapped parking decal from my rearview mirror before taking out my cell phone.

My investigation had gone in directions I couldn't have predicted, but it was still a murder investigation. No matter what else happened, I had to follow the evidence, and right now, I had a big piece of evidence I hadn't even considered. I took out my phone and called the Marion County Coroner's Office and asked to speak to Dr. Hector Rodriguez. It took a few minutes, but eventually I got him on the phone.

"Ash, hey," he said. "You could have just called my direct line. You didn't need to go through the switchboard."

"I would have, but I'm not on my normal phone. I'm calling about a body the Bureau was supposed to let you have access to. It was a floater found in the Ohio River near Madison."

Rodriguez grunted. "Yeah, that one. I've got it. You free this afternoon?"

"If necessary, I can make time."

"Please do. We need to talk."

I nodded to myself and turned on my car. The engine let out a deep-throated growl that made several people inside the restaurant in front of me look out the window. This car might be a little fun after all.

"I'm a couple of blocks from the Castleton Square Mall. I'll be at your office as soon as I can."

Dr. Rodriguez and the rest of the coroner's office worked out of an old, converted warehouse a couple of blocks from Lucas Oil Stadium, the home of the Indianapolis Colts. Despite its rather humble brick facade, the building functioned well. There were multiple autopsy theaters, offices for the staff, and space to store both old records and corpses. I rarely heard people complain about the place, but dead bodies rarely complained about anything.

I parked in the lot out front and went inside, where the receptionist directed me to autopsy room 2 in the basement. As I descended the stairs, the temperature dropped, and an antiseptic smell began seeping into my nose. I wished I had worn a sweater. Hector Rodriguez was inside the autopsy room, leaning over a counter to read a report while he ate an apple. Jacob Ganim's body rested on a cold metal table about five feet from him. Harsh bright lights illuminated the work space, while music played softly from somewhere nearby. A woman was singing about a breakup many years ago.

"Never imagined you as the sentimental type," I said.

Dr. Rodriguez looked up, his brow furrowed as he chewed his apple.

"The music," I said, nodding in the vague direction of the radio. Recognition dawned on his face, and he nodded.

"My internet radio station. Apparently, it thinks I'm an Adele fan," he said, putting his apple down and then sliding to a sink to wash his hands. Once he had his hands cleaned and dried, he snapped on a pair of latex gloves and walked to the exam table. I followed a few feet back.

No matter how many times I saw the corpse of a murder victim, it was hard to get over the indignity of a violent death. Not only was a man or woman's life snuffed out early, but the victim's body would also be photographed, sliced up, and examined dozens of times over by dozens of people. After the autopsy, the pictures would be displayed in front of juries and lawyers, and, oftentimes, the body would be kept in cold storage for months or years until trial. The victim didn't even get the decency of a timely burial. Seeing Jacob Ganim displayed on the autopsy table felt like a violation almost as bad as the one that took his life.

"This was an interesting one," said Rodriguez. "What can you tell me about him?"

I sighed and raised my eyebrows as I looked at Ganim's body. They had found him in the water, so his skin was puffy and loose. There was a deep laceration on his neck and what looked like bruises across his torso.

"Unfortunately, I'm limited in what I can say," I said. "He was a law enforcement official who worked undercover. He was fished from the Ohio River. Cause of death was unknown, but I'm guessing it had something to do with that cut across his throat."

Rodriguez nodded. "Yeah. He died from exsanguination due to a laceration on the anterior aspect of his neck. Cut was approximately seven centimeters below his chin and seven centimeters above the suprasternal notch. The cut itself was clean and deep.

There's damage to the underlying thyroid cartilage, supraglottic part of the larynx, soft tissue, blood vessels, and musculature corresponding to the surface injury. In addition, there's a cut along the fifth cervical vertebrae measuring four centimeters in length and at a depth of two millimeters."

"Ouch," I said, looking from Rodriguez to the body.

"Damn near took off his head," said Rodriguez. "This guy was used to pain, though."

"What do you mean?"

"As part of the autopsy, I took X-rays over his entire body. This guy was tortured severely sometime in the recent past. Nearly every bone in his right hand has been broken, and there are indications none of the fingers were set properly after his injury."

I leaned against a nearby counter and crossed my arms, thinking.

"This guy would have had health insurance. Why wouldn't he have gotten medical attention?"

"You'll have to answer that one," said Rodriguez. "I'm just telling you what I've found."

I nodded. "What could have done it? Was this an accident, you think?"

"No," said Rodriguez, shaking his head. "The amount of remodeling on the bones indicates that the first break occurred about four weeks before the last. This was systematic. If I had to guess, somebody took a hammer to his hand, one finger at a time."

That wasn't the kind of thing that happened to very

many FBI agents, although it did explain the pain medication I found on him.

"Anything else?"

"Yeah. There's significant damage to his shoulders and wrists. I've only seen this kind of damage once before. It was from an older man who had been a guest inside a North Korean prison. According to his family, that victim had his wrists bound behind his back and was then strung up by his hands. It would been excruciating."

I drew in a breath, taken aback. "Anything else?"

"He's broken five ribs and been shot in his right knee. Both injuries occurred at roughly the same time as his hand injury—I'd say about four years ago. You said this guy was a police officer?"

"Something like that."

Rodriguez took a step back and leaned against the counter beside me to stare at the body.

"If a live patient came to me with these X-rays, I'd refer him to a psychiatrist to make sure he wasn't going to hurt himself. Then I'd refer him to a social worker who could help him apply for disability. I don't know what happened to him, but your victim was in pain every day of his life."

I nodded and crossed my arms, thinking. I had begun to think Ganim was a rogue FBI agent addicted to pills. And maybe he was, but clearly he was more than just that. This was a man willing to endure pain for his cause. What that cause happened to be and why someone would kill him for it, I had no idea. I knew someone who might have, though, and it was past time she talked to me.

"I appreciate the work you put into this," I said, pushing off from the counter. "I'll see myself out. I've got to drive to Franklin before it gets dark."

Chapter 24

I hit the outskirts of Franklin about an hour after I left the coroner's office. Lauren Collier's neighborhood wasn't far from that. The rain had tapered off by the time I parked, but the sky hadn't cleared. A cold breeze whipped through my shirt as I opened my door. At times, it felt like summer was right around the corner, but spring still had a way of reminding me that we were still in its grasp.

I grabbed the autopsy report and pictures I had received from Dr. Rodriguez and then straightened my shirt and jacket before heading up the walkway of Jacob Ganim's widow's house. A young girl opened the door when I knocked. Like her father, she had olive colored skin and dark hair. She was younger than my daughter but older than my son. Probably six or seven, if I had to guess. I knelt in front of her and smiled.

"My name is Ashraf, and I'm a police officer. I'm looking for your mommy. Is she home?"

Before the little girl could answer, Ms. Collier's strident voice whipped through the house.

"Get away from him, Maya," she said, hurrying down the hallway. The little girl shrank back, and I stood. Ms. Collier's throat was red and her eyes were narrow as they bore into me. "Lieutenant, I thought I made myself clear the last time you were here. You're not welcome at this house, you're not welcome to talk to my daughter, and you're not welcome to talk to me. Get out."

"Not this time," I said, shaking my head. "We need to talk about Jacob Ganim."

"Daddy?" said the little girl, taking a step forward. Ms. Collier looked back at her and softened her voice.

"Please go in the basement. You can watch *My Little Pony* if you want. Mommy needs to talk to this man."

The little girl slowly nodded and began walking down the hall, trailing her fingers on the wall. When she disappeared around a corner, Ms. Collier turned to me.

"I'm getting the phone, and I'm going to call the police."

"Okay," I said, nodding. "If you're going to do that, be sure to tell them your ex-husband was involved in the plot to murder President Crane's family and everyone at Westbrook Elementary. I'm sure the police and the FBI will be right over."

She scoffed. "I don't have to listen to you."

"You don't have to, but you really should," I said. "Your ex-husband infiltrated a group of Islamic men building a summer camp. While he was supposed to be investigating that group, he was secretly investigating another case entirely. In the meantime, that peaceful group had their lives put through the wringer. They've now been arrested for something they didn't do. I don't know what's going on, but your ex-husband was in the middle of it. Who was he? And please don't tell me he was just an FBI agent."

"Jacob had flaws, but he was a good man. If he infiltrated this *peaceful* group, he did it for a reason, probably because they're not so peaceful."

I nodded and drew in a breath. "Maybe you're right. I don't know yet. I do know your husband isn't the man everyone thinks he is. Who did he actually work for?"

She blinked and then crossed her arms. "He was an FBI agent."

"No more lies, okay? I'm getting tired of them," I said, shaking my head. "If Jacob had been an FBI agent, you would have called a security officer at the FBI when I showed up the last time. That security officer would have done a preliminary background investigation of me, found out that I correctly told you I was a police officer, and then he would have called the US Attorney's Office in Indianapolis with a complaint. The US attorney would have then called the Marion County Prosecutor's Office, who would have then alerted my boss.

"Instead, you called a *military* officer. That *military* officer called my boss from the White House. Just for future reference, the former spouses of FBI agents don't usually have those kinds of contacts within the government."

Ms. Collier's eyes bore into mine as she weighed whether to speak to me. Finally, she leaned against the door frame, her posture softening.

"What do you want, Lieutenant?"

"Answers," I said. "I was called into this case to investigate your husband's murder. Not bragging, but I'm a pretty good homicide investigator. After this long on a case, I've usually got a pretty good idea of who my murderer is. In this case, I don't even know who my victim is."

Some of the heat left her eyes. Her shoulders dropped as she took a step behind her and reached to a purse on a table beside the front door. My back stiffened, and I dropped my right hand to the weapon on my belt. With shaking hands, she pulled out a pack of cigarettes and lit up.

"I quit a couple of years ago when we were trying to get pregnant," she said, exhaling. "Now just seemed like the right time to start again."

"I'm sorry if I make you nervous."

"You're not sorry," she said, tipping her cigarette to knock off a length of ash. "Men like you are never sorry."

I looked her in the eye.

"Okay, sure. I'm not sorry. The FBI found pictures in your ex-husband's home that implicate him in the attack on Westbrook Elementary in New Hampshire."

She scoffed and shook her head. "I don't think so. My husband wouldn't do that."

"I agree. Somebody's setting him up to take a fall. I was in his house earlier, and the pictures weren't there. They were when the FBI returned this afternoon. That's partly why I'm here now. I need to know who your ex-husband was. You can start by telling me who tortured him."

"I don't know what you're talking about."

Out of instinct, I almost called her out without thinking. As I watched her, though, her expression went from surprise to confusion. She was being honest. She had no idea someone had hurt her ex-husband. I considered how I wanted to approach this. Even if they were divorced, Ms. Collier clearly had some feelings for her husband. Maybe she didn't love him, but she had cared for his well-being, nonetheless.

I narrowed my eyes at her.

"Can you tell me what your ex-husband did for a living in 2014?"

"Was my husband tortured in 2014?"

And now, Jacob was her husband instead of just her ex-husband. She did care about him. That made this tricky.

"There are indications that he was hurt then, yeah."

"What kind of indications?" she asked, her voice growing hard. She looked to the autopsy report I was carrying. "And what's on those papers?"

"This is the autopsy report. It includes pictures. You don't want to see them."

She nodded and swallowed hard. "How did he die?"

"Someone took a knife to his throat and cut his carotid arteries. His body was disposed of in the Ohio River. He would have died very quickly. There would have been a minimal amount of pain."

She looked away from me as tears began forming at the corners of her eyes. I wanted to say something, but I had done enough next-of-kin notifications to know nothing I said would help. She brought a hand to her face, but she didn't wipe away her tears. Instead, she balled it into a fist and exhaled deeply and slowly, getting control of herself.

"He knew his murderer," she said.

"That's one possibility," I said, nodding.

"No," she said, shaking her head. "I'm telling you. Jacob knew and trusted his murderer. He never would have let a stranger get that close to him."

"I'm sure he was a capable man," I said, speaking slowly and trying not to sound too paternalistic, "but we can't discount the possibility that he was murdered by a stranger."

She looked at me as if I had just told her the sky was neon green.

"You have no idea who my husband was, do you?"

"No, I don't."

"Wait here," she said, taking a step back into the house. Before I could say anything, she pulled the door shut and disappeared. With everything else going on, I didn't have a lot of time, so I hoped whatever she was about to show me was worth it.

I pulled my jacket around me tight as a cool breeze blew off the wet road behind me. A minute passed, and then another. I was about to knock on the door again when Ms. Collier opened it. She looked at me up and down.

"Come in, but take off your shoes."

She held the door open and stepped back. I hesitated but then walked inside. The entryway was warm and clean. A TV blared from somewhere in the house. It smelled as if she were making spaghetti sauce. Before she could change her mind, I slipped my shoes off and smiled.

"Thank you. It's getting a little chilly out there."

She nodded and then shut the door before walking deeper into the house to an eat-in kitchen. There, displayed on a granite countertop, were half a dozen photographs of a man in a military uniform. There were also display boxes with medals. In the formal pictures, Jacob Ganim wore a green beret adorned with a US Army major's oak leaf. I had never been in the military, so I didn't know what the ribbons on his uniform meant, but he had a lot of them.

"Jacob was a soldier," she said, holding up a wooden display case that held a bronze cross. "This is a Distinguished Service Medal. It's only been given out a couple dozen times in the past twenty years. He couldn't tell me how he earned it, but people respected him for it. It's given for extraordinary heroism in combat. The only higher honor is the Medal of Honor."

She picked up another display case with three medals inside.

"He earned the Silver Star three times for gallantry in combat," she said. "My husband was one of the most intelligent, capable soldiers in the United States Army. He spent years in combat zones. No one snuck up on him and killed him from behind. He was murdered by someone he trusted."

I didn't know whether I bought that completely, but

it potentially explained a few things.

"As I said earlier, there are indications from his autopsy that he was tortured in 2014. Was he in the Army then?"

She hesitated, but then nodded. "Yes. Jacob was a clandestine officer with the Defense Intelligence Agency."

"So your husband was a spy," I said, narrowing my brow.

Ms. Collier smiled wistfully.

"Jacob was a lot more than that."

Chapter 25

A woman pushing a stroller passed their car without looking inside. Her blonde hair bounced on her shoulders, while her baby kicked his feet in the air and grabbed his toes. Butler al-Ghamdi shifted on his seat. Kamil Salib, Daniel Hakim, and he were in Daniel's Volvo station wagon. The air smelled pungent, like a locker room after a big football game. Hockey gear lay strewn about the back of the car.

Butler hadn't done anything like this before, but he had seen enough movies and read enough books to know how it worked. Ideally, he would have watched the house for several days. He would have known when his target arrived and left for work, when her boyfriend got up in the morning, when they went to sleep...everything about their lives.

Instead, he had spent the past twenty-four hours at a summer camp owned by a fool. Nassir Hadad and his friends thought Butler needed help. They thought they could persuade him to turn his back on God. They thought they could "fix" him.

He wasn't broken.

The world was at war, and Butler had decided to become a soldier. He was tired of sitting on the sidelines. What's more, God had already shown Butler that he had made the right choice. While Nassir and his friends sat in prisons operated by the federal government, Butler sat in a car outside Kim Peterson's home.

The FBI had come to the camp while Butler was at a lumberyard twenty miles away. If Butler had doubts before, they were quashed then. God wanted him to complete the mission Hashim Bashear had given him. He wanted Butler to become a soldier like the men he was with. That was exactly what Butler planned to do.

Daniel stretched in the driver's seat and then turned and reached to the backseat to pat Butler's leg.

"Stay awake, brother," he said. "This is your day."

Butler didn't need the reminder. He knew what he had to do. Daniel turned forward again to watch the house. They had been there for over an hour, watching and talking through their plan. Butler knew it well enough now that he could have recited it in his sleep. They still needed to steal a car—preferably a Toyota Camry or Honda Accord—but that was the easy part. The hard part would come this afternoon.

Butler was more than ready.

Sweat trickled between his shoulder blades and down his back. He felt every breath he took. His revolver bulged from his right hip pocket. He hadn't wanted to carry a pistol, but Daniel had insisted on it. Butler's rifle —a Bushmaster M4A2 Patrolman AR-15 semiautomatic —was in a hard case beneath the hockey gear. After losing most of their gear to a fire the night before, they had scrambled to buy new weapons from collectors on the Internet.

The AR-15 was one of four rifles they had

purchased that afternoon. It was smoother and more powerful than any weapon Butler had ever held. Combined with its thirty-round magazine, the rifle made him a formidable fighter. His revolver felt like a toy in comparison.

He watched the apostate's house from the street. Kim Peterson, his target, had red hair and thin lips. When he had seen her earlier, her hips had swayed like a prostitute's when she walked. She was probably ten years older than him, and she lived with a man who wasn't her husband. In nearly every picture he had seen of her, she wore a low-cut blouse that showed the entire world her breasts. She should have been ashamed, but women like her had no shame.

Still, God was merciful. Had all else been equal, she'd have to account for her wicked decisions at the end of her life, but it wouldn't have been Butler's place to punish her for those sins. Unfortunately, she had done far worse than live a life of immodesty. She had hidden six female apostates in her basement, each of whom threatened a community Butler loved.

Hashim Bashear had tracked the women from Raqqa, Syria, to their final destinations in the United States. Their own families had shipped them away so they could live sinful, wicked lives without the guiding influence of men like Hashim Bashear and other rightly directed clerics. More than anything else, it was sad. Had they stayed in Syria, they could have had husbands and children and a household to run...everything a good woman should want.

They threw away this precious gift so they could spread malicious lies about the men, women, and community they left behind. These women had known God's commands. That, above all else, bothered Butler.

Circumstances had forced him to seek the straight path, to fight for it, to find those rightly directed teachers to lead him. These women, though, had received perfect instruction inside the Islamic State and ignored it. Even that, he could have forgiven. Had they merely run, had they stayed silent about the world they left, perhaps they would have been allowed to live.

But they did more than run.

Kim Peterson made documentary films. Hashim Bashear had shown him the trailer online for her newest movie. Supposedly, it was a feature-length exposé of life within the Islamic State before it fell. In actuality, it had no more truth than the popular novels his English teachers had forced him to read in school. That was why she and the women in her care had to die. She and the women hidden in her basement could not be allowed to besmirch God and His people with impunity. He relished the thought of killing them.

Though he had never shot a human being, Butler had killed before. He had grown up in the suburbs of Dayton, Ohio. On the coasts, hunters may have been looked down on as backward, but in the Midwest, hunting was a part of life and a rite of passage for a lot of young men. He knew what it felt like to take a life. He'd feel that again very soon.

Butler drew in a breath and felt a calm stillness as righteousness flowed through him. He had been a boy when he first met Hashim Bashear online. In many ways, he still was. Today, though, he would truly become a man. He leaned forward, his voice hard.

"She's not coming back," he said. "We have work to do. Let's go."

Daniel nodded and turned the car on. As they left, Butler looked over his shoulder at Kim Peterson's house again. When he saw it next, he would bring God's righteous anger with him and leave only after having completed his holy mission. Kim Peterson and the apostates she hid would die by his hand.

It filled him with pride.

Chapter 26

From the very start, I had been in the dark about critical details of this case. Unfortunately, now that I was starting to learn some of those details, I was just as confused as ever. I looked at the photos on the table, and then I looked at Ms. Collier.

"What happened in 2014?"

She blinked and looked down. "I don't know precisely."

"What do you know?"

She looked up and then brushed a stray lock of blonde hair behind her ear. "Jacob was born in Baltimore, but his mother and father were from Iraq. He spoke Arabic fluently, and he grew up in an Islamic household. His superiors at the DIA used him. They helped him infiltrate an insurgent group in Iraq. I didn't know what he did there, but eventually he ended up in Syria. That was when everything fell apart."

I waited a moment as she gathered herself to speak. She looked down and touched his picture as tears began to spring from her eyes.

"I don't know how it happened, but they figured out he was an American. They held him captive and tried to ransom him to the highest bidder. Before they could sell him, a Syrian rebel group freed him. They smuggled him to Turkey, and then he made his way to Ramstein Air Force Base in Germany."

That must have been why he had anti-anxiety drugs and antidepressants in his room at Nassir's camp. The man probably had severe PTSD. Unfortunately, everything she had just told me reinforced my belief that he had no business in the field. Jacob Ganim had deserved to retire in peace. Instead, he was undercover again. This time, he didn't make it home.

"I'm very sorry for what happened to him," I said. "That was 2014. What was he like today?"

She didn't say anything.

"Ms. Collier?"

She looked at me and blinked before looking down again.

"Jacob and I were together since I was in college and he was in the Army. He took a consulting job with the FBI, and we eventually moved to Indianapolis. We got married in 2015 when I found out I was pregnant."

She smiled wistfully. "I thought he'd settle down."

"But he didn't," I said, encouraging her to keep speaking.

"No, he didn't," she said. "Even when he worked for the FBI, he would disappear for months at a time on assignment. When he was home, he had a psychiatrist at the VA. He was getting help. Every now and then, he'd come home, and he'd joke and smile and be a good daddy. Then there were days when he'd be moody and angry all the time. He never hit me or our daughter, but he scared me sometimes.

"Then, one day, he told us he had to leave for good.

I signed the divorce papers two weeks later and never saw him again. That was a year ago. I haven't talked to him since."

I nodded to myself, thinking. I had a much clearer picture of my victim, but it didn't get me closer to his murderer. Ms. Collier was probably right, though: This was not a man murdered by a stranger. He would have been too well trained for that. He let somebody into his life, and that somebody killed him.

"I understand he was likely limited in what he could tell you, but did your husband ever mention anything about human trafficking to you?"

She shook her head. "No."

"Did he have any siblings? Maybe a sister?"

Again, she shook her head. Unfortunately, that left me nearly back where I started. A man like Jacob probably made enemies while working for the DIA. He could have been killed by any of them. At the same time, he probably made more than a few enemies working for the FBI. They could have killed him. Or maybe he was killed for the freelance investigation he was clearly running. Or maybe he was even killed for his involvement with Nassir and his group.

Everything I found just brought me more questions. It was getting frustrating.

Ms. Collier didn't need to hear that, though. She had lost her husband. Her daughter had lost a father. She needed support. Even if I couldn't give much, she deserved everything I had.

"Jacob had a house in Indianapolis," I said. "He has pictures of the two of you together in his hallway. He's got a lot of pictures of your daughter. He may not have talked to you, but he cared about you."

Her lower lip trembled, and she nodded.

"We used to live there together. I moved here after the divorce," she said. "Thank you for telling me about him. But I think I need you to leave now."

"I'm sorry for your loss," I said. "I'm going to do my best to find out who killed him."

She nodded and gave me a weak smile that didn't reach past her lips. I put on my shoes in the entryway and walked back to my car.

I had spent almost two hours to find out my victim worked for the Defense Intelligence Agency and that his ex-wife still loved him. As much as I appreciated being able to tell her about her husband, I had wasted time I didn't have to waste. With a forty-eight-hour deadline, I had to move.

Once I got back in my car, I put on my seatbelt and immediately began heading back to Indianapolis. If Ms. Collier couldn't tell me why her husband was taking pictures of young Islamic women, I'd ask the man who was hiding them. I didn't remember his name, but I knew him. He had a seat on Indianapolis's Interfaith Council. More than that, he was the imam at a mosque I had once visited. That was more than enough to track him down.

I drove toward the interstate but pulled into the parking lot of a gas station before getting on. There, I used my phone to begin searching the websites of mosques around town. I found the man within about five minutes. His name was Omar Nawaz, and he looked like he was about thirty years old in his pictures. I put his mosque's address in my phone's GPS and headed out.

The drive was easy and quick. Omar Nawaz's mosque was in a residential neighborhood full of single-story homes, most of which were sided with rough clapboard. Its parking lot was about half-full with congregants on their way to *maghrib*, the fourth of five daily prayers performed by devout Muslims. I parked and unclipped my badge from my belt and put it in the front breast pocket of my jacket so people inside could see it. Then I called my dispatcher for some backup.

The nearest patrol vehicles were just two or three minutes away, so I didn't have to wait long. I told the officers that I planned to speak with a man who had a history of running from the police and requested they wait in the parking lot in case he tried to escape. Hopefully they wouldn't be needed.

The mosque had a heavy wooden door. Warm air rushed out at me the moment I opened it. There were a couple of people in the lobby. Several looked at me nervously at first but then relaxed, probably because I had the same light brown skin and black hair they did. My parents had come from Egypt. This group was my community, and they knew it.

All but one of them, at least.

Omar Nawaz stood ramrod straight and looked at

me from the center of the room with the stunned, terrified gaze of a teenager caught trying to buy a keg of beer with a fake ID. I walked to him and smiled.

"I hope I'm not too late for *maghrib*," I said, looking around at the other men and women. There were six or seven of them, and they were starting to move toward the prayer hall. I smiled to a few people. Most of them smiled back. "It's been a couple of years, but I had *fajr* with your congregation a while ago. They're a good group."

"They are," he said. He took a deep breath and plastered a fake smile on his lips. "If you'll excuse me, I need to get ready."

I gave him a matching fake grin and lowered my voice so no one else around us could hear.

"You're going to run again, aren't you?"

The smile left his face.

"Please do the right thing," I said. "Lead your congregation in prayer, and then come talk to me."

He looked down as if he were thinking. Then he nodded and took a step to join his congregants in the prayer hall. I watched him walk for about ten feet. He wore a loose-fitting tan *thobe*—a flowing tunic that reached to his knees—a matching pair of slacks, and a navy blue coat. On his feet, he wore the same tennis shoes he had worn when I saw him at the motel southeast of town.

Before reaching the door to the prayer hall, he turned to look at me. The lizard part of my brain, that unevolved remnant of humanity's hunter-gatherer past, saw him lower his center of gravity; it saw his skin flush just a little, and it saw the fear in his eyes. I knew instantly he was going to either attack or run. Either way, he'd have a bad day.

"I just want to talk," I said.

As if those were the magic words, he sprinted toward the front door. I sighed.

"Asshole."

Chapter 27

The officers outside would grab Nawaz before he could get too far, so I wasn't too worried about catching him. That he would run rather than talk to me, though, didn't bode well for my interview. Most of the congregation had moved to the prayer hall, but a few people remained with me in the entryway.

I looked at a man and a woman nearby. The man put his arm around his wife and turned so that he stood between the two of us. His eyes were wide open, and his body was stiff. He didn't know I had chased Nawaz from a hotel, or that Nawaz might have been involved in a crime. He only knew that his imam was scared of me. That made him see me as a threat. I hated that this job sometimes made innocent people afraid of me, but I couldn't back down now.

"Where's Omar's office?" I asked. The man hesitated and then pointed to a hallway behind me. His hand trembled. "Thank you."

I hurried down the hallway before anyone could stop me. Nawaz's office was on the end of the hallway. He had a big, wooden desk and flimsy black bookshelves that looked as if they had once been flatpacked and sold in a big box store. He had books—mostly religious texts, but also a well-loved copy of the first Harry Potter book—stacked on his desk. It wasn't a welcoming space, but it looked well used.

I walked around the desk, hoping to find a laptop or at least an appointment book. Instead, I found his cell phone. I hit the home button to turn it on, but it wouldn't let me access anything without Nawaz's fingerprint. I thought I could work around that, so I put it in my pocket and walked back toward the entryway.

Someone in the congregation had begun leading the group through *maghrib* in Nawaz's absence. I stayed outside the prayer hall and paced for a few minutes.

Eventually, a pair of uniformed patrol officers walked through the front door, dragging Nawaz with them. His ears were red, and he kicked his feet. The officers had secured his hands behind his back with a pair of cuffs.

"Here you go," said one of the officers. "You think you can handle him?"

Two officers held Nawaz upright. He scowled at me, but he didn't try to break free and attack. That was always nice.

"If these guys let you go and take off the handcuffs, what are you going to do?"

"Call my lawyer," he said.

I looked to the officers and nodded. "You can let him go. Do you mind sticking around in the parking lot for a few minutes?"

"Not at all," said a uniformed sergeant, removing Nawaz's cuffs. He patted the imam on the shoulder. "No hard feelings, buddy. There's no law against running from us, but in this neighborhood, it gives us reasonable suspicion that you're involved in some kind of crime. We're going to run you down and talk to you every time."

Nawaz scowled again and looked at me. "And this is the work you do? You arrest innocent men simply for refusing to talk to you?"

"Oh, yeah," I said, my lips straight as I nodded at him. "That's why I got into this business. It's my life goal. I want to expend great amounts of energy to momentarily inconvenience powerless people who annoy me."

Nawaz screwed up his face. "What?"

"It's sarcasm," I said, pulling back my jacket to show him my badge. "As you've probably guessed by now, I'm a police officer. I've got some questions for you."

"I will never talk to you," he said, lifting his chin slightly.

I let him see me ball my hands into fists. Interrogations and interviews were more of an art than a science. My goal was always to get information or a confession, but how I went about doing that varied with every individual. It was theater, a story told for one person alone. Nawaz thought he was getting the better of me, that he was making me angry. And if that's what he wanted and expected, that's what he'd get.

"I'm working a murder," I said, raising my voice. "Can't you just talk to me?"

"You're here because I'm a Muslim," he said. "You look like one of us, but you're not. You hate us."

I wanted to roll my eyes, but I held back.

"My feelings toward you and people like you don't matter," I said, getting into the role and spitting the words out as if I were disgusted by him. "A man matching your description was seen at the scene of a murder. That's it. I tracked you to a hotel, and you ran away from me. I just want to talk. If that wasn't you at the crime scene, we have nothing to talk about."

I looked toward the prayer hall, hoping no one would come out and recognize me from Islamic events around town.

"And your true colors come out," he said, lifting his chin. "I've seen you before, you know. You were on the Interfaith Council. The police set that up so you could watch us. Or did you do that on your own?"

I didn't know what planet this guy came from, but I nodded as if he had caught me in some grand conspiracy.

"We watch your community, okay?" I said. "My parents came from Egypt, so I fit in well. Happy?"

"Very," he said, smirking. "You're a snake."

"I'm a man doing my job," I said, continuing the lie. "A witness saw a man matching your description at a murder scene."

"I wasn't there," he said. "Now leave."

"I wish your word were good enough, but it isn't," I said. "We've got fingerprints. They match you, we've got a problem. They don't, you'll never see me again."

"So you've got to fingerprint me now," he said. "You have no shame."

"I lost that a long time ago," I said, speaking honestly

for the first time in this conversation. I reached into my pocket for his cell phone but kept my eyes on his. As he looked at me, I popped his black rubber case off with my thumb so he wouldn't recognize the phone at a glance. "I just need your thumbprint on my phone. An app will scan it and compare it to the fingerprint at the crime scene. If you weren't there, you'll be cleared, and you won't see me again."

Nawaz didn't blink. I felt as if I were in a staring contest, which worked out just fine for me. I held out his phone, making sure not to blink so he wouldn't have the chance to look down. He pressed his thumb against the phone's screen without looking.

"Happy?"

I looked down to make sure he had unlocked the phone.

"Yep," I said, nodding and turning away. "Thanks."

"Did I match?" he asked. I looked around to see him cross his arms and smirk.

"No, you're good," I said. "Thanks. I appreciate your cooperation."

I turned to walk away. Nawaz cleared his throat.

"Who did I supposedly murder?"

I turned around for just a second and blew out a long breath, thinking quickly.

"A guy named John Doe, but you're cool. Your fingerprint didn't match."

He started complaining that the United States was turning into an oppressive, dangerous police state, but I ignored him. Outside, I thanked the uniformed officers and told them they could go. After that, I walked back to my car, where I quickly disabled the security features on Nawaz's phone so I could turn it on again without his thumbprint. After that, I started browsing.

Despite having a reasonably nice camera, his phone had no pictures. Either he deleted his photographs, or he didn't take any. Both were odd behavior for a modern man. Since he didn't have any pictures to study, I focused on his list of outgoing calls. Not surprisingly, the same numbers kept showing up day after day. I wrote them down and began systematically calling them on my own phone.

The first number belonged to the switchboard at a local hospital. Nawaz was probably keeping up with ill congregants. The second number belonged to the hotel I had chased him from. That wasn't too surprising if he had spent time there. I entered the third number and listened to the phone ring four times before the voicemail system kicked on.

"Hi, this is Kim Peterson at Kim Peterson Photography, and I'm not in right now. If you're interested in having me shoot your wedding, please leave your name and number and I'll get back to you as soon as I can. If this is an emergency or a personal call, you probably know where to reach me."

I looked through Nawaz's phone. Of the past hundred calls he had made, nine went to that photography studio, which was odd for a man who didn't seem as if he were a fan of photography. I wrote the number down and circled it before looking through his text messages.

He contacted a lot of people, but his conversations were mostly benign. Most focused on his duties as an imam, but he had a few personal conversations as well. Nothing mentioned Jacob Ganim, Nassir, or Michael Najam.

I put Nawaz's phone on the seat beside me and called my dispatcher for Kim Peterson's home address. It took some back and forth because there were a number of women named Kim Peterson in the region, but we searched Facebook and Instagram to narrow it down to a twenty-six-year-old woman who lived with a man named Imran Avari in Irvington, a historic neighborhood about five miles east of downtown Indianapolis.

I put their address in my phone's GPS and headed out. Even with traffic, the drive didn't take long. Kim Peterson and Imran Avari lived in a quaint bungalow with gray siding and a small front yard. The moment I stepped onto the front porch, I unholstered my firearm.

The front door was open, and there was blood on the ground.

Apparently, I wasn't the only one calling on Miss Peterson today.

Chapter 28

I stepped over the blood on the threshold and walked into the living room. My heart thudded against my breastbone. The front shades were drawn, leaving the room mired in shadows. I wanted to turn on the light, but I didn't want to risk contaminating a crime scene. The blood led down the front hallway, as if someone had been shot and then dragged through the house.

Before going any farther, I got on my phone and called my dispatcher for backup. The nearest officers were four or five minutes out. I wanted to stay outside and wait for them, but if someone was hurt inside, five minutes was too much time to waste. I slipped my phone in my pocket and gingerly stepped down the hallway, hoping to avoid the blood on the floor where possible.

I found the first body inside the kitchen. It was an approximately thirty-year-old dark-skinned man, probably Imran. He lay on his belly at the end of the blood trail. I couldn't see his wounds, but he wasn't moving. He wore a pair of gray slacks and a matching suit coat, making him look like a banker or a lawyer just home from work. A cell phone rested on the ground beside him, as if he had tried to call for help.

I felt his neck for a pulse but found nothing. He was dead, but rigor had yet to set in, and his skin was still warm. As cold as the house was with the front door hanging open, he couldn't have been dead long. A couple of minutes, maybe.

His killer very well might have been in the building still.

I walked over the body, my weapon held in front of me. Beads of nervous sweat had begun to form on my head and drip into the corners of my eyes. I blinked them away.

An open door on the other side of the kitchen led to a finished basement. There, I found seven bodies, all women. Six of the women wore hijab, while the seventh had red hair and wore a low-cut blouse. All seven women had clung to one another as they died. Their blood painted the wall and ceiling, and the air held a mix of gunpowder, metallic smelling blood, and rose oil perfume. The sight was almost overwhelming. I didn't know who these women were, but they didn't deserve to die like this.

I walked around the room. There were twenty or thirty shell casings piled in the center of the room. The shooter must have stood still, then. He had looked in their eyes, had heard them scream, had probably listened to them beg for mercy.

And then he executed every one of them.

The victims were young. Some of them were probably only fourteen or fifteen, five or six years older than my daughter. They looked like my kids' babysitters. They should have been down there talking about boys or playing video games or whatever teenage girls did now. Instead, they were dead. They barely even had a chance to live.

I felt each girl's throat for a pulse, but none of them would ever draw breath again. These were children. Early on in my career, a sight like that would have brought me to my knees. It still bothered me, but my reaction now was colder and angrier. My left hand balled into a fist, and I drew in a long, slow breath. Anyone who could execute seven women like this didn't deserve to breathe. I hoped I got the chance to send him to hell.

Briefly, I closed my eyes and said a prayer for the families of the dead. Then I took a step back, being careful to avoid disturbing the crime scene further.

That was when I heard it.

It was a rustle, a sound almost below my threshold of hearing, and it came from my right. Instantly, every muscle in my body went tight. Slowly, I pivoted. There was a single closed door on the far wall. It probably led to a laundry room, or maybe a bathroom.

Blood rushed in my ears as I stepped forward.

If the shooter was in the house, I had no doubt he'd fire at me the moment he saw me. It was entirely possible, though, that we had another victim, maybe even one who needed help.

I shuffled across the room and stood near the door, listening.

Silence.

I took a step back, drew in a quick breath, and counted down five in my mind, preparing myself. When I reached one, I kicked the door as hard as I could. The wooden frame splintered, and the door flew open. I swept the room with my pistol.

Out of nowhere, pain exploded through my face, and I felt myself falling. A loud gong reverberated through the room, deafening me. For a moment, I didn't know what the hell had happened. Then a shape blurred past me as somebody ran. A metal folding chair clattered to the ground.

For a second, I could barely focus. The figure ran toward the stairs and then turned to me, fumbling for something in his pocket.

I raised my firearm. Despite the ringing in my ears and the dizziness coming over me, my hand was steady. Something stirred in me, a dark whisper from the recesses of my mind. I'd be doing the world and the court system a favor if I killed him. He may have been reaching for his keys, but he might have been reaching for a gun. The department would clear me. They might even give me a medal. My finger slipped inside the trigger guard. A couple pounds of pressure, and this guy would die. Nobody would even miss him.

I'd know what I had done, though, and I didn't want to be that man anymore.

"Hands in the air right now."

The figure stopped moving, and I blinked some of the fog out of my eyes. My righteous anger began to dissipate as I got a better look at him. He was as much a kid as his victims. There were the wisps of a mustache on his upper lip and black hair on his head. He had light brown skin and a worried expression on his face. He pulled his hand out of his pocket and held them at his shoulders.

"Do not move," I said. "If you reach into your pocket again, I will kill you."

He seemed to nod. We stayed like that for a moment, and then I started to sit up. A fresh wave of dizziness came over me, and I fell back and blinked hard.

The kid hesitated and then took his chance and ran. I pushed myself to all fours and then stood. For a second, I thought I'd fall down, but eventually my adrenaline overcame my nausea and dizziness, allowing me to sprint after him. I reached the kitchen in time to look down the front hallway and see the kid jumping off the bungalow's front porch and onto the lawn. The moment his feet touched the grass, a car took off from the curb to my left.

I was going to lose him.

I ran out of the house and reached the front walkway just as the boy I was chasing reached the car. It was a current-model, gray Toyota Camry. The kid dove into the backseat, and the car took off. I ran to the street. I didn't have time to get my phone out to take a picture, so I focused on the license plate. The car had Indiana plates registered in Hamilton County. The first numbers were eight five eight, but I didn't see anything beyond that.

As the car drove away, I holstered my firearm and took out my phone to call it in. In the distance, I could already hear sirens as patrol cars closed on our position. My dispatcher picked up very quickly.

"This is Lieutenant Ash Rashid. I need all available

units to close on the 5000 block of East Clair Street in Irvington. Officers should look for a gray Toyota Camry with a license plate that begins with numbers eight five eight. Assume the driver and passenger are armed and extremely dangerous. Both are wanted for arrest in a multivictim homicide. In addition, call Tactical Air Patrol. I need a bird in the air now. The suspects are teenagers, but they have shot and killed at least six people."

I paused for a moment to make sure the dispatcher was getting everything. I didn't hear a sound from the other end of the line.

"You should be typing right now," I said. "Move."

The keys started clicking in rapid succession.

"You have patrol officers en route right now. I will call in additional support teams."

"Thank you," I said. I hung up the phone and balled my hands into fists. I had so much adrenaline coursing through me that my legs practically itched. I couldn't stand still.

I closed my eyes and took deep breaths, forcing my mind to clear so I could think analytically. Judging by the shell casings in the basement, the victims were shot by a high-powered rifle. If the shooter had walked through the neighborhood carrying an AR-15, he would have been noticed. People would have called the police. Very likely, then, he was either dropped off in front of the house, or he had the weapon concealed somehow.

As I thought through the crime scene, I found myself growing calmer. None of the windows or doors in the house had looked broken, so the shooter had probably been let inside—very likely by Imran Avari, Kim Peterson's boyfriend. He shot Imran first and then methodically walked through the house to look for other victims. He ultimately found them in the basement, shot them, and hid. I must have come in before he could escape.

If that scenario was right, the rifle must have still been in the house because the shooter didn't have it when he left. Why didn't he shoot me, though? And who was he? How did he know to come to Kim Peterson's house? Why would he gun down people he likely didn't even know? Did he know Jacob Ganim, too? Did he kill him? If so, why?

None of my questions had easy answers, and I was getting real tired of asking them.

The first uniformed officer screeched to a stop in front of the house about two minutes after the shooter fled. Since I had already secured the scene inside, he stayed on the front porch and started a log book. I listened to the radio in his squad car as his fellow patrol officers scoured the surrounding neighborhood. For the first few minutes, the search was mostly fruitless. Then I sat up straighter.

"Dispatch, Baker-19 requests 10-51 at Irvington Community Elementary on Julian."

The officer's call sign indicated that he was a patrol officer from the eastern district, and he was requesting assistance from the fire department at an elementary school a couple of blocks from my location. He must have been on the job for a while because we had stopped using ten-codes for radio communications years ago. I waited and let the dispatcher coordinate with him for a moment before keying the radio.

"Baker-19, this is Major Case. Settle my curiosity and tell me what's on fire."

"Major Case, it's a single-vehicle fire involving a recent model, gray, four-door sedan."

I closed my eyes and swore to myself before keying the microphone.

"Confirmed, Baker-19. Keep the scene secure. I'm on my way."

I got out of the patrol vehicle and drove my borrowed Mustang to the school. It was only about five blocks from the house, so the drive only took a few minutes. Under normal circumstances, I probably would have used the GPS on my cell phone to find the location. I didn't need it today, though. The plume of black smoke rising from the parking lot led me right there. When I arrived, a patrol vehicle with its lights flashing blocked the entrance, but there were already a couple of people standing to watch the car burn.

I parked on the street and flashed my badge to the officer.

"You Major Case?" he asked.

"Yeah. I'm Lieutenant Ash Rashid," I said, nodding. "You call in the license plate yet?"

He looked over his shoulder to the burning heap.

Had the shooter parked that vehicle during a school day with a full parking lot, we might not have found that car for hours. Hell, had he driven just a couple of blocks away to the grocery store up the street, he could have gotten away for even longer. He didn't, though. Instead, he set the car on fire, setting up a literal signal to come and find the vehicle. He could have been taunting us, but just as easily, he might have been trying to tie up our resources and send us on a fruitless chase.

"Yeah. Plate was stolen. It belonged to a pickup truck in Carmel. We're trying to track down the owner."

"Any sign of the driver?"

The officer shook his head. "No, but there's something you need to see in the far corner."

He pointed to the northwest corner of the lot. I looked at the section of asphalt and then back to the officer.

"You going to tell me what it is?"

"I figured I'd let you come to your own conclusion."

I grunted and started walking. At first, I thought he might have been messing with me, but then I found a pile of cigarette butts and a small puddle on the asphalt. I snapped a picture with my cell phone as the scenario started coalescing in my head. There were at least two people and probably a third involved in this murder. Two drove getaway cars, and a third did the shooting. The first driver parked in the elementary school lot. He kept his air conditioner blasting and smoked five cigarettes while he waited. The second driver parked near Kim Peterson's house and let the shooter off. He was the diversion. The first driver had the real getaway vehicle.

I swore under my breath and walked back to the officer I had been talking to earlier.

"When CSU gets here, have them bag the cigarette butts and vacuum the parking spot. Maybe we'll get lucky, and they'll find some fibers from the vehicle that was parked there."

"You not sticking around, Lieutenant?"

I drew in a breath and then looked at the car before shaking my head.

"No. I'm no use here, and I've got to get back to another crime scene. Good luck, and thank you. You did good work."

"Thanks. Good luck to you, too."

I walked back to my car with my hands in my pockets and my gaze low as I tried to work out what I knew and what I didn't know.

Whoever my shooter was, he was dangerous. He had the foresight to know he needed an escape plan after the massacre at Kim Peterson's house, and he had the prescience to realize his original getaway car might be spotted. His escape plan, then, had two steps. First, he'd get away from the house in one car. Then he'd call our attention to that car by lighting it on fire while he escaped in another.

The plan was methodical and effective. It anticipated the police response and accounted for it in a very surprising way. The bad guys got away, and I had no idea where they were despite a massive police presence in the area. Frankly, it made my head spin.

I had been attacked by a teenager. That teenager looked as if he had been driven away by a second teenager. Those were the facts, but I couldn't believe a sixteen-year-old kid had decided to do all this on his own. Someone else was directing this, someone who could think tactically and analytically, someone who had a motive to murder everyone in that house and the ability to talk at least two teenagers into committing the crime. Whoever this mastermind was, he was dangerous.

And I didn't have the first clue who he could be.

Chapter 29

Sami Beran's blue and white postal carrier uniform stuck to his chest and back. Even late in the afternoon, it was warmer out than he had expected. He had been assigned to this route for three years now. He knew the neighborhood and the people within it. He also knew their sins.

Most of the families on his route probably considered themselves Christians, but they only went to church on Christmas and Easter. None of the Jewish families he served were devout, and the very few Muslim families on his route lived decadent, sinful lives. By their lifestyles, they had declared war on God and all that was decent. They deserved what was coming to them.

He opened the rear door of his mail van and pulled out a package. It was Memorial Day weekend. In less affluent areas, that meant families would have gone to the local public pool or park for a little fun. On Sami's route, though, that meant families went to Miami or Hilton Head or places more exotic. He double-checked his clipboard before pulling his van's rear door shut.

The home in front of him had a four-car garage and big windows out front. It was owned by a twice-divorced physician and her two kids. The doctor had put in a stop-mail order from Friday to Tuesday, probably so she and the kids could take a vacation. Unlike many of the homes on his route, this one didn't have an alarm. It would work very well.

He hurried up the front walkway and then knelt beside the fake rock that held the family's spare key. He was inside in moments. The package in his hand held a simple black-powder explosive with an ignition device fashioned from an old cell phone. By itself, his bomb could damage a kitchen table, but it wouldn't hurt the house. It didn't need to, though.

Sami carried the package to the kitchen and left it on the counter beside the refrigerator before pulling the gas stove from the wall to expose the half-inch flexible yellow cable. He cut it with a pocketknife, and instantly, a hiss filled the air. Sami coughed and left the building, pulling and locking the front door shut behind him.

According to Hamza Bashear, an engineer by trade, the house would fill with approximately two thousand cubic feet of natural gas in the next twenty-four hours, becoming something akin to a giant pipe bomb.

When Sami reached his van again, he looked over his shoulder at his remaining packages and checked another address off on his list. Four to go. Truly, tomorrow would be a glorious day for God.

Chapter 30

I drove back to Kim Peterson's house. Where there had been one patrol vehicle before, now there were half a dozen with their lights flashing. I parked about a block away and unclipped my badge from my belt so I could attach it to the front pocket of my jacket. One uniformed officer stood near the front porch with a log sheet, while four or five others interviewed the neighbors, many of whom had exited their homes to stand on their front lawns and watch.

The uniformed officers had the scene in hand, so I called Captain Mike Bowers, the commanding officer of IMPD's Crimes Against Persons division.

"Mike, it's Ash Rashid. I'm at the home of Kim Peterson. We've got a lot of bodies in the house. You sent anybody out here yet?"

"Nancy Wharton. Elliot Wu's going to be second. I've got the entire division on notice, though, in case we need additional resources. Are you still working for the Bureau?"

"Sort of. It's a long story," I said. "Nancy and Elliot are both good, but this is going to be a bigger case than the two of them alone can handle. Go ahead and call in everybody you've got. And you need to be on the scene to deal with the media."

Bowers paused. "If you think this investigation is that big, maybe major case should take it."

"No," I said, shaking my head. "I can't be on TV right now. It's a long story."

"All right. I'll get more people down there. Nancy and Elliot shouldn't be too far away. Anything I should tell them before they arrive?"

I thought through my answer for a moment. "The victims are connected to the case I'm working for the Bureau. My case with the Bureau is somehow connected to the attack on Westbrook Elementary. You connect the dots."

Bowers swore under his breath. "I'll call Kevin Havelock at the Bureau, then."

"The Bureau isn't going to be the most reliable partner right now. I don't know what's going on over there, but it's probably best we stay out of their internal politics. And it's best you don't mention me to them at all. They think I'm in custody right now."

Bowers swore again. "Tell me you didn't break out of federal custody."

I didn't respond, so Bowers repeated himself and requested an honest answer.

"You want me to be honest, or do you want me to tell you I didn't break out of federal custody?"

"What the hell are you doing, Lieutenant?"

I caught movement to my left and saw a gray, unmarked Crown Victoria sedan pull to a stop on the side of the road. Detectives Wharton and Wu stepped out.

"I'm working the death of an undercover FBI agent, but it's veered off in an unexpected direction," I said, nodding to Detective Wharton as she walked toward me. "Wharton and Wu are here. I've got to go."

I hung up before he could say anything else. I knew Nancy Wharton reasonably well, but I had only met Detective Wu a couple of times. Bowers wouldn't have promoted him to homicide, though, if he weren't good at his job. While I talked to him and filled him in on what had happened at the house, Detective Wharton went inside to see what was going on there.

Homicide work was a painstaking process. On TV, the detectives solved cases through brilliance and superior forensic science. In real life, most homicide investigations were closed through legwork and self-made luck. You knocked on enough doors and talked to enough people, you were bound to find somebody who saw something. One eyewitness could open a case right up.

Detectives Wharton and Wu would talk to the neighbors, they'd research everyone the victims had called recently, and they'd crawl through the house with technicians from Forensic Services. In total, they'd spend thousands of manhours trying to solve a crime that had taken moments. And even then, that wasn't always enough. It was the system we had, though.

After Wu interviewed me, I went to my car and sat in the driver's seat, knowing Detective Wharton would likely want to talk to me next. The first news van showed up a few minutes later. Uniformed officers kept them well away from the house, but even still, I stayed in my car to avoid being inadvertently caught on camera.

After that, things moved quickly. Forensic Services arrived and took over the search inside the house. They were followed by three vans from the coroner's office. Dr. Rodriguez and his fellow forensic pathologists were going to be busy for a while.

As I sat, I called Kevin Havelock to fill him in on what had happened. He offered to send additional resources, but I declined. As I started to hang up, he cleared his throat.

"Before you go, Nassir's been released. So have the other men we picked up."

"How?" I asked, furrowing my brow.

"Bad press combined with a directive from President Crane directly to the director of the FBI."

"That's good," I said, nodding.

"Maybe," said Havelock. "Right now, the United States government is conducting one of the largest investigations in the history of law enforcement. We have agents on almost every continent on the planet and every specialty in law enforcement investigating the attack on Westbrook Elementary, and a lot of their findings are pointing toward Indianapolis. Something big is about to happen in our neck of the woods. Jacob Ganim was in the middle of it, and he happened to hang out with your brother-in-law an awful lot."

I couldn't deny that, so I nodded. I started to tell him I planned to go back to the mosque I had been at earlier so I could interview Omar Nawaz, but then I saw Detective Wharton walking toward my car. She had her hair pulled back from her face, and her jacket flapped in the wind. She had the intense expression of a woman who knew the exact importance of the case she had just picked up.

"Thanks for the update," I said. "I'll keep you informed if I find anything."

I hung up before Havelock could respond. Detective Wharton gave me a small but genuine smile as I stepped out of the car.

"Hey, Ash," she said. "It's been a while. How have you been?"

"Can't complain. Kids are growing, my wife is healthy, and I still have my hair."

For a brief moment, her smile widened but then disappeared.

"When my husband turned forty, his hair migrated to his back. It's nice that yours has stayed put," she said, turning. "Come on. There's something in the house I want you to see."

I kept my head down and followed her to the house, where I signed a log sheet before going inside. It looked as if Captain Bowers had requested the crime lab send every tech on staff to the scene because there were people in every single room. Considering we had eight bodies strewn through the house, that was probably the correct move.

I followed Detective Wharton to one of the bedrooms, where Detective Wu knelt beside a low bookshelf. He looked up at me and then to Wharton.

"You have an extra pair of gloves?" he asked.

She nodded. "I'll find some. In the meantime, show Ash what you found."

Detective Wu nodded and pulled a book from the shelf. It had a faux leather cover and probably held three hundred pages or so. There were no marks on the outside to indicate its contents.

"We found these on a bookshelf. There are more in a box downstairs."

"Okay," I said, nodding and catching his gaze. "What are they?"

"I was hoping you could tell us," he said, cracking the book open to a lined notebook page covered in neat, black script. "The victims looked Middle Eastern. I thought you might be able to read it."

I studied it but then shook my head. "I can't, but I know people who can. This is Persian."

He sighed and nodded. "Okay. Thanks, anyway. Now that we know it's Persian, I'll call somebody about a translation. Maybe we'll get lucky."

I nodded toward the bookshelf. There were almost a dozen notebooks on it, none of which had exterior markings.

"Are all these notebooks written by the same person?" I asked.

Wu shrugged just as Detective Wharton came back in the room with a box of gloves. I took a pair of gloves from her and thanked her before snapping them on my hands.

"I can't tell," said Wu. "Some are in pencil, and some are in pen. I don't know the language, so that's all I can figure out."

"May I?" I asked, gesturing toward the books.

"Help yourself," he said.

I picked up another book. It, too, was in Persian, but it looked like different handwriting. I put that one back on the shelf. The writer of the second book I picked up, though, wrote Modern Standard Arabic with a very neat, very practiced hand. It almost looked like type from a printer. I picked up a third book and found Modern Standard Arabic again, but the script was sloppy. This was a different writer entirely.

"You find something?" asked Detective Wharton.

"Yeah, we've got different writers and different languages," I said, glancing up. "Give me a minute. I'm reading."

Wharton crossed her arms but nodded. My heart started beating a little faster with every word. It almost felt as if I were reading a novel, but I knew the stories in that diary were all too real.

"Today, *rijaal al-hisbah* came for the Abidi family," I said, reading. I glanced up and saw curious expressions looking back at me. "*Rijaal al-hisbah* is a reference to men who guard against those who sin. They're the state religious police in certain predominantly Muslim countries. They arrest and punish those who disobey their government's particular interpretation of Islam."

"What countries?" asked Wu.

I raised my eyebrows and tilted my head to the side. "I don't know every country, but Saudi Arabia, Afghanistan under the Taliban, parts of Syria, parts of Nigeria, the Islamic State."

"So places I probably don't want to visit," said Detective Wharton. "Go on. Keep reading."

I looked back to the diary.

"Yeah, okay," I said, finding my place again. "Today the *hisbah* came for the Abidi family. We weren't allowed to cry. Anisa tried to run, but they caught her. They dragged her to the street by her hair. Somebody had told Brother Faiz that they were Shia, so he lined the family up outside their house and made them kneel in the dirt. Then he made all the neighbors come and watch. Faiz said that all Shia are apostates and should be slaughtered like lambs. Then he and his men slit the family's throats in front of us.

"I braided Anisa's hair last week while she played with a doll on my lap. Now I have her blood on my clothes, and I can't wash it off. This can't be what God wants. I don't want to be here anymore."

That was the end of the page. Neither Wharton nor Wu said anything. We all knew, though, that this wasn't a novel. This wasn't a story. This was a young woman's life, probably one of the young women I had found dead in the basement. She had escaped hell only to find the devil in her new home.

I slipped the book back on the shelf and stood up. Omar Nawaz, the imam I had spoken to earlier, knew who these girls were. He knew what they had been through. If I had to guess, he knew who was after them. The two of us needed to have a long conversation.

"If you guys need someone to translate these, I will later," I said. "But right now, I've got somebody to see."

Chapter 31

It was night by the time Ahmed and Omar Massoud reached the parking lot. Yellow trucks spread in front of them. The tire and auto center to their left had closed two hours earlier. The overhead lights were harsh and bright but sporadically placed so that they left light and dark spots on the asphalt.

They had watched that lot for an hour. Even though the business was closed, customers still came by periodically to drop off trucks and return paperwork to the store's mailbox. They didn't look out of place.

Ahmed pointed to a white paneled van.

"That one would be the easiest to drive," he said. "Probably gets the best gas mileage, too."

Omar shook his head. "Too small for what we need."

"We'll get the next size up, then," said Ahmed, pointing to a truck. "I'll be driving this thing, so I don't want something too big."

Omar walked toward the truck and looked at the sign on the window before shaking his head.

"Load capacity's only three thousand pounds. We need something bigger."

Ahmed walked toward his brother and lowered his voice. "How big is this bomb Hamza's building?"

Instead of answering, Omar looked toward the twenty-six-foot truck, the biggest truck on the lot. Ahmed felt himself shrink just a little.

"That's a big truck."

"It's a big bomb," said Omar, reaching into his pocket for a safety hammer their mother had given them in case they ever got stuck in a car after an accident. It had an attachment to cut seatbelts and a hardened steel point perfect for breaking through safety glass. He walked to the truck, climbed onto the steps beneath the driver's door, and broke the driver's side window. "If we're fast, we'll be done before the rental place even knows their truck is gone."

Ahmed nodded as his brother opened the door and started sweeping glass outside. Neither of them had ever stolen a car before, but they had watched internet videos on how to do it. They had the truck running within ten minutes of stepping foot onto the lot. Ahmed drove, while his brother navigated and watched for the police.

Truly, though, God was on their side. They had a clean getaway, a full tank of gas, and a truck with a ten-thousand-pound load capacity.

Ahmed hoped that was enough.

Chapter 32

The sun had been down for a good hour by the time I left the crime scene. Omar Nawaz had been at his mosque the last time I saw him, but there was a good chance he had left after prayer. If he had just talked to me, the people in Kim Peterson's house might still be alive. That was the problem with this case. Everyone had something to hide, and everyone had someone who wanted them dead.

The moment I turned my car on, my cell phone started ringing. I answered without looking at the screen.

"Yeah?"

"Ashraf, I'm out of jail, but I need your help."

The voice belonged to Nassir. I had wanted to talk to him tonight anyway, so I was glad he called.

"I'm glad you're out. I'm on my way to visit Omar Nawaz. You know him?"

"He's the imam at a *masjid* on the east side of town," said Nassir, his voice almost distant. "I've only met him a couple of times. He's competent."

Coming from Nassir, that was a high compliment for any clergyman. It meant Nawaz lived those things he taught rather than just paying lip service to ideals.

"Glad to hear it. You said you need help. What do you need?"

"We need you to come to the camp."

I blinked a few times. "I'm in the middle of a major case, and your camp is an hour away."

"I know," said Nassir. "This is an emergency."

"And we can't solve this over the phone?"

"No," said Nassir, his voice low. "We screwed up. It's important. I need your help."

"Eight people are dead. Omar Nawaz might know their murderer. Is your screwup more important than that?"

Nassir's voice caught in his throat. He cleared it.

"I'm sorry, but yes. A lot of people could get hurt because of us."

I leaned back on my seat to think. It felt like I had been working this case for years instead of just forty-eight hours. I rubbed my eyes. I needed to interview Nawaz, but he was still a peripheral figure in this whole thing. Nassir was closer to the hub, the center of the wheel that connected everything. Jacob Ganim, the dead women, the attack at Westbrook Elementary in New Hampshire, the warehouse and fire…Nassir may not have known what was going on, but somehow it all came back to him. If he thought a lot of people could get hurt because of what he did, he was probably right.

"I'm on my way."

Nassir thanked me several times before hanging up. I buckled up for the hour-long drive. Before leaving, I texted my wife to let her know that I was okay and that I loved her. She didn't know the FBI had arrested me that afternoon, and I didn't tell her. She worried about me. I loved that about her. I loved everything about her, in fact. She and the kids were my whole world.

After texting her, I called my dispatcher and asked her to have some uniformed officers pick up Omar Nawaz for safekeeping.

Once I had the preparations made, I took I-465 to I-65 and headed south toward Nassir's camp. There were few cars out, allowing me to make good time with little stress. The trees around Nassir's property were dense and thick, but once I had left their canopy, the sky opened up with a seemingly endless number of stars. It was unfortunate that the federal government would likely seize the property before this was all through because it was certainly a pretty spot.

I found three cars beside the main building at the camp. I parked beside Nassir's Cadillac and got out. Crickets and other nighttime insects sang from the woods near the building, while a breeze caused the trees to gently sway. I followed heated voices inside the building. Nassir, Saleem al-Asiri—the guidance counselor from Illinois—and Asim Qureshi argued as they sat at a round table. Saleem held a bag of frozen peas against his face. There was a bloody handkerchief on the table in front of him.

I cleared my throat. Asim looked at me and nodded.

"Thank you for coming. We didn't know who else to call."

I nodded to him and then looked to Saleem. "What's wrong with your face?"

He lowered the bag of frozen food, revealing a bruise on his cheek and the makings of a black eye.

"If someone at the FBI did that to you," I said, "you

need to talk to your lawyer. I can't help with that."

Saleem shook his head. "This was the work of one of my students. Butler al-Ghamdi."

I crossed my arms and raised my eyebrows. "The kid you caught buying ammunition online and brought here?"

"Yes," said Nassir. "When the FBI came and arrested us, he was out buying lumber. He hid from them because he thought they were going to kill him. They undid everything we were trying to accomplish. He was already radicalized. Now he thinks he has to act."

I swore under my breath before looking up, my eyebrows raised. "And you guys want me to find him?"

"We *need* you to find him," said Saleem. He licked his lips. "I made a mistake."

"Yeah, you did," I said. "We're past pointing fingers, though. I need his cell phone number. Since he's clearly a threat, I'm going to bring the FBI in on this."

"There's more they're not telling you," said Asim, his arms crossed as he glared at Saleem and then Nassir. "He and his friends broke into the armory and took some very dangerous things."

I let the statement hang for a moment before speaking, expecting someone to say something.

"Excuse me? You have an armory?"

"Butler wasn't the first young man we've helped," said Nassir. "He ordered ammunition. Other boys had guns and knives and things like that."

I didn't say anything at first, but my face started to warm as my temper rose. Finally, I couldn't take the silence.

"What the hell were you guys thinking?" I asked. No one answered, so I threw up my hands. "That's a real question. What the hell were you thinking? These weren't Boy Scouts caught breaking the speed limit. These were young men primed to commit mass murder, and you took them to a summer camp."

"We thought we were helping," said Nassir.

"Yeah, and because of your help, there's now a dangerous kid out there with God only knows what."

Saleem sat straighter. "To be fair, we have a pretty good idea of what they took. We have an inventory."

I squeezed my hands into fists so tight the skin over my knuckles turned white. Then I took deep breaths, trying to calm my temper. It only partially worked, but a slow, simmering anger was probably appropriate given the situation. I looked at Asim.

"You said Butler and his friends robbed the armory," I said. "What friends?"

Asim looked to Saleem. He sighed before speaking.

"There were three of them," said the guidance counselor. "Butler and two other boys I didn't know. They were vicious. As soon as they got here, one of the boys punched me in the stomach. The other kicked me in the face when I fell down."

"They wanted his key," said Nassir.

"So they beat you up for the key," I said, nodding. I looked to Nassir and then to Asim. "How many people know about your armory?"

"Not many," said Nassir. "It's a pretty close group."

"And yet these kids knew all about it," I said. "Where is it? Could they have just found it on their own?"

"It's connected to the storm shelter beneath the barn," said Asim, his arms still crossed. "The FBI didn't even find it."

And if the Bureau *had* found the armory, Nassir and his friends never would have seen the sun against except through bars.

"If it's well hidden and no one knows about it, how did these kids find it?"

Nassir and Asim looked to Saleem. He cleared his throat.

"I told him," he said. "They had a gun to my head and were asking where we put Butler's ammunition. They would have killed me if I hadn't told them."

I crossed my arms. "I'm not buying that. If these kids are willing to commit mass murder, they'd kill you to keep you from talking."

Saleem looked down. "Butler told them not to. He said he wanted to do it. So the other boys went to the armory to get the guns, while Butler remained behind. As soon as his friends were gone, Butler started crying. He apologized and begged me to forgive him, but he wouldn't give me the gun. He said we'd both be dead if that happened. He shot into the wall twice and told me to hide in the office until they were gone."

I didn't know whether I believed the story, but it didn't matter. There were three dangerous kids with guns on the loose.

"When did this happen?" I asked.

Nassir and Asim looked to Saleem.

"A couple of hours ago."

"Does Butler have dark brown skin and shortly cropped hair?"

"Why?" asked Saleem.

"Because a young man with dark brown skin and shortly cropped hair just killed eight people in Indianapolis who were connected to this case," I said. Nassir's face paled, while Saleem and Asim looked as if someone had just punched them. I took that as a confirmation of my question. "I need Butler's cell phone number."

"What are you going to do?" asked Saleem.

"What you should have done," I said, allowing a hint of coldness into my voice. "I'm going to call the police. They'll track him down and arrest him."

"If you do that, a lot of people will die," said Saleem. "Butler is in over his head. Call him. Talk to him. Maybe there's another way out. He can help you. Maybe he can even lead you to his friends. If the police try to pick them up, those boys will shoot back. They're willing to die. They think this is what God wants from them."

Everybody I met lately seemed to think that God either wanted them to murder somebody or die for a cause. Frankly, I was getting a little tired of it.

The worst part was that Saleem was probably right. If these guys really had perpetrated the attack in Kim

Peterson's house, they wouldn't hesitate to open fire on our police officers. Maybe worse than that, our officers wouldn't hesitate to fire on them. This would need to be handled delicately.

"I will do what I believe is right in accordance with my professional judgment," I said, speaking slowly as I tried to come up with a plan. "I will take him into custody as gently as I can, but I'm not going to put my life or the lives of anyone under my command in danger. Now, I'd like an inventory of your armory."

Nassir and Asim went to the office to get the list, while Saleem stayed put. He didn't say anything, and I didn't have anything to say to him. Instead, I looked at my phone. I had one bar, and it seemed steady. Maybe the wind was blowing right.

"How old is Butler?" I asked.

Saleem sputtered something and then sat straighter. "Fifteen."

"The other boys about the same age or older?"

"Older. They were probably college age."

"What were they driving?"

He thought for a moment and then leaned forward. "A red Ford pickup. It was old and had rust on the wheel wells."

"And Butler didn't want to go with them?"

Saleem blinked. "He was scared. I think he thought that if he didn't go with them, they'd kill him."

It met the criteria, then. This would work. I called my dispatcher at IMPD and gave her my badge number and name.

"I'd like to request an Amber Alert be put out for Butler al-Ghamdi. He's a fifteen-year-old boy last seen near a campsite in Brown County, Indiana. He was abducted with threats of violence by two men in their early twenties. Both men should be considered heavily armed and extremely dangerous. They were last seen driving a late-model Ford pickup truck. I believe Butler is in imminent danger of death or serious injury and request that civilians call the police upon sighting the victim. Law enforcement should be on notice that the abductors will fire upon any perceived threats. The victim will likely fire as well. I'm not sure of his mindset. All due precautions should be taken."

I stayed on the line for another few minutes while the dispatcher took my information down. Since I was a lieutenant, my requests were given a little more weight than those from an average officer, and I felt pretty confident we'd have the alert issued within the hour. Once that happened, Butler's name and description would be on every TV in the state. They'd find him. I just hoped the boys gave themselves up without a fight.

A moment after I made my call, Nassir returned with a printout on which he had written quite a few notes.

"This is a complete inventory. I've circled those things that were taken."

Though they hadn't taken everything, the inventory took an entire page. There were rifles, pistols, bomb components, and a lot of suspect electronic gear. I looked at it and sighed.

"How many troubled young men have you guys helped?"

Nassir hesitated before answering. "Eight, but none of them have ever committed an attack after we worked with them. They learned."

"Except Butler," I said, scanning those items he had circled. Before anyone could say anything, I cleared my throat. "So, according to your inventory, they took four pistols, three AR-15 rifles, and twelve boxes of ammunition, each of which held twenty rounds."

"That sounds right," said Nassir.

I looked at him and then to Saleem and Asim. "And none of you thought it was a bad idea to store this stuff at a summer camp?"

They didn't answer, which wasn't too unexpected. I looked at Nassir.

"Do you have his cell number?"

He pointed to a handwritten number at the bottom of the sheet. I stood and placed a call. I didn't particularly want Nassir and his enablers to listen to the conversation, so I grabbed the inventory, left the building, and walked down the gravel driveway while Kevin Havelock's phone rang. When he answered, he sounded groggy.

"I get you up from a nap?" I asked.

"Yeah," he said. He cleared his throat. "I haven't slept for a while. What's up?"

"I need a trace on a cell phone. Bowers call you about the murders yet?"

Havelock paused. "No. What murders?"

"Jacob Ganim had photographs of women in his basement. Somebody tracked those women down and killed them this afternoon."

"Jesus," said Havelock, his voice clear. "You have any idea who did it?"

"Possibly the owner of the cell phone I need you to track down."

"This connected to Ganim's murder?"

I exhaled a slow breath. "Ganim, my brother-in-law, the dead women, the attack on Westbrook Elementary, they're all connected. I just don't know how yet."

I gave him the number.

"Okay," he said. "Give me five minutes. If it's on, we'll find it."

I thanked him, hung up, and sat down against the base of a tree just off the side gravel roadway. For five minutes, I stared at the stars. It was peaceful. I wished it could have lasted, but time doesn't stop for men like me. My phone rang just as I was starting to relax.

"Yeah?" I said.

"Phone is in a fixed location near the Indianapolis International Airport. Hasn't left the general vicinity for almost an hour."

I rubbed my eyes and gave myself a minute to think about how to approach this.

"Get a team together. Search the location and see what you can find. I'm going to head to Indianapolis and talk to an imam who did something really stupid."

Chapter 33

Kamil Salib's hand hovered over the aluminum alloy frame of his AR-15 rifle. It was loaded. The optics were dialed in. He had additional ammunition in a bag at his feet. Now he just had to wait.

He had been awake for almost twenty-four hours straight, and he should have been exhausted. Instead, he felt more alive than he ever had in twenty years on Earth. His parents thought he was in his dorm at the University of Illinois. They thought he was two years from completing a degree in engineering that would land him a middle-class job and lifestyle. They wanted him to marry a good Muslim girl and have children.

He would have done that gladly had he been born into a better world. That wasn't the life he had ahead of him, though. His destiny was to become a soldier for God. His mentor, Hashim Bashear, had shown him that. Now, Kamil would make Hashim proud. Still, his stomach fluttered.

"I'm nervous," he said, looking to his friend, Daniel Hakim. The two men sat on a deer blind built into the crotch of an oak tree approximately twenty feet from the ground. The wooden structure had been painted black, making it difficult if not impossible to see against the night sky, while the foam insulation they sat on muffled the sound of their movements and blocked their infrared signature to anyone on the ground. They were as safe in the trees as a newborn babe would be in her mother's arms.

"There's no need to be nervous," said Daniel. "We have God on our side."

Daniel was right, of course. At twenty-five, he was five years Kamil's senior and had years of experiences Daniel would likely never have. He was strong and confident. More than that, he had walked the straight path every day of his life. Kamil couldn't have asked for a better mentor or friend.

The plan this evening had come together hastily and took the combined efforts of five people to prepare. The actual execution came down to Kamil and Daniel, though. Kamil's hands trembled with nerves, but he could knew he could do it. He had to.

Lieutenant Ash Rashid had nearly derailed Butler al-Ghamdi's mission that afternoon by showing up at Kim Peterson's house unexpectedly. Had he been there five minutes earlier, Butler probably would have been dead. As it was, Butler succeeded and survived relatively unscathed, but Rashid almost ruined everything.

They needed to deal with him and fast.

Hashim Bashear had come up with the plan, and Hamza Bashear had worked out the details. Butler suggested using himself as bait in order to lure the detective to a location at which Kalim and Daniel could ambush him, but Hashim said it wouldn't work. The detective was too intelligent and cynical for that. He'd sniff out an ambush and come with such overwhelming force everyone would die.

The plan Hashim had devised was subtle and precise. It took advantage of the detective's nature and had levels he'd never see through.

"Do you think Butler went through with it at the camp?" he asked.

Daniel nodded without looking at him.

"Butler is a soldier who has already proved himself. It will be your turn this evening. I'll be with you. With God, no one can stand in our way."

Kamil nodded and drew in a breath. It had already been a day of firsts for him. He had stolen his first car—a Toyota Camry—and he had been involved in his first operation, but he had yet to fire a weapon except at paper targets. God willing, that would change tonight. Kamil didn't know why they had to kill the people they did, but it wasn't his place to know. He was just the weapon. God was the true marksman.

Tonight, Ashraf Rashid would die, and nothing could stop that.

Chapter 34

By the time I reached the interstate, it was past the time my wife would be putting the kids to bed. I had barely talked to them all day. I needed my kids more than they knew. I chose to be a police officer because of them. I was a reasonably bright man. I had a law degree, and I had some money saved up. If I had really wanted to, I could have hung a shingle and become an attorney in private practice.

That wasn't my calling, though. I was a dad. If I had a purpose on Earth, that was it. Though I had originally joined the police force because I needed a job, I stayed because I wanted to make the world safer for my children —and for other children. Sometimes I succeeded, and sometimes I failed, but everything I did came back to them. I wished I had gotten to hear their voices today.

I put the thought out of my head and focused on the drive. I didn't have lights or a siren in the Mustang, but the roads were mostly empty except for long-haul truckers. The left lane was clear, and my car had a big V-8 engine. All in all, it meant I made pretty good time.

About twenty miles from Indianapolis, I got a call from Agent Havelock. Since I didn't like to talk while driving, I pulled off on the side of the road and turned on my emergency blinkers.

"Havelock," I said. "What's going on?"

"You want the good news or the bad news?"

"What's the good news?" I asked.

"We found the warehouse and checked it out. Nobody got hurt."

I nodded. "Okay. That's good news. What's the bad?"

"We didn't find anybody. We found your suspect's cell phone, but it looked as if he had dropped it."

I swore under my breath and then rubbed my eyes. "Okay. Any idea what they were doing in the warehouse?"

"Yeah. They were making explosive devices. We found some snipped wires, a pair of soldering guns, and a few printed circuit boards. We didn't find any explosive material, but our bomb-sniffing dog indicated that he smelled some."

I closed my eyes. "You told me earlier that you had signals intelligence that said something big was about to happen in Indianapolis. Could this be it?"

"It might be part of it," he said. "I'm bringing in a technical team to dust the place for prints and see what we can find. The warehouse next door has security cameras on its exterior, so I've already got agents trying to track down video. Might be able to find something there. This building is owned by a freight logistics company that went belly up, but this is a busy area. Somebody will have seen something. We'll work the scene and see what turns up."

It sounded like a reasonable plan, but before I could say that, my phone started buzzing, indicating an incoming call. I glanced at the screen. It was Nassir. I told Havelock I'd call him back and then answered my brother-in-law.

"Nassir," I said. "You okay?"

"Butler's here."

I paused for a second, surprised.

"He's at your camp?"

"Yes," said Nassir. "He's scared. He didn't want to go with the other boys, but he didn't think he had a choice."

That was one possibility. The other one—the one I found much more likely—was that he was in the middle of everything, and he was playing Nassir and his friends.

"Okay," I said, nodding. "Can you put him on the phone? I'd like to talk to him."

"Hold on," said Nassir. I waited for a new voice to come on the line.

"Hello?"

"Butler, yeah. This is Lieutenant Ash Rashid of the Indianapolis Metro Police Department. I'm glad you called. Seems you're in a little bit of trouble."

"I'm sorry. I didn't mean for any of this to happen. I fell in with a bad crowd and got in over my head."

It was a lot of clichés for one sentence, but I wasn't there to critique his word choice.

"I'm glad you realize that. How are we going to fix this?"

The kid's voice was shaky. "I know where the guns are."

"That's a good start," I said. "Are they being stored with any explosive devices?"

"We never had explosives," said Butler, quickly. "The

guys aren't into explosives. They took over a house. It's halfway between Indianapolis and Terre Haute."

So much for the benefit of the doubt. This guy was a liar. Now I needed to give him some rope and let him hang himself.

"What do you mean they took over a house?"

"They found it online and broke in," he said. "It's like a cabin. It's for sale, so they knew nobody would be in it."

"Okay," I said. "Are they at the cabin right now?"

"No," he said. "They're probably looking for me. If you go now, you'll be able to get the guns and leave. You can arrest them when they come back. That's what I'd do."

I nodded to myself. "You know these guys, so if that's what you'd do, that's what I'll do. What's the address?"

As he said it, I pinned my phone between my shoulder and ear and wrote it down on a notebook I kept in my jacket pocket.

"All right, Butler," I said. "You sit tight at Nassir's camp. I'll check out the cabin and arrest your friends. They won't bother you again."

"Thanks, Lieutenant," he said, his voice much lighter than it had been a moment earlier. "You've saved my life."

"I'm just glad you did the right thing. Stay with Nassir and take care of yourself. I'll take care of this cabin."

He thanked me again before hanging up. Next, I

called the Brown County Sheriff's Department and asked them to pick Butler up and put him in custody. This little shit wasn't going anywhere. Then I called Agent Havelock back.

"So I just got a phone call from Butler al-Ghamdi, the owner of the cell phone found at your warehouse. He lied his ass off and denied having anything to do with explosives. He wants me to go to an abandoned house so I can arrest his partners before they hurt anyone."

Havelock paused for a second. "Sounds like an ambush."

"That was my assessment, too. Can you put a team together to ambush their ambush? The house is halfway between Indianapolis and Terre Haute, so you're not too far from it."

"Yeah, we can do that," said Havelock. "I've got eighteen tactical officers here, so I'll send a small team to scout the location and put together a plan of assault. Where are you?"

"South of the city, about forty-five minutes from the airport."

"Then get your car in gear," he said. "By the time you get here, we should have some more information about what to do."

"I appreciate it," I said, already looking over my shoulder so I could get back in traffic. I gave Havelock the address and then wished him luck before hanging up.

The drive to the airport was uneventful. I found Havelock and his agents right where I expected them in the warehouse's parking lot. Havelock and a second agent were huddled around a laptop on the hood of an SUV. I parked nearby and flashed my badge to the first agents to walk to my car. They nodded and directed me toward their boss. Havelock nodded a greeting to me and then looked to the man beside him.

"Ash, this is Special Agent John Rose. John, this is Ash Rashid."

"Nice to meet you, Agent Rose," I said, shaking his hand. I looked to Havelock. "Any news?"

Havelock looked to Agent Rose.

"My advance team has arrived at the location, but there's no sign of your bad guys. The cabin's empty."

So our ambushers stood us up. Reminded me of dating in high school.

"Has your team been inside the house?" I asked.

Rose shook his head. "Not yet. They're deployed throughout the woods nearby, but they're staying back. We've scanned the house with infrared scopes, but it's totally empty. There's a red pickup truck in the driveway, but it looks as if it's been there for a while."

I thought for a few moments. Even if the bad guys weren't at the cabin, they chose this particular spot. There may not have been anything there, but we needed to check it out anyway.

"If the house is empty, we don't need a tactical team," said Havelock. "Ash and I can go in and check it out. The rest of the team can go back to Indianapolis."

Agent Rose drew in a deep breath and then nodded.

"The cabin's remote, so backup will be slow to get there in case of emergency. You okay with that?"

"Our other option is to tie up an entire tactical team for a wild goose chase," said Havelock. "If there's an attack in the city, we're going to need every tactical officer we can get. Lieutenant Rashid and I will be fine in the house. Keep your advance team in place. If we run into problems, we'll have six armed officers on site."

"If that's how you want to do it," said Rose. "My team and I will head home."

"That's what we're doing," said Havelock, turning to me. "And that means you're driving, Ash."

That sounded fine with me. Before leaving, I thanked Agent Rose for his help and wished him luck in the city. He said the same to me. We all headed out at the same time, although we turned in opposite directions on the interstate. Havelock and I settled into an easy silence as we drove.

Since we were already west of the city, the drive only took about half an hour. A black SUV awaited us on the side of the road as we neared the address. I parked, and an FBI agent wearing black tactical gear stepped out of the heavy vehicle. His name was Ken Hanson, and he was the advance team's leader. I shook his hand. He had a firm, rough grip.

"So what do we have?" I asked, looking around. At this time of night and this far from the city, the night felt oppressively dark. Last year's leaves covered the forest floor, while this year's leaves formed a canopy overhead that blocked out all but the barest hint of moonlight.

"There's been no movement since my team arrived," said the agent, turning and pointing in a southerly direction. "There's a ridgeline directly south of the house. I have a man stationed there with an infrared scope. He's got clear sightlines into the house, but he's not seen anyone inside. I've got a man to the east in a slight valley. He's got sightlines to the house and the road, but nothing's moved. And finally, I've got a man on a hill to the west of the house. No sign of movement there, either.

"I can't guarantee the house is safe, but there's nobody in it, and it doesn't look as if anybody's been in it for quite a while."

Agent Hanson probably couldn't see me, but I nodded and looked to Agent Havelock.

"You want to drive or walk?" I asked.

"Might as well drive," he said. "If the house is empty, nobody's going to shoot up the car."

I reached into my pocket for my keys. "Then let's go."

Chapter 35

Special Agent Scott Kaler had positioned himself on top of a ridgeline beside an old oak tree approximately half a mile from the house, giving himself a sweeping view of the valley below him. He thought about his five-year-old daughter. He loved that girl with everything he had. He loved her mom just as much. This was supposed to have been his night off, and he had the whole evening planned. First, they would go play miniature golf, and then they'd have dinner. Afterwards, they'd go home, Kayla would go to bed, and Scott and his wife would relax on the couch with a movie. There was a good chance he would have even gotten lucky.

Now, he was stuck in the woods. Neither Kayla nor his wife had wanted him to leave, but they understood he had a job to do. Since he wouldn't get the chance to tuck her into bed that night, he had sung her a song right before he left, and now he couldn't get the damn thing out of his head.

"Are you humming, Kaler?"

It was Special Agent Santiago Muniz. Kaler swept his rifle's infrared scope across the valley below him, searching for movement, before keying in his microphone.

"Negative. That must have been Agent Havelock. Must have swiped a radio. I hear he's into show tunes."

"He does have quite the spring to his step now that

he's sleeping with that lady from Homeland Security," chimed in Agent Nicholson.

"That's enough, guys," said Ken Hanson, the seniormost agent in the group. "We're here to do a job, not gossip about the boss."

"Copy that," said Muniz.

"You hear anything about this detective we're covering?" asked Nicholson. "I hear he's a dick."

"I hear he's killed more people than cancer," said Muniz. "Guys from DC picked him up this afternoon. He has a file half an inch thick."

"That's enough," said Agent Hanson. "Both of you. I want this line silent except for mission-specific communication."

Kaler heard the conversation, but he didn't pay attention. Instead, he drew in a slow, even breath and panned the rifle across the valley. As his gaze swept to the west, he saw a figure he hadn't seen before. Kaler estimated him at about twelve hundred yards distant. The sniper pulled the microphone to his lips and centered the crosshairs of his scope on the man's chest, already mentally calculating the figures he'd need to make the shot.

"Hanson, we got anybody west-southwest of the house?"

"Negative, Kaler. You see movement?"

Kaler adjusted his scope for the distance and wind speed. "Affirmative, sir. I got a shot. You want me to light him up?"

"Our rules of engagement are to shoot only if we're shot at. We don't want to shoot the neighbors if we don't have to. Does he have a weapon?"

Kaler watched for a moment.

"I can't tell from my position."

"Then get into a position in which you can tell," said Hanson.

"Affirmative," said Kaler, reluctantly taking his eye from the scope. He pushed off from the ground but didn't stand upright. Instead, he crouched as low as he could, trying to stay in the shadows as he eased himself closer to the man he had seen. About ten yards away, he found a tree that had fallen, giving him a decent place to set up again. When he scanned the surrounding woods, the figure he had seen was gone.

"Hanson, my target is MIA. I can't find him again."

"You sure he was there?" asked Muniz.

"Yeah," said Kaler. "What do you think, boss? Now seems like a pretty good time to call in air support to me."

He waited a moment, but Agent Hanson didn't respond.

"You read me, Ken?"

Again, he waited, but again, no one responded.

"Ken. I need you to say something," he said. He paused for a five count. "Anybody in visual contact with Hanson?"

"Negative," said Muniz and Nicholson, almost in unison.

"Shit," said Kaler, scanning the area for his target

again, and again finding nothing. "We've got a problem."

The house was about two hundred yards from the road, and as I turned down the driveway, my headlights illuminated the woods around us, catching a possum or raccoon by surprise. Its dark eyes stared at us, reflecting my headlights back at us like a pair of tiny mirrors. Then the animal turned and ran.

With the house for sale and foot traffic at a minimum, this was probably a pretty safe area for small animals to bed down for the night. More than likely, we'd find some vermin inside.

"Kind of nice to see nature every now and then," said Havelock, nodding toward where the animal had been. "At my house in Indianapolis, I only see feral cats and sewer rats."

I glanced at him as I pulled the car to a stop behind a Volvo station wagon parked in the driveway. "What kind of neighborhood do you live in?"

He chuckled as he opened his door. "Apparently a bad one."

I smiled a little and stepped out into the night. It had cooled off considerably from earlier that day. Something —a mouse or another rodent, likely—rustled the leaves to my right. I looked around, but I couldn't see Havelock's agents anywhere, which wasn't too unexpected. Every one of them wore black tactical vests and black pants. They blended into the night. It was nice knowing they had my back if anything happened.

"Doesn't look like anyone's been here for a while," said Havelock.

I nodded, but I wasn't sure that I agreed with him. There were dry, dead leaves and twigs randomly scattered across the driveway and on top of the pickup. The wind could have scattered the debris, but there was something wrong. I walked to the truck and ran my hand across the roof. My fingers came away with a thin layer of grit. It was an old car, and it certainly wasn't clean, but it didn't look abandoned, either.

"There's no pollen on the truck," I said, nodding to the woods around us. "There are a couple of pine trees out there. If this car had been here for as long as we're supposed to believe, it'd be covered in pollen as well as leaves."

Havelock reached to his waist and unholstered his weapon.

"You still want to go in?"

I thought for a moment and then nodded before walking toward the home. "If your team says the house is empty, I believe them. We're not going to go in through the doors, though. Too likely they're booby trapped."

Havelock agreed, so we started peering into windows with our flashlights. The house had some furniture, but no people in it. Though it didn't look it from the driveway, it was a surprisingly large place with lots of windows, all of which were locked and intact.

Unfortunately, I couldn't pick a window lock the way I could a deadbolt. We'd do some damage getting in, but the Bureau's insurance would pay for it.

I used the butt of my pistol to break a window in the laundry room and then gestured for Agent Havelock.

"After you," I said.

Havelock didn't hesitate to go through the window. I climbed through after him. Broken glass crunched beneath my feet. There were hookups for a washer and dryer along the wall to my right, and there was a thin layer of dust on the vinyl flooring. Nobody had been in this room for a while.

I unholstered my firearm and walked toward the door. The hallway was clear. A door to the left led to the garage—also empty—while the hallway to the right led to the kitchen, great room, and entryway. We swept the kitchen quickly. Almost all the cabinets were open and bare. Those that weren't open had a layer of dust on them as thick as the layer that had been on the floor. The pantry held a single box of Corn Flakes.

The dining room and entryway were both empty and clear, and I couldn't find any indication that Butler and his friends had wired the front door. It all left me wondering what the hell we were doing there.

Our team outside had cleared the woods, and by all accounts, the house was empty. I didn't know the first thing about Butler, but none of the people I had found in my investigation were stupid. Butler and his friends had brought us here for a reason, but for the life of me, I couldn't figure out what it was.

Havelock and I left the entryway and walked into the living room. There, we found a pair of couches and a coffee table. Curiously, there were a lot of papers on the table. Havelock knelt down and picked up a photograph, one of dozens spread across the table. It depicted Jacob Ganim at Nassir's farm. He wore a sweat-stained hoodie sweatshirt and jeans that were covered in a layer of dirt. Nassir and Qadi stood beside him. Both were similarly attired, and both were carrying shovels. Everyone was smiling.

"So now we know Butler and his friends were watching Jacob Ganim," said Havelock, returning the picture to the stack. "If they knew we were coming, why would they leave the pictures in the middle of the room? Why wouldn't they destroy them?"

I didn't know how to answer, so I looked away. Havelock and I were in the center of an open room. There were clear sightlines to the hill outside. That was when I realized why the bad guys hadn't destroyed them.

"Duck."

Almost the instant the words left my lips, the first shot came through the window. By then, it was too late. Havelock's blood splashed all over my face as he went down.

Chapter 36

The instant the shot rang out, Kamil Salib knew he had just killed a man. Life was a precious, sacred gift from God, and to take it without just cause was a sin punishable by an eternity in hell. Kamil hadn't murdered anyone, though. This was righteous.

"They're in the trees," shouted a voice beneath him.

Kamil had one job that evening: kill the detective and then escape. The pictures on the coffee table had been Hashim Bashear's idea. He knew how the police thought. He knew they would search the home, and he knew the pictures would draw their attention. Kamil's partner, Daniel, would provide as much cover as he could, but it was up to Kamil to do the job.

He lined up another shot, waiting for a head or other limb to pop up. He slowed his breathing and counted backwards from ten, trying to calm himself.

And then a round thwacked into a tree nearby. He flinched but didn't let himself panic. The FBI agents didn't know where he was exactly, but they were trying to find him. Everything had gone according to Bashear's plan. Like American soldiers overseas, the FBI agents came in with night-vision technology. It gave them a decided advantage after dark, an advantage that filled them with confidence.

It also made them predictable. Suspended in a black hunter's blind with foam insulation beneath him, he was a ghost able to wreak havoc in the material world.

Kamil held his breath as another shot rang out beneath him. This one thudded into a tree farther away than the first.

"Keep shooting, asshole," he whispered as softly as the wind rustled. "It just makes it easier for us to find you."

With each second that passed, Kamil's hands grew steadier, and his breath grew even more steady. He put his eye to the scope of his rifle again and waited. Though he was prepared to pull the trigger, he didn't need to shoot anyone. He just needed to keep the men inside the house contained long enough for the second part of Hashim's plan to start.

Special Agent Kaler sprinted through the woods toward the spot in which his supervisor and friend Ken Hanson should have been. At the same time, he keyed his microphone.

"Sound off. What's your status?"

"Unhurt," said Muniz. "I'm moving to higher ground."

"Nicholson?" asked Kaler.

"Unhurt as well," he said. "The shooter's near me, but I can't find him. He's in the tree somewhere. Have we got air support incoming yet?"

"Hanson had the sat phone," said Kaler. "I haven't

got reception on my cell. We can't stay here and wait for help. We've got to get back to the car."

"How'd we miss these guys?" asked Muniz. "We swept this area."

"I have no idea," said Kaler, still moving. "Keep your eyes open. You see anybody unfamiliar, light him up. With the bad guys above us, we are sitting ducks. We'll regroup at the car and use it as cover to get Rashid and Havelock out of the house."

"Agreed," said Muniz.

"On my way," said Nicholson.

Kaler took his hand off the switch on his radio and took a deep breath. The ground was uneven and rough, and he ran in a zigzag pattern from tree to tree for whatever cover he could get. Another shot rang out, and he dove to the ground at the base of an eastern white pine tree. The tree's needles wouldn't give him cover, but at least they concealed him.

"Anybody hit?"

"It was to the east," said Nicholson.

"I got him," said Muniz. "He's in a tree stand."

"Light his ass up."

Almost the moment the words left his lips, something thwacked into the ground at Kaler's feet. He stared at it for a moment, dumbfounded.

It was an arrow with a barbed tip.

Then another slammed into the ground at his feet. If the pine needles above him hadn't deflected it, that arrow might have killed him. Kaler skidded on the ground, to get to the other side of the tree and hopefully out of the shooter's reach.

No wonder they hadn't heard Hanson go down. He probably got shot with a bow and arrow. It seemed almost medieval.

Gunfire erupted to his east as Agent Muniz opened fire. Rounds from the agent's M4 carbine slammed into the tree stand, tearing it to bits. Within seconds, something heavy thudded to the ground.

"Splash one," said Muniz.

Kaler looked at the arrows on the ground. The angle from which they had come was approximately fifteen degrees from the vertical and to the northeast. Kaler raised his rifle and fired half a dozen shots in the approximate direction.

Then he ran as hard as he could in the opposite direction until he could put his back to an old oak tree.

"Who's firing?" asked Nicholson.

"I am," said Kaler. "He's northeast of my position in a tree. He's got a bow and arrow, and he's dangerous with it. You're not going to hear him coming. We need to get back to the car and call in air support."

"What do you want to do about Robin Hood?" asked Muniz.

Kaler took a deep breath. "We'll get a bird in the air and flush him out."

"Shit," I said, holding my hand over Agent Havelock's throat. Blood oozed between my fingers and down my wrists. Havelock croaked something but then choked as blood trickled out of his mouth. "Stop talking. You're making it worse."

Had someone not been shooting at us, I would have held a clean cloth to his throat and kept him immobilized until an ambulance could pick us up. If we stayed in the middle of that room, though, we were dead.

"We've got to move, and it's probably going to hurt. Sorry about this."

Havelock might have said something, but it came out as a choked gurgle, which meant he had fluid in his lungs. As a police officer, I had gone through some first-aid training, but not enough to deal with this. I grabbed him by the shoulders and manhandled him onto his belly. I didn't know if that would help get the blood out of his lungs, but with an active shooter targeting us, it was all I could do.

I crawled to what I thought was the relative safety of the kitchen, dragging him behind me. The FBI agent's blood made him slide easily over the hardwood floor. We weren't safe in the kitchen, but the windows were higher and smaller, limiting the shooter's view inside.

I sat Havelock up and leaned him against the cabinets as I ripped at his shirt. The fabric wasn't clean, but infection was the least of his worries at the moment. I held a bunch of cloth against the wound on his neck.

"Keep breathing," I said. "Come on, man."

For a brief moment, he flicked his eyes toward me and held my gaze. Then he reached up to my wrist. We stayed like that for thirty or forty seconds. With every beat of his heart, I could feel his blood soaking the fabric more and more. His eyes were distant, and he had an almost peaceful expression on his face. I didn't know what Havelock was seeing, but it wasn't me, and it wasn't this hateful house.

"Stay with me," I said, adjusting him to sit him up straighter and pressing the cloth harder against his throat. "You're going to be okay. Just keep breathing."

Gradually, I felt the grip on my wrist weaken. Then his hand dropped to his waist. The serene expression never left his face. A doctor could probably have explained exactly what was happening, but I didn't need an explanation. Havelock was dying. I kept the cloth pressed as hard against his neck as I could, but already his heartbeat began to grow weaker.

"Don't give up on me," I said. "You're getting out of here. I'm going to get you home."

I didn't know whether he understood me, but he blinked slowly. Then he looked at me. That serene, calm expression twisted into something violent. He gurgled and coughed blood. I rolled him onto his belly again, hoping the fluid would run out of his lungs. He coughed again, and then he stopped moving.

"No, no, no," I said, rolling him back over. His eyes were open, but they had no life in them at all. I put my hands together in the center of his chest and began a

CPR cycle. Unfortunately, that opened the wound on his neck even further, and blood began flowing out onto the floor again, covering it in a slick film. That same blood coated my arms nearly up to my elbows, but I kept going.

When I hit thirty compressions, I looked at him in the eye again. For a brief moment, I thought I caught a glimmer of something, but it might have been my imagination. I held my hand to his throat. He didn't have a pulse, so I began compressing his chest again.

"Come on, Kevin," I said. "Don't give up."

I got five compressions in before I heard the crack of a high-powered rifle. The window behind me shattered. Glass rained down on my back and head, and a round slammed into the floor to my right, shattering the porcelain tile.

"Shit."

I tried to duck, but the floor was so slick with blood that my limbs went out from under me. My body went flat, and my belly hit the floor. I didn't bother getting up that time. Instead, I crawled on all fours as fast as I could toward the hallway that led to the laundry room and garage. That didn't put me any closer to getting out of the house, but there weren't any windows for someone to shoot me through, either.

As I lay there catching my breath, someone outside shouted. Then I heard shots. They were higher-pitched than the rifle used to shoot Havelock, and they came in rapid succession. The FBI agents outside must have been firing back. I looked to Havelock's body.

"They're coming for us," I said. "I'm going to get you home."

I took a couple of deep breaths. And then, as I turned my head, I smelled it for the first time: smoke. My stomach contorted. This wasn't wood smoke from an abandoned campsite. This had a chemical undertone that seemed to coat my lungs, and it was growing stronger.

I shot my eyes around the hallway. Little light penetrated this part of the house, so I pulled out my cell phone and held it up, using it as a flashlight. A thick haze hung in the air. It seemed to be coming from a door near the garage.

I coughed into my shirt sleeve and hurried down the hall. Already, the air near the ceiling was growing thick, so I crouched low beneath the layer of smoke. The hallway seemed to grow warmer with every passing moment, and smoke began to burn my eyes. Even if I could put out a fire, I didn't know how much longer I could stay around that kind of environment.

When I reached the door, smoke billowed from beneath and around it. The knob burned my hand the moment I touched it. It was like something out of one of the campy horror movies my wife loved, only this one might actually kill me. I didn't bother opening the door. The burn on the palm of my hand told me everything I needed to know: This house was gone.

I coughed violently into my sleeve before looking up and down the hallway for an exit. A door led to the laundry room, but its window opened to the same side of the house as the front room. Even if I made it through the window without being shot, the nearest cover would have been at least ten yards away. I'd be cut down well before I made that.

The kitchen had windows on both the north and south side. The shooter wouldn't be able to get me if I went out the south-side window, but the landscape dropped off steeply. It was about a two-story drop. That was an option, but it might have left me with a broken leg in the middle of a gunfight in some very deep woods.

The garage opened to the west. So far, no shots had come from that direction, but that didn't mean I'd be safe there. Still, it was probably my best bet to survive. I sprinted to the kitchen but stopped before going more than a foot or two inside. Smoke roiled near the ceiling. The fire was spreading beneath me even as I hesitated. Havelock's blood had spread around him so that it gave the floor a thin reddish-brown sheen. Tempered glass crunched beneath my feet.

Agent Havelock and I weren't friends, but I respected him. Character mattered to me, and he had died trying to keep other people safe. He didn't deserve to die in that house, and he didn't deserve to be left behind as I escaped.

And yet, there wasn't a damn thing I could do about it.

The house was burning around me, and a shooter stalked us from outside. I couldn't expose myself to grab a dead man. I had to focus on the living, and that meant getting the hell out of there while I could.

"I'm sorry," I said for the second time that night.

I watched for another moment and began to feel the heat beneath me. The floor joists were probably catching now. I didn't have time to hesitate. I kept my head down and ran toward the garage.

The homeowner had evidently used the room for storage because there were boxes stacked throughout the space. I didn't expect the garage door opener to work, but I hit the button beside the back door anyway. As expected, nothing happened, so I pushed boxes out of the way and pulled the manual release clamp.

The door's sharp metal edges bit in the burned palm of my right hand as I lifted it. Smoke wafted around me as I muscled the door open. The night was quiet outside. If I could get to my car, I could get out of there and get to somewhere safe. Behind me, the house had started crackling and popping as wood burned.

I darted forward, crouching low and staying in the shadows wherever possible. When I reached my car, I started to open the door but stopped when I caught movement in my peripheral vision. There was a man to my right. He had his back to a tree, and his left hand was cocked back near his cheek. I blinked twice, sure my eyes were deceiving me.

He had a freaking bow and arrow.

"Police officer," I yelled, unholstering my firearm and raising the barrel toward him. "Drop your weapon."

Immediately, gunfire rang out from my left. Tree

bark near the archer exploded as rounds thwacked into it. The archer ducked low but didn't take his eyes from his target. He was young and had brown skin. He could have been in high school. I shook my head and kept my weapon pointed at him.

He was about twenty-five yards away, which I presumed was well within the reach of a competent archer. At a firing range, I could hit a man-sized target nine out of ten times at that range. It was a lot harder in the field with someone shooting back, but this guy's weapon was about four hundred years out of date. I had him dead to rights.

"Drop your weapon now."

He slowly pivoted toward me.

"Don't do this," I called, taking a step forward. A fresh volley of shots thudded into the tree behind which the archer stood. He adjusted his stance. No one had ever pointed a bow and arrow at me like that before, but I recognized a man taking aim at me when I saw it.

I didn't let him loose an arrow.

The sound of my firearm reverberated through the trees around me as I squeezed the trigger. The first shot missed. The second clipped his arm. Somehow he kept his bow up. There was a grimace on his face. With each shot, I found myself praying that he'd just go down. He didn't, though. I fired again, and then again—seven shots in total—closing the distance between us with each shot. When he finally fell, I was no more than thirty feet from him.

"Target down," called a voice from the woods to my left. "We're clear."

I slipped my firearm into the holster on my belt and turned around as something inside the house crashed. There were flames in the windows now. I walked to the archer and found a black-clad FBI agent already leaning over him, feeling the archer's neck for a pulse.

"It was a good shoot," he said without looking at me. "Where's Agent Havelock?"

My voice caught in my throat. Whether that was from the smoke I had inhaled or something else, I didn't know. I coughed, though, to clear it.

"He was shot in the neck. He didn't make it, and I couldn't get him out."

The agent looked at me, then. He stood quickly.

"Jesus, you're covered in blood. You shot?"

"No, this is Havelock's blood," I said. I drew in a breath and felt the adrenaline begin to wane. My hands started trembling, and I felt cold. "I tried to keep him alive. It didn't work. Where's your team?"

The agent drew in a breath. "I'm it."

Meaning, we had lost a lot of FBI agents tonight. If I had heard him say that at any other time, I probably would have had some kind of emotional reaction. Now, though, he might as well have told me he just searched for new car insurance. I felt empty.

"I'm sorry."

"Me, too," he said, standing over the body and allowing me to have a good look at the man I had shot.

The moment I saw his face, I felt my shoulders drop. I swore and ran a hand through my hair.

"Don't feel bad for this guy. He took out three FBI agents tonight. He got what was coming to him."

"I'm not mad because I shot him," I said. "I'm mad I didn't get to question him. He drove the getaway car this afternoon for a kid who murdered eight people in Indianapolis."

Chapter 37

Since neither of our cell phones worked out there, we had to search the woods for Agent Hanson's body and his satellite phone. It didn't take long. Hanson had an arrow in his back, which, by its placement, had probably pierced his lung. I couldn't remember having worked a murder involving a bow and arrow, but I had worked a lot of murders involving shots to the chest. Even if we had gotten to him right away, we were so far from a major hospital that he probably would have died on the way.

The agent I was with—Scott Kaler—used Hanson's satellite phone to call for help. We had a medical helicopter hovering over us in ten minutes and an FBI helicopter overhead very shortly thereafter. The Bureau helicopter helped us pinpoint the location of the other two tactical officers who had died. One had been killed by a bow and arrow, while the second had been shot. We sent the medical helicopter away without it having to land. The dead didn't need their services.

The entire evening felt surreal. The house continued to burn, but thankfully, the nearest trees were far enough away that they didn't catch fire. I moved the Mustang I had borrowed so its gas tank wouldn't heat up and explode, and then I sat on the hood while the first responders arrived.

I didn't know Agent Havelock well. I never even knew whether he had a family or a significant other. I knew him only as an FBI agent willing to do whatever it took to get his job done. He believed in his agency, though, and he believed in the men and women who worked for him. For now, the best way I could honor his death was to close the case we'd started. Knowing the little I did about him, I thought that would be what he wanted.

When the FBI arrived, it came in force, bringing generators, powerful lights, dozens of agents, and a portable command truck from which Havelock's deputy could oversee the investigation. The moment they saw me, their forensic technicians took my blood-soaked shirt, jacket, and pants as evidence and gave me a pair of navy blue sweatpants and matching sweatshirt.

After that, I mostly sat and thought.

It would take the FBI a while to get up and running. From what I understood, Agent Havelock had kept our investigation compartmentalized so that only people directly involved with it knew about it. Combined with his disagreement with his own agency's counterterrorism division, this could get ugly very quickly. I was content to stay out of it. My department had enough office intrigue; I didn't need to involve myself in the Bureau's office politics.

I stayed at the crime scene almost four hours and led agents from the FBI's Office of Professional Responsibility through everything Havelock and I had done. They listened to what I had to say, but they reserved judgment and said very little. Even when staying silent, though, their body language spoke volumes about their thoughts: Havelock and I had screwed up.

If he had lived, most of the scrutiny would have fallen on Havelock's shoulders. With his death, the blame would fall on a lot of people.

Eventually, Havelock's deputy, the second-most powerful special agent in the Indianapolis field office, walked to me. I was sitting inside my borrowed Mustang, watching the team work. He nodded to me, and I got out of the car. The agent was probably in his early forties and had neat brown hair parted on the left side, dark blue eyes, and slightly inset cheeks His hands were in the pockets of a dark blue windbreaker. He was taller than me and quite a bit larger. He looked like a professional football player approaching middle age.

"Lieutenant Rashid," he said, holding out his hand. When I reached out to shake it, he squeezed hard and refused to let go. I had to squeeze back to keep my knuckles from cracking. "I'm Special Agent Garret Russel. Kevin Havelock was a friend of mine. He spoke highly of you."

"He was a good man," I said, trying to pull my hand back. The agent didn't release his grip.

"He was my kid's godfather and the best man in my wedding," said Russel, finally dropping my hand. His eyes were hard and angry as they stared into mine. "I just thought you should know."

"I'm very sorry for your loss."

He looked down and then stepped closer to me.

"You were his partner on this operation. You left him in there."

"There was nothing I could—"

"Shut up," he said, interrupting me. I didn't want a fight, so I let him talk. "Kevin was my friend, and you let him die. I don't give a shit about your excuses. You let my friend die. That's it. That's all I've got to say to you. Now get out of here before I do something you'll regret."

I slowly took a step back and nodded. Before I could get in my car, he cleared his throat.

"To be clear, you're off this case, and your consulting position within the FBI is terminated as of this moment."

"I understand," I said.

"If you keep investigating, I'll arrest you for obstruction of justice," he said. He leaned into me and lowered his voice. "And if I find out you were negligent or complicit in my friend's death, you won't like what'll happen to you. Is that clear?"

I gritted my teeth and balled my hands into fists before speaking.

"You're pissed. I get that. You have every right to be pissed," I said, standing straighter and holding my ground. "That doesn't give you a right to threaten me. Agent Havelock died standing right beside me. I wish it hadn't happened. Agent Havelock died doing his job, though. It could have very easily have been me. I'm sorry he's gone, but his death is not my fault."

His eyes looked at me up and down. "We'll see. Now get out of here. If I need you, the US Attorney's Office will call you."

I wanted to tell him off, but that wouldn't help anybody. Hopefully, he'd calm down and realize that I had done what I could to help Havelock. The operation had gone sideways. We should have gone in with a bigger team, we should have brought a helicopter to the site… we should have done a number of things differently. The bottom line was, though, that we had done the best we could with the information we had. If Agent Russel refused to acknowledge that, he was at fault.

I got back in my car and drove east toward the city before pulling into a rest stop near Plainfield. At that time in the morning, there were a few long-haul truckers sleeping but very few cars. The FBI may have wanted me off this case, but this wasn't just their case now. We had a lot of dead people in Indianapolis at Kim Peterson's house, and we needed to find out who killed them before anyone else died. If I happened to find Jacob Ganim's murderer along the way, so be it.

I called my boss at IMPD. Captain Mike Bowers answered after a few rings. His voice was distant and sleepy.

"Ash," he said. "It's five in the morning. What do you want?"

"Anybody at the Bureau call you recently?"

He sighed and lowered his voice. "What'd you do?"

"Kevin Havelock is dead. A couple other agents I didn't know died as well. We were ambushed while searching a house early this morning."

Bowers didn't say anything, but I heard him exhale a long, slow breath.

"You all right?"

"I made it through okay," I said. "I've been removed from the investigation we were working, but I've got information we need to move on."

"Did you share it with the FBI?"

"They're not interested in talking to me right now, which is why I need you to call their liaison. Kevin Havelock and I were working an antiterrorism case. He was convinced something bad was coming our way. I don't know what's going to happen, but he was right. We've got a lot of people dead already, and we're going to have more unless we act."

Bowers paused.

"You're going to have to be a little more specific than that."

"The guys who killed Agent Havelock stole assault weapons, pistols, blasting caps, and detonators from an idiot who shouldn't have had them in the first place. I don't know what they're doing, but the Brown County Sheriff's Department has a suspect in custody who does. I need him brought to Indianapolis and put in a box. I'll interrogate him as soon as I can."

Bowers inhaled deeply. "Have your suspects made specific threats?"

"We found a warehouse by the airport in which they made explosives. I think they're tied to the terror group who attacked Westbrook Elementary and the president.

They like spectacles, and we've got the Indy 500 in a couple of hours. We need to move."

"Christ in a handbasket," said Bowers. He paused. "Are you sure about this? Because if you're wrong, we're all going to look like idiots."

"If I'm wrong, yeah, we'll look like idiots. But if I'm right and we don't do anything, our image will be the last of our concerns."

Bowers sighed. When he spoke, his voice sounded more resigned than angry.

"All right. We've got almost a thousand officers assigned to the Speedway, but I'll call the chief and see whether we can get some more. I'll also call Homeland Security for assistance and the Brown County Sheriff's Department about a prisoner transfer."

"We need this guy as quickly as possible. Tell them to go lights and sirens."

Bowers grunted. "I have done this thing a time or two, Ash, but I appreciate your enthusiasm."

"Yeah, sorry. I know," I said, softening my voice. "Thank you. I'm on my way downtown."

He grunted again and hung up. I put my car in gear and started driving south toward downtown. Years ago, I had had a desk in the homicide unit's bullpen in the City-County Building. After being promoted to lieutenant and given command of the major case unit, I had needed an actual office. Unfortunately, my department didn't have the space, so it borrowed a storage unit from the prosecutor's office and put a desk inside it for me. To call it a shithole would have been insulting to public restrooms everywhere, but it was home away from home. In just a couple of hours, the entire city would turn into a veritable parking lot as race fans made their way to the Motor Speedway, but that early on a Sunday morning, it was passable. I parked in the secured lot near my building, took the elevator to my floor, and sat down at my desk.

Television detectives oftentimes turned interrogations into battles of wits in which they tricked suspects into saying things against their interests. Real life wasn't like that. Interrogations were about leverage and using that leverage to show a suspect that confessing was in his best interest—even if it never was. It was all theatrics and lies, and I was pretty good at it.

This case was going to be a little different. Butler al-Ghamdi was fifteen years old. Nassir hadn't introduced me to him, but I thought I had met him in Kim Peterson's basement, right before he hit me in the face with a folding chair and escaped in a Toyota Camry. Even if he hadn't committed those murders, he had involved himself in a conspiracy to murder four FBI agents. We had this guy dead to rights. He'd die in prison.

And it wouldn't matter to him.

I had worked a lot of murders involving teenage shooters under the influence of older people. Just three or four years ago, I picked up a fourteen-year-old boy who had murdered a seventeen-year-old girl and her nineteen-year-old brother. He had never seen either of them before, but he hid behind some trash cans at their house and then shot them both as they came home from the grocery store with their grandmother.

We found the murder weapon within moments of arriving at the scene, and we arrested the kid an hour later based on the grandmother's ID. Eventually, we found the shooter's footprints and fingerprints at the scene, we found gunpowder residue on his hands and clothes, and we got video footage of him at a convenience store half a block from the shooting five minutes after the shooting. We even had multiple eyewitnesses in nearby houses ready to testify that they saw the shooter running from the crime scene. The case wasn't airtight, but it was close.

And yet, the kid refused to tell us why he did it.

The prosecutor's office offered him a sweetheart deal: If he rolled over on the shot-caller, we'd charge him as a juvenile. He'd spend the next six years in a facility for juveniles, but he'd get out on his twenty-first birthday with a high school diploma and a potential future. Instead of taking that deal, he spat in our faces and said he'd never talk. The prosecutors charged him as an adult, took him to trial, and won. He was sentenced to life without the possibility of parole.

That kid will never again see the sun set as a free man. He'll never get married, have children, have a career, or do any of the things that make life worth living. What's more, he knew he could avoid that future if he just told us who gave him the order to kill those two teenagers. He refused, though. He thought it was more important to protect his boss than to protect himself. When he grew up and realized what he had lost, I was pretty sure he'd regret his mistake and wish he could do it over again. It'd be too late, though.

I didn't know Butler al-Ghamdi, but I knew kids like him. He believed in a cause and was willing to forfeit his life for that cause. Given time, I had little doubt he'd realize he had made a mistake, but I didn't have time to give him. I needed him to talk now, which meant I needed a different kind of leverage on him than I'd typically get on a suspect.

I needed him to hurt.

Butler al-Ghamdi was from Mount Vernon, Illinois, so I looked up their police department on my computer and gave them a call. My request was odd, but the watch commander agreed to it. It was all I could ask for.

After my phone call, I locked my office and walked to the City-County Building, where IMPD had its official headquarters. Thousands of people worked in that building, so it took a while to get an elevator up to Captain Bowers's floor. There, I found him in his palatial office, talking to somebody on the phone. He put his hand over the receiver.

"Your suspect's on his way. Get a cup of coffee, go to the conference room, and have a seat. I've got morning briefings, but somebody will let you know when al-Ghamdi gets here."

Bowers returned his attention to his phone call, so I did as he asked. The sun had risen about halfway in the sky, filling the conference room with morning light. I pulled a chair to the window and drank my coffee.

My shoulders and chest felt heavy, and the muscles in my legs and arms ached. I hadn't realized until that moment how tired I was. I sipped my coffee. Kevin Havelock had looked tired at the end, too. I closed my eyes and said a prayer for his family. Before I could finish, my phone beeped, signaling an incoming text message.

I fished it out of my pocket and found a picture of two young girls in the backseat of a squad car. They wore pajamas, and they looked scared. Then I got another text and another picture. The second picture showed a man and a woman sitting side by side in the back of another cruiser. Zip ties secured their hands in front of them. The woman wore hijab and a loose-fitting blouse and dress while the man wore jeans and a sweater. Neither looked at the camera, but both had tears on their cheeks.

I took my phone to the copy room and used a computer there to print them out. They were a little blurry, but they'd work just fine. I shoved them in a manila envelope. Captain Bowers walked into the conference room just as I was returning to let me know Butler al-Ghamdi had arrived. That meant it was showtime.

I took my pictures to the homicide unit's office suite and found the correct interrogation booth. Butler was already seated at the room's only table. He had his head in his arms and looked as if he were trying to sleep. A lot of suspects did that to try to show me how cool and collected they were. A lot of those same suspects left that room with shackles on their wrists and ankles and tears on their cheeks. It didn't impress me much.

I walked in and cleared my throat.

"Wake up, sleeping beauty," I said, pulling a metal folding chair out from beneath the table. Butler slowly raised his head. His eyes were red and puffy, and his hair was mussed. He smirked at me. I had only gotten a quick look at him at Kim Peterson's house, but I recognized him. It would take some work before we had enough evidence for trial, but my eyewitness account alone would have been enough to charge him with multiple homicides.

"Did you search that cabin?" he asked.

"Yeah," I said, nodding. "We met your friends there. Both are dead. Since you set me up, we'll be charging you with felony homicide for that. I'm pretty sure we'll be charging you with the murders of everyone at Kim Peterson's house as well."

His smirk grew. "I'm fifteen. I'll be out on my twenty-first birthday."

"That's possible," I said, nodding and sitting down. "It's also possible you'll be charged as an adult and sentenced to multiple life sentences. Considering your actions led to the deaths of several law enforcement officers, I wouldn't make too many long-term plans if I were you."

He crossed his arms. "I'm ready for that."

"I know," I said, nodding. "You're a real badass."

He didn't respond except to look away. I gave him a

moment to think. Finally, he looked at me and shrugged.

"Seems like you've got your answer," he said.

"I didn't ask a question."

He scoffed and shook his head. Again, I gave him a moment to think. Then I cleared my throat as he looked at me again.

"How do you like your family?"

He didn't say anything, but he did furrow his brow, clearly confused.

"You're the big brother, right?" I asked. "You've got two younger sisters. One of them has braces. The other likes to wear My Little Pony pajamas. Do you like them?"

"My family is none of your business," he said, shifting and leaning back, probably in an attempt to look cool. I merely nodded.

"You love your mom and dad?"

He narrowed his eyes at me, but then he laughed and sat a little straighter.

"That's clever," he said. "You gonna tell me I'm not being a good role model to my sisters. Is that it? Are you going to tell me I'm bringing shame on my parents? Because I don't care."

"No," I said, lowering my voice. "I'm asking whether you love them."

He didn't say anything. Instead, he shook his head and smirked again. I glanced up to a bubble suspended from the ceiling.

"The surveillance cameras and microphones are off," I said. "You don't have to worry about anything you say in this room getting out. Everybody will know you're still a tough guy. Just tell me: Do you love your family?"

He didn't say anything for about a minute. I didn't push. Finally, he snorted and nodded.

"Yeah. I love my family. How's that make you feel?"

I smiled, but I didn't let it reach my eyes.

"I'm glad. I've got an older sister, and I think the world of her. There's no relationship in the world like the relationship between siblings." Before he could respond, I cleared my throat. "The FBI and I aren't sure what exactly is going on, but we know you and your friends robbed Nassir Hadad's camp of weapons and ammunition. We know you and your friends were building explosive devices in a warehouse near the airport. We also know you set us up in an ambush in which your friends and numerous agents died. We think you're planning some kind of attack. You want to tell me about that?"

"There is no God but God, and Muhammed is the messenger of God."

"I'm glad we've got that sorted out," I said. "The FBI has received nonspecific intelligence that an attack is forthcoming. You're involved. What's going on?"

He started repeating the *Shahada*. I didn't plan to sit through it a second time, so I opened the envelope in front of him and then showed him the photos. He stopped speaking midsentence.

"What are you doing with my family?" he asked.

"Officially, we're bringing them to town to talk to you," I said, lying through my teeth. "The station psychologist thinks it might make you more likely to admit what you've done if you can talk to people you trust first. Frankly, though, you're never going to talk. I know it, and you know it."

He said nothing, so I leaned forward, bringing our faces to within a few inches of one another.

"You killed a friend of mine. I'm bringing your family into town because I know your friends are planning an attack. I'm going to make sure it hurts you as much as it hurts everyone else."

His face went pale. "What are you talking about?"

I leaned back and crossed my arms.

"The Indy 500 starts at a little after eleven. The track and stands will be pretty safe because there are bomb-sniffing dogs and police officers everywhere. What's more, everyone who goes through the gate and every bag and cooler they carry will be hand-searched by police officers. The gates themselves, though, are a bottleneck. Three hundred thousand people started lining up at six this morning to go through those gates. They'll wait for hours. Many of them will have purses, coolers, backpacks, handbags, you name it. We won't have any idea what any of those people are carrying until we search them. For all we know, they could be carrying pipe bombs and assault rifles."

He drew in a breath. "So?"

"Here's what I think is going to happen: You and your friends are going to attack the 500. You're smart guys, so you know you won't get past security with explosives or guns. You don't need to, though.

"You'll attack the people waiting outside. Maybe you'll have coolers full of explosives, maybe you'll just drive a truck into a crowd, killing everyone in your way. Either way, you'll kill a couple thousand people on national TV, you'll terrify a country that loves major sporting events, and you might even surpass September 11th as the deadliest terror attack perpetrated on American soil. There's not a lot we can do to stop it, either, short of cancelling the race."

He seemed to think for a moment, but then he started smirking.

"Scared yet?"

"Honestly?" I asked. He nodded. "I'm terrified, but at least I won't be alone. Your mom's going to be at the north gate. Your dad will be at the south gate. Your sisters will be at the east and west gates. If a cooler goes boom in that crowd, your family's going to feel the shrapnel."

The smirk left his face. Then he shook his head and leaned back.

"You can't do that. They're my family. You're going to get them killed."

"That's the idea," I said, hating myself for saying it even as the words left my lips. I smiled and stood up. "Have a good one."

He called me a motherfucker as I stood. Time wasn't on my side, but I needed to break through his anger and force him to come to grips with everything he'd lose if he allowed his friends to carry out an attack. I needed him, in other words, to believe that I was such a cold-hearted bastard that I'd let children die just to make myself feel a little better.

So I pulled the door shut without another word and let it lock behind me. He screamed even harder, but the walls mostly muffled the sound. Since I didn't know when he'd come to his senses, I grabbed a cup of coffee in the break room and then sat in front of a computer monitor to watch.

For the first few minutes, he just screamed. Then he gave the door the finger. After that, he kicked over the folding chair opposite him. It clattered to the wall. He went on like that for about an hour before he put his head down and started crying.

That's what I had been waiting for.

I walked back into the room. When he looked up from the table, his eyes were tinged with red, and there were tears on his cheeks.

"I hate you."

"I'm not overly fond of me at the moment, either," I said. "What's it going to be? You risk letting your sisters die, or do you want to tell me what's going on?"

He held his hands in front of him and closed his eyes. "I don't know what's going on."

I shook my head and started to leave the room without saying anything, but he stood quickly.

"Wait. I don't know what's going on, but they went to Nassir Hadad's camp this morning. They had to do something there. You've been there. You know where it is. I bet they're there right now. Once that sheriff picked me up, Nassir was alone."

"Is Nassir involved?"

"No," he said. "Nassir's an idiot who thinks he can change the world by being nice to people. We were using him."

"Who do you mean by we?" I asked.

"Hashim Bashear and the men who work for him. That's all I know. Hashim Bashear. That's the man you need to look for."

I blinked a couple of times and then crossed my arms. "Last time you suggested I go somewhere, I got shot at, and then the house I was in burned to the ground. I'm going to need a guarantee that I won't die this time. I'm going to take your mom. If I get shot at, at least I'll have a human shield."

"Nobody's going to shoot at you," he said, shaking his head. "They won't know you're coming. They may not even be there anymore. They didn't tell me what they were doing. I was supposed to get caught. The less I knew, the less I could say."

It made sense, so I nodded. "All right. I'll check out the camp. Thank you."

"So you're going to keep my mom safe, right? I mean, you're going to let her go home once you check out the camp?"

I stopped and looked at him. He had tears in his eyes again as he begged me.

"Your family was never in any danger. Right after the

Mount Vernon police took that picture, everybody went home."

For a moment, he just stared at me. Then his serious, worried expression lifted, and anger took its place. He started screaming that I was a motherfucker again. Technically, as a father of two children, I supposed it was true, so I didn't take offense. I shut the door with him screaming behind me. In the hallway, I called Captain Bowers.

"Mike, it's Ash. I need you to call the state police and get their southeastern emergency response team together. I know where the bad guys are."

Chapter 38

Captain Bowers and I left within five minutes of al-Ghamdi's admission. Though we had the authority to make arrests anywhere within the state of Indiana, as a practical matter, we stayed in Indianapolis. If a suspect left the city, we worked with the Indiana State Police or whatever local law enforcement agency had jurisdiction in our suspect's location. In this case, with Nassir's camp a good sixty miles from the city, we called the Brown County Sheriff's Department, who then called the Indiana State Police for assistance. That left us as bystanders.

The first call came in while Bowers and I were on the interstate heading south. We had been in the car for almost an hour, but with race traffic already heavy, we had barely left the city. I was driving, while Bowers sat in the passenger seat of his department-issued SUV. Bowers answered and put the phone on speaker and set it on the console between our seats.

"This is Captain Mike Bowers with IMPD. I'm with Lieutenant Rashid. We got stuck in traffic, so we're about fifty miles north of you. What's going on?"

"Good to hear from you, Captain. This is Colonel Adrian Holtz with ISP. This is a courtesy call to let you know that we've got search warrants in hand, and we're about to hit the camp. We've got forty-eight officers and two aircraft incoming. If you were a little closer, I could ask them to postpone until you arrive, but I don't think we can keep our birds in the air long enough for you to get here."

"Go when you're ready," I said. "There are buildings all over the property, and you're going to have to search all of them. You need to be careful of a large garage on the northwest side of the camp. It looks like a pole barn, but the walls are thick concrete covered in aluminum siding. There's a storm cellar and another secure room in the basement. If you've got bad guys on the premises, that's where I'd look for them. Other buildings have much more standard construction."

The colonel paused for a moment. "Is this Lieutenant Rashid?"

"It is, yeah," I said, taking my eyes off the road for just a moment to glance down.

"Any other threats I should be aware of?"

He couldn't see me, but I shook my head. "Not that I know of."

The colonel paused again. I thought I heard the click of keys for a brief moment.

"Okay, gentlemen," he said. "We'll be assaulting the location shortly and will take anyone we find into custody. We'll be in touch."

Bower wished him good hunting before hanging up. I drove in silence for another few minutes before he looked at me.

"Still think your brother-in-law is innocent in all this?"

I started to say yes, but then I hesitated. "I hope so, but I don't know. Butler al-Ghamdi said he was an idiot and that everyone was using him, but I've never known my brother-in-law to be stupid. Aside from that, of all the people in the world, why did they pick him?"

Bowers shrugged. "You said he was monitoring kids online. Maybe they were monitoring him, too, and found an easy mark."

I raised my eyebrows and nodded. "It's possible, but I can't help but feel that I'm missing some connection."

Bowers grunted. "If there's a connection, we'll find it. First, though, we need to focus on shutting this down."

I agreed, and we drove for another half hour before taking the exit for Columbus, Indiana and heading west toward Nassir's camp. Within ten minutes, cell reception was intermittent at best on the narrow, hilly back roads. Within fifteen, we had no reception at all. I had expected that. Eventually, we turned onto the small side road that led to Nassir's camp. A pair of state police cruisers guarded the gate. I flashed the lights hidden in our SUV's grill and rolled down my window as a uniformed officer walked toward us.

"I'm Lieutenant Ash Rashid. Beside me is Captain Mike Bowers of the Indianapolis Metro Police Department. Colonel Holtz inside?"

"Yeah," said the officer, taking a step back and pointing further into the compound. "He's at the big building. Just follow the drive. You'll find it."

I nodded and started to lift my foot off the brake but

then pressed down again before the big car could move.

"You guys make it out okay?"

The officer nodded and closed his eyes before drawing in a quick breath.

"We did, but we found a body."

"Oh?" I asked, raising my eyebrows. My heart began to pound against the bones of my chest. "What'd he look like?"

"I didn't see him," said the officer, taking a step back. "Heard he had dark skin and black hair, though."

I nodded and pressed my foot on the accelerator. Bowers put a hand on my shoulder as gravel hit the undercarriage of the car and sprayed behind us.

"Easy there, Ash," he said. "They found somebody, but it doesn't mean it's your brother-in-law."

I took my foot off the gas.

"I've seen enough people die lately," I said. "I'm getting tired of this."

"It's almost over," said Bowers, taking his hand off my shoulder and pointing ahead of us to a row of marked state police cruisers, SWAT tactical vehicles, and marked state police SUVs on the lawn. "Let's park and find out what's going on."

I nodded and parked at the end of the row of vehicles and then clipped my badge to the neck of my sweatshirt so everybody could see it. The sweatpants the Bureau forensic technicians had given me when they took my clothes at the cabin didn't have belt loops, but I wore a belt anyway. Primarily, it kept my firearm at arm's reach.

Combined with the two days of growth on my chin and the fact that I hadn't slept in almost forty-eight hours, I looked like a hobo with a badge, but I didn't care. This case had gone on long enough.

A uniformed patrolman started walking toward us the moment Bowers and I got out of our car. He was taller than me but rail thin. As he started to hold up a hand to stop us, I pointed to my badge and walked past him.

"There are two officers at the front gate," I said. "You think they would have let me pass if I wasn't expected?"

The patrolman stammered a response but didn't try to impede me further. Bowers said something to him, but I wasn't paying attention. My focus was on Nassir. He and his friends had certainly committed crimes—you can't just stockpile explosive devices and firearms you confiscated from troubled teenagers—but none of those crimes warranted the death penalty. He was trying to do the right thing. Maybe he was an idiot, but he didn't deserve to die.

The closer I got to the building, the lighter my feet seemed to become. Once I saw people inside, I couldn't stop myself from running. When I arrived at the clubhouse, two uniformed police officers caught me on the porch.

"Whoa, buddy," said one. "What's going on?"

I drew in a deep breath, nodding to the screen door ahead of me. "I'm Lieutenant Ash Rashid. I need to see the body."

A third figure—this one wearing a colonel's silver eagle on his collar—came out of the building. He nodded to his troopers, and they let go of my arms. He looked at me up and down.

"Are you sure you're all right, Lieutenant?"

"I haven't slept in a while, but I'm fine. Have you identified the body yet?"

"No," said the colonel, shaking his head. He looked over my shoulder. "Are you Captain Bowers?"

I turned so Bowers was to my left and the colonel was to my right. Bowers nodded.

"Yeah. Lieutenant Rashid is anxious to see the body. It might be his brother-in-law."

Colonel Holtz took a step back and gestured toward the door. "By all means, go in. Don't touch anything. You know the drill."

I put my hands in my pockets so I wouldn't accidentally touch anything and walked past the officers into the clubhouse. A breeze blew through the windows. A man and a woman stood in the center of the room. The woman wore black pants and a black blazer, while her partner wore dark jeans and a white long-sleeved shirt. They turned as I walked in.

I didn't know either of them, but they both wore detective badges on lanyards around their necks. I nodded a hello to each of them.

"I'm Lieutenant Ash Rashid with IMPD. I might be able to identify your body."

The man nodded and took a step back. I stepped forward, feeling my gut contort. The police officer at the gate was right. The victim was an Arab man, but it wasn't Nassir. This was Omar Nawaz. He wore a beige *thobe* beneath a dark brown sport coat. His legs were tucked beneath him as if he had been kneeling when he died. A single gunshot wound marred his forehead. It was a small-caliber round with just enough power to penetrate the frontal bones of his skull but not enough to blow out the back. The round would have ricocheted off the bones of his skull, tearing his brain apart.

This was an execution.

I saw all that at a glance as my mind slammed pieces together. Nassir barely knew Omar. He hadn't come out there to build that summer camp. None of the men in Nassir's group attended Omar's mosque as far as I knew. He had no reason to be at that camp, and yet here he was.

It was right in front of my face. I should have seen it. Ganim had a dozen or more surveillance pictures in his basement, and Omar was in every single one. I had thought Ganim was interested in the women, but they weren't his target at all; that was all Omar. He wasn't some do-gooder out to help Syrian refugees; he was one of the villains, and he had hid right in front of me.

I didn't know who the bad guys were, but he was working with him. That's how Butler and his friends found Kim Peterson's house. Omar had led them right there. Now, his former partners had killed him because he was a loose end.

"Lieutenant?" asked the female detective. I felt my nostrils flare as I drew in a breath.

"Your victim is Omar Nawaz. He's the imam of a mosque on the near-east side of Indianapolis. He's the only person you found on the property?"

"Yeah," said the male detective. "We searched every building as best we can tell."

"Did you search the garage to the northwest?"

He nodded. "It was empty."

"Even the storm cellar?"

The two detectives looked to one another.

"There's a storm cellar?" asked the female.

Instead of answering, I left the building and began running northwest. A couple of people followed, but I didn't pay much attention. The building was just a couple hundred yards away, so it didn't take long to reach. All of its doors were open, but no law enforcement officers had stayed after searching it. Like the detective in the clubhouse said, though, it was empty. The stack of fertilizer it had once held was gone.

I looked over my shoulder. Captain Bowers and the two state police detectives had followed. More uniformed officers followed at a leisurely pace just down the hill.

"Mike, walk around the building and see whether the tank of diesel's empty," I said. Bowers nodded and disappeared while I looked at the two detectives and then pointed to one of the garage stalls. "There used to be a pallet full of fertilizer there. It was a couple thousand pounds at least. There should be an invoice in the office detailing how much exactly."

"Okay," said the male detective, drawing the syllable out as if he were confused. "This is farm country. Why do we care about fertilizer?"

"Because when you mix diesel and ammonium nitrate fertilizer, it creates a very powerful explosive," I said, speaking slowly. "You're working an antiterrorism case, and some very bad people just stole the ingredients for a very big bomb."

He held up his hands and started taking a step back. "If this is a terrorism case, shouldn't the FBI be involved?"

"They are involved," said Bowers. "They're working another end of the investigation. Why don't you go back to Mr. Nawaz's body and supervise the investigation there? We'll call you if we need anything."

The two detectives hesitated but then left. Bowers turned to me.

"So what now?"

"We find Nassir," I said, walking around the building until I came to a pair of doors that led to the storm cellar. There wasn't a lock, so I simply pulled them open and walked down the concrete steps. The cellar was dark, so I held up my phone as a torch. It was a large, open space maybe forty feet by forty feet. Concrete columns and steel beams held the ceiling up about eight feet above my head. Had the worst come to pass, Nassir and his crew could have fit a lot of people down there in a tornado.

Nassir had said their armory was connected to this

storm cellar, so I walked to the nearest wall and ran my hand across the concrete, looking for a seam or hidden door. I found one behind some steel shelving along the wall directly opposite the entrance.

Bowers and I dragged the metal structure away, and I ran my hand along the concrete for a handle or some other device to open it. Fortunately, the door didn't need a handle. All I had to do was push on it.

The instant the door opened, nearly blinding light filled the cellar. I squinted into the newly uncovered room. Four bare light bulbs in fixtures along the ceiling illuminated the space. It was about half the size of the storm cellar, and along the exterior walls, there were metal shelving units similar to the ones Bowers and I had moved a moment earlier. There was a body on the ground.

"It's Nassir," I said, running inside and then kneeling beside him to feel his throat for a pulse. It was strong and regular, and his breath seemed unobstructed. He lay on his back as if he had been put there. He had a bruise the size of a grapefruit on his temple and forehead, but there was no blood on the ground. He was hurt, but not mortally. Clearly, they had clubbed him with something, maybe the butt of a rifle. Even if he wasn't bleeding externally, we needed to get him to the hospital for a CT scan to make sure his brain wasn't bleeding.

I looked to Captain Bowers.

"Go back down to the clubhouse and call for an ambulance. We need to get him to the hospital."

Bowers nodded but hesitated before leaving.

"Were you exaggerating about the amount of fertilizer they stole?" he asked.

I shook my head and looked from Nassir to him. "No."

"Tell me you and Havelock had a plan for tracking these guys down."

I smiled a mirthless smile at him. "Given that Havelock's dead, even if we had a plan, I'm not sure how much trust I'd put in it."

Bowers nodded and left the room without saying anything. He didn't need to say anything, though. We both knew the stakes. Very bad men were going to kill a whole lot of people very soon.

And we were the only people who could stop that from happening.

Chapter 39

A few minutes after Bowers left, a car pulled up behind the building, and four doors slammed shut in quick succession. Several people rushed into the storm shelter, but I couldn't see them well from the room Nassir and I were in. At least one of them, though, had a camping lantern because the room outside the armory lit up.

"Lieutenant Rashid?" called a voice.

"In here," I said. "We're in the back room."

Footsteps shuffled toward me, and then four uniformed male officers burst into the room. Two of them looked like they were in their mid-twenties, a third looked about my age, and the fourth looked as if he could have retired at any moment with a full pension. The two young guys carried fishing tackle boxes and lanterns, while the other two carried a stretcher.

"Is he breathing?" asked one of the young guys as he set his tackle box and lantern on the ground and then snapped a pair of latex gloves on his hands.

"Yeah, he seems to be breathing fine," I said, furrowing my brow at the back brace. "What did Mike tell you?"

"Just that we had a medical emergency," said one of the other officers. "We're the team paramedics."

"I think he's just knocked out."

One of the young guys looked almost disappointed, but the others kept their emotions to themselves and got to work over Nassir. They checked his pulse, his capillary response, and then they felt his skin to see whether it was clammy. Then, once they determined he probably was okay, they broke open a smelling salts ampule and held it under Nassir's nose. For a moment, nothing happened. Then his eyes popped open, and he shuddered.

"How are you feeling, Mr. Hadad?" asked the older officer.

Nassir's eyes fluttered, and then he tried to sit up but fell backward before he could.

"Dizzy," he said. "And thirsty. Who are you, and what am I doing here?"

"They're police officers," I said, kneeling beside him. "You're okay."

For a moment, he stared at me, confused, and then comprehension dawned in his eyes.

"Ashraf, they came to the camp after the police left. They had guns. They didn't tell me what they wanted. They shot Omar Nawaz."

"I know," I said, nodding. Unease began to build in my gut. "Why did they kill Omar and not you?"

His eyes flicked to the ceiling, and then he shook his head. "I don't know."

The question was more important than he probably realized. My investigation kept coming back to him, and yet he denied a connection at every turn. I wanted to believe him, but it got harder at every turn.

"Think hard," I said. "They killed Omar and left his body to rot. You're alive. Why? We need an answer to that question."

"I don't have one," he said, sitting up again. This time, he didn't fall backwards. "I don't know what's going on. They came to my home and murdered a man in front of me. I don't know who they were, or what they wanted. Aside from Omar, I hadn't even seen any of them before."

I locked my eyes on his and held his gaze for a few moments.

"You are right in the middle of this, Nassir. If you want to stay out of prison, your explanations need a lot more detail," I said. "Where are the other men who live here with you?"

"They went home after we were arrested," he said. "They're with their families. Rana made it clear that I don't have a family anymore. So I came here."

I wanted to tell him that was his own damn fault, but this wasn't the time for family squabbles.

"How many people came?"

His eyes went unfocused for a moment. Then he looked at me again.

"At least ten. They were boys, mostly, but there were two older men, too. One was named Hashim."

I nodded. Butler al-Ghamdi had mentioned someone named Hashim. We were getting somewhere.

"How did they get here?"

He furrowed his brow. "They drove. What do you think, they took a train?"

I forced a smile to my face to hide my annoyance at

the answer.

"What did they drive?" I asked.

"Cars."

My hands balled into fists without my conscious effort. I almost smacked him. Instead, I clenched my jaw and drew in a deep breath. Nassir cleared his throat and looked away.

"What kind of cars did they drive?" I asked. "Four-door sedans? SUVs? Convertibles? Pickup trucks? Did you see what they drove, Nassir? The people who came to this camp are going to kill a lot of people. Talk."

He blinked a few times. "A truck. The kind you move in. It was yellow. And minivans. One was gray. The other was light blue."

"Good. So twelve people came," I said, nodding. "Were they white? Were they black? Brown? Asian? Latino? Native American?"

He drew in a breath and closed his eyes as a pained expression crossed his face.

"They were brown," he said. "All of them, I think. They looked like us."

I nodded to the uniformed officers with me. "One of you go tell your boss and Captain Mike Bowers to start calling truck rental companies. We want to see whether anybody's rented yellow moving trucks to Arab-looking men in the past couple of days."

Three of the officers looked to the older guy. He nodded to one of the young men.

"Do as he says," he said. "Run."

The guy disappeared, and I looked to Nassir again.

"Tell me about the fertilizer upstairs. Where is it?"

Nassir furrowed his brow. "We haven't touched it since Qadi bought it. It's hard to find time to fertilize when you're in federal custody or when crazy people attack you."

"So you haven't touched it at all?" I asked, lowering my chin.

"No," he said, his voice growing indignant. "We haven't touched it. Why are you asking?"

"Because it's gone," I said. "The men who killed Omar and knocked you out took your fertilizer. That's probably why they brought a truck. How much did you have?"

He drew in a breath. "I don't know how much Qadi bought. He got a good deal. I'd have to look at the computer to be sure."

I put a hand under his armpit to help him stand. "Then we're going to your office."

Nassir stood up easily, but he leaned against me at first for balance. Then he blinked and waved me away.

"I'm fine," he said. "Give me a minute. The blood just rushed to my head."

I looked to the uniformed officers who were starting to stand and gather their gear.

"It's not far to the clubhouse, so I'll just walk him down. We'll meet you there."

"Are you sure you're okay walking?" asked the older uniformed officer.

"He's fine," I said, squeezing Nassir's tricep so he wouldn't say anything. "He's not even wobbling anymore."

"I am fine," said Nassir, glancing at me and then to the officers. "We'll walk."

The officers seemed leery of leaving us alone, but I didn't care. I led Nassir outside and stepped close to him as the uniformed officers began loading up their SUV.

"Are you positive you didn't recognize any of the men who came here earlier?"

He gave me a bewildered look. "I already told you no."

"I get that, but I was hoping you could tell me the truth now. These bad guys you didn't recognize murdered a man right in front of you. Instead of killing you, they clubbed you over the head and dumped your body in a secret room only known about by people you trust. You see the problem I'm having?"

Nassir slowed his gait.

"I don't know what to tell you," he said. "Butler al-Ghamdi knew about it. He could have told others."

It was a reasonable answer, but it didn't truly respond to my concerns. I stopped walking. Nassir took another few steps but then stopped as well and turned to me.

"I need your help," I said. "If you're telling me the truth, there are twelve men intent on hurting innocent people out there. What's more, they've got guns, trucks, and potentially explosives."

"Like I told you earlier, this is a summer camp," he

said. "I never intended—"

"Just stop right there," I said, interrupting him. "Jacob Ganim came here to see you. The terrorists who attacked Westbrook Elementary blamed you. You brought Butler al-Ghamdi to Indianapolis, and he killed seven innocent people. He set up an ambush that killed four FBI agents. I never would have met him if not for you. Today, I came back here and found out that your bulk purchases of fertilizer and diesel fuel happened to be stolen by terrorists. That's an awful lot of coincidences, don't you think?"

"I made some mistakes," he said. "I admit that, but I'm not a terrorist. I'm building this camp for my daughter. How many times do I have to tell you that?"

I folded my hands in front of me. "Is it possible somebody else in your group wants to hurt people?"

"I've known these men for twenty years. They wouldn't hurt anybody. They're good people."

"All of them?" I asked. Nassir nodded. "What about Saleem al-Asiri? He brought in Butler al-Ghamdi. Have you known him for twenty years, too?"

Nassir hesitated before answering. "No, but he's a good man."

"Where'd you meet him?"

Again, Nassir hesitated.

"Nassir, I don't have time for this," I said. "People are going to die unless we do something now."

Nassir blinked and then looked down. "I met him on Facebook. We know some people in common. They vouched for him."

"Somebody vouched for Michael Najam, too, and he turned out to be an undercover FBI agent," I said, nodding. "How long have you known him?"

Nassir didn't say anything for a few minutes, but then he closed his eyes.

"We're not stupid."

"I didn't say you are," I said.

"Then you implied it," he said, opening his eyes to glare at me. He threw out his hands. "Of course it's possible he isn't who he says he is. It's also possible he's exactly the man I think he is. I can only judge him based on what I've seen, and I've seen a good Muslim who loves his family and community."

Neither Nassir nor I said anything for a moment, but we did step out of the road as the state police SUV passed. I didn't know what the officers had heard, but very likely Bowers and Colonel Holtz would get a report that Nassir and I had been seen arguing. I drew in a deep breath and closed my eyes.

"Do you at least understand where I'm coming from?" I asked. "I'm not asking these things lightly, Nassir. There are real lives at stake."

"I know," he said, softening his voice. "I also know what it's like to be accused of something I didn't do simply because I was in the wrong place at the wrong time."

"I get that, and I'm sorry," I said. "We need to work together, though. I'd like to find out how much fertilizer you had so I can know how big a bomb the terrorists can make, and then I'd like you to start calling your friends. We'll pick them up."

"You still think the men who volunteer at this camp are terrorists?"

"Call it a precautionary measure," I said.

He called me a bastard and started walking again. As long as he did as I asked, he could call me whatever he wanted. We reached the clubhouse within five minutes. By that point, nearly everyone was outside. There had been a lot of people in there earlier, so hopefully we hadn't damaged the crime scene too badly.

Bowers crossed his arms and looked out over the grassy field in front of us.

"Colonel Holtz has every officer under his command calling truck rental places to look for stolen yellow trucks or any yellow truck that was rented to Arab-looking men. I also called the Bureau to let them know what's going on. They've got five hundred agents on the ground near the Motor Speedway. IMPD has another thousand uniformed officers in the same area. We're ready to act at the first sign of trouble. Nassir tell us anything?"

"Nothing helpful beyond what I already told you," I said. "These guys could be anywhere. We don't even know whether they're going to hit the 500."

He looked at me. "Can you think of a better target?"

"No, which is why I doubt they're going to attack it. These guys aren't dumb. They've shown that over and over again. They're not going to get within five miles of the Motor Speedway. Put yourself in their position. You've got a massive bomb in Indianapolis. Nobody knows what you look like, but every law enforcement official within a hundred-mile radius is looking for a bright yellow moving truck at the Indianapolis Motor Speedway. What are you going to attack?"

"I'm still going after the Indy 500," said Bowers. "That's where everybody is. These are terrorists. They want to make a statement and get their faces on TV. That's what terrorism is about."

I shook my head. "That's not how this group operates. They're playing a different game. They knew they couldn't kill President Crane, so they didn't even try. Instead, they attacked his family. They sought a vulnerability and attacked that. Where are we vulnerable with almost every officer in the region focused on the race?"

"Everywhere but the race."

"Yeah," I said, nodding. "And that's the problem."

Chapter 40

Nassir came out of the building a few minutes later with two stacks of documents, each of which likely had twenty or so pages. He handed one to me and the other to Bowers. I raised my eyebrows.

"What am I looking at?"

"A list of everything we have at this camp, who bought it, how much he paid, when he purchased it, and when it was last used," he said. "It's everything we have."

"So the fertilizer's on here?" I asked, raising my eyebrows.

"First page, fourteenth entry," said Nassir. "I checked. Two months ago, Qadi purchased forty-four hundred pounds of noncoated ammonium nitrate 34-0-0 prill-form fertilizer from a farm supply store online. We have yet to use a single bag."

I looked down at the spreadsheet and nodded when I saw the entry.

"Okay, thank you," I said, looking to Bowers. "This could be a big bomb."

"They steal anything else?" asked Bowers, turning pages.

"The stuff from the armory," said Nassir. "That's on page seven. Ashraf knows about it."

"The armory?" asked Bowers, raising an eyebrow and glancing at me.

"It's what they called the room in which we found

Nassir," I said. "They had some guns there."

Bowers flipped pages and read for a few moments. Then he glanced at me.

"That's a lot of firepower," he said, flicking his eyes toward Nassir. "They take anything other than guns and ammunition?"

I started to say no, but Nassir made a noise in his throat that stopped me. I looked at him and raised my eyebrows.

"Something you want to tell the group?"

"They took some tools," said Nassir. "The list is on page eight."

"What kind of tools?" asked Bowers.

Nassir drew in a breath and raised his eyebrows. "Two soldering irons, some wire cutters, a spool of rosin-core solder, and some thin copper wire. We confiscated them from a young man who, we thought, was making bomb components. He was really trying to make homemade speakers. That's why I didn't say anything."

Even if the original kid had used the tools to make speakers, they had likely been put to a completely different use now.

"Anything else?"

Nassir looked down and ran a hand across his face. I repeated my question.

"A box of prepaid cell phones," he said. "I forgot we even had them until I checked the inventory. Saleem bought them because none of our cell phones worked out here. He thought the prepaid carrier would work better, but they didn't. They've been sitting on a shelf in the armory for months. They've never even been activated."

My extremities started tingling as I flipped through pages. Each phone—nineteen of them—had its own line on the spreadsheet telling us the model number, the date of purchase, the price, and, most importantly, each phone's serial number. I looked to Bowers.

"Get on the phone and call the FBI. They have better technical resources than we do. If the bad guys took these phones, either they're part of a bomb, or they're being used for communication. Either way, we might be able to track them."

Bowers nodded and pulled out his cell phone and put it to his ear. Then he pulled it away and looked at the screen.

"I've got no reception," he said. "Check your phone. Somebody's got to have a connection."

"Forget it," I said. "There's a hill behind the building. Your phone'll work up there."

Bowers nodded and ran. I focused on Nassir. He looked small and forlorn.

"We need to talk about Saleem," I said. "He brought Butler al-Ghamdi to this camp, he happened to be here when Butler and his friends came back to rob the place, and he told them about your armory. Now he brought cell phones that are probably being used by terrorists. That might be a coincidence, but are you sure he's the man you think he is?"

"I don't know anymore. Maybe bringing him in was a

mistake."

"Do you know where he is?"

Nassir blinked and swallowed. "After the FBI released us yesterday, he said he was going home. As far as I know, nobody's spoken to him since."

I pulled out my cell phone. "What's his cell number?"

Nassir didn't have the number memorized, but he read it to me from his own cell phone. I entered it into my phone's address book.

"Thank you."

Nassir sat on one of the porch's rocking chairs while I ran up the hill after Captain Bowers. He was already on the phone when I arrived, so I stood a couple yards away from him and placed my own call to Paul Murphy. He answered after three rings. Wherever he was, it was as quiet as a tomb.

"Paul, it's Ash. What are you up to?"

"Just sitting around the office and waiting for somebody to kill somebody else. What are you up to?"

"Working a case. I need you to run a cell phone for me. It's owned by a guy named Saleem al-Asiri. He's from Dayton, Ohio."

"You never just call to talk anymore, Ash," said Paul. "Remember when we were young, and we could just stay up all night talking? What happened to us? We used to be so good together."

"You're hilarious," I said, my voice flat. "Now get a paid of paper and a pencil. He's supposed be in Dayton, Ohio, right now. If he is, great. If he's here in

Indianapolis, though, he might be involved in a plan to kill a lot of innocent people. Either way, I need to track him down."

I read Paul the number, and he said he'd start making some calls to find him. As much as Paul liked to joke around, he knew when to shut up and work. A lot of our younger detectives could have learned from him. I thanked him and looked to Captain Bowers. I didn't know who he was talking to, but his voice was subdued. I put my hands in my pockets and waited. After about ten minutes, he hung up and slipped his phone back in his pocket.

"It took some arm twisting, but the Bureau's on it," he said. "I talked to Special Agent Garret Russel. He's taking over Kevin Havelock's position until Washington sends a permanent replacement. You need to watch out for him."

I nodded and started walking down the hill. "He let me know that. I think I'm done here. You ready to go?"

"Yeah."

We walked back to Bowers's SUV and found the state police tactical team already packing up. I had the feeling we'd need them before the day was through. I drove while Bowers stared at his phone, waiting for a signal. He finally got one a few miles from the interstate. Special Agent Russel at the FBI hadn't gotten information about the phones yet, but he and the US Attorney's Office were in touch with the wireless carrier's legal office. Hopefully something would happen soon.

Once I got on the interstate, I put on the lights hidden in the SUV's grill and floored it. We hit the outskirts of Indianapolis in less than half an hour and were heading toward the city's inner core when Bowers's phone rang. He spoke for a moment and then put the phone on speaker and rested it on the console between our seats.

"You mind repeating that, Agent Russel?" he asked. "You're on speaker. I've got Lieutenant Rashid with me. He leads our major case squad."

Agent Russel grunted. "All nineteen cell phones have been activated and are dispersed throughout the city. Seven are in residential neighborhoods, three are in the zoo, one is in the botanical gardens near the zoo, six are near the Indianapolis Motor Speedway, and two are in the Circle Center Mall."

We had a lot of locations to search, but we had a lot of officers.

"Nassir Hadad counted twelve people at his camp," said Bowers. "Assuming those twelve each have a phone to coordinate with the others, what are the other seven phones for?"

"Remote detonators, decoys, backups…we don't know," said Russel.

I tilted my head toward the phone so it could pick up my voice.

"Can we just work with the phone company to turn them off?" I asked. "If they're remote detonators for a bomb, that might be the conservative thing to do."

"We could do that if we were morons, Lieutenant," said Russel. "Since we're not morons, I'd rather not."

I wanted to respond, but Bowers held up a hand and shook his head at me.

"Agent Russel, this is Mike Bowers. I'm curious why Ash's suggestion is such a bad one. Wouldn't we disable the bomb if we disabled the detonator?"

"Not necessarily," said Russel. "We don't know how they're using these phones. If they're acting as remote detonators, it's possible that disconnecting them from the telecom's network will close or open a circuit and set off the bomb. And if the bad guys are just using them to coordinate, they'll know we're on to them if we turn off their phones simultaneously."

"What do we do, then?" asked Bowers.

"We're still figuring that out," said Russel. "When my team has a plan, we'll let you know."

"That's not good enough," I said. "Here's a plan that works. We put together nineteen tactical teams. We'll put at least one member of the bomb squad on each team. Our tactical officers will track the bad guys down via their cell phones and arrest them before they can hurt any civilians. If the threat involves an explosive device, our bomb squad tech will examine the device while the tactical team evacuates the area. It's not ideal, but it might be the best we can do."

Almost immediately, Russel chuckled, but there was little humor in the sound.

"IMPD doesn't have enough tactical officers—let

alone bomb technicians—for an operation that large," said Russel. "It's not going to work."

"You're right," I said, nodding. "We don't have enough officers, but you've got several hundred special agents from your counterterrorism division in town. I imagine some of them have had weapons training. We can also call the state police. They've got their own SWAT team. Like I said, it's not ideal, but it might be the best we can do."

"Half-cocked thinking like that is what got my friend killed, Lieutenant."

Bowers immediately reached for the phone, but I started talking before he could cover up the microphone.

"Bad men with guns killed your friend," I said. "I'm sorry about Agent Havelock. I truly am. He was a good man. He died, though, because an asshole shot him with a sniper's rifle. I did everything I could to save his life."

"Neither of you should have been in that building in the first place," said Agent Russel. "Modern law enforcement doesn't have room for cowboys or gunslingers, Lieutenant, which means that as far as I'm concerned, you have no place in this conversation. From now on, I'll be discussing the FBI's response to these incidents with Chief Reddington."

The line went dead. Bowers sighed and flicked a finger across his phone's screen to hang up before slipping it into his pocket.

"Could have gone better," he said.

I didn't answer and instead reached to the console

beside me to turn on the siren and clear out some cars ahead of us. They got to the side of the road quickly enough that I didn't even have to let off the gas. The buildings of downtown Indianapolis loomed just ahead of us, and I drove straight toward them.

Eventually, I had to slow down as the road narrowed and became more crowded, but I kept our lights and siren on, which kept us moving. When we reached our destination, I parked in the employee garage beneath the City-County Building.

The building was quiet. On a weekday, thousands of men and women ambled about those hallways, but on a Sunday—race day, no less—the place was relatively empty. There wasn't even a guard outside the parking garage, just an automatic meter to read your parking pass. Bowers and I took the elevator to his floor. Where most of the building felt calm and tired, IMPD's executive-level floor buzzed with energy. Men and women ran through the hallways, carrying folders and talking on their phones.

When he saw us, a uniformed lieutenant with dark skin and a bald head began hustling us down the main hallway.

"Chief Reddington needs you guys in the conference room. We've got a lot going on right now."

Bowers and I hurried toward the conference room. There were a dozen men and women inside, and everybody seemed to be talking at once. Chief Dan Reddington sat at the head of the conference room table. The DHS liaison—a civilian whose name I couldn't remember—sat beside him. Both of them were engaged in what looked like a heated discussion with an attorney from the Indiana Attorney General's Office. When Reddington saw us, he excused himself from his conversation, crossed the room, and took both me and Bowers by the arm and led us to the comparative quiet of the hallway.

"I'm glad you two are here," he said. "Agent Russel has been keeping me apprised of events around town. He's in his own command center at the FBI fieldhouse. Have you guys heard about the nineteen cell phones?"

I crossed my arms and nodded. "Yeah. We know about them."

"Agent Russel's plan is to put together nineteen small tactical units of about fifteen officers each. It's possible the cell phones we're tracking are being used as part of a remote detonation system for explosive devices. As such, each tactical team will have at least one member of our bomb squad. The idea is that the tactical team will be able to evacuate the area, while the bomb squad member assesses the device. We'll either disarm it—or, more likely, put it in a containment vessel for safekeeping.

"IMPD alone doesn't have enough officers with the required level of tactical training, so we're coordinating with Homeland Security, the FBI, and the state police to put together teams. You've gone up against these guys, Ash. Given what you know about our opponent, do you have any objections to the plan?"

Bowers had a tight smile on his face. I put my hands

in my pockets and shook my head, pretending as if this were the first time I had heard the idea.

"The plan's risky, but it might save some lives. We need to tell our teams that the bad guys—and I think their leader is named Hashim Bashear—recruits from within the US. They're probably going to be teenagers. They might be black, they might be white, or they might be something else entirely. We can't know ahead of time. Based on what I've seen, though, they're dangerous. They will not hesitate to kill."

Reddington nodded slowly. "I'll relay the warning to our teams. Hopefully, we won't have to shoot anyone on national TV."

"Yeah, let's avoid doing that if we can," I said.

Reddington thanked me and left to call our SWAT team's commanding officer. Bowers left as well to make sure the detectives under his command were ready to work. I grabbed a cup of lukewarm coffee from the break room and then found a quiet corner in the conference room while everyone worked. I was exhausted, and the longer I sat, the heavier my eyelids seemed to become. Before I relaxed, though, there was something I needed to do.

I pulled out my cell phone and dialed my home number. Hannah picked up quickly.

"Hey," I said. "It's your husband. Sorry I didn't call last night. I got wrapped up with work."

"I thought so," she said. "Plus, I figured that if you were dead, it would have made the news. You doing okay?

You sound tired."

She didn't know how close her joke cut.

"Yeah, I'm okay. It's been a rough day. I don't have a lot of time, but I wanted to call and say I love you. I don't feel like I do that enough."

"You probably don't, but I'm gracious enough not to mention it."

I smiled for what felt like the first time in days. Then I looked up as somebody's cell phone rang. And then another rang. And then another and then another. Within moments, seemingly everyone in the room was on their phone.

"Hey, honey, I need to go. Do me a favor: Don't go out today."

"Something going on?"

"Yeah, but I probably shouldn't talk about it," I said. "I'll call you later. I love you."

I hung up the phone before she could say anything. I looked at Captain Bowers, one of the few other people in the room who didn't have a cell phone pressed to his head. He looked as confused as I felt.

Within maybe ten seconds of the first phone calls, I heard heavy footsteps pounding down the hall. Curious, I walked toward the door and found a uniformed officer running from the direction of the stairwell. I didn't remember his name, but he was the patrol division's watch commander for this shift. I stepped aside so he wouldn't slam into me. He nodded his thanks and then leaned heavily against the doorway as he caught his breath.

"What's going on, Chris?" asked Captain Bowers, nodding to the officer.

"We've got shots fired at Monument Circle. I've already pulled everybody I could from the building, but we've got at least five casualties so far. Reports are two male shooters, both with semiautomatic rifles. They might be wearing body armor. We're not sure. We've got about three dozen officers en route."

I closed my eyes again and swore under my breath as a heavy, nervous feeling began to build in my gut. If these two shooters had cell phones from Nassir's camp, we would have had a tactical team on them already. I was wrong. Our teams were in the wrong places. Whatever Hashim Bashear and these bad guys had planned, it was starting.

And we weren't nearly ready.

Chapter 41

Everybody in the room started talking at once. Mostly, it seemed as if they were trying to figure out whose fault this was. I tuned them out and checked my firearm. It was a Sig Sauer P226 chambered for a .40-caliber Smith & Wesson round. It had a good balance of stopping power, ammunition capacity, and weight. I would have preferred a rifle, but this would have to do.

I started toward the door but felt a hand on my shoulder before I could reach it.

"Where are you going, Ash?"

I turned to see Captain Bowers. He had crossed his arms and gave me a knowing look.

"Monument Circle. There's an active shooter."

He paused before speaking.

"Let me get this straight," he said, narrowing his eyes at me. "You plan to go after two active shooters, both of whom have tactical rifles. They're possibly wearing body armor. They're probably carrying other weapons as well. Your hope is, what, that they'll run out of ammunition by the time you arrive?"

"Following the cell phones was my plan," I said, lowering my voice. "Agent Russel might have taken credit for it, but I came up with it, and I was wrong."

"You weren't the only person to sign off on it, Lieutenant," said Bowers. "I heard it, Agent Russel heard it, Chief Reddington heard it, probably everybody in this room heard it and had the chance to raise objections. It was the best plan we could come up with given the information we had. We were all wrong. Now we've got to do our jobs and coordinate a response."

I looked across the room at the window and then to Captain Bowers.

"I'm the lowest-ranked officer here. This isn't my place. I should be out there."

"And if you were a sergeant wearing a tactical vest and carrying a rifle, I'd let you go," said Bowers. "But you're a lieutenant in a sweatshirt. Like it or not, you carry a gold badge now. You're a command officer. It's not always easy, but this is what we do. We coordinate, we plan, and we let the very well trained officers who work for us do their jobs. Think you can handle that?"

I bit back my initial response and nodded.

"Yes, sir," I said.

Bowers nodded and held my gaze for a moment before taking a step back. "If it means anything, I'd rather be out there, too. There are a lot of days I wish I had stayed in uniform."

"I know the feeling."

Bowers and I stayed still for a few moments, but then Reddington called him over. I walked to the window and looked out. My hands trembled, and my feet itched. Intellectually, I understood why I had to stay, but every part of my body told me to ignore Bowers and run four blocks up the street. I drew in deep breaths, forcing myself to remain calm. It was almost surreal looking out that window on empty streets. Four blocks away, people were dying. For all I knew, I had lost colleagues.

The feeling was like an ember in my gut, and I couldn't do a damn thing about it. After a couple of minutes, my phone buzzed, and I answered without looking at it.

"Yeah?" I asked, silently praying I wasn't about to receive a report of other active shooters around town.

"Ash, it's Paul. I've spent the last half hour arguing with the general counsel at a telecom company about Saleem al-Asiri. I finally got a location on him, and now I feel like I just wasted a lot of time. When'd you pick him up?"

I covered my left ear with a hand to block out some of the conference room's background noise.

"We didn't pick him up."

"Then why is he here?"

I furrowed my brow, not understanding. "What do you mean?"

"His phone company gave me his coordinates," said Paul. "He's at 39.77 degrees north and 86.16 degrees west. That puts him at 200 East Washington Street. Here."

"He's in the building?"

"Yep," said Paul. "Or close enough to it."

My heart started pounding. I didn't really know who Saleem was, but he was connected to this. Not only that, he had absolutely no business being anywhere near this building on a Sunday morning—especially not this

Sunday morning.

The shooting at Monument Circle had cleared most of the police officers out of the building, but even on a Sunday, there still would have been hundreds of civilian city workers. I let some of my pent-up energy enter my voice.

"Who's in homicide with you right now?"

"Emilia Rios, Nancy Wharton, and Elliot Wu. I think Wu and Wharton are interrogating somebody in the box."

I thought for a minute. "Tell Wharton and Wu to get their suspect outside. Then I need you and Emilia to clear the rest of your floor. Make sure it's empty. Lock every door you can. Then take the stairwell to the lobby and wait for me."

"You're ordering me to take the stairs," said Paul. "If this is a fat joke, I don't appreciate it."

"There are a pair of shooters with tactical rifles at Monument Circle right now. If Saleem is here, we've got a problem. I don't want you stuck in the elevator if he starts shooting. Get going. I'm going to need you."

Paul paused for a moment. Then he drew in a breath. "I'm on it."

I hung up my phone and walked to the head of the conference table beside Chief Reddington. He and Bowers were talking about something, but I didn't bother getting their attention.

"Hey," I said. "I need everybody to listen up."

For a moment, the room quieted but then conversations picked up again. A few people shook their heads, annoyed. I cupped my hands around my mouth.

"Hey, shut up," I yelled. Everyone in that room was a command officer of one sort or another. Many of them had dozens of officers reporting to them. A couple had hundreds. Even Chief Reddington didn't order them around, but that was exactly what I planned to do.

"We screwed up and sent our tactical units to the wrong locations. We've got shooters at Monument Circle, and it's very likely we've got another in the building. We don't know what floor he's on, but his name is Saleem al-Asiri. He's approximately sixty years old and has light brown skin and graying hair. We do not know what kind of weaponry he has, but he's not here for the scenery. It's time to put on our big-boy pants because we are the only law enforcement officials left on site.

"Captain Bowers, call the watch commander and mobilize every uniformed officer in the area. Chief Reddington, call Agent Russel and let him know that we've got an active threat in our building. Somebody needs to call the canine unit because we need a bomb-sniffing dog. It'd be nice if we could get some bomb squad officers here, too. Everybody else, call your teams and tell them they need to start sweeping their floors."

There were a dozen people in that room, and they all stared at me as if I were crazy. Then I clapped my hands as hard as I could.

"Fucking move."

"Richey, call the bomb squad," said Chief Reddington, his voice calm and smooth. "Tracy, get in touch with Sergeant Ableson with the canine unit.

Everybody else, you heard your orders. Get your squads together and start sweeping the building. If you aren't IMPD, stay in the room. We'll lock down the floor."

Nobody panicked, but people got out of there in a hurry, leaving just three civilians, Chief Reddington, Captain Bowers, and me. I had met all three civilians, but I could only remember two of their names. Two were attorneys, while the third worked in public relations. All of them looked scared. Reddington looked to me and then to them.

"Folks, why don't you go to my office? There's a TV, and there are sodas in the minifridge. Relax as much as you can."

Reluctantly, they nodded and left. Reddington crossed his arms.

"That was a surprising thing you did," he said. "My subordinates don't oftentimes bark orders at me."

"Given the circumstances, I thought it was necessary," I said, glancing at Bowers. Smartly, he kept his mouth shut.

"It might have been," said Reddington, raising his eyebrows. "For the sake of your job, you should probably consult with me before you give orders to people who can ruin your career with a phone call. Now what do you need?"

"Good tip," I said, nodding. "At any rate, in addition to the cell phones, we've been looking for a yellow moving truck. Anybody find it?"

Reddington flicked his eyes to Captain Bowers and

then to me. He shook his head.

"Not that I know of," said Reddington.

I looked to the two men. Bowers was in his mid-fifties. Reddington was a little older. Both were in reasonable shape, though.

"Are you two armed?"

Reddington looked at Bowers. The captain drew in a breath and sighed.

"You think the moving truck is around here," said Bowers, "and you need help searching the parking garage."

"Yeah. I thought it was best if I didn't bring that up with a dozen people in the room."

Reddington narrowed his eyes. "What threat does a moving truck pose?"

"If it's here, it's probably carrying a bomb roughly the same size and composition as the one Timothy McVeigh used to attack the federal building in Oklahoma City in 1995."

For a moment, neither man said anything. Then Chief Reddington drew in a long, slow breath.

"Okay," he said, nodding. "I'm going to go to my office and get my firearm. We'll escort the civilians there out of the building, and then we'll check the parking garage. Are you armed, Mike?"

Captain Bowers nodded. "Yeah."

"Then let's go," said the chief.

We hurried to his office, where Reddington explained the situation to the three civilians still inside. They seemed more than a little relieved at the prospect of getting out of the building. Before leaving, he tossed his suit coat onto his couch and grabbed a pistol and holster from a locked drawer in his desk. We took the stairs to the lobby, where we met Emilia Rios and Paul Murphy. Both detectives carried police-issue M4 carbines, and both wore black tactical vests over their torsos.

"Stairwells are open and clear," said Emilia. "We've had forty or fifty people come down already, but nobody shot at us or threatened us in any way. Detectives Wu and Wharton are in their car in the parking lot across the street with a guy they were interrogating. If we need them, they can let their suspect bounce. They don't think he's a flight risk."

"I'll get them, then," said Reddington. "Ash, fill your partners in on what we've got."

The chief jogged out of the building, and I turned to Emilia and Paul. I didn't give them many details, just that we were looking for a yellow moving truck that might have been holding a very large bomb. Emilia looked at Captain Bowers.

"Is it too late to call in sick today?"

"Yes, it is, Detective," he said. "That goes for you, too, Sergeant Murphy."

"She's the sick one," said Paul. "I'm the coward."

Bowers looked to Emilia. "I hope you get over your illness very quickly," he said. Then he looked to Murphy. "And I hope you grow a backbone."

"Already on it, sir," said Paul, rolling his shoulders. "If this van is down there, how many suspects do we anticipate finding?"

Bowers looked to me.

"Not a clue," I said. "Nassir said twelve men came after him at his camp. If two are at Monument Circle right now, we could have up to ten here."

Paul looked at us and then toward the exterior door. Detectives Wu and Wharton and Chief Reddington were hurrying across the street.

"If I'm counting correctly, we'll have seven on ten," he said, nodding. "It sounds like a terrible porno."

"Or a really good one," said Emilia, brightly. "It all depends on the director."

"You two should probably stop talking now," I said, pulling my firearm out of its holster to chamber a round. "Reddington's coming in. Check your firearms. We've got work to do."

Chapter 42

The City-County Building was a twenty-eight-story building that housed the consolidated offices of Marion County and the city of Indianapolis. On a weekday, the building held a lot of relatively important men and women, and most of them had marked spots in the garage beneath the building.

The seven of us took the stairwell down and emerged into a poorly lit concrete garage that smelled just faintly of mold and sewage. There were a couple dozen cars and thick concrete jersey barriers to funnel traffic to where it was supposed to go. To the right of the stairwell was an elevator that led to the cells in which the sheriff's department held men and women on trial. To my left was an inclined ramp that led out of the building.

Nothing moved.

"Fan out," I said. "Stay behind the barriers. The suspects we're tracking are bad dudes. Don't try to take them on yourself."

I got a chorus of nods as my team spread out. Our footsteps seemed to echo inside the enclosed space. I crept past one barrier and then to another, expecting a dark form to pop up at any moment. None did, but that didn't stop my heart from pounding.

The garage wasn't big. It had a single story and perhaps a couple hundred parking spots. A moving truck shouldn't have been able to hide in there.

"Hey, Ash," whispered a voice to my left. Emilia Rios knelt behind a concrete jersey barrier and pointed toward the entrance ramp. I thought she was telling me a car was coming down, but she wasn't. The nose of a heavy truck poked out from a shadowed spot beneath the ramp. My fingers trembled.

It was here.

I looked to my left and right and started forward. Emilia followed. By the time I reached the truck, my entire team had seen what we were doing and joined us. The truck's engine was warm but not hot, which meant the bad guys had likely stashed it here earlier today. Emilia climbed onto the truck's running boards to look in the cab while Bowers and I walked to the rear. The rolling rear door was padlocked shut.

TV detectives probably would have shot the padlock and opened the door without a problem. In real life, it didn't work like that. The lock itself was maybe an inch and a half square, giving us a very small target to work with. Not only that, the bumper it rested on was solid steel. Any round that hit that would ricochet and possibly kill the shooter. And even if I hit the lock, bits of shrapnel would tear me apart. Shooting it out wasn't an option. I needed a plan B.

"Look around for something I can use to break the lock," I said. "Crowbar, hammer, anything."

For the next few minutes, we scrambled around the parking lot for tools. Thankfully, Detective Wu had a better head on his shoulders than the rest of us and ran outside to his car in which he kept a pair of bolt cutters in his crime scene kit. I cut the lock, handed him the cutters, and rolled the rear door open to expose a nightmare.

The truck's cargo hold held at least a dozen black fifty-five-gallon drums. Wires connected each barrel to the one beside it and led into a duffel bag on the floor.

"Shit," said Paul, his voice so low I almost didn't hear it.

"Unless you know anything about electronics or explosives, you should get out," I said, reaching up and grabbing onto the handle built into the side of the truck for leverage as I stepped up. The duffel bag held what looked like a home's electrical panel. I knew how to wire a circuit, but I didn't know the first thing about explosives. If our bomb squad had an hour or two to study this thing, they might have been able to disarm it, but it was well beyond me. I looked over my shoulder. "Unless one of you happens to be an explosives expert, I suggest we back away slowly and hope we don't set this thing off inadvertently."

"That sounds like a pretty good plan to me," said Paul, already taking a few steps back. I climbed down and gently stepped off the rear bumper, taking my first couple of breaths. I waved my arm in the direction of the garage's exit.

"Everybody get back. We need to close off the area and wait for help."

Everybody but Chief Reddington started walking.

He was already on the phone. When he looked at me, his face was almost white. Then he started waving his arms frantically.

"Everybody out of the building," he said. "We've got to go. Right now. We've got explosions all over the city."

For a moment, nobody moved. Then something inside the truck started beeping. I had been holding a nervous energy inside me for hours. Finally, I let it go and sprinted. The team ran beside me. As I neared the exit, I grabbed Chief Reddington's arm.

"How many people are upstairs?"

"More than I care to think about."

The last time I talked to my wife, I'd told her I loved her and asked her to hug our kids for me. If I kept running, an awful lot of people would never get to see their kids again. They'd never wish their spouses goodnight again. They'd never get the chance to tell their loved ones how much they meant to them. I, at least, got that chance.

My footsteps slowed and then stopped. There were probably hundreds of people in that building. I was a police officer. I swore an oath to protect people. I didn't put on my badge to run when others needed me.

"Ash," said Bowers, slowing and then stopping in front of me. "What are you doing?"

"My job," I said, turning back into the building. Almost instantly, I heard heavy footsteps behind me. I didn't care. I reached the truck within seconds. The device in the back kept beeping. I didn't know what that meant, but I assumed it wasn't good. My hands shook, but that was the least of my worries. Bowers pounded to a stop beside me.

"What the hell are you doing?"

"There are people inside the building. We've got to move the truck," I said, pulling the door handle. The door was locked, but the window was broken, allowing me to reach inside. Bowers climbed onto the running board on the other side. The moment I got in, I unlocked his door. The bombers must have stolen the truck because the ignition wires were already cut. That saved me some time.

"What the hell are you doing?" asked Bowers.

"Reaping the benefits of a misspent youth," I said.

With the plastic panel beneath the steering wheel torn and the wires cut, getting the car to start was a simple matter of twisting the correct wires together and then sparking the ignition. The entire process took about ten seconds, but with a giant bomb in the back, it felt like a year.

The truck started with a rumble, and I threw it into gear.

"You stole cars when you were a kid?" asked Bowers.

"No, I took autoshop in high school," I said, pressing the gas pedal. The big truck jumped forward. "I wanted to be a mechanic. My mom had other ideas."

Bowers nodded but didn't say anything. He had his eyes closed, and his lips were moving. He was praying. Probably wasn't a bad idea.

It took us another thirty seconds to leave the garage.

When we burst into the light of the street, it seemed almost impossibly bright. A car to my left honked. I didn't care. I didn't let off the gas. I just floored it out of there and hung a right, blowing through a stoplight.

"You know where you're going?"

"Yep," I said. "Parking lot. When I stop, get out and run."

Bowers nodded. In most cities, natural barriers—rivers, lakes, oceans, harbors, etc.—forced developers to go up. They built skyscrapers and massive multistory parking garages. Indianapolis didn't have that same geography. Here, our relatively flat landscape allowed developers to take a more relaxed approach. They used every inch of space we had, but instead of putting up an eight-story parking garage, they might just put in one giant surface lot.

Like the one catty-corner to my building.

"Hold on, Mike," I said, pressing on the gas hard. The big truck didn't jump, but it sped up as I turned the wheel. There wasn't an easy way into the parking lot, so I made my own entrance. I hit the curb hard and almost flew out of my seat. Thankfully, the truck had enough momentum to keep going. The front of the truck smashed into a minivan and pushed it out of its spot. Then I hit a sedan and tiny two-seater before coming to a stop several rows deep in the lot. A lot of people were going to be pissed when they got home from the mall, but hopefully they'd forgive me.

"Get out," I said, already opening the door. Bowers

and I jumped out of the big truck and ran hard for about three hundred yards to a row of oversized concrete planters built into the sidewalk across the street. When I reached them, I slid on the ground and felt the asphalt tear through my sweatpants. I didn't care as long as I had something heavy and stable between me and the truck. Bowers came to a stop beside me and tensed. Neither of us breathed for a moment.

And nothing happened.

I glanced at Captain Bowers and chuckled a little, a quick release of tension. Then I heard Bowers beside me exhale a long sigh of relief.

"You know," I began, "in the movies, the truck would have—"

An explosion ripped through the air before I could finish the sentence. The shock wave hit us first. Even with a concrete planter between us and the blast, it was a visceral blow to every part of my body, like being punched by God himself. The ground shook hard enough that had I been standing, I would have been knocked down. A split second later, the sound hit. It was raw noise that assaulted my ears and overcame my senses so that it was all my brain could process. Instantly, dirt and glass and pieces of metal started slamming into the planter and raining down on the ground around us. A thick cloud of debris enveloped us. I held my breath.

For a very brief moment, the world became a very small place for me. All I knew was noise and dust. Eventually, I blinked grit out of my eyes and breathed again. The smoke was pungent and sharp, like something from a refinery. As my senses gradually returned, I found that my body didn't hurt. That seemed like a good thing. As I leaned forward, dirt and glass fell from my shoulders. Something had cut my right hand, but it looked superficial. I was okay.

"You all right, Mike?"

I could barely hear my own voice above the ringing in my ears. Bowers looked at me and blinked and then pointed to my hand.

"You're bleeding."

His voice was even fainter than mine. Since he could talk, he was probably okay. The two of us stayed still for another minute as the world gradually came into focus.

Then I stood on wobbly legs and looked around. It was an odd scene. The sky was bright blue to the west and north, but it was marred by a massive plume of smoke from the south. Every car on the street had broken windows, and if I listened closely, I could hear car alarms all around me. The parking lot in which I had stashed the truck was a hellscape of black smoke and flame. There was a massive crater where there had once been a truck.

I pulled out my cell phone. The screen was cracked. I didn't know whether that was from the blast, or whether I had fallen on it. Either way, it didn't work.

Captain Bowers stood beside me. He had blood on his chin and right cheek.

"You all right?" I asked for the second time. The

ringing in my ears wasn't quite as intense as it had once been, but it hadn't subsided completely. Bowers looked at me and nodded.

"I think so. You?"

"Fine," I said, walking around the planter to the side that had taken the brunt of the blast. Several pieces of metal had become embedded in the concrete, and shards of glass littered the ground. The gingko tree the city had planted was little more than a stick at that point, but the planter itself took the impact with little visible damage. I knew without a doubt that it had saved my life.

I rubbed dirt from my face and sat down. Bowers sat near me. People were starting to come out of the nearby buildings. Most looked shocked. A few were in tears. Bowers patted my shoulder and pointed to our left. There was a man running away. Seemed a little late for that.

"Weren't we looking for a sixty-year-old Arab guy?" asked Bowers.

I focused on the runner. He looked as if he were the right height, and he had graying hair. He had the right skin tone, too. I couldn't see his face, but he sure looked like Saleem al-Asiri from behind. My mind must not have been working at a hundred percent because it took me a moment to realize that I probably should have been chasing him.

I stood and took off. Saleem was about a block ahead of me on Washington Street, but he was an old man who had just weathered a massive explosion. It didn't take long to catch up to him. A younger suspect, I probably would have tackled and held down. Saleem, I grabbed by the arm and pushed against the glass window of a mortgage processor.

"Were you hurt in the explosion?" I asked.

He bent over and put his hands on his knees but didn't say anything.

"If you're thinking about catching your breath and running, I wouldn't."

He nodded and eventually stood straighter.

"You can't arrest me," he said. "I have diplomatic immunity from the Syrian Arab Republic."

I grabbed him by the shoulder and pushed so that he faced the window. Then I ran my hands across his chest and legs to search for weapons. He had a cell phone in his pocket with a string of text messages in Arabic. I skimmed them and then looked to Saleem.

"I will see you in paradise, my friend," I said, roughly translating his last text. "God is great. Your sacrifice will be remembered."

Saleem turned around but didn't respond.

"I'm guessing you were supposed to die in the explosion," I said. "You were probably supposed to take this phone with you, too."

"If you arrest me, I'll die in prison," he said. "You can't do that. I'm a Muslim. You won't do that to one of your own."

I slipped his phone into my pocket. "You tried to murder hundreds of people. You're not one of my own."

"I'll tell you everything I know," he said. "Just let me

go."

"I appreciate your enthusiasm, but I'm not the one who makes deals. Now shut up. You're under arrest."

Chapter 43

There were one-hundred and forty-seven people in the City-County Building at the time of the explosion. All but one, a social worker putting in extra hours on a Sunday morning, survived. The woman who died had a heart attack upon hearing the blast. Paramedics tried to revive her, but there was nothing they could do.

Seven people—two bad guys and five civilians—died at Monument Circle. Another eight civilians and two state police officers died when three teenage gunmen opened fire at the Indianapolis Motor Speedway. Those three teenagers along with three other gunmen at the Indianapolis Motor Speedway were shot and killed by our tactical teams. The race went off without further hitch. Most of the fans probably didn't even realize something had happened.

In addition, two gunmen were arrested at the zoo without incident, one was arrested at the Botanical Gardens after firing several errant shots at a docent, two were arrested in the Circle Center Mall before they could fire a shot, and one was arrested crying in the men's room at the Art Museum.

The terrorists didn't just go after human beings, either. Three houses exploded around town when the natural gas in them ignited. Our tactical teams and the Indianapolis Fire Department managed to vent four others without incident.

In total, fourteen civilians, eight misguided young men, and two police officers lost their lives. We arrested six teenagers the day of the explosion and charged them with dozens of crimes. It took a couple of days, but thanks to Saleem al-Asiri's phone and contacts, the FBI tracked the group's ringleaders—Hashim and Hamza Bashear—to a small town in Texas near the US-Mexico border. When Border Patrol agents tried to make an arrest, Hashim and Hamza pulled out pistols. Both men were killed before getting a shot off.

Saleem al-Asiri disappeared from federal custody shortly thereafter. Whether he got a deal or whether the CIA had taken him to a secret prison in Thailand for further questioning, I didn't know. I didn't care. He wouldn't hurt anyone again.

Dalia Bashear, Hamza Bashear's young wife, was arrested in Italy a couple of days later, trying to make her way to Afghanistan. I didn't know what would happen in that case. The US government wanted her to stand trial for the same charges as her husband, but the Italian government refused to extradite criminal suspects if those suspects were to be tried for crimes for which the death penalty was a potential punishment.

Considering she was accused of murdering the president's wife and family, that one was going to get ugly. It made me glad I didn't have a more important job. I felt for her kids. They had lost everything in an instant. I hoped and prayed the system worked for them. Maybe they'd even get adopted by a nice Italian family. If so, they might be able to escape living in a society that knew them only as the children of people who had killed the beloved wife of a former president.

For my actions that day, Chief Reddington nominated me for a Medal of Valor for heroism, and Captain Bowers nominated me for IMPD's Medal of Honor, the highest award the department could give. The review board agreed unanimously on both medals and scheduled a special award ceremony to take place in five months. As much as I appreciated being recognized for my service, I didn't feel heroic. Supposedly, my work had saved hundreds of lives, but a lot of people still died. If Hannah let me, I planned to call in sick that day.

When Kevin Havelock had approached me with this assignment, I had thought I knew what this investigation would cost me. I'd hurt people I cared about. My community, my friends, my family. I didn't have a damn clue about the cost, though. Now Kevin Havelock was dead. Three other FBI agents were dead. Eight civilians were dead. Six boys too young to understand the world they had stepped into were dead. Kim Peterson and her boyfriend were dead. Six young women from Syria were dead. Jacob Ganim was dead.

Now I knew the cost of my investigation. It wasn't time or money, but lives. The thing that scared me the most, though, was that I'd do it all again in a heartbeat if it meant stopping something worse from happening.

All of that passed through my head as I carried eight pounds of marinated boneless skinless chicken thighs to my grill. A week had passed since the bombing, and I had spent it writing and reading reports and researching my case and the people involved. I had answers to most of my questions now.

I wished I didn't.

Nassir wasn't charged with a crime, but US Marshals seized the assets of Safe Haven, LLC, claiming the holdings company had clearly become involved in matters of domestic terrorism. The onus, then, was on Nassir and his attorneys to prove that his camp and its assets weren't involved in criminal activity.

They had filed paperwork, but I think Nassir understood his idea of a summer camp for refugees would never happen. Maybe his heart was in the right spot, but he and his friends had made mistakes. After losing his summer camp, Nassir moved home to his house in Indianapolis. My sister moved in with me for a couple of days while she and Nassir figured things out. That was okay by me. With our lives falling apart around us, I liked having an eye on her.

"Hey, Dad," called Megan from the lawn as I put chicken on the grill, "can we put up the badminton net today?"

I closed the lid to keep the temperature high.

"Sure. Uncle Paul and Miss Emilia are on their way. When they get here, just ask them for help."

It was a perfect day for a backyard barbecue. The sun was high overhead on a cloudless spring afternoon, bees were buzzing from one spring flower to another, and my kids were playing well together in the sandbox in the backyard. I was surrounded by the people I loved most in the world, but I couldn't relax. I had a lot on my mind.

Rana, my sister, came out of the back door and onto the deck. She had her hair down, and she wore a flowing green dress and black leggings. She sipped at a coffee mug. She looked more comfortable and relaxed than she had in a long time. I guess that came with not having Nassir around.

Rana put her coffee mug on the top rail of the deck and sat on a chair near me.

"You've really got to talk to your wife about her coffee," she said, looking into her mug. "This can't be healthy."

I cleared my throat and looked at my watch to time the chicken. Since the meat was boneless, I gave it six minutes a side.

"Hannah makes me coffee every morning, and I've kept my mouth shut for almost twelve years now. I love her, and I love that she's so thoughtful that she makes it for me," I said, looking from Rana to the kids. I lowered my voice. "God has given us all gifts and natural talents. I hope yours is discretion."

"My lips are sealed," she said, picking up her coffee mug again and watching the kids play. At six minutes, I flipped the chicken. At twelve minutes, I took the meat off the grill, covered it with aluminum foil, and took it inside to rest. Emilia Rios knocked on the front door as I was in the kitchen. She had brought a salad, and once she put it down, Hannah gave her a hug. Paul came a few minutes later with a pot of baked beans, which Hannah put in the oven.

After that, Rana and Hannah started talking about Hannah's newest book in the kitchen, so Paul, Emilia, and I went outside to the deck. It wasn't a party. The occasion was too somber for that.

"So did you go to Kevin Havelock's funeral?" asked Paul.

I shook my head and looked over the lawn. Megan and Kaden had started playing soccer with Emilia.

"Agent Russel made it known that I wasn't welcome. I paid my respects at his grave this morning."

"That's rough," said Paul. "You doing okay?"

"The FBI's Office of Professional Responsibility cleared me in the shooting."

"That's not what I asked," said Paul, smiling just a little.

"That's the only answer I have."

We slipped into silence and watched the kids and Emilia run around the yard. After a few minutes, Paul joined the soccer game and played goalie. It was fun to see everybody running around and laughing. As soon as Hannah took some potatoes out of the oven, lunch would be ready, but our last guest had yet to arrive. I hadn't expected him to be on time, though.

Nassir was never early.

I went inside and grabbed a soda from the fridge. Nassir knocked on the front door about ten minutes later.

He had tulips in a clear glass vase.

"I would have brought food, but I'm not a good cook," he said. "I thought Hannah would like these."

"She will," I said, taking the flowers. "Come in. We need to talk."

I led him from the entryway, through the living room, and then to the kitchen. Rana was there, and she immediately crossed her arms. Hannah grimaced. She had known Nassir was coming, but she didn't know exactly why I had invited him.

"Nassir," said Rana, her voice cold. She looked at me and raised her eyebrows. "Ashraf, can I see you outside for a moment?"

"You can. Nassir's going to be with us," I said.

Rana furrowed her brow but followed us outside anyway. I waved to the kids, Paul, and Emilia. Eventually, they got the hint and came to the porch, too. Megan smiled at her uncle.

"Are you here to play badminton, Uncle Nassir?" asked Megan.

Nassir looked at me and then to her. He knelt in front of her and smiled gently. "I'm here to visit, but I'm not sure how long I can stay."

Megan looked at me with a confused look on her face. Before she could say anything, I smiled.

"Sweetheart, can you and your brother go inside with *Ummi?* I think she needs some help making cookies for desert," I said. I then looked to Paul and Emilia. "I need you two to stay here."

My daughter had no idea her aunt and uncle were in the midst of a difficult split, but she could sense that something was wrong. She went back to the lawn, where she grabbed Kaden's hand and led him inside. I watched them go and then looked to the adults. Paul clearly wanted to say something, but I held up a hand to stop him. He took the hint. My sister didn't. She looked over her shoulder at Paul and Emilia and then turned to me, her expression simultaneously angry and hurt.

"If you think you need your friends here to break up a fight, you're wrong," she said. She looked at Nassir. "If he's here, I'm leaving."

"I'm sorry," said Nassir. "For everything."

"It's far too late for apologies," said Rana. She looked at me again and then drew in a breath. "I appreciate what you're doing, but an afternoon picnic won't fix my marriage."

"I'm not here to fix your marriage," I said. "I'm here to talk to you about my investigation."

Rana took a step back. Nassir sighed.

"I thought that was over," he said.

"After today, it will be," I said. "I'm closing the case."

"Then why am I here?" asked Nassir.

"Because even after everything was over, I was left with a lot of questions," I said. "For the past week, I've been working with Jacob Ganim's ex-wife to figure out what actually happened to her ex-husband and what led to the attack on Indianapolis."

Nassir walked to my table and pulled out a chair to

sit down. Rana did likewise near him. Paul and Emilia both looked confused, but then I gestured to the table.

"Why don't you two take a seat, too? This will take a few minutes."

The two of them sat down, and I leaned against the deck's railing.

"Three months ago, I was hired by Special Agent Kevin Havelock to investigate the death of an undercover FBI agent named Jacob Ganim. Nassir, you knew him as Michael Najam."

Nassir nodded. "I know."

"At the time of his death, Ganim worked for the Defense Intelligence Agency and was on permanent assignment with the FBI's counterterrorism task force. In 2014, Jacob Ganim was stationed in Raqqa, Syria. He was given a position within the *hisbah*, the state religious police. Unofficially, his job was to plot troop movements within the city and report them to his superiors in Washington. While in Syria, he also assisted resistance fighters who were smuggling people out of the city.

"As a *hisbah* officer, Jacob worked under the guidance of a cleric named Hashim Bashear. Bashear believed that Arab Muslims were a superior race and that they deserved their own homeland. He wanted an Islamic State within the Islamic State. To fund this dream, he used his connections within the Islamic State to traffic young people to wealthy families in Saudi Arabia and Qatar and other Middle Eastern states. The boys and girls whom he helped escape were treated as property. They were bought and sold and abused by their owners.

"Hashim couldn't do this alone. He had an entire network, including a man named Waleed Ayad. Waleed Ayad has a brother-in-law in the United States. His name is Saleem al-Asiri, and he was a guidance counselor at a high school near Dayton, Ohio."

Nassir's shoulders slumped. He covered his face. "I'm sorry. I didn't know."

"I'm not quite done yet," I said. Nassir nodded and sat straighter. My sister's face was blank, but she was paying close attention. "Jacob Ganim's cover was blown somehow in Syria. Nobody seems to know how it happened, but he was arrested and tortured over the course of several weeks. Before Hashim Bashear's men could extract the information they wanted from him, Kurdish fighters from Turkey overran their camp. Ganim was rescued and eventually made his way to Ramstein Air Force Base, at which point he was flown home.

"Fast forward a couple of years, and the Islamic State is in disarray. Hashim Bashear believes Muslim fighters across the world need an accomplishment they can rally behind. They need an attack on the order of September 11th. About six months ago, the DIA received word that a major attack was being planned. They didn't know details, but they knew it involved Hashim Bashear. Ganim tracked one of Bashear's associates—Saleem al-Asiri—to a property in Brown County, Indiana. That's why he became interested in Nassir's group."

Nassir stared down at his hands. When he looked at

me, his eyes were red.

"It was my fault," he said. "Jacob was a good man. He'd be alive if it wasn't for me."

"Jacob did his job. He died doing something he believed in. Don't blame yourself for that," I said. "I talked to Saleem al-Asiri. Whether Jacob joined your group or another, Saleem was going to kill him. He recognized Jacob from a picture his brother-in-law had given him."

"What about the girls who died?" asked Emilia, taking a step forward.

"They were women Hashim had trafficked," I said. "Kim Peterson and her partner were videographers. They shot wedding videos, mostly, but they were making a documentary about human trafficking in the Islamic State. According to Saleem al-Asiri, Hashim knew that if people learned he had sold good Muslim children into slavery, his own supporters would turn against him. He had hoped to kill the women during a larger attack on Indianapolis, but my investigation made him change his timeline. I was getting too close to Omar Nawaz, the crooked imam who was hiding them."

Rana looked from me to Nassir and then back to me.

"So you're saying my husband had nothing to do with the attack?"

"It felt like every piece of evidence I had pointed to him, but he was just in the wrong place at the wrong time."

"That's good news," said Paul.

I didn't say anything. Emilia furrowed her brow.

"Why did Saleem al-Asiri join Nassir's group?"

"The FBI thought Nassir just had bad luck," I said. "Saleem was going to join some group. They thought he happened to find Nassir and took advantage of what looked like a good opportunity."

A curious smile formed on Emilia's lips. "But you don't think that."

She said it as a statement, not a question. I nodded to her.

"The FBI gave me access to some documents that made me change my mind. If you remember, the attack on Westbrook Elementary was filmed by a very expensive commercial drone. After the attack, the FBI found that drone and traced it to an online purchase at a camera shop in New Jersey. The drone had been delivered to a warehouse leased to Safe Haven, LLC, in Indianapolis. You and Paul should remember that warehouse because it burned to the ground before we could search it."

"I remember," said Emilia, nodding. "So Saleem ordered the drone?"

I looked down and shook my head. This was the moment I had dreaded, and I didn't know whether I could go through with it after all. My heart thudded in my chest, and I swallowed hard.

"The drone was an expensive piece of hardware, so the camera company that sold it required a signature certifying that it had been delivered in good shape. It was signed for by Nassir Hadad."

Rana closed her eyes. "How could you, Nassir? You killed all those people…"

"It wasn't Nassir's handwriting on the form," I said, my voice lower and sharper than I expected. "It was our mother's. The FBI knew it wasn't Nassir's signature, but they didn't know whose it was. I recognized it the moment I saw it. You remember how you practiced it, Rana? You'd spend hours just signing her name. You got so good at it that *Ummi* couldn't tell your signature from her own."

Rana leaned forward. The world seemed to go quiet around us.

"Ashraf," she said. "I need you to listen very closely. I don't know what you think you've found, but I'm sure there's a perfectly rational explanation."

I allowed my anger to flow freely into my voice. I knew that anger would turn to pain soon enough, but for now, I allowed myself to feel it.

"That was my initial reaction, too. I thought there must have been a mistake, but the drone wasn't the only shipment from that camera store. Someone also ordered some very high-end surveillance equipment. Coincidentally, that was also delivered to Nassir at the warehouse and signed for by him in our mother's handwriting. That surveillance equipment was then placed in the home of Jacob Ganim."

"I don't know what's going on, Ashraf," said Rana, starting to stand, "but I'm going home. If you want to talk to me like this, you can talk to my attorney."

I looked to Paul and Emilia. They stood up and walked toward my sister.

"Don't you dare do this," she said.

"That surveillance equipment connected to the neighbor's wireless router. The moment I entered Jacob Ganim's house during my investigation, an alarm went off on your phone. You then called me with some bullshit story about a home invader.

"While I raced to your house, you called Saleem al-Asiri, who cleaned out Ganim's house and put incriminating pictures of Westbrook Elementary in his basement in place of the ones I saw. Saleem already admitted everything, and FBI technicians found the app on your phone. They also found that you had cloned Nassir's address book on his cell phone. That's how you knew the phone number of my burner cell."

Rana closed her eyes but didn't say anything. Nassir looked to his wife. He had tears on his cheeks.

"I am curious about one thing," I said. "Why did you go after President Crane's family instead of him?"

Rana opened her eyes again. She looked almost relieved.

"You're not going to ask why I became involved with Hashim Bashear? Why we decided to kill anyone?"

Nassir gasped and covered his face. Paul put a hand on his shoulder and then whispered to him. The two of them left the deck. Emilia stayed put near my sister.

"I've done this job a long time," I said. "I learned to stop caring about people's motives long ago except as a means to catch them."

"You've never believed in anything bigger than yourself your entire life, Ashraf," she said. "How sad the world must be for you."

"I'm not going to get into an argument about this," I said. "You participated in the murders of hundreds of people. I don't care what your reasons are."

Rana looked directly in my eyes. Then she leaned forward and whispered so that only I could hear.

"We went after the first lady and her family because it was easier than killing President Crane. His limo was armored. Her SUV wasn't. How does that sit with your morality?"

"I suppose that's a sensible answer. Thank you," I said, nodding. I looked to Emilia. "Detective Rios, please arrest my sister. I don't want to see her right now."

Emilia nodded. Her voice was subdued as she put a hand on Rana's shoulder.

"You heard the lieutenant. You're under arrest. If you go quietly, I won't put cuffs on you until we get to my car."

Rana looked to me. "Our father would be ashamed of you right now. He was a good Muslim. He'd know that what I did was right."

"I never met him," I said. "But that's probably for the best. If he'd be proud of you and what you did, I'd be ashamed to be his son. Good luck, Rana."

She didn't fight or say anything else. She just walked out. Emilia kept one hand on Rana's elbow and the other over the firearm on her hip. I stayed where I was, leaning against the deck's railing. Eventually, Hannah came out.

"What just happened?" she asked. "First, Nassir came by crying. Then your sister and Emilia came by. It looked like Emilia was arresting her. What just happened?"

I blinked and felt my cheeks grow hot. Hannah must have sensed what I was feeling because she walked toward me and put her arms around me.

"What just happened?" she asked again.

I clenched my jaw and drew in a deep breath before speaking, feeling a well of anger and sadness in equal measures build in my gut.

"I did the right thing."

Hannah took a step back and covered her face. "Don't tell me Nassir was involved in that attack."

"It wasn't Nassir. Everything seemed to come back to him, but it wasn't him. I focused on the wrong person."

For a moment, Hannah just stared at me, not comprehending what I had said. Then tears came to her eyes.

"I'm so sorry," she said, closing her eyes.

"I am, too," I said, reaching for her hands. Hannah and I stayed like that for a few minutes, and then she stepped forward for a hug. I felt her tremble against me, so I rubbed her back.

"I'm so sorry," she said again and then again, whispering. "I don't know what to say."

I pulled my face back and forced myself to smile as I looked at her. The more I looked in her soft, kind eyes, the easier that smile became. I held her for a few minutes. Eventually, Megan opened the back door. I had seen pictures of Hannah as a child, and Megan could have been her twin. She looked at both of us dubiously.

"Are you guys going to kiss?"

"Not right now," said Hannah. "What do you need?"

Megan looked back at the door. "Are Uncle Paul and Uncle Nassir coming back? Because I still need somebody to help me put up the badminton net."

"I'll call them in a few minutes and see," I said. "You go in and keep your brother company."

She tilted her head to the side. "You are going to kiss, aren't you?"

"Probably," I said.

"Gross," said Megan, turning to go back inside. "That's seriously gross."

Hannah and I watched her leave without saying anything for a few minutes.

"Rana is my sister," I said, finally. "I love her, and I always will, but I didn't choose her. I don't know what's going to happen to her, and I'm so mad at her right now that I'm having a hard time feeling anything else. Whatever happens, though, I'm not alone. I've got you and the kids, I've got Paul, Emilia, even Nassir and Captain Bowers. I've got more family than I know what to do with."

Hannah patted my chest. "Yeah, you do, and we're

not going anywhere."

My wife and I stayed like that for a few minutes. I didn't know what came next in my life. My sister would probably go on trial, and I'd have to answer a lot of questions. The media loved stories like this, so reporters would probably beat down my door any moment. They'd spin it every way they could so that no one would know the truth. I would know, though. Nassir and Hannah would know. Eventually, even my kids would know. We'd lean on one another and get through it together, though. Because that's what family does. For a brief while, the night sky might grow dim for us, the stars and moon might seem to disappear, but there was always hope with the coming dawn.

Enjoy this book? You can make a big difference in my career

Reviews are the lifeblood of an author's career. I'm not exaggerating when I say they're the single best way I can get attention for my books. I'm not famous, I don't have the money for extravagant advertising campaigns, and I no longer have a major publisher behind me.

I do have something major publishers don't have, something they would kill to get:

Committed, loyal readers.

With millions of books in the world, your honest reviews and recommendations help other readers find me.

If you enjoyed the book you just read, I would be extraordinarily grateful if you could spend five minutes to leave a review on Amazon, Barnes and Noble, Goodreads, or anywhere else you review books. A review can be as long or as short as you'd like it to be, so please don't feel that you have to write something long.

Thank you so much!

If you like my Ash Rashid series, you'll love my Joe Court series.

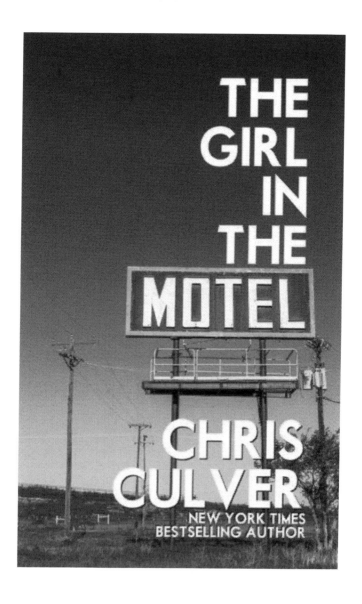

The past is never gone. It's merely forgotten.

Detective Mary Joe Court sleeps with a shotgun beside her bed and a loveable bullmastiff at her feet. For the past twelve years, she's hidden from a nightmarish past, but with every passing day, her scars fade, and her heart grows lighter. Now, for the first time in her life, she looks forward to her future. She's happy.

Then she finds the body.

Someone shot the victim in her chest and left her to die in a cheap motel. Joe knew her well. She grew up with her. They were sisters, of a sort.

Twelve years ago, the victim put a gangster in prison. Now that gangster's out, and he's looking to settle scores—Joe included.

Joe has fought to leave her past behind. Now, she has to face it or lose everything she cares about. Because the killer hunting her will tear apart her carefully constructed life piece by piece until there's nothing left.

Unless Joe gets him first.

The Girl in the Motel is available

Chris Culver

now at major booksellers!

Stay in touch with Chris

As much as I enjoy writing, I like hearing from readers even more. If you want to keep up with my world, there are a couple of ways you can do that.

First and easiest, I've got a mailing list. If you join, you'll receive an email whenever I have a new novel out or when I run sales. You can join that by going to this address:

http://www.indiecrime.com/mailinglist.html

If my mailing list doesn't appeal to you, you can also connect with me on Facebook here:

http://www.facebook.com/ChrisCulverbooks

And you can always email me at chris@indiecrime.com. I love receiving email!

About the Author

Chris Culver is the *New York Times* bestselling author of the Ash Rashid series and other novels. After graduate school, Chris taught courses in ethics and comparative religion at a small liberal arts university in southern Arkansas. While there and when he really should have been grading exams, he wrote *The Abbey*, which spent sixteen weeks on the *New York Times* bestsellers list and introduced the world to Detective Ash Rashid.

Chris has been a storyteller since he was a kid, but he decided to write crime fiction after picking up a dog-eared, coffee-stained paperback copy of Mickey Spillane's *I, the Jury* in a library book sale. Many years later, his wife, despite considerable effort, still can't stop him from bringing more orphan books home. He lives with his family near St. Louis.

Printed in Great Britain
by Amazon